PENGUIN CLASSICS

KADAMBARI

BANA (also known as Banabhatta) was a seventh century Sanskrit scholar and poet. He was Court Poet during the reign of King Harshavardhana (606–647 AD); besides *Kadambari,* one of Bana's principal works is the *Harshacharita,* a biography of the king. The other works attributed to him are *Candikasataka* and a drama, the *Parvatiparinaya.*

*

Dr Padmini Rajappa pursued her cherished goal of mastering the Sanskrit language under the guidance of teachers in the Department of Sanskrit, University of Poona and from the Bhandarkar Oriental Research Institute.

KADAMBARI

BANA

Translated with an introduction by
PADMINI RAJAPPA

PENGUIN BOOKS

An imprint of Penguin Random House

PENGUIN BOOKS

USA | Canada | UK | Ireland | Australia
New Zealand | India | South Africa | China | Singapore

Penguin Books is part of the Penguin Random House group of companies
whose addresses can be found at global.penguinrandomhouse.com

Published by Penguin Random House India Pvt. Ltd
4th Floor, Capital Tower 1, MG Road,
Gurugram 122 002, Haryana, India

Penguin
Random House
India

First published by Penguin Books India 2010

10 9 8 7 6 5 4 3 2

ISBN 9780143064664

Typeset in Sabon by Eleven Arts, New Delhi

Printed at Manipal Technologies Limited, India

www.penguin.co.in

MIX
Paper | Supporting
responsible forestry
FSC® C043100

Contents

Acknowledgements

I would like to express my gratitude to Vijaya Deshmukh for introducing me to the Sanskrit language. My special thanks are due to Yashodhara as well as Bhagyalatha Pataskar for having taken me through the intricacies of the grammar of Panini. I am grateful to Dr. Saroja Bhate for putting me in touch with Yashodhara and for having encouraged me in the study of the language.

It was Dr. Saroj Deshpande who introduced me to Bana and taught me how to unravel his tangled style. I express my sincere thanks to her.

My very special thanks are due to Lalitha Ganguly for those countless hours of study without which this translation would not have been possible; and to young Surabhi for having read the manuscript and pronounced it interesting.

I am deeply obliged to Satya Saran for reading the first few chapters and encouraging me to submit the manuscript to Penguin Books.

My grateful thanks to Paromita for getting the work into shape with careful editing. It has been a pleasure working with her.

Introduction

Early examples of Sanskrit prose are found mainly in sacred literature. Some of the Vedic *samhitas*—like the *Krishna Yajur Veda*—contain prose sections. The *Brahmanas* and the *Aranyakas* are for the most part composed in prose, while the *Upanishads* are a mixture of prose and poetry. The early prose of the scriptures is simple but it charms the readers with its delightful similes and metaphors. Secular Sanskrit literature, on the other hand, has always shown a partiality to metrical composition—talented poets are known to have gone to the extent of rendering existing prose works into verse in the genuine conviction that they were thereby refining and purifying the works concerned.

However, the tyranny of metre could not continue without being challenged, at least by some writers. Prose—being a freer medium—made it certainly easier for writers to give full rein to their creative imagination without being shackled to metrical precision. With the full development of *samasa*, the grammatical technique of forming compound words, prose is believed to have come into its own; it is said that writers could now express several ideas together, succinctly. On reflection however, they perhaps merely exchanged one form of tyranny for another, for what they wrote was certainly not the simple easy prose of the early days.

The three most important prose writers in classical Sanskrit were Subandhu, Bana and Dandi (Daṇḍin), all of whom lived in the late sixth and early seventh centuries AD. All the three wrote more or less the same kind of prose, ornate and complicated in different degrees. All the three were burdened with the necessity of using compound words. Subandhu is thought to be the earliest and the most difficult to read.

Dandi is probably the most readable of the three. Two works are credited to him, namely, *Kavyadarsha*, a work on poetics, and *Dashakumaracharitam*, a collection of stories describing the adventures of ten princes. Although in *Kavyadarsha* he does commend the style of writing characterized by long compounds, in his own creative work, *Dashakumaracharitam*, he tempers it with racy idiomatic language. His stories are realistic and full of humour and his characters are drawn from all stations of life, both high and low.

Banabhatta, with whom we are here concerned as the author of *Kadambari*, is also a product of the same culture. His language too is anything but easy, with long compounds packed into long sentences that run to several pages. He too gets lured by the tempting charms of the Sanskrit language only to lose his way in verbal mazes. And he is prolific in the use of figures of speech or *alamkaras*, especially in the descriptive passages that abound in his work. In fact almost every idea in these passages is couched in a literary figure of speech. Although many of his alamkaras are indeed beautiful, in the midst of such profusion it is inevitable that unhappy and laboured similes and inappropriate metaphors should at times creep in, as they do in *Kadambari*.

But despite these disconcerting habits that he shares with his literary contemporaries, *Kadambari* is a beautiful work, a fascinating fairytale told with great feeling. Bana's strength lies in his skill as a storyteller and a creator of characters vibrant with life and individuality. Besides, he is a writer who reveals his own mind through his characters; he expresses his opinions and convictions through them, a feature not common among Sanskrit writers. The mind that is thus revealed is amazingly modern, humane and sensitive, especially for the seventh-century India in which he lived.

Bana tells us something of his personal life in his other great work, *Harshacharita*. So we know that he was born the son of a wealthy Brahmin in a town called Pratikuta on the banks of the Shona River, a tributary of the Ganga, sometime towards the end of the sixth century AD. His mother died while he was still a child and his father too passed away when Bana was but fourteen years of age. Then followed several years of wandering around the country in the company of congenial companions drawn from all walks and all stations of life. He seemed to have counted among his friends, drummers, bamboo cutters and music teachers; astrologers, workers of spells and magicians. He rubbed shoulders with erudite Brahmins as well as thieves, gamblers and plain rogues. He had women friends as well. These bohemian years no doubt broadened his mind and instilled in him a healthy irreverence towards many of the established orthodoxies. It was in the course of his wanderings that Bana met King Harshavardhana. After several vicissitudes the relationship between poet and King stabilized and Bana spent a long time at the court of King Harsha.

~

Bana probably borrowed the plot of *Kadambari* from a fable preserved in one of the dialects of Prakrit, essentially as oral tradition. In the eleventh century a Kashmiri poet named Somadeva, having rendered several of these tales into Sanskrit verse, put them together in a compendium called *Kathasarithsagara—An Ocean of Story Rivers. Makarandikopakyanam*, which figures in this compendium, bears enough similarities to *Kadambari* for us to concede that Bana must have taken the plot, albeit in a skeletal form, from it. However, with his considerable skill as a storyteller, he develops it in his own way. He introduces many changes in the plot; he invents new characters and alters the nature of several others to make the story more effective. In the process he removes the brittleness of the original story. He introduces enough realism into the *kavya* to prevent the characters from becoming two-dimensional stereotypes. Like modern writers he weaves skeins of suspense into it concealing the real identity of several of the characters till the very end, including that of the hero Chandrapida. Again like modern writers he uses the dramatic technique of irony by making his characters use words the real significance of which is unperceived by the speakers themselves. Thus *Kadambari* as we now have it is a delightful romantic thriller played out in the magical regions between this world and the other, in which the divine and the earthly blend in idyllic splendour.

Bana died without completing *Kadambari*. We now have the kavya in two parts, a *Purvardha* and an *Utttarardha*, the first and the second halves. Whatever is written by Bana himself goes as Purvardha, although if one considers the length of the work alone it constitutes more than half. His son Bhushanabhatta or Pulinabhatta wrote the second half, the Uttararardha. The son is full of humility in undertaking to finish his father's work cut short by death. He compares himself to a farmer's son who merely gathers the fruits of the labour of his father who has done all the work, sowing good seeds in fertile soil and caring for the crop until it grows and ripens.

Bhushanabhatta does not say if his father discussed his work with him. But we do find that all the threads introduced in the

Purvardha have been satisfactorily gathered up and braided into a neat plait by him. In fact the Uttarardha is more eventful than the Purvardha with the resolution of all the 'mysteries' introduced in the beginning. The 'death' and 'resurrection' of Chandrapida and the revelation of his real identity, the story of the antecedents of Vaishampayana, the parrot, the revelation of the real identities of Patralekha and Indrayudha, all these take place in the Uttarardha. Bhushanabhatta could hardly have depended on the fable *Makarandikopakyanam* because most of these events are not found in it. Even more commendable is the congruity in the characters as they appear in the Purvardha and in the Uttarardha. By deft touches he manages to sustain the vibrancy of Bana's characters. Further, by making the future cast its shadow on the earlier events Bhushanabhatta sustains the suspense skilfully. Vilasavathi's inexplicable unease at her son's departure, the increasing depression of Chandrapida himself on his way back to Hemakuta the second time and the terrible flagging of his spirit as well as the dreary appearance of the once beautiful lake, all these poignantly portend the approaching calamities.

The only jarring note in the Uttarardha is the somewhat unseemly and venomous outburst of uncontrolled fury on the part of the venerable minister Shukanasa over his son's strange behaviour. Perhaps there were compelling reasons for Bhushanabhatta to introduce this scene. Did he feel it necessary to intensify the potency of Mahashveta's curse on Vaishampayana by adding the angry father's to it? Or was he trying to give some scope to the *raudra rasa* to come into play which is otherwise absent in the work? Whether it is worthwhile doing it at the cost of reducing the nobility of Shukanasa's character is something only the reader can decide.

The plot of *Kadambari* as conceived by Bana is too good for the story to have been left incomplete; despite the occasional display of awkwardness and the somewhat tortuous style of writing the son has done yeoman service both to the father and to lovers of literature by completing the work so creditably.

~

Apart from his great skill in describing natural phenomena like sunrise and sunset, forests and rivers and depiction of character Bana excels in delineating several rasas in varying degrees of intensity. It is these rasas that make Kadambari a beautiful work. And it is the elegant portrayal of the rasas that has earned for Bana the title of Mahakavi.

What is a rasa? The Sanskrit writers on poetics believe that whenever a particular emotion, love, fear or anger or something else is portrayed on stage or in the pages of a book it creates a response in the spectator or the reader by activating certain innate emotional capacities present deep within him. As a consequence he experiences the same emotions, not in any personal or realistic sense, but in a universal way that he shares with others exposed to the same artistic event. This would constitute the manifestation of rasa. It is thus a purely aesthetic experience, and no matter what the dominant emotion created, enjoyment would be intrinsic to it.

Bharata, the author of the *Natyashastra,* who probably lived in the first century BC talks of eight basic emotions or *sthayibhavas.* They are *rati* (love), *hasa* (humour), *shoka* (sorrow), *krodha* (anger), *utsaha* (energy), *bhaya* (fear), *jugupsa* (repugnance) and *vismaya* (wonder). These may give rise to eight rasas: *shringara* (the erotic), *hasya* (the comic), *karuna* (the pathetic), *raudra* (the furious), *vira* (the heroic), *bhayanaka* (the terrible), *bibhatsa* (the odious) and *adbhuta* (the marvellous). Rasas are the very soul of any literary work—prose, poetry or drama.

Love or *shringara* in both its manifestations, *vipralamba* (separation) and *sambhoga* (union) is the dominant rasa of

Kadambari, which is a love story—the romantic love between Chandrapida and Kadambari, as well as that of Mahashveta and Pundarika forms the dominant emotion of the story. It is the charming depiction of the first appearance of this love that leads to the rise of the romantic sentiment, the shringara rasa. The beauty, valour and nobility of Chandrapida, the ascetic other-worldly splendour of Pundarika, the charming naiveté and unconscious voluptuousness of Kadambari, the unusual ethereal loveliness of Mahashveta shining through her ascetic appearance, the magical charm of the Acchoda Lake and Hemakuta, the bursting forth of spring, the divine fragrance of the *parijata* flower, all these are the necessary ingredients that create the ambience for the rise of the rasa; the extreme sensuality of the love experienced by the characters, who act out their intense erotic feelings for the lover, forms a powerful catalyst.

The love itself is projected in a larger-than-life mode with an immensely exaggerated portrayal of the emotions, while the time scale in which it develops is extremely compressed, which gives it extraordinary urgency. No sooner do they meet than they fall in love intensely. No sooner do they fall in love than they are in the grip of uncontrollable, overwhelming passion. No sooner does fate separate them than they fall into terrible despair, with the physical taking complete control again—Kadambari wilts and takes to her bed. Mahashveta would have done the same thing but before she reaches that stage Pundarika dies, succumbing to the enormity of his physical longing for her. Chandrapida's heart splits when confronted with the utter hopelessness of his love for Kadambari. The rapidity with which the romance unfolds, the highly exaggerated expression of the emotions and the extreme physicality of their manifestation both in the first flowering and in the vipralamba stage, all these together create the shringara rasa.

Vipralamba shringara is of course inextricably mixed with shoka or sorrow. There is a great deal of it in Kadambari in the distress of the lovers in separation. In addition Bana skilfully portrays the parental agony of the king and Vilasavathi as well as Manorama and Shukanasa over the fate of their dear children.

But shoka is overshadowed first by shringara and then by adbhuta, the sense of the marvellous which pervades the whole work creating a magical atmosphere. Similarly vira rasa too is ambient throughout the work in the heroic personalities of the three great royals, Shudraka, Tarapida and Chandrapida, in the ascetic power of the sage Jabali, as well as in the quiet heroism of the two women—Mahashveta with her arduous ascetic discipline and the shy, innocent Kadambari taking on the awesome responsibility of caring for Chandrapida's body. Together these two rasas raise the experience of romantic love to levels not attainable among the merely mundane and conventional sequence of events. It is only proper that such a larger-than-life romance should be played out in the midst of celestial marvels and characterized by endeavours of awesome magnitude.

Fear and disgust have no place in an ethereal romance. Bana therefore contrives a little to bring in a few touches of these emotions. He introduces a description of a desolate forest with a Chandika temple built on one side of it and administered by a tragi-comic Dravida Dharmika, a south Indian priest. A very tenuous connection is then established between the main narrative and this digression. Bana makes Chandrapida pass through this forest on his way back to Ujjayini in a distressed state of mind, having left Hemakuta in some confusion as to whether Kadambari loves him or not. He worships at the temple and pitches camp there for a few days finding some relief from his mental agony in the antics of the eccentric Dravida priest. The only purpose of this episode seems to be to give some scope for the sentiments of disgust and unease, if not fear, to come into play. The dry desolation of the forest, the ever-present fear of attack from wild animals, the half-dried wells with leaves rotting in the scanty water giving out a stench, the gruesome remnants of the animal sacrifices carried out in the temple—all these combine to give rise to a strong sense of disgust mixed with a sense of unease. Tantalizing hints of human sacrifice add to the sense of disquiet. In the Uttarardha, Bhushanabhatta describes a *chandala* settlement in similar fashion but fails to match the vividness of Bana's descrption of the forest.

There is humour in Kadambari, but it plays, not surprisingly, a subordinate role. There is one graphic description of a funny situation, the spectacle of the vassal kings in riotous confusion to bid farewell to King Shudraka, who having dismissed his court, was merely going in to have his bath. Similarly the description of the disfigured body of the Dravida Dharmika and his eccentricities is meant to be a comic diversion. A more subtle humour lurks in Bana's tongue-in-cheek description of the exaggerated fragility of the Gandharva women of Kadambari's *antapura*. But his best effort lies in endowing his main characters, Tarapida and Chandrapida with a delightful sense of humour that finds expression at unexpected places in the narrative.

~

A kavya without alamkaras is no kavya at all. Alamkaras are adornments, figures of speech that embellish the language and help to express an idea in a picturesque and striking manner. Properly used, alamkaras could convey emotion effectively and heighten the mood. On the other hand indiscriminate use of these figures of speech merely to exhibit the command of the writer over the language would defeat their very purpose by making the writing tedious to read and rob it of all emotional content. Anandavardhana, the author of *Dvanyaloka,* a well-known treatise on Sanskrit poetics, lays down stringent rules for the use of alamkaras in any piece of work. Alamkaras may be used only to evoke a rasa; in fact it should flow naturally in the build-up of the rasa, in the brimming of the emotion; the poet should never make a special effort to insert figures of speech as special effects. While many of Bana's figures of speech fill the prescription admirably there are several that do not.

Bana uses similes (*upama*) and metaphors (*rupaka*), *utpreksha* (poetic fancy which suggests that the subject and object of comparison may be identical on the strength of some similarity), *atishayokti* (hyperbolic expression), *parisankhya* (enumeration) and *virodha* (contradiction) to name but a few. He is especially effective in handling utprekshas in the descriptive passages in *Kadambari*. The series of utprekshas that he uses in describing the magical beauty of the Acchoda Lake is a good example. They bring out graphically the vastness of the lake and the amazing clarity of its waters. To the poet the lake appears *as though the quarters have melted, as though the very expanse of the skies has liquefied and flown down, as though Mount Kailasa has melted, as though moonlight itself has taken a watery form . . . .*

Bana uses the same figure of speech in trying to convey the unusual loveliness of Mahashveta:

Enveloped in that intense white splendour, she appeared as though she was enshrined in crystal, immersed in milky water, veiled in fine white Chinese silk, as though hidden inside a mass of white autumnal clouds . . .

A series of metaphors brings out the saintliness, austerity and humanity of the sage Jabali:

He is the rushing waters of compassion, the bridge across the ocean of existence, the very reservoir of forgiveness; he is axe to the dense bower of desire, a veritable ocean of undying bliss; he is the leading steps for those

descending into the river of study, he is touchstone to the
gems that are the various disciplines of knowledge; he is
forest fire to the fresh growth that is attachment, he is the
incantation that arrests the serpent of anger, he is the sun
that lights up the darkness of delusion . . .

The heroic proportions of the *shalmoli* tree with the white cotton
pods on its top branches are brought out effectively with the
alamkara called *atishayokti*:

The horses pulling the sun's chariot move close to the
white-cotton-covered top of the tall shalmoli tree; they
are exhausted with galloping around in the skies. Is it the
foam that spurts from the sides of their mouths that is
whitening the tops of the high branches?

Parisankhya and virodha are two figures of speech used by Bana
to great effect. But both are based on pun on words, which makes
translation difficult. Bana uses parisankhyas to tell us how great
the ashrama of Jabali is, a sanctified spot of incomparable peace
and purity:

It is a place where there may be impurity in the smoke
from the altar but never any in the character of the people;
where redness may be seen in the beak of the parrots but
no flush on the face of men due to rage; where sharpness
is found on the edge of the kusha grass, but none in the
temperament of men, and where the plantain leaves may
sway unsteadily but not in the minds of men . . . .

In the figure of speech virodha, a phrase, appears to be a
contradiction in terms, but only until the pun is resolved.
Shudraka is described as *mahadoshamapi sakalagunadhishta* and
kupatimapi kalatravallabha. The first phrase means, at first
glance *although he is full of great faults, he is the abode of all
virtues*, which is absurd. But the word *dosha* also means *arm*.

The hidden meaning of the phrase is *although he possesses great strength of arms, although powerful he is still the abode of virtues*. Similarly the obvious meaning of the second phrase is, *although he is a bad husband he is the beloved of his wives*, which is contradictory. Here the compound word *kupati* may be dissolved in two ways. *Ku pati* means *bad husband* but *kuh pati* means lord of the earth, as *kuh* means *the earth*. Therefore the phrase actually means although *he is the husband and protector of the earth he is still the beloved of his wives*.

There are many figures of speech in *Kadambari* especially in the passages describing grand palaces, forests, sunrises, sunsets, moonlit nights and so on. At times Bana gets so carried away by the sheer momentum of the alamkaras following each other in a torrent that infelicitous figures of speech too rush in. There occurs for instance, in the description of the Vindhya forest the following phrase: *chandramurtiriva satatamrksha sarthanugata harinadhyasita cha*. Bana is comparing the forest to the moon. The simile is based in the first place on the pun on the word *rksha*, which means both 'the star' and 'the bear'. *Anugata* means both 'full of' or 'filled with' and 'followed by' or 'attended by'. To paraphrase the figure of speech, the Vindhya forest is like the moon because just as the moon is attended or followed by the stars the forest is filled with bears. Secondly, just as the moon has the deer seated on it (in the form of a mark) the forest too has deer settled in it. This is mere play on words, which loses all its meaning in translation. But the question is can one at all draw any comparison between two such dissimilar things as the moon and the Vindhya forest?

Yet another simile likens a region of the same forest to the flag flying on Arjuna's chariot. *Kvachit partharathapatakeva varanarakranta: Just as Arjuna's flag is dominated by the monkey emblem, in some parts, the forest too is overrun by monkeys.*

Here too the question arises whether a forest can be compared to one little flag on the basis of a single figure of the monkey appearing on it.

There are other similes, which if taken seriously would be considered inappropriate, infelicitous and uneasthetic; they go against the very rasa that Bana is trying to invoke. Here is an example of one such simile. The sage Jabali is compared to an elephant of noble proportions. *Prashasta varanamiva pralamba karnabalam.* The point of similarity rests on the compound word *karnabalam.* When applied to the noble-proportioned elephant it means that the animal has prominent ears and a long tail but when applied to the sage it means he has long hair growing from his ears. The compound when it applies to the elephant means 'he whose *ears and tail* are long'; when applied to the sage it becomes an adjectival compound meaning 'he whose *ear hair* is long'. *Bala* means a tail as well as hair.

Bana is at his best when he uses *swabhavokthi.* The writers on poetics are not agreed on whether swabhavokthi might be termed an alamkara at all. Be that as it may, Bana rises to great heights when simply describing a scene; the comedy of the princes rushing hither and thither at the dismissal of the court by Shudraka, the beauty of the Pampa Lake, Tarapida talking of his longing for a son, Pundarika's travails on his deathbed, the love play between Kadambari and Chandrapida or Mahashveta falling in love. With very few figures of speech thrown in, these passages brim with rasa.

~

The highest achievement of Bana as a creative writer is the delineation of character. In spite of the fabulous nature of the story all the characters in *Kadambari* are full of life, and drawn with great subtlety.

According to the literary convention established since the time of Bharata, the hero of a great work must have a great character. He should be of exalted lineage, and endowed with great prowess and knowledge; he is the *dhirodatta nayaka,* the valiant-exalted hero. If he has a finer side to his character that exhibits sensitivity to beauty of all types, then he is a *dhiralalita nayaka*, valiant-elegant hero. In general Bana follows the traditional prescriptions in casting his hero Chandrapida. He is the only son of a great king who rules over the whole earth. He is extraordinarily handsome. He is also a brilliant scholar who masters all the branches of knowledge. His physical prowess is incomparable. His favoured diversion is the thrill of the hunt. Chandrapida has a finer side to his nature as well. He is keenly sensitive to beauty of all kinds; he is captivated by the beauty of the Acchoda Lake and its surroundings, of the haunting music of Mahashveta as it floats over the lake. He is well versed in all the arts and his knowledge of music is so profound that he is able to discuss fine points of the mechanics of it with Kadambari's friends. Clearly Chandrapida qualifies to be a *dhirodatta-dhiralalita nayaka*.

But Bana, in addition to the prescriptions of tradition contributes something of his own to make Chandrapida come alive, an individual with interesting facets of personality. He comes through as a young man who has a mind of his own, who thinks for himself and forms his own opinions on matters of significance. One significant example would be his vehement condemnation of the practice of courting (embracing?) death when a dear one dies even when the dear one happens to be the husband, an amazingly modern concept.

His virtues no doubt dazzle us. He regards his father with love mingled with respect. He is ever obedient to his father's wishes; he is always deferential to Arya Shukanasa and is full of warm affection for his friends, Vaishampayana and Patralekha. He is dutiful and hardworking.

But at the same time Bana makes him endearingly human; he is full of irrepressible youthful impulses that captivate us. He forms easy friendships with people whom he likes, such as Mahashveta, Madalekha and Keyuraka. He loves his mother dearly but he is impatient with her caresses. He is a great prince who goes on a victory march over his vast kingdom dispensing equitable justice to his subjects and vassals, yet gives in to his impulsive curiosity about the *kinnara* pair; he must chase after them. And he must question Mahashveta about her strange life although he is quite aware of her distress at reliving her memories.

He is mischievously amusing when he chooses to be, as when he keeps the *gandharva* women in splits of laughter with his playful banter on the affair of the myna and the parrot. A great warrior, a great administrator, yet he is touchingly at a loss how to handle his affair with Kadambari. He is not sure if she really loves him. With typical adolescent awkwardness he hides his love from his parents and searches desperately for an excuse to go back to Hemakuta.

Kadambari is the heroine or the nayika of the kavya. Bana again follows tradition in making her a maiden born of an exalted lineage. She is of course extraordinarily beautiful as a nayika should be and very young, thus in every way a suitable partner to Chandrapida. Bana goes out of the way to emphasize her extreme youth, her artless innocence, and the almost unnatural bashfulness that constantly seizes her and her overwhelmingly affectionate nature. Mahashveta is very different. When the two women are presented side by side the contrast is striking. They are both gandharva girls brought up in identical fashion, yet Mahashveta, from the beginning, is shown to be bolder and surer of herself. Attracted by the divine beauty of Pundarika, she takes the initiative in striking up a conversation with him and Kapinjala. After fate strikes her a cruel blow by felling her lover, she changes her life completely, and becomes an ascetic with a mission in her life, namely union with her beloved. Her spiritual merit is considerable as the ashrama trees of their own accord shower their choicest fruits for her.

When we meet Kadambari for the first time in the kavya she is surrounded by her friends and attendants spending her time in somewhat childish diversions. Bana also goes to some length to impress upon us the fragility of Kadambari and her friends, and he seems to use subtle mockery in describing her exaggerated physical helplessness. With the vivacious and ready-witted Madalekha on one side and the stately Mahashveta on the other, one wonders why Chandrapida falls in love with Kadambari at all!

Then we see her transform with love. Under the intensity of that novel emotion she gets over her bashfulness enough to reveal her feelings to Chandrapida. She even sends him the priceless *seshahara* as a token of her love and then goes and visits him dressed in charmingly simple clothes. But she is still tongue-tied and quite unable to express her deep love for him in words.

When the curse leads to Chandrapida's 'death', all of a sudden Kadambari finds herself in unprecedented circumstances as she is made to bear the unimaginably grave and agonizing responsibility of caring for her lover's body, on the proper preservation of which her whole future happiness rests. The exaggerated physical helplessness and fragility disappear. The crippling bashfulness gives place to quiet self-possession. The frivolous pastimes are abandoned and she too becomes a woman with a mission in her life, the resurrection of Chandrapida and her union with him. As the story draws to a close Kadambari occupies centre stage, a role Bana surely intends for her to acquire although it is his son who actually puts the finishing touches to her character.

Let us now take King Tarapida and Arya Shukanasa, king and minister, magnificent men both, each a past master in his own chosen field. Tarapida's greatness lies in the battlefield, where valour and strategy shown by him have won him dominion over the whole earth. Shukanasa on the other hand is a scholar profoundly versed in statecraft. He is almost Kautilyan in the thoroughness with which he manages the affairs of the vast kingdom although he intensely dislikes the political philosophy of Chanakya. The two are more than king and minister; they are great friends and inseparable, for we almost never meet one without the other. The king defers to Shukanasa's opinion on all occasions. As the king leans on the arm of the minister as they walk together he seems to lean on him mentally and spiritually as well.

But there is something about the king that makes him greater in our eyes than the erudite wily minister; not merely greater but more lovable, more human. It appears as though Bana presents the two together only to drive home the subtle difference between the two. The king shows a deep natural wisdom acquired in the school of life, while the scholarly minister seems bookish. Tarapida has led a fuller life. Therefore he could assume the role of adviser to his erudite minister when the latter is shaken to the core with the disappearance of Vaishampayana. Shukanasa's reason forsakes him and all his scriptural texts fail to come to his aid. He succumbs to an uncontrollable rage hurling the most loathsome invectives against his own child without even waiting to find out what exactly has happened. It is then the king who stops the flow of curses and in the fullness of his experience advises the minister to show compassion to the poor confused youth. He gently chides the minister for heaping curses on his own child. He talks at length about the aberrations that could occur in the wildness of youth and advises restraint. Later, when he sees Chandrapida, his only child, 'lying dead' he shows amazing self-control, and wisdom and magnanimity as well in letting the care of Chandrapida remain in the hands of the young gandharva princess. Again it is Bana's son who wields the brush for the finishing strokes in a manner that would surely have won the father's approval.

Tarapida is indeed a charming character in literature. As a great king he is full of valour, he is the lord of the earth. He is a great lover who enjoys his women with abandon. But he is a caring husband too who spares the time to share the joys and sorrows of his wife. When the longed-for son is at last born the king gives himself wholeheartedly to the raptures of fatherhood. He suffers from no inhibition in demonstrating his tender love for his son. The king's sense of humour is delightful. As he teases his wife's bashfulness over her pregnancy or his son about his budding manhood we see the warmth and ebullience of his many-sided personality.

Vaishampayana remains a shadowy figure in the background. As the parrot he is the raconteur, although unlike narrators in general he is vitally concerned with the fortunes of his characters. Both as the son of Shukanasa and as Pundarika we see him only in the death throes of love which leaves him somewhat one-dimensional.

When we have Chandrapida condemning the practice of sati or Arya Shukanasa bitterly railing against Kautilyan statecraft known for its deviousness, inhumanity, and unscrupulous aggrandizement of the ruler at the expense of the subjects it is Bana speaking to us through the mouthpiece of his characters. His humanitarianism and liberalism take us by surprise for the age in which lived, the medieval age, is certainly not known for either. As a liberal he ridicules the pretensions of many of the rulers to divinity; he jeers that they may even labour under the delusion that they have two more hands concealed beneath the two that are visible, and a third eye hidden under the forehead. He is openly critical of the sycophancy that creates and nourishes such delusions in the minds of the rulers. Many of his remarks and descriptions would fit the ambitions and strivings of many in today's world.

~

I have not attempted a literal, word for word translation of Bana's *Kadambari*. I have tried, to the best of my ability, to bring out the spirit of his work.

As described earlier alamkaras are plentiful in *Kadambari*. Many of them depend on pun on words, which are difficult to translate without slipping into paraphrasing the idea contained in them. I have taken the liberty of omitting altogether those figures of speech which are, to my mind, infelicitous and far-fetched. I have however included a few of them so that the reader might get an idea of how Bana has made use of double entendre to craft his figures of speech.

Finally, there are certain conceits that are peculiar to Sanskrit literature, conceits that one repeatedly comes across in all literary work. They are, just to name a few: that the cobra carries a gemstone on its hood; that an elephant has pearls inside its temples; that there is an immense store of wealth lying at the bottom of the ocean; that there is a stone called *chandrakanta* which melts in moonlight. One encounters most of these in *Kadambari*.

There are also certain misconceptions with regard to natural phenomena. That the rays of the moon are cool to the touch is the least offending of the lot. At the other end of the spectrum is the thesis that conception is possible without the male sperm although, according to the saintly wisdom of Jabali, a foetus thus conceived will perish, if not immediately then sometime soon, without enjoying a full lifespan because it is the male essence that imparts strength to the child both physical and spiritual. The reader should treat these with indulgence considering the period in which this work was written.

Prologue

–1–

Once upon a time there was a king named Shudraka who reigned over the whole earth. He was a great king, a second Indra. All the rulers of the world without exception bowed to his authority. He had subdued them all, by intimidation and by conciliation. He had thus become Lord Protector of Dame Earth. On him were seen all the marks of a great sovereign, a *chakravarthi*.

Like Lord Vishnu, Chakradhara, the wielder of the discus, Shudraka too carried the discus and the conch—as signs—on the palms of his hands. Like Shiva he too had vanquished Manmatha—by his surpassing beauty. Like Kamalayoni, the one born on the lotus and the rider of the *rajahamsa*, the stately swan, he too had quelled the pride of the rajahamsas—the powerful monarchs of the world.

Supreme in valour, Shudraka performed marvellous deeds, and great sacrifices. He was verily a mirror in whom all learning found its reflection. He was the source of all arts, the fount of all aesthetic sensibility and truly a storehouse of all virtues.

It may well be said that the god Dharma found his abode in Shudraka's dutiful mind, Yama in his righteous anger. Kubera resided in his kindness and Agni in his valour. The strength of his arms reflected the stability of the earth and the brilliance of his eyes was the splendour of Lakshmi. Saraswati lingered in his learned speech and Chandra shone from his lustrous face. In his might there was Vayu and in his incomparable intellect there was Brhaspati. In his beauty of form there was Manmatha and in his splendour Savitr. Exhibiting all these divine perfections Shudraka was indeed the very image of the Vishvarupa of Lord Narayana.

When Shudraka ruled there was peace on earth. The people led noble and happy lives. There was deviousness only in the twisting trellises of their windows, blemishes only on the sheaths of their swords, due to disuse; there was spying only in lovers' quarrels, vacant houses only on ludo boards. The only tears shed were those caused by the smoking sacrificial fires; the only whipping known was the whipping of the horses and the only bow that twanged was the bow of Manmatha.

Shudraka's capital was at Vidisha, a city so vast that it could have been the womb that gave birth to all the three worlds. It was so righteous a city that one could well wonder if the noble Krita Yuga of yore, in fear of being assaulted by Kaliyuga from all sides, had compressed itself to the dimensions of this city and taken refuge in it.

Vidisha was skirted by the river Vetravati whose waves were continually shattered by the bouncing breasts of the beauties of Malwa frolicking in the water. The waters were often stained a twilight-red by the vermilion on the forehead of the battle-victorious elephants diving into them. Her banks resounded with the chattering of the excited swans.

Having subdued all the three worlds King Shudraka was free of all worries and bore the burden of ruling lightly, like the armlets on his arms. Besides, he had able ministers to assist him in the task. These ministers were men of the noblest lineages, wiser than Brhaspati himself. Their minds were clear as crystal due to their constant study of the sacred and secular texts. They were alert and selfless and affectionate. Is it any wonder then that the king's youthful days were spent in the pleasurable company of the vassal princes who had come from far and wide to pay him homage—all comparable to him in age, learning, comportment and valour. They too had honed their intellects in the study and practice of the various arts; they too were experts in all forms of literary composition. Endowed with magnificent physiques with hard, well-developed muscles in their chest and arms they too had proved their valour by vanquishing repeatedly the enemy elephants and riding on them like lion cubs. Yet they were invariably modest and full of courtesy.

The king's time was spent mostly in the company of these princes in various pursuits. He would, of course, go hunting with them, seemingly intent on emptying the forest of animals, with the incessant discharge of his arrows. But he was interested in gentler pastimes as well. He was fond of making music; he would play on the *mridangam*, his armlets swinging and his earrings tinkling like bells; or he would strum the veena. Sometimes he would organize learned seminars at which he would try his hand at composition; or he would discuss points in philosophy. Sometimes he would listen to the reading of literary works of various types as well as the *itihasas* and the *puranas*. Or he and his friends would devise various literary and language games to divert their minds. They also spent some of the time in ministering to the comforts of the visiting ascetics.

Whether it was a result of his excessive preoccupation with acts of valour, or whether it was a natural feature of his innately lofty mind, whatever it was due to, Shudraka's indifference to women was most bewildering. The king was in his prime and was exceedingly handsome. His antapura was full of women of noble descent whose beauty and charm could have put Rati in the shade. They were modest and appealing as well. The ministers, for their part, were importuning the king on the necessity of producing heirs to the throne. But all this had no effect on him. If anything the king appeared at times to exhibit a positive hatred towards all pleasures of the flesh.

Early one morning, when the thousand-rayed sun had barely risen and the skies were still doused in the pinkish hues of dawn, with the lotus buds just opening, the *pratihari*, the female doorkeeper approached the king who was already seated in his court. She was beautiful, but somewhat intimidating, because a starkly unfeminine sword hung on her right side, like a serpent seen on a sandalwood branch. Her high breasts were pale with a thick smear of sandalwood paste which brought to mind the image of the twin temples of Indra's elephant Iravata rising from the waters of the Mandakini. Her reflection fell on the shining crowns worn by the assembled princes, and it seemed as if the vassal princes were bearing aloft on their heads a symbol of their king's authority. Autumnal in her swan-white robes the pratihari appeared like the patron goddess of the kingdom in material form.

She drew near the king and, placing both her lotus-hands on the ground, spoke these words: 'Sire,' she said, 'there is a chandala woman at the gate waiting to be admitted to your presence. She is of such a magnificent appearance that one wonders if she might be none other than the Rajyalakshmi of Trishanku, now come to our part of the world after that king was thrown away from the gates of heaven. She carries with her a parrot in a cage and speaks thus: "It is the king who is the rightful owner of all that is the finest of the earth just as the ocean is the storehouse of all the finest gems. As this bird here is a marvel I have come to place it at his feet. I therefore beg to have the pleasure of seeing the king." My lord, please command me as to what is to be done.'

Overcome with curiosity, the king exclaimed, his glance sweeping over the assembled princes, 'Why not indeed! Please show her in.'

Soon the chandala woman entered the court, ushered in by the pratihari. Her eyes took in the king who was seated surrounded by his tributary princes—like Mount Meru of the golden peaks with the lesser mountains huddled all around it out of fear of Indra's thunderbolt. His body, decked with dazzling jewels, brought to her mind an overcast sky shot through with myriad rainbows. The king sat on a throne of black marble protected by a canopy of silk, white as the foaming celestial Ganga. Four pillars, studded with precious stones and hung with streamers of pearls, fixed in place by chains of gold, held the canopy aloft. Attendants wielding golden-handled deer-hair fans were fanning the king. His left foot rested on a white crystal stool. The nails of his right foot resting on the floor appeared somewhat darkened, possibly due to the dark rays emanating from the black stone floor. Or could they have been dulled by the deep sighs of his vanquished foes, as they lay prostrate at his feet? The shining rubies embedded in the seat tinted his thighs, reminding one of Hari, suffused with the blood of the slain Madhu and Kaitabha. His white-as-foam silk garment had pairs of swans painted in *gorochana* on the borders. The tassels hanging from them were dancing in the wind. His chest was painted white with the exceedingly fragrant sandalwood paste on which was printed a saffron hand mark; it appeared as if a piece of the young morning sun had fallen on the snow-clad Himalaya. His face was encircled with a string of pearls, 'as though the star clusters believing his face to be yet another moon have gathered around it,' as the chandala woman thought to herself. The king was indeed handsome, with arms of noble proportions, a high nose, eyes like fully bloomed white lilies and a clear forehead like the crescent moon.

Having been ordered by the pratihari not to approach too close to the monarch the chandala woman stopped at some distance. She tapped the ground once with the bamboo staff that she held in her pink lotus-soft hand by its well-worn handle, as if to draw the attention of the entire court. At once all the assembled princes turned their faces in unison—as a herd of elephants would at the sound of the *tala* instrument—away from their king and fixed their gaze on the chandala woman.

She was young, and dark like Mohini who beguiled the asuras into parting with the nectar. Indeed she was like a walking sapphire doll. Her body was covered down to her ankles in a dark-coloured robe. Over her head she wore a red silk veil. It was like the red rays of the morning sun falling on a field of blue lilies. On one of her ears there hung a *dantapatra,* an ivory ear ornament whose radiance seemed to render her cheek a little pale, even like the rays of the rising moon lightening the darkness of the night. Her brownish tilaka done in gorochana was like a third eye. Her slender waist could have been grasped by one hand, like the floral bow of Manmatha.

She was like autumn with her wide eyes like white lily blooms.

She was like the rainy season with her cloud mass of dark tresses.

She was like Shri with the lotus lustre of her palms.

An old man with white hair had come ahead of her; his body was trim and youthful and seemingly unaffected by age. Behind him was a boy with unruly black hair who held a golden cage. It looked as if it had been inlaid with emeralds, so vividly green was the parrot within.

As the woman stepped near, the light-yellow lustre rising out of the anklet on her uplifted foot suffused her entire body with a golden glow, as though Agni, unable to accept that one created with such extraordinary beauty should have been placed so low in the ritual scale, sought to rid her of her caste impurities by his purifying embrace.

Hers was a beauty that arrested the mind, like unconsciousness.

It captured the eye, like sleep.

It was as ethereal as it was untouchable.

She was a beautiful painting fit only to be gazed upon. And the king gazed upon her forgetting even to blink.

And he thought to himself, 'How unworthy the ground on which Brahma has displayed his genius for creating form. Why has he, having fashioned so beautiful a form—a form that surely surpasses the entire stock of beauty in the world—placed her in a caste that is out of bounds for sensual enjoyment for the high-born? I do believe that Brahma himself fearing pollution must have created her without ever touching her. For how else could such unblemished loveliness have come into existence? How can such lustre reside in limbs sullied by touch while being fashioned? Pity that Brahma should have brought together things that do not go with each other. Astonishingly attractive she is, yet she repels me because of her birth.'

The king's thoughts wandered on these lines. Meanwhile, the chandala woman, bold and quite confident of herself, bowed before him; her earrings, made of fresh shoots, slid down a little as she did so. Then she sat down on the polished stone floor.

The old man who had come with her advanced a little and, placing the cage with the bird in it in front of the king, said, 'My lord, this bird here is no ordinary parrot. He is learned in sacred literature, well versed in the theory and practice of politics, expert in expounding mythology and history, an excellent musicologist with a profound understanding of the intricacies of the twenty-two *shrutis*. He is an accomplished student of poetry and drama, as well as ethics and the sagas of contemporary kings. He has written his own works as well on these subjects. He is an expert analyst of humour. His understanding of musical instruments of all varieties is incomparable. He is a seasoned critic of dance and is accomplished in the art of painting; he is wily in the game of dice and resourceful in mediating in lovers' quarrels. He is knowledgeable about horses and elephants and a connoisseur of human beauty, both male and female. Thus, this parrot called Vaishampayana is, in short, the most wonderful of all the wonderful things of the world. As the king is the rightful owner of all things excellent, even as the ocean is the holder of all that is precious, this woman, my lord's daughter, has brought the parrot over to you. Do kindly accept the gift.' Having said these words the old man withdrew.

At once that astonishing bird turned towards the king and raising its right leg in salute hailed him in clear and well-modulated tones; then it recited the following verse in his praise:

Nestling close to their smouldering hearts,
The breasts of the women of your foes,
Bathed in their tears and shorn of jewels,
Seem under a vow of penance.

Utterly amazed, the king turned to his prime minister Kumarapalita, a grand old Brahmin, wise and learned as Brhaspati, seated close to him on a priceless seat of gold and exclaimed, 'Did you hear the words spoken by this bird so precisely and melodiously? It is wonder enough that it could speak, and speak so well, using such pure, distinct and grammatically chaste turns of phrases so elegantly put together.

But even more amazing is that he conducts himself like a refined human being with knowledge even of court etiquette. Did you see how he raised his right foot, hailed me and then recited the panegyric on me? I have always thought that in general the awareness of birds does not go much beyond fear, hunger, sleep and the urge to mate. This bird here is really a marvel.'

Kumarapalita smiled and replied, 'My lord! What is so strange about it? I am sure your majesty is aware of the fact that birds like the parrot and the myna are quite capable of repeating the words they hear. It is also known that these birds do acquire a certain proficiency in speech perhaps due to the influence of a previous birth or as a result of training in the present one. In any case, in days of yore these creatures used to be capable of as clear an enunciation as human beings themselves. It was only as a result of the curse of Agni that the speech of the parrots and the other birds became unintelligible and the tongue of the elephant became garbled as well.'

—2—

The king sat discussing the bird with his minister until the drums sounded and the conch blew announcing the noon hour. The hot-rayed sun was already up in the middle of the sky. It was the king's bathing hour; he rose and dismissed the court.

All at once there was a great commotion among the princes present in the court. They too rose and rushed about, vying with each other to be the first in saluting their departing sovereign. Their armlets slipped; the crocodile-shaped tips of their *patrabhangas* tore at each other's clothes. The necklaces swung wildly when the princes collided with each other. The fragrant vermilion powder, applied on their shoulders, rose in clouds of dust, tinting the atmosphere red. The *malati* flowers decorating their topknots shook and the bees hovering over them swarmed up. The blue lilies hanging from their ears kissed their cheeks.

Pandemonium reigned over the court and all of a sudden it had become very noisy. A medley of sounds filled the air. The tinkle of the gem-embedded anklets, that sounded like the excited cackle of the white swans, was heard at every step taken by the fan-wielders carrying the chamara fans on their shoulders. The precious gemstone-studded girdles swinging on the hips of the court women skipping hither and thither jingled charmingly. The high, piercing calls of the house cranes rent the air.

The sound of the stamping and hurrying feet of the princes in the courtroom caused the very earth to tremble. The pratiharis, staff in hand, shouted loud and long in a bid to disperse the throng in front of the king. 'Watch out, watch out' they cried and their voices echoed back from the towers lengthening their syllables. As the princes rushed about bending low in salute their *chudamanis*, the crest jewels, shook and the serrated edges of their crowns grated against the stone floor as their heads touched the ground. When they fell one on top of the other their earrings rubbed against the floor producing ringing sounds. Along with these harsh tones the sweet benedictions sonorously repeated by the bards walking ahead filled the air.

Having dismissed his court the king politely requested the chandala woman to rest for a while; he also ordered his betel-box bearer to carry Vaishampayana inside.

Then, like the setting sun with its weakened rays, like the sky shorn of the moon and the stars, the king, having shed all his jewels, entered the gymnasium where there lay a collection of tools for exercising the body. The king performed his daily exercises in the company of princes of his own age. The exertion adorned his body with beads of perspiration. On his cheeks they appeared like slightly crushed *sinduvara* blossoms; on his chest they lay like the scattered pearls of a broken necklace, snapped due to relentless exertion; on his forehead they were like droplets of ambrosia oozing out of the surface of an eight-day-old crescent moon.

Meanwhile, ahead of the king the hurrying attendants were assembling the materials for his bath. Staff-wielding officers led the king to the bathing ground exercising diligently their authority in clearing their sovereign's path, even though at that noon hour there were very few people around. There was a huge white canopy erected in the bathing area under which the minstrels had already gathered. In the centre was a large golden basin filled to the brim with scented water. Close to it was placed a crystal bathing stool. On one side were the smaller pots, also filled with fragrant water. The mouths of these pots were darkened by the hovering bees swarming there attracted by the sweet scent. It gave the impression that the pot mouths were being veiled by dark strips of cloth as though to ward off the heat of the sun.

With his head smeared with gooseberry paste ground by seductive women the king stepped into the basin. The women, their bosoms bound tightly in silk cloth, attended him on all sides. Their bangles had been pushed up their slender arms; their earrings had been fastened up, and the hair falling in curls around the ears had been tucked away. Goddesses of the bath, they were ready with water pots in their hands.

The king, in the midst of these high-breasted beauties, was like a male elephant frolicking in the water surrounded by his females.

Soon, the king rose from the tub and climbed on to the flawless crystal stool, like Varuna ascending a white swan.

Then the women bathed him. Some of them carrying pots made of emerald were suffused with the dark lustre of the gem, like the lotus flower darkened by the dark green of its leaves.

Others with silver goblets were of the hue of nights flooded with the flowing white rays of the moon. Yet others, their bodies bathed in perspiration with the effort of lifting the water-laden crystal pots appeared like water nymphs. Some held the pots raised, with their slender fingers curled around the sides, their nails scattering brilliant rays all around. They were like the figures of goddesses on the water-fountains, with water streaming out of their splayed fingers.

Soon, the conch blew its shrill ear-splitting note announcing the end of the king's bath; the cymbals clashed and the drums sounded. The music of the veena and the flute also rose, accompanied by the uproarious chorus of the choir of bards. The tumult spread and filled every nook and corner of the world.

The king rose from his bath and donned clean white garments as fine as the moult of snakes. His newly bathed, clean body shone like the autumn sky at the end of the rains. With a length of white silk cloth that looked like a silvery cloud, he wound a turban round his dark head; it looked like the white streams of the celestial Ganga winding their way around the dark flanks of the Himalayas. Having worshipped the spirits of the ancestors with sanctified water and prostrated himself before the sun the king entered the shrine of Shiva.

In the shrine he prayed to the deity and performed fire sacrifices. Then he made his way to the anointing chamber where his body was rubbed with sandalwood paste mixed with fragrant musk and camphor and saffron. His hair was decorated with the extremely sweet-scented malati flowers. Changing his clothes once again and wearing only earrings by way of jewellery the king, with just a few of his princely companions deemed worthy of his company at the table dined, relishing the taste of his favourite dishes.

When he finished his meal the king washed his hands and then inhaled fragrant smoke. Accepting the *tambula* he rose from the clean-swept stone floor. The ever-present pratihari rushed to extend her hand, calloused by the constant wielding of the cane, a tender shoot withered before its time, to help the king up. Followed by a few attendants designated for the private apartments the king entered his private audience chamber.

Hung with clean white cloth on all sides, the walls of the chamber appeared as if made of crystal. The floor was cool, as it had been sprinkled with sandalwood and the highly fragrant *kasturi*-scented water. The dark polished stone floor had a thick carpet of flowers spread on it, like the night sky strewn with the star clusters. A collection of dolls placed in the room looked like an assemblage of the household deities. The room was splendid with a profusion of golden pillars, all washed clean with scented water. The fragrance of joss sticks pervaded the room. The bed was covered with a sheet as white as rain-depleted clouds and imbued with the fragrance of flowers. Silk pillows were piled up near the headboard. The legs of the bed stood on gem-inlaid pedestals; there was a footrest on one side, also inlaid with precious stones and the cot itself stood on a platform.

The king reposed on the bed; close to him squatted his sword-carrier on whose lap lay his slender sword. She pressed the king's feet with her lotus-petal-soft hands. Talking of various things the king spent a pleasant hour in the company of his vassal princes, ministers and friends.

Then, unable to contain any longer his curiosity about the parrot he ordered the pratihari to bring Vaishampayana over from the interior apartments. The pratihari genuflected, placing both her hands on the ground and replied deferentially, 'As your majesty commands' and then hastened to do his bidding.

In a short while, Vaishampayana made his appearance before the king. His cage was held by the pratihari who was followed by the *kanchuki*, the chamberlain, leaning on his golden staff. The kanchuki was an old man; the upper part of his body was rather bent and his hair had turned white. Clad in a white tunic, indistinct of speech due to age, and able to move only slowly, he had followed Vaishampayana, drawn by his love of birds.

Informed by the kanchuki that Vaishampayana had been bathed and fed by the ladies of the palace, the king now turned to the parrot and inquired, 'Was there at all anything to your taste to eat?'

Vaishampayana answered 'My lord. Was there anything at all that I left without tasting? The bittersweet juice of the *jambuphala* of blue-pink lustre resembling the koel's eyes, I drank to my heart's content. Then I had a go at the white-red pomegranate seeds as brilliant and as moist as the blood-soaked pearls torn out of the mad elephant's temple by the claws of the lion. I mauled the gooseberries from the east, green as the lotus leaves and sweet as the juice of the grapes, as much as I wished. Is it any wonder that everything served to me by her ladyship with her own hands should turn into veritable nectar?'

The king listened to this speech a little impatiently and said, 'Well let us leave all this aside now; please do satisfy our curiosity. Tell us everything from the very beginning. Where and how were you born? Who is your mother and who your father? Who named you Vaishampayana? How did you acquire Vedic knowledge? How did you become familiar with the sciences and the arts? Is it a boon or are you someone else living inside the body of a bird? How old are you and how were you captured and put inside a cage by the chandalas? And finally, how did you end up here?'

Vaishampayana, subjected thus to a barrage of questions, remained pensive for a while as though he were collecting his thoughts. Then he replied courteously, 'My lord. It is a very long story. But listen carefully if you are interested.'

The Parrot Speaks

3

The great Vindhya forest touches the wooded shores of the eastern and western oceans and adorns the Madhyadesha; it is like a girdle to the earth. Wild elephants roam the forest and water the trees with their streaming rut fluid. Is it therefore any wonder that the trees in the forest have grown so very tall? Their tops densely covered with white blossoms give rise to the illusion that they are in fact carrying aloft the heavenly constellations.

The forest is full of excited cranes that keep pecking at the new shoots of the pepper creepers. There is a pervasive fragrance of the tender bay leaves crushed by the baby elephants. A carpet of new leaves covers the ground. Surely it is the *alaktha*-stained feet of the tripping forest nymphs that have stained the leaves that now shine like the flushed cheeks of a Kerala damsel intoxicated with wine.

The flowing juice of the pomegranate seeds crushed by thousands of parrots soaks the ground. Broken bits of the papaya fruit and leaves rain down as the ever-restless monkeys keep shaking the trees. The blue-throated peacocks dance in the midst of the new red shoots, like Nilakanta doing his cosmic dance in the russet twilight of the final dissolution. Pollen dust flies up incessantly.

The forest, with its *khadgas*, the restless rhinos, and the red sandalwood trees is like Katyayani, the sandalwood-paste-smeared goddess wielding her sword, or *khadga*. Full of *rikshas*, or the bears, and the deer, the forest no doubt mimics the moon; for the moon too carries the mark of the deer on itself and the *rikshas*, or the stars, ever surround it. The forest is like the Lanka of the Ten-Faced Ravana, for the one has rows of tall *shala* trees teeming with monkeys and the other has shalas too, tall mansions, once overrun by the monkeys of Rama's army.*

The boars have dug the earth deeply with their sharp horns; is this indeed a preview of *pralaya*, the ultimate deluge? Beds made of tender clove leaves are found here and there on which the weary travellers must have rested at night. The edges of the forest are lined with mature coconut trees, *ketaki* shrubs, prickly cacti and the *bakula*. The many betel nut groves with the entwining betel creepers are surely bowers for the forest nymphs to dwell in. The densely growing thickets of cardamom that darken the forest exude a strong scent, as though, having been constantly soaked by the rut fluid of the elephants they too have absorbed its powerful smell. Overgrown with *shara* grass, dense with *tamala* trees, the forest is impenetrable with thick growths of cane and the hollow bamboo.

The forest seems at times and at places to flaunt the trappings of a sovereign state as it were, as its herds of deer wave their

---

* *These are a few examples of the use of pun by Bana. Words in Sanskrit quite often have more than one meaning which makes it highly suited for pun. In the above paragraph the comparisons are made on the strength of certain keywords with more than one meaning, e.g. khadga means 'rhinoceros' as well as 'sword'; riksha means both 'bear' and 'star' and shala is the name of a tall tree and also means 'mansion'.*

chamaras or bushy tails, and bands of wild elephants circle around, the one an insignia of royal power and the other an arm of the defence force. There is a fragrance of sandalwood and musk in the midst of *aguru* and *tilaka* trees; does the forest then also mimic the courtesan who applies sandalwood paste on herself and puts on *aguru-tilaka*, the beauty spot, on her forehead? There is the lovesick cooing of hundreds of koels; does it not imitate the indistinct prattle of courtesans intoxicated with wine?

The forest appears delirious where the palm trees, or the tala, rustling loudly in the violence of the wind, *vayuvega*, sound like the wild handclapping, or tala, of one in the virulent grip of a fever, vayuvega. Elsewhere it seems to be in mourning; where other palm trees, having lost all their fronds, the *talapatras*, in the strong wind, vayuvega, seem like widows shorn of their ear ornaments, the talapatras.

There is fear in the air. Where the ground is full of thorns the forest seems to be breaking out in gooseflesh as though in fear of the roaring lions. These reverberating roars sound like an army roused to battle, the sounds of arrows being discharged mingling with loud war cries. There is an actual battle being fought too. The *Bhil* commanders hunt down hundreds of lions for the pearls still sticking to the tips of their claws, pearls torn out of the temples of the wild elephants.

Death lurks close. One can see rows of tiger pugmarks. There are bands of wandering rhinos. The wild buffaloes too roam at will. Verily is it the city of Yama, the god of death.

It was on these Vindhya ranges, right in the heart of the Dandaka forest that the venerable sage Agasthya lived a long time ago and his hermitage was famed throughout the worlds as the very birthplace of Dharma. Agasthya's greatness is well known. It was he who once drank up the waters of all the oceans at the request of Indra; and it was he alone who could control

the erring Vindhya mountain when out of envy for the golden
Meru, it spread its own peaks all across the sky obstructing the
progress of the sun's chariot in defiance of all the *devas*. It was
Agasthya again who digested the demon Vatapi by the fire in his
stomach. Gods and asuras bowed low before him. Hailed as the
tilaka on the face of the goddess of Dakshina, the southern
direction, Agasthya's power was fully revealed when he brought
Nahusha down from the heavens by merely an angry roar.

Agasthya's hermitage was beautiful in those days with all
the trees planted and nurtured by his wife Lopamudra, as her
own children. Their son Dridadasyu added to the purity of the
grove. Vowed to celibacy, Dridadasyu, *palasha* staff in hand, his
forehead marked with three lines in sacred ash and clad in a
kusha grass garment with a *munja* girdle tied round his waist,
would go from hut to hut carrying a begging bowl made of
green leaves and beg for his daily food.

All around the edges of the hermitage there used to be
the dark and shady parrot green plantain groves. The river
Godavari wound round the hermitage in a thin single stream;
she was like a widow in mourning with all her hair woven into
a single plait. And she seemed intent only on reaching her
'dead' husband, the ocean, whose waters had already been
swallowed by the sage.

It was around here a long time ago, that Rama lived happily,
for a while, with his wife Sita in a hut put up by Lakshmana at
a place called Panchavati, in order to serve the sage Agasthya—
Rama who gave up his kingdom to fulfil his father Dasharatha's
promise, Rama the destroyer of the Ten-Headed One. Panchavati
now remains deserted, the ascetics of those ancient times all
having gone away long since; yet the rows of white pigeons sitting
quietly and closely packed together amidst the dark branches
create the illusion that the trees are really columns of smoke
freshly issuing up from the sacrificial altars. The glossy red young

growth of leaves on the creepers makes one wonder whether they have acquired that vivid redness from the soft palms of Sita while she was gathering flowers for the rituals. Or is it the blood of the numerous rakshasas killed by the deadly arrows of the sons of Dasharatha that, having soaked the roots, is still staining the fresh growth of leaves?

The horns of the aged deer have turned blunt with the passage of time; surely they are the deer once looked after by Janaki herself. Now when they hear the deep roar of thunder in the newly formed clouds of the rainy season they remember the sound of Rama's bow that used to reverberate in all the three worlds. They cast their eager eyes in all the ten directions and not finding him anywhere stand still, their eyes filling with tears of longing as they let the half-chewed grass slip from their mouths.

It was here that the golden deer, egged on by his companions, deceived Sita and led her Lord far away. And it was here that Rama and Lakshmana were both caught in the agony of the loss of Sita; it was as though Rahu had at once swallowed both the sun and the moon. Their sorrow forecasted the destruction of the Ten-Headed One and made the three worlds tremble with fear.

The hunters who now roam the forest still see, after all this time, the likeness of Sita drawn on the floor of the cottage by her grieving husband, seeking some relief from the agony of separation. And they fancy it could be the real Janaki come up from her abode in the bowels of the earth just to cast her longing eyes once more on the spot where Rama used to live.

—4—

Not too far away from Agasthya's hermitage—that still harbours the relics of incidents of long ago—there is an astonishingly large lake named Pampa. Has Prajapati—goaded as much by Varuna's anger at Agasthya for having drunk away all the waters of the oceans of which he, Varuna was the overlord, as by his own jealousy at the prowess of the rishi—created this lake, ocean-like in its expanse so close to the hermitage just to taunt him perhaps? Or has the firmament fixed in place by the eight directions to stay aloft till the end of the Yuga fallen down betimes?

The waters of the Pampa are never placid. The *shabara* women who keep plunging into the lake disturb them with the bounce of their well-rounded breasts. The countless creatures living in the lake agitate the waters, as do the myriad diving birds. The sound of the ripples is heard constantly. The waves tossed up by the wind rain down cold sprays. A forest of blue and white lilies and lotuses grows in the water. The just-opening lotus blooms covered with droplets of honey resemble the 'eyes' on the peacock feathers. The hovering bees cast a shadow on the blooms.

Drunk with the nectar in the lotuses the female swans turn coquettish and make merry. Secure in the solitude of the forest the water-sport loving nymphs descend into the lake for bathing. The flowers in their tresses add their own fragrance to the water.

From somewhere comes the enchanting sound of the ascetics filling their *kamandalus* with water. Groups of white swans swim in the midst of the recently opened white lilies; their presence may be inferred only by the sound of their cackle.

The sandy shores of the lake are caught in the pollen dust of the *ketaki* growing on the edges of the beach.

The waters close to the shore are stained pink and red by the colour dripping from the washed and saffron-dyed bark robes of the hermits living in the ashramas close to the lake. The wind blowing through the tender shoots of the trees fan the waters.

The shores of the lake are darkened by rows of densely growing *tamala* trees with their dark coloured bark.

The hermits stand in the water and do penance. They scatter the flowers used in worship on the shore. The soft fresh grass growing on the ground remains always moist with the water sprayed by the leaping fish and the beating wings of the water birds. The peacocks dance in their bowers. The flowering bushes on the shores fill the air with fragrance as though the goddesses of the forest are scenting the air with their own breaths. Like masses of clouds coming down to drink the waters of the lake in the illusion that it is the ocean, mud-stained forest elephants come ceaselessly to drink of the waters of the Pampa.

Such is the beauty of the Pampa Lake, which is unfathomable, seemingly unbounded and certainly incomparable.

On the western shores of the lake close by the row of those hoary palms that Rama pierced through with a single charging arrow, stood a huge and ancient *shalmoli* tree. A great old python of the proportions of the trunk of a celestial elephant lay permanently wound around the roots of the tree forming as it were, a bank to hold the water in. The tree's high branches had spread far and wide in the sky as if seeking to measure the extent of the horizon. Or was it trying to emulate Shiva's flying hair when he danced his cosmic dance with his thousand hands all stretched out? Perhaps the tall old tree swaying in the wind was merely clinging to the shoulders of Vayu with its outstretched branches in the fear of losing its balance!

Thick creepers twined around the tree like the raised tendons of old age; thorns covered it like old-age spots. The tree was ancient. But it was very tall. The rain clouds laden with seawater would steal their way through the branches wetting the new green leaves. But even these clouds had not seen the top of the tree, which was perhaps taking a peek at Indra's fabled garden!

The top branches gleamed with bunches of silk cotton, but these could just as easily have been mistaken for the foam collecting at the mouths of the sun's horses exhausted by their trek across the skies pulling their lord's chariot behind them.

Truly a terrace for the forest spirits from which to observe the world beneath, the shalmoli stood proudly on the banks of the Pampa, a friend of the Vindhyas, lord of the entire Dandaka forest and a prince among trees. On it were countless nests, built at the edges and junctions of the branches, inside the hollows of the ancient bark and amidst the foliage, built with ease and confidence because of the availability of unlimited space. In these nests there lived innumerable families of parrots and other birds come from different regions; they lived with a sense of security and freedom from all fear of danger because of the great height from the ground. And the old tree for its part with its somewhat attenuated foliage managed to look full and dense whenever these birds nestled on the branches during the day or at night.

Passing the night in their own nests, every morning the birds would fly away in formation in search of food, dark streaks across the sky. As though Balarama in his inebriation had scattered up the dark waters of the many-streamed Yamuna with the tip of his ploughshare. As if the dark lilies blooming in the celestial Ganga had been plucked and cast down by Indra's elephant. The swiftly flying birds would now look like a moving emerald floor, now like a series of moss patches in the sky-lake. Their fast-beating plantain-leaf-wings would seem to be fanning the quarters distressed with the fierce heat of the sun's rays. When they flew the sky looked as if it was decked with rainbows.

Having first satisfied their own hunger they would fly back to the nests to feed the young ones left behind; they would keep flying in over and over again with the juice of various fruits and ripened grain sprouts. Brimming with overwhelming love they would then take the young ones protectively under their wings and spend three *yamas* of the night.

In an old hollow on this tree there lived an old parrot with his mate and it was to him that I was born as his only son in his declining years. My mother passed away soon after I was born. Bitterly grieving the loss of his beloved companion my father, because of his great love for me, somehow contained his virulently swelling sorrow deep within his heart and devoted himself single-handedly to raising me.

My father was so old that his tattered feathers were like *kusha* garments! His shoulders having lost their muscular tautness had become slack. His wings had lost the ability to fly up high in the sky. His uncontrollably trembling limbs made it appear as if he were forever trying impatiently to shake off the enfeebling senility coming upon him. Unable to fly far for food, he would collect the cereal from the kernels fallen on the ground from the other nests, and gather the bits of fruits crushed and dropped by the other parrots. With his yellowed beak worn to the softness of a *shevali* stalk and whose tips were cracked he would first feed me and then partake of whatever was left after I finished.

One morning the sky was just beginning to redden with the break of dawn. The moon, which had earlier risen on the celestial Mandakini, was now slowly descending into the waters of the western ocean; with his setting russet rays the moon resembled an aged swan whose feathers had been dyed red in the nectar of the red lotuses amidst which he had been wandering. The expanding vault of the lightening sky had turned the colour of the fur of an old deer. The elongated warm red rays of the sun were like threads drawn out of heated lacquer! They were like the lion's mane dipped in elephant blood! They were sweeping away, like a broom made of red ruby sticks, the stars still left scattered on the floor of the sky. The setting *saptarishi* constellation was suspended in the northern sky as though the sages were about to descend into the Manasa Lake for the performance of the morning rites. On the shores of the western ocean the mothers-of-pearl washed ashore broke open and the myriad pearls whitened the sands; it was as though the red-rayed sun had edged away the stars down on to the ground.

The rain of dewdrops was awakening the peacocks; the lions were yawning; the stud elephants were being woken by their female companions. The lotus fields were waving in the dew-laden morning breeze, which dried the beads of perspiration on the love-sated shabara women. Showering everywhere the honey gathered from the lotus blooms, pleasing the bees by wafting the fragrances of the flowers, intent on teaching rhythm to the swaying creepers, the gentle breeze blew, languorous with the morning coolness. The bees sang the wake-up song for the lotuses and drummed at the rut-stained cheeks of the elephants. Gathering their wings together as the blue night lilies closed their petals they raised a high-pitched murmur.

The forest deer too were slowly coming awake, the hair on their chest dusty with lying on the barren salt-encrusted ground. Their eyelashes were still gathered up tight as if glued together with molten lacquer; their eyeballs were still rolling with the remnants of sleep.

The other animals of the forest were also beginning to stir as the mass of rays, Indian madder-red streamed down, like the downward facing *chamara*s of the sun-elephant climbing up the sky.

With the sun already in the eighth part of the day, it had brightened everywhere. The parrots had already flown away in their favoured directions. The young ones lay in the nests, hidden, quiet. In the silence that reigned the tree appeared deserted. My father remained in the nest. As for me, weak as I was due to my infancy, with my wings just beginning to grow, I had snuggled close to my father in the hollow of the tree.

All of a sudden there was a commotion in that great forest and all the animals were in a panic. I heard the rapid beating of the birds' wings, the shrill trumpeting of the elephant calves, the loud buzzing of swarms of disturbed bees, the hoarse cry of the high-nosed wild pigs running hither and thither and the reverberating roar of the lions just awakened in their caves. Shaking the very trees of the forest, uproarious like the Ganga coursing down to the earth behind Bhagiratha, striking fear in those forest nymphs who heard it, the tumult of hunting rose.

— 5 —

Hearing the pandemonium of the hunt I began to tremble, I had never heard anything like that before. My tender ears were practically deafened and I was agitated and confused. Seeking to ward off the peril I crawled under the age-loosened wings of my father perched close to me. Feeling somewhat secure under his wings I listened to the shouts of the hunters.

'Do you get here the fragrance of the lotus plant crushed by the charging leader of the elephant herd? Here is the smell of the *badramusta* grass chewed by the boars. And the pungent scent of the *sallaki* tree broken down by the young elephants. Hark! Listen to the rustle of the fallen leaves. The dust rises here from the anthills destroyed by the sharp-edged horns of the wild buffaloes. Here is a herd of deer. There is a herd of elephants. Pay attention to the cry of the peacocks and the call of the partridges and the ringing tones of the ospreys.

Do you see the slushy footprints of the boars and the grass-green saliva of the ruminating deer that has so recently fed on this tender grass? Yonder is the path taken by the *ruru* deer indicated by the dry leaves soaked with drops of its own blood. There is the bloody trail of the lion marked with the savage impressions of its claws. This blood-soaked place here is doubtless where the forest deer gave birth recently to her young ones!

Oh! Uneven like a braid is the ground of the forest! Follow the trail of the chamari. The ground is dusty here with the dried dung of the deer, enter quickly. Climb up the trees. Listen to that noise. Take hold of your bow. Be careful now. Unleash the dogs.'

Thus as my father and I sat listening, a huge crowd of hunters, somewhat hidden from our view by the denseness of the trees, shook the entire forest, by the commotion they caused, shouting commands to each other.

Soon the roar of the lions hit by the arrows of the shabara hunters echoed from the caves of the forest like the deep reverberating sounds of a well-oiled *mridanga*. The king-elephants separated from their distressed herds, alone and helpless trumpeted loudly; it sounded like thunder in the rain clouds, their screams mixing with the sound of the incessant beatings of their trunks. The piteous cries of the deer, their tear-filled eyes rolling in agony as they got caught in the jaws of the aggressive hunting dogs, rent the air. The female elephants whose mates had just been killed wandered around followed by their young stopping every now and then to listen with fear to the commotion of the hunt and let out long mournful calls for their lost mates. The milch rhinos desperately looking for their newly born young ones, that had strayed away, wailed loudly and heartrendingly.

The birds were flying up to the tops of the trees helter-skelter. The earth seemed to quake with the stamping feet of the hunters, all running together behind the game. The bows drawn up to the ears, they released a shower of arrows sounding like the mating call of the ospreys. The sharp-edged swords of the hunters swished through the air and were heard to fall on the tough shoulders of the forest buffaloes. The hunting dogs growled incessantly. The forest filled with these sounds seemed to tremble.

But as suddenly as it had begun, the commotion ceased; the forest became as quiet as a cloud mass that had rained down all its water, as still as would become the stormy seas after the wind had fallen. My fears abated and I was overcome with curiosity. I moved slightly away from under the wings of my father but staying well within the hollow, I stuck my neck out a little and directed my eyes, as yet weakly focused, towards the source of the noise, eager to find out what it was all about.

What met my eyes struck me with amazement.

Were they the dark waters of the Yamuna scattered into a thousand streams by the thousand-handed Kartaviriya?

Was it a forest of dark tamala trees being blown about in the wind?

Could it be that the darkest hours of the night of the great dissolution had all struck together?

Was it a forest of collyrium-dark stone pillars being shaken by an earthquake or a flood of pitch darkness fleeing the harassing rays of the sun?

Had the lions living on top of the peaks pulled at the dark clouds, which then fell and shattered into a thousand bits?

Like the retinue of the god of death running hither and thither, like a band of fiends rising up from below the earth, splitting the ground as they did so, as if all the dark deeds of the world had come together; as though the entire collection of the bitterest curses of the hermits of Dandakaranya were on the move, as though a myriad comets had come down to destroy all the creatures of the earth, the terror-inspiring army of thousands of shabaras saw I, messengers of death, coming towards me from deep inside the forest.

Right in the centre of this huge army was its leader, hard as if cast in iron, Ekalavya come to life again. He was in the first flush of youth with the hair on his face just beginning to sprout; it was now a mere dark stain, so much like an elephant calf with its cheeks adorned with the first streaks of the rut fluid. The blue-lily lustre streaming from his body flooded the forest. His abundant dark, curly locks came down to his shoulder like a lion's mane darkened by the rut fluid. He had a broad forehead and a high, intimidating nose. In his left ear he wore a serpent hood gem whose pink rays had lent their colour to that side of his body, as though the bed of tender leaves on which he was wont to lie had painted his left side pink.

Having held the cheeks of the elephant that he had just killed, his body seemed anointed with its rut fluid and smelt sweetly of the *saptaparna* and the paste of *krishnaguru*. Attracted by this fragrance, swarms of bees hovered over his head looking like a canopy of peacock feathers, or an umbrella of dark tamala leaves.

As if subdued by the strength of the hunter's arms and pressed into his service by fear, the Vindhya forest blew away the sweat pouring down his cheeks by waving her leaf-hands. His slightly bloodshot eyes, symbolizing the russet twilight preceding the night of doom of the deer of the forest, seemed to lend their colour to all the directions. His hands reached down to his knees, seemingly fashioned on the measurements of the trunks of the celestial elephants. His forearms were calloused and rough with the constant handling of exceedingly sharp weapons, as he hunted animals to offer to the goddess Chandika.

His broad dark chest was like a rocky expanse on the Vindhyas; it was now adorned with drops of slightly dried deer blood interspersed with beads of sweat, like a necklace of the black and red *gunjaphala* strung alternately with pearls from the temple of the elephant. His abdomen was lean and his swarthy sturdy thighs mocked at the rut-stained pillars to which elephants were usually tied. The innate ferocity of the tribe had left habitual frown lines on his forehead even in the absence of anger, as though the goddess Katyayani pleased by his devotion had branded him for her own, with her *trishul*. This, with the constantly knitted eyebrows gave a terrifying aspect to his face.

Hunting dogs of different colours followed the shabara leader. Exhausted with the day's effort their pink tongues were hanging down. They had necklaces of cowries hung around their necks. Small of stature yet they were veritable lion cubs in their ferocity.

The leader was also surrounded by his comrades-in-arms, almost all of whom carried in their hands the spoils of the hunt— the bushy tails of the deer, the tusks of the young elephants and of course the pearls torn out of the elephants' foreheads. Some carried loads of meat like veritable rakshasas; others wore around their waist, the skin of the lions they had hunted, like the *pramatha ganas* of Shiva; and some held like the Jain ascetics, peacock feathers in their hands.

My attention was once again drawn to the commander; a child of the Vindhyas to be sure but he was also an aspect of Yama, the god of death come down to earth. He was young in years yet old in experience for he had killed men of all ages; he was a sibling of sin, a charioteer of the unrighteous *Kali Yuga*. He had the freedom to live his life as he wished yet he was totally under the command of Durga. He was fearful to look at, yet his great strength and power had endowed him with a grave and solemn appearance. His name, which I came to know later, was Matanga.

I thought 'Alas! The life of these hunters is one of ignorance, their conduct one spurned by the wise. Their food is flesh, their drink liquor and their profession hunting. Their sacred chant is the howl of the jackals. Their preceptors from whom they learn right and wrong are the owls, their confidants, the hunting dogs.

They draw their practical wisdom from the call of birds. Their celebration is drinking alcohol. Their aides are the poison-tipped serpent-like arrows and the only music they know is what stuns and destroys the helpless deer. Their wives are women captured by them as part of their loot. Their worship is with the blood of animals and their offering, flesh. Their ornaments are the serpent gems and their body lotion the sweat of the elephant in rut. They destroy the very forest they live in.'

— 6 —

Such were my thoughts when Matanga, exhausted with all the wandering in the forest and wishing to rest awhile, placed his bow under the very shalmoli tree on which I lived, and sat down on a leaf seat hurriedly brought over by one of his attendants. Yet another shabara youth rushed over to the gleaming waters of the Pampa Lake—gleaming like melted pearls, like the cat's-eye-gem, and so clear that its presence could be perceived only by touching its icy coolness—and brought over some of that water, astringent with the pollen of the lotus buds, in a leaf cup along with freshly plucked lotus stalks, cleaned of all mud. Matanga drank the water and ate the lotus stalks like Rahu swallowing the phase of the moon. Refreshed, he got up and followed by his retinue, which too had slaked its thirst with the water of the lake, slowly moved away in his chosen direction.

However, one of the old shabaras a fierce looking man who had obviously been unsuccessful in hunting deer was on the prowl for flesh of some kind. When the leader disappeared from sight the old hunter, wanting to climb the tree, looked up at us, the little ones in the nests as if calculating how many of us might be there; he seemed to drink our life blood with his rapacious eyes, like a vulture greedy for the taste of bird flesh.

In that moment of sheer terror inspired by the look of him, life seemed to flee from the young ones. Is there any act of cruelty at which the pitiless would draw the line? The old shabara climbed up the tall shalmoli, as tall as several tala trees arranged one on top of the other, touching the very clouds with the tips of its branches, as effortlessly as if he were climbing a mere flight of stairs. And there they were the helpless young ones, with no strength developed as yet to be able to fly away. Some were so recently born that they were still shrouded in a pale pinkish glow and looked no different from the blooms on the shalmoli tree. Some with their wings just beginning to grow were like the new petals of the lotus. With the tips of their beaks just beginning to turn red, some of the little birds had the beauty of slightly opened lotus buds. Some in very early infancy were utterly helpless and the trembling of their unsteady necks seemed like pathetically futile efforts at warding off the calamity. It was these defenceless creatures that the cruel old shabara caught hold of, one by one from inside the nests, as though they were fruits to be plucked at will, killed them and threw them on the ground.

In the face of this utterly monstrous, irremediable and deadly calamity, my father's body shook even more than normal. His eyes brimmed with tears and rolled in fear. He threw his unfocused glances here and there and his mouth went dry. Quite powerless to ward off the danger, but at the same time overwhelmed with helpless love for me, intent only on my safety, but unable to think of any remedial course of action, he simply covered me with his enfeebled wings now further weakened with fear and sat supporting me under his chest, hoping it would serve the purpose of saving me at that juncture.

The old hunter moving relentlessly among the branches drew near the opening of our hollow. He thrust his evil hand in, repulsive and fearful like an old snake; it smelt of raw meat and the marrow of the wild boars of the forest; it was a veritable incarnation of the staff of Yama, the god of death. He pulled my father out who wailed piteously and pecked at his hand again and again with his beak. The shabara then killed him by wringing his neck. As for me, perhaps due to the smallness of my body that had now shrunk even more with my limbs all drawn up close in fear, or simply because I still had life left in me to live, he did not see me hidden under the wings of my father. He threw my dead father down on the ground.

I too fell along with him with my neck placed between his legs and concealed by his chest. As I held myself very quiet and more important, as I was not destined to die just yet I found myself fallen in the midst of dry leaves blown together in heaps by the wind. The shabara failed to notice me as I was well hidden by these dry leaves and I was not hurt either.

Now, there was a big tamala tree not too far away from the spot where I had fallen. The shabara beauties would often use the flowers of the tree to adorn their ears; its lustrous blue leaves surpassed the dark glow of Sri Krishna's body. The new leaves were so dark that one might fancy that they were the tresses of Lady Vindhya herself. The branches of the tree were so dense that under them, there was no light even during the day.

It was under this tree that I sought to take refuge before the hunter could get down from the treetop. With my body well camouflaged by the decayed leaves I moved away from the lap of my dead father, the pitiless creature that I was, although it would have been meet and proper for me to have died with him then and there. My childish nature was as yet unable to comprehend love, and functioned entirely on the inborn sense of fear. I supported myself on my wings just beginning to grow, and stumbling every now and then I crawled to safety under the tamala tree. I had indeed managed to sneak out of the cavernous mouth of death.

In the meantime the shabara descended from the tree and collecting the dead parrots strewn on the ground in a leaf cup and binding them together with creepers serving as twines hurried away in the same direction as the leader.

I had just been granted a fresh lease of life. But I was stunned by the recent death of my father and exhausted by the fall from such a great height. My body was still trembling with terror and I found myself seized with a crippling thirst.

I calculated that the evil one would, by now, have gone far away. Therefore raising my neck a little and casting my still panic-stricken eyes all around me I came out from under the tamala tree and tried to go to the water to appease my thirst. The slightest movement in the grass would terrify me that it was the cruel one that had come back.

I had not grown my wings fully as yet; nor was I very steady on my feet. With the result I fell again and again on my face or on my side. Supporting myself on one wing I dragged myself on the ground. Unused to such exertions I was soon worn out. At every step, I would stop, raise my head and take laboured breaths. My body became ashen with dust.

And I thought, 'How very strange that even when placed in such dire straits the creatures of the earth cling to life. There is nothing sweeter than life to all creation. My noble father is dead and yet here I am breathing still and all my senses are intact. I seem to have already forgotten all that my dear father did for me. How selflessly he cared for me right from the day of my birth, reining in the grief unleashed by my mother's death. What varied ways he devised to feed and protect me. I seem to have forgotten all that. Vile indeed are the life forces that do not allow me to follow my benefactor in death. Lust for life turns everyone selfish.

'Even in this state of bereavement the desire for water grips me. The shores of the lake must still be far away, from the distant cackle of the swans, so similar to the tinkle of the anklets of the water nymphs. The cranes' call too sounds muffled and faint is the fragrance of the lotuses. This is the most trying part of the day with the sun right in the middle of the sky. His rays are spreading the heat like a shower of fiery embers. My thirst increases. I am unable to move even a little as the hot dust rises and my limbs droop. No longer do I seem to be in control of my body. My heart is distressed and my sight is dimming. Just as well. Even if I do not wish it cruel fate may yet bring about my death at this very moment.'

─7─

B ut help came from an unexpected quarter.
  Not too far away from the lake was a hermitage in which lived a sage named Jabali. Harita, the son of this sage came right at that moment along with his companions to this very lake near which I lay dying, to have his bath and perform his daily rites.

The young hermit Harita was truly like a son of Prajapati. His mind was clear and lucid as a result of a careful study of the arts and sciences. He was so splendid that he appeared like another Agni, difficult to gaze upon. His body seemed as if sculpted out of the halo of the sun, and his limbs, fashioned out of rainbows. It would be still more accurate to say that his body seemed plated with molten gold. His glowing presence lit up the place, like the morning sun, nay, like a forest fire.

Harita's thick hair fell down to his shoulders; it had been purified with the waters of many a sacred spot and shone like burnished copper. Some of it was collected and tied into a knot on top of his head. He looked like Agni when the god came craftily disguised as a Brahmin youth to destroy the Khandava forest. A crystal *rudrakshamala* hung around his right ear. It brought to mind an army standing guard at the fortress of dharma. His forehead was marked with three lines in sacred ash symbolizing the threefold vows taken to desist from all worldly pleasures.

As he walked down to the lake he carried a crystal pitcher in his left hand. His body was wrapped in a lustrous black and white deerskin that fell over his shoulders. The sacred thread lay over his left shoulder looking delicate as though made out of lotus stalk; it was so light that it moved in the wind; and when it did it seemed to try and count the ribs on his spare chest. In his right hand he held a *palasha* staff, to the tip of which was attached a leaf cup filled with flowers from the creepers gathered for purposes of worship.

The deer that had grown up on the handfuls of grass fed to them by the hermits now followed them to the lake. In a show of touching affection they would often dig up the mud with their horns for the hermits to use when they bathed. Some of that mud was still stuck to the tips of their horns.

The compassionate of the world are so full of the milk of human kindness that they offer it freely with no expectation of reward. Spotting me lying in such a helpless state Harita was overcome with pity and said to his companions: 'This young one of a parrot with undeveloped wings has somehow fallen down from the top of the tree here. He might even have slipped out of the mouth of a hawk. He is just barely alive. Look how he gasps for breath and how he keeps falling on his face and opens his mouth over and over again. His eyes are almost closed and he cannot hold his neck erect. Let us take him to the water before he dies.'

He picked me up and reached the lake where he put aside his water jug and the staff. By then I had given up all my exertions

except keeping my head raised. Harita himself then took some
water from the lake and fed me drop by drop with his fingertips.
A few drops fell on my body as well. As I revived he placed me
in the cool moist shade of the lotus leaves growing near the
shore and then went about his bathing rituals.

Harita was already cleansed of all impurities, with the
performance of Yoga.

Yet, now, after finishing his bath, he recited verses for
sweeping his sins away as though there were any still left. Then
he offered freshly opened lotus flowers and leaf cups of water to
the sun. After which he gathered up his washed white bark
garments; the white garments on his golden body appeared as if
the young morning sun and moonlight had come together.
Fanning out his wet hair with his palm he picked me up, and
followed by all the other young hermits, their hair dripping after
their bath, slowly wended his way to the hermitage.

After travelling just a short distance I beheld a hermitage of
such surpassing beauty that it could truly have been called
paradise on earth. It was surrounded on all sides by dense groves
of trees, ever laden with flowers and fruits—such as the tala,
tamala, *tilaka*, *hintala* and *bakula*. There were groves of coconut
palms, with the trees entwined with creepers of cardamom.
Lodhra trees, *lavali* creepers and *lavang* bushes abounded; their
leaves trembled in the wind. There were flowering mango trees
from which pollen rose and spread attracting the bees. Pollen
from the *ketaki* doused the hermitage in a sea of yellow. The
creeper-slim areca nut trees swayed in the wind, becoming a
swing for the forest nymphs. When the wind blew there was an
incessant shower of a mass of white flowers from the densely
growing trees as though it were raining stars, as though the trees
were conferring benediction, expiating all sins.

Close to the hermitage there was much activity. The sages
were walking about followed by their disciples who were carrying

materials for worship like *samidh, kusha* flowers, earth and so on. They were also chanting the scriptures sonorously.

The three sacrificial fires were continuously being fed with clarified butter. Pleased with the devotion, the fires sent out lines of smoke as if to build a flight of stairs, a bridge, to lead the ascetics right away, in their very mortal bodies to heaven.

The waters of the hermitage wells were pure as though they too had partaken of the sacrificial merit of the place. The ever-widening series of ripples in the well water reflected a row of suns leading one to wonder if the 'Seven Sages,' the constellation of Saptarshi had plunged into the water impelled by their desire to meet the holy men of the hermitage. It was different at night; with myriad white lilies in full bloom, it now appeared as if the stars and planets had come down to pay homage to the hermits.

In the courtyards in front of the huts in which the hermits lived the *shyamaka* grains were spread out to dry in the sun. There were also piles of gooseberries, cloves and *karkandu* and an abundance of fruits such as the plantain, breadfruit, mango, *phanas* and tala.

The disciples were loudly reciting their lessons; having heard the incantations all their lives the parrots were repeating them fluently while the mynas were chanting the Vedas. The forest cranes pecked at the offerings laid out to the *vaishvadevas*. And close to the wells the cygnets ate the *nivara* offerings. The deer were licking the young children of the sages caressingly. The half-burnt kusha grass, samidh and flowers on the still simmering altars crackled sibilantly.

The elderly hermits, who were blind, shuffled in and out of the sacred grove clutching at the sticks held out to them by the friendly monkeys who led the way. The elephants watered the trees bringing the water in their trunks. The peacocks fanned the sacrificial fires by waving their outspread feathers.

The delicious aroma of rice being cooked with ghee for the oblation filled the air.

On one side of the hermitage the guests were being looked after. On another the forefathers were worshipped. Some of the sages were absorbed in reading; others were deep in philosophic discussion, and still others in profound yogic meditation.

Some were carrying out one practical chore or the other, such as putting up the thatched huts, in which they lived, or cementing the courtyard with cow dung, or sweeping the insides of the cottages. Most of the residents of the hermitage were variously busy, cleaning the skin of the black buck, washing their bark garments, collecting samidh, drying the lotus seeds according to the sacred rules or stringing the rosary.

Such a place as this hermitage had never existed before in this age of Kali, where falsehood was unknown and lust never even heard of. It was a place where 'soiled' meant only being soiled by the smoke of the sacrifice, not by one's own bad deeds. It was a place where redness was seen only on the beaks of the parrots and never in the flush of anger on men's faces. It was a place where sharpness resided on the tips of the kusha grass but never in the temperament of the people. And it was a place where only the cuckoos had bloodshot eyes, never men inflamed with lust.

There was *pakshapatha* in this grove to be sure as the cocks shed their feathers but of bias, pakshapatha in learned discussions, there was none indeed. There was much circling, *bhranti,* round the fire, but never was there any confusion, bhranti, with regard to theological points! The praises of the eight Vedic deities, the *ashtavasu,* were indeed heard constantly—but of greedy adulation for worldly wealth, *vasu,* there was none.

And it was a place where downward motion, *adhogati,* was seen solely in the roots of the plants and trees.

— 8 —

A t the very centre of the hermitage, there was an *ashoka* tree with lacquer-red leaves. The black buckskins and the water jugs of the hermits hung from its branches. There were to be seen all around the base of the tree, the palm prints of the daughters of the hermits, made in yellow scented powder. The young ones of the deer were drinking water from the moat-like basin around the tree. The ropes made of darba that the young hermit boys used to secure their kusha grass garments with, were all seen tied round the tree. The ground near the tree was paved with cow dung and had just been decorated with fresh flowers. Although the tree was not very big, its circular canopy provided a vast area of shade under it. It was here, that I first saw the great sage Jabali, seated under the red ashoka tree.

Around him were other great sages who too had performed the most vigorous penances. Like the seas surrounding the earth, like the great mountains ranged around Mount Meru, like all the sacred fires flaming around the main sacrificial altar, like the *kalpas* encircling Absolute Time, were the sages gathered around Jabali, the greatest of them all.

Lady Old Age had embraced the sage all over. She trembled in his trembling limbs as if she were in fear of his curses; like one inebriated she stumbled in his stumbling gait. She was the penitent smeared with sacred ash, who had made his body pale. The sage's lustre was as blinding as the brilliance of the sun at *pralaya*, the final dissolution; yet like the foaming Ganga gushing down the head of the Lord of the Animals, like milk oblation on the flames of the sacrificial fire, she had fallen fearlessly on his head covered with moonlight-white hair. Like a lover she had caught hold of his hair.

His long white hair was pulled up on top of his head, a victory standard hoisted in the name of righteousness, having won the allegiance of all the sages of the world by his spiritual power. The matted strands could well be the sacred ropes, for ascending to heaven. A soaring tree of austerities was the sage and his *jata,* the flowering merit of all that penance. The three lines drawn in sacred ash across his broad forehead were like the three streams of the Ganga winding their way across the rock surface of the Himalayas. Like the downward bent rays of the moon, his age-slackened eyebrows fell over his eyes. The brilliance of his teeth lit up the area in front of his face; the rays that streamed through his parted lips as he uttered the ceaseless *mantras* were like shoots of truth, materializations as it were of the purity of his mind and body, his compassion and his scholarship.

His cheeks were hollow in their emaciation; his chin was pointed and his nose high, and the eyes piercing under scanty eyelashes. The beard fell down to his navel. Taut veins bound his neck closely, reins with which he controlled the unruly sense horses as it were. Actually his entire body was so closely laced with prominent veins that he was like an ancient kalpa tree entwined with the stems of old creepers shorn of all leaves. The raised rib cage had bones far apart. The sacred thread hanging from his shoulders moved on his gaunt, immaculate chest like a slender wave that rose in the wind, like a tender lotus stalk floating around on the clear waters of the Mandakini. He was counting the *akshamala* of crystal beads that hung from between the moving fingers of his hand, akshamala that resembled the goddess Sarswati's necklace of huge brilliant pearls.

He wore a bark garment silken in appearance and spotless, as if washed in the waters of the Manasa Lake. Had it been woven with moon rays or with the foam on the nectar? Perhaps it is the virtues of the world that constituted the warp and weft of the garment. Be that as it may, the white garment wrapped him like a second layer of old age. A crystal goblet filled with Ganga water rested on a tripod close to him, like a white swan nestling close to a cluster of white lilies.

Could there be any doubt that it was Jabali who bestowed some of his own steadfastness on the mountains to make them immovable, who gave of his profundity to the oceans to make them deep? The power of his penance, doubtless, he gave as brilliance to the sun, his equability, as coolness to the moon and it was his own utter sinlessness that he must have shared with the skies to make them blemishless too.

'Behold the splendour of tapas,' I thought. 'This great sage is full of peace, and his body pure and flawless like tempered gold, yet the light from his eyes strikes us like lightning. Although he is totally detached his great majesty instils fear in those who approach him for the first time. Even the lesser brilliance of sages with meagre merit, sages who are quick to anger—like the leaping fire in the dried *nalakasha* flowers—is, by its very nature hard to bear. Then, need anything be said about great sages, venerated in all the three worlds, whose sins, if any, are constantly washed away in the waters of their penance, who can see the entire world as clearly as a gooseberry resting on an open palm by the power of their divine insight, and who never hesitate to destroy evil. Merely to utter their names confers merit; how much more meritorious an actual meeting with one of them should be. Blessed is this hermitage, which is under his command. Blessed is this entire earth guided by this earthly Brahma. And blessed are these other hermits here who have the good fortune to gaze upon the great one, day and night and serve him single-mindedly and listen to his sacred utterances. All knowledge rendered turbid in this age of Kali has regained its clarity in him, just as the rivers muddied in the rainy season become clear again in the autumn.

'Even the sun's rays skirt the sacred grove as though cowed by the greatness of the sage and his ashrama, shrouded with the smoke of many a sacrificial fire. The flames of these fires are gathered up and gently sway in the wind as though they too are paying homage to the sage. They devour the mantra-sanctified offerings avidly, indicating their love for him. The breeze, that carries the fragrance of the flowers on the creepers of the grove and rustles the silk-like bark garments, approaches the sage slowly as though a little unsure of itself. Even the elements bow before the austere might of the saintly.

'With him the earth shines as if blessed with two suns. Secure in his hold she trembles not any more. And the birds and the animals of the sacred grove live together forgetting their natural antagonisms. This snake here wishing for a respite from the heat has crawled under the dense feathers of the peacock that imitate an expanse of fresh green grass speckled with the lustrous eyes of the antelopes. And this young one of the deer, leaving its own mother drinks the milk flowing at the udders of a lioness, along with his friends, the lion cubs. As for the lion, he sits with eyes half-closed in enjoyment, while the elephant calves pull at his mane; and the monkeys having given up their innate restlessness bring fruits to the children of the hermits.

'He is the rushing waters of compassion; he is the bridge across the ocean of existence; he is the very reservoir of forgiveness; he is axe to the dense bower of desire and a veritable ocean of undying bliss; he is the leading steps to those descending in to the river of study; he is touchstone to the gems that are the various disciplines of knowledge; he is forest fire to the fresh growth that is attachment; he is the incantation that arrests the serpent of anger and the sun that lights up the darkness of delusion.'

I was lost in my own thoughts when Harita placed me on one side of the very same ashoka tree under which sat his father. He then touched his father's feet and sat down on a kusha grass

seat placed not too close to the sage. At once all the sages turned
their curious glances at me and exclaimed 'Harita! Where did
you come by this baby parrot?' And Harita replied, 'When I
went for my bath there he was fallen from his nest on the tree
on the shores of the lotus lake. He had wilted in the heat of the
sun; he was covered with hot dust, and hurt by the fall from
such a great height and barely alive. Poor thing! He was quite
unable to climb back into his nest on top of that tall tree. Taking
pity on him I brought him here. He has not grown his wings yet
and so he cannot fly. In fact he can survive only if we place him
in a hollow in one of our hermitage trees and our children feed
him with nivara grain and the juice of fruits. It is indeed the
sacred duty of people like us to protect the orphaned. Once his
wings grow and he acquires the ability to fly he will fly away
wherever he wants to. Or having got used to this place perhaps
he will choose to live with us.'

Jabali, becoming a little curious, inclined his head slightly
and observed me for a while with his gentle eyes. His quiet gaze
washed over me like a shower of sanctified water. Then, as though
some kind of recognition was dawning on him, his eyes came to
rest on me over and over again. Finally he said 'This parrot is
just experiencing the fruits of his own insolence'.

The great sage Jabali could see equally well into the past,
present and the future, by the power that his penance had
conferred upon him. With his divine sight he could see the entire
world as though it rested on the palm of his hand. He knew the
past lives and could foretell future events. He could estimate the
life span of a person by merely looking at him.

The entire assembly of hermits that knew well the powers of
the sage became excited with a lively curiosity. 'What kind of
offence did this creature commit? What was the reason for it?
And when did this happen? What was he in his previous birth?
And how come he is now born a bird?' Full of questions, the

hermits begged the sage to enlighten them. For they all knew very well Jabali's miraculous powers.

The sage replied, 'It is indeed a long and astonishing tale. But it is late now, very little of the day is left. Our bathing hour approaches, and the time for your prayers is passing. Please rise now and perform your daily duties. Later at night when you sit down to relax after having partaken of your evening meal of fruits and roots, I shall tell you the story from the very beginning, what this bird was in his earlier life, and what his guilt was that has now brought him to this predicament. But first see to it that the bird is refreshed with some food. I am sure when I am narrating the story of his earlier life, he will listen as though he is dreaming of it all, and later remember everything without omitting a single detail.'

With this the hermits had to be content. Jabali then rose and went about his daily ablutions with the other hermits following suit.

Night was about to fall. The setting sun sported the redness of red sandalwood. Faint-rayed, the sun was shrinking in lustre as though the heat-drinking sages with their upturned faces and eyes fixed on him, were drinking away the abundance of his glow. Fleeing from the plains of the earth and the fields of lotuses, the sun's rays, at the end of the day clung like birds to the tops of the trees and to the peaks of the mountains. As though to avoid touching the rising saptarishis the sun drew in his ray feet. When the thousand-rayed sun finally went down, pink twilight rose, like reefs of coral from the shores of the western ocean. Very soon the hues of the evening twilight dripped over everything.

It was time for some of the sages to sit down to meditate. From somewhere came the heart-stealing sound of milk gushing out as the ritual-worthy cows were being milked. The young girls of the grove went about placing the cooked offering to the deities of the four directions. The sacrificial altars were being covered with green kusha grass.

No sooner had her lord the sun set, than the lotus plant, full of distress, undertook penance for a speedy reunion with him. She closed her petals and it became her kamandalu; the white swans that swam around her served as her white garments, the white lotus stalk her sacred thread, and the rows of hovering bees, her rosary.

Immediately after the sun set, the stars rose in the heavens; could they be droplets of the water spray that rose after the sun had splashed into the western ocean? Soon the evening redness disappeared; had the water thrown up by the sages as they worshipped their special deities with raised faces washed it away?

Quickly the twilight faded. Stricken by that disappearance as it were, night donned blackbuck-skin-dark mourning; and a blinding darkness seeped into everything except the heart of the sages.

In due course the nectar-rayed moon rose. Like the ocean-filling, swan-whitened waters of the Ganga coursing down from the heavens, the swan-white moonlight streamed down from the skies. Like the swans, white as freshly bloomed *sinduvara* blooms, back from the seas at the end of the dark cloud-covered rainy season, the white rays of the moon hovered over the white lily-covered waters of the lake. The earth became whitewashed with the lime-dust-like moonlight. A cool, gentle, moist, evening breeze started blowing, fragrant with the strong scent of the blooming white lilies. The hermitage deer sat in repose enjoying the breeze, the mouth moving in rumination, the face stilled, the gaze dulled and the eyelashes knitted in somnolence.

The night had barely lost half a yama when Harita, his evening meal over, approached his father with the other sages. He carried me with him. His father was seated alone on a cane seat, a little away, on one side of the moonlight-drenched sacred

grove. Jalapada, a disciple fanned him gently with a fan made
of deerskin, pure as darba grass. Drawing close Harita said, 'Here
is the entire group of sages, full of curiosity, gathered around
you expectantly. The little bird too has had its rest. We are now
ready for the story, the bird's deeds in his previous life and what
is to become of him in the future'.

That great sage Jabali glanced at me perched right in the
front and at the gathered group eager to hear the story. He said,
'Well, listen then if you are interested', and began to talk slowly,
musingly . . .

Jabali Speaks

There is in the kingdom of Avanti, a city named Ujjayini, of surpassing beauty, a city more splendid than the city of the gods, and an ornament to all the three worlds. On account of the virtue of its people it is celebrated as the womb of Krita Yuga.

The great god Mahadeva is the presiding deity of the city of Ujjayini. Has the great lord, He who is the cause of all creation, preservation and destruction, created this city as yet another earth for his very special abode? Have the oceans then come and surrounded the city in the form of the deep moat around it, going right down to the nether world, believing it is indeed a second earth? Are these just tall whitewashed ramparts that ring Ujjayini, or is it really Mount Kailasa of the soaring snowy peaks that has now come to this city, drawn by the presence there, of Pashupati, the lord of the animals?

The market streets of Ujjayini are wide and long and are filled with a wealth of merchandise—conches, mother of pearl, pearl, coral and emerald. Fine sand-like gold dust is everywhere. Surely, this was how the golden sands of the ocean floor must have looked after the waters had all been drunk away by the great Agasthya.

Rows upon rows of art galleries in the city are all decorated with paintings, the pictures depicting the devas, asuras, siddhas, gandharvas, and vidhyadharas. Are these really picture galleries or could they be the actual aerial vehicles of the divinities come down to earth to watch the lovely women gathered at the never-ceasing festivals of the city?

The city squares are adorned with magnificent temples that look like the Mandara ranges splashed with the milk of the milky ocean while being churned. They have golden domes and the white flags flying on top look like the streams of the celestial Ganga. There are also innumerable Jaina and Buddhist viharas.

The city is shady with dark green woods which have wells in their midst for watering the trees. White-washed platforms are built around these wells, and machinery consisting of assembled pots unceasingly waters the groves. The breeze wafts the fragrance of the flowers from the woods. Flying pollen from the ketaki bushes makes the countryside appear dusty.

The worship of Kama, the god of love goes on in the city as one hears the auspicious ringing of bells. Bright coral-red chamaras and flags are tied everywhere. Over every house is also hoisted, on a pole made of the wood of the *bakula* tree, the love god's own flag with its fish emblem.

But the city is not given to fun and frolic alone; continuous chant of the Vedas is also heard which washes away the moral impurities, if any, of the city.

The innumerable fountains of Ujjayini rumble imitating the deep sounds of a muted mridangam. Water sprays thrown up by these fountains refract the rays of the sun into rainbows. In this rainy-day-like atmosphere, the excited peacocks open out their feathers in an arc and dance in abandon, creating a commotion with their raucous calls.

Myriad lakes dot the city. They are resplendent with an abundance of lilies, the blue ones in the periphery and the white ones in the centre, so beautiful that one could gaze at them forever. Everywhere there are turrets made of ivory, white like foam that brighten the city. They are framed with a dense growth of plantain trees.

The river Shipra flows around Ujjayini. Her turbulent waters rise in huge waves possibly in a bid to wash the skies above. Or, she could be knitting her wave-eyebrows in violent jealousy of the Ganga seated on the crown of Shiva.

The city is home to men of brilliance and sophistication whose fame is known to all the three worlds. Immeasurably wealthy yet without flaunting it, and unbiased in all their dealings they are like living *smritis*, for what these texts advise they carry out impeccably. They construct *sabhas* where the learned meet and discuss the affairs of the city. They make *avasthas*, dwellings for pupils and ascetics. They sink wells, and put up drinking water dispensing centres. They make gardens, build temples, bridges, and water fountains.

They are strong yet have their future world in mind; they are valiant yet full of courtesy; they speak sweetly, but they speak the truth. They indulge fully in *kama*, sensual pleasures and enjoy thoroughly their *artha,* riches, but they remain ever rooted firmly in a deeply ingrained sense of *dharma*, righteousness. They are tranquil and soothing like the spring breeze and they are compassionate towards all life like those of the Jaina faith.

They are also erudite, full of wit and humour, with a mastery of the languages and scripts of practically all the countries of the world. Splendidly turned out, even-tempered, and generous, they are unbeatable even in the game of dice.

On the top floors of the tall mansions the women of Ujjayini make music. Their sweet melodies attract the horses of the sun's chariot. As the horses slow down and bend their heads as if to listen to the music and the flag of the chariot falls forward it seems as if the sun when he passes every day is paying homage to Mahakala, resident in the city.

The women's ornaments are so brilliant that they light up the city at night and darkness never seems to fall. The *chakravaka* pair never separates. And the lamps of love are rendered redundant. The night attains the yellow radiance of a morning with a young sun, as though the quarters have been set ablaze by the fire of Madana.

Beholding the beautiful faces of the women asleep on the terraces of the mansions, the one marked with the image of the deer, roused to passion, descends and wanders among them in the guise of his reflection on the sandalwood scented waters splashed on the cool stone floors.

In the noble city of Ujjayini, there is *asthithi* or shaking only in the *gamakas* of music and the beat of the mridanga, there is no shaking the people from their righteousness. The pangs of separation are only for the chakaravaka couples at night, the men need never go away from their lovers in search of wealth. It is the flags that flutter in the breeze; the people never tremble due to any kind of distress.

What more need be said in praise of the city when He, whose shining toenails are kissed by the glittering crowns of the devas and asuras: He, whose razor-sharp trident tears into the demon Andhaka: He, whose crest jewel, the crescent moon is for ever scratched by Parvathi's anklets: He, whose body is enveloped in the ashes of the burning Tripuras: He, at whose feet rises a pile of broken bangles slipping from the outstretched, supplicating hands of the bereaved Rati, grieving for the destroyed Manmatha, seeking to propitiate the Lord into forgiveness: He, on whose flaming tresses falls the celestial Ganga and loses her way: He, the Lord Mahakala Himself, forgetting his love of Kailasa has now made Ujjayini His home?

─10─

In this remarkable city of Ujjayini, there ruled a king called Tarapida, comparable in greatness to Nala, Nahusha, Yayati, Dhundhumara, Bharata, Bhagiratha, and Dasharatha.

Tarapida had become the lord of the whole world by the might of his arms that were like the trunks of the celestial elephants, and was proud of being the refuge of the entire world; he mitigated the calamities of the world. Wise and energetic, and powerful, his mind never tired of political analysis; and he was deeply read in jurisprudence. He was an equal third to the sun and the moon in splendour and brilliance. He was also extraordinarily handsome; the world readily believed that he was another Manmatha that Hara must have created, taking pity on Rati's inconsolable grief over the loss of her husband.

Tarapida's body had become immaculate with the performance of countless sacrifices. No wonder Rajyalakshmi, driven by her impulse to be with men of valour came to him lotus in hand, to embrace him unashamedly, having abandoned her own lotus field, having rejected even the pleasure of residing on the chest of Narayana.

All verities flowed out of King Tarapida, just as the pure streams of the celestial Ganga, the resort of all the ascetics of the world, flowed out of the feet of Madhusudana.

Always cool, the king was yet the cause of burning anguish in his opponents; firm and steady of mind, he was restless only in ever being on the move in his kingdom. Himself without blemish of any kind he was the cause of the tearstains on the lustrous faces of the women of his enemies.

Kali had shaken dharma to the very roots; ignorance and excessive sinfulness had soiled it. King Tarapida re-established dharma on a firm foundation, like Shiva stabilising Kailasa shaken by the Ten-Headed One.

A veritable incarnation of god Dharma, Tarapida was like a deputy of Narayana on earth, a true remover of all the suffering of the people.

The princes of the entire world subjugated by the power of Tarapida's arms came to him, in supplication, eyes rolling in fear, hands joined over their heads like lotus buds and bowed low, their crowns touching the king's feet. And they came from all directions.

In the east, they came from as far away as Udayashaila, whose mid slopes were washed by the waves of the ocean; the flowers on whose trees appeared more dense than they really were as the stars moved through them; and whose sandalwood trees were drenched by the nectar that oozed out of the rising moon.

In the south they came from around that distant bridge across the sea that Nala, the monkey leader, son of Vishvakarma had built with thousands of rocks; where the army of monkeys ate away almost all the *lavali* fruits with the result very few were now left; where one could still see the footprints left by Rama which the nymphs were wont to worship, coming up from the waters. And where myriad scattered pieces of seashells, crushed when the rocks were broken for the bridge, had made the stone surfaces starry with their glitter.

In the west they came all the way from the Meru mountain whose crystal clear streams seemed to wash over the very constellations in the sky; whose rock faces had been polished smooth with Narayana's armlets grazing against them, as he was engrossed in churning the milky ocean for *amrita*; and whose back was stamped upon by the moving feet of the devas and asuras pulling at Vasuki wound round it and whose peaks were drenched in the spray of nectar.

In the north they came from the faraway Gandhamadana mountains, home to a sacred grove called Badarikashrama that was marked with the footprints of Nara and Narayana. On the peaks of these ranges one could hear the tinkle of the ornaments of the lovely women of Kubera's city. The streams of Gandhamadana had been sanctified by the daily ablutions carried out by the Seven Sages, and its mid-slopes were fragrant with the *saugandhika* flowers, bunches of which were once cut away by Bhima.

Rajyalakshmi never left the shade of King Tarapida's umbrella as though distressed by the heat of his valour. Even Indra, the lord of the devas coveted the unique and incomparable powers of King Tarapida.

To this day mankind listens to Tarapida's story believing it would contribute to its welfare. The people celebrate the story as auspicious. They recite it over and over again like an incantation and commit it to memory as though it were the Vedas themselves.

This great king Tarapida was served by a great Prime Minister, a Brahmin named Shukanasa, a deeply erudite man full of Vedic learning, who had been close to the king right from his childhood. Highly skilled in the interpretation of law, he was an expert navigator of the ship of state. His was an intellect unfazed in the presence of difficulties; and he was a man of great firmness and stability. A river of truth, an exponent of virtues, a teacher of propriety, an upholder of righteousness, Shukanasa like Adisesha was equal to bearing the burden of the entire earth. He was indeed unique and unparalleled in the kingdom. He was to Tarapida what Brhaspati was to Indra, Kavi to Vrshaparvana, Vasishta to Dasharatha, Vishvamitra to Rama, Dhaumya to

Yudhishtra, and Sumati to Nala. It may be said of him that wisdom itself, by resorting to him attained many more dimensions, bore many more fruits, like a creeper attaining luxuriance of growth by finding refuge in the strength of a great tree.

Shukanasa had firm control over the kingdom. Thousands of his spies had fanned out over the wide world bounded by the four oceans. The Prime Minister would know of any event, as soon as it happened anywhere in the world, as if it took place right in his home. The vassal princes could hardly take a deep breath without the Prime Minister knowing about it.

With the power of his arms that were like the sacred staffs planted at the performance of the rites of war, arms that were the refuge of the whole world and splendid with the lustre of the sword they wielded, arms that were veritable comets that brought doom to the foes, Tarapida, whilst still young had brought all the seven islands of the earth under his suzerainty. With the welfare of all his subjects secured, he now entrusted Shukanasa, his friend and minister with the responsibility of day-to-day administration. With all opposition put down with a firm hand, the king felt relieved, and reducing his own workload he sought pleasure in youthful dalliance.

A great lover, the king made continuous love to the sensuous women of his antapura who were only too willing to please their king. Their floral ear ornaments falling on to their passion roughened, flushed cheeks and wilting away, they would shower their nectar-sweet, enticing smiles on the king like a flood of sandalwood water. Their blue-lily eyes would shoot amorous glances at him. The brilliance of their jewels would blind him like flying vermilion powder. Their creeper-slender arms, like a garland of *champa* flowers, would encircle him. Thus roused to passion the king would then give himself wholly to the love sport.

The king would nibble at the lips of a courtesan and as she feigned to shake him off by waving her arms, her gem-inlaid armlets would tinkle sweetly. The bed would soon become grainy with the splintered pieces of her broken earrings; the krishnaguru pattern drawn on her breasts thrilling at the touch of the king would leave its own imprint as well on it. The king's hair would get stained with the alaktha juice from the raised feet of the courtesan. The gorochana tilaka on her forehead would run in the perspiration that bathed them in the aftermath of love.

Sometimes the king indulged in water sports with his women. A courtesan would keep throwing water mixed with *kumkum* at him like a shower of Ananga's golden arrows, turning the king's body yellow. His white garments would become pink with the *laksha* water thrown at him by yet another courtesan. Still another would spray water mixed with musk and his body would become spotted with it; and yet another would mark him with her handprints in sandalwood paste. At times the ripples in the palace ponds would turn white from the running sandalwood paste on the women's breasts. The alaktha from their restless, tinkling, anklet-adorned feet would drench the swan pairs. A variety of flowers would shower down from the women's tresses into the water. The waves would break when they swung their high hips. The water foaming with the incessantly moving arms of the frolickers would create patterns on the surface.

The king would drink wine out of the mouths of the belles and delight in the taste of it just like a bakula tree. Or the women would kick him with their feet, and just as the ashoka tree when kicked by women would burst forth into red blossoms, the king's body too would turn red with the alaktha of the women's feet and he would be roused to passion.

At times the king, like the scented elephant would wander in the woods and gardens fragrant with wild flowers. The flowers worn on his ears would fall on his wine-flushed cheeks and he would lisp sweetly under the influence of wine. Or like a swan delighted with the sweetly tinkling anklets of the women, he would enjoy himself among the lotus fields. Or like the king of the animals, with a garland of kesari flowers around his shoulders he would roam on the hillocks made for sport. Sometimes of a twilit evening in the waning period of the moon hiding under a dark veil, the king would steal out to keep his tryst with a damsel.

Along with a few close friends Tarapida would also often attend music concerts as well, with the *veena, venu* and *muraja* playing in the central apartments of the palace that had windows with golden doors, and where the pigeons, the colour of *krishnaguru* would huddle in their holes.

Need anything more be said? Tarapida simply revelled in all that delighted him, all that was not expressly forbidden by the *shastras*, giving no thought to the present or the future; only because he had already fulfilled all his kingly duties and not because he was indifferent to the task of governing. And such indulgence in sensuous pleasures was indeed an added ornament to a king who had accomplished everything to the satisfaction of his subjects; in others it would be a matter for ridicule, a cause for derisive laughter. However in order to keep alive the love of the people the king gave audience every now and then and even sat on the throne when the occasion demanded.

Shukanasa ruled effortlessly and with great ease helped by the power of his intellect. The love of the subjects for their king and minister increased manifold. The assembled vassals accorded the minister the same degree of respect they showed to the king, and treated him with equal deference. Shukanasa commanded as vast an army as the king did himself. When the minister marched out the sound of the stamping hoofs of his impatient cavalry deafened the whole world. With the weight of the moving forces the earth trembled and the mountains shook. With the dust kicked up by the commotion the very rivers became dusty. Lusty shouts of victory were heard continuously. With the vassals raising their golden handled umbrellas all together, the ten directions often lost the day.

— 11 —

Many years passed in this fashion. The king had experienced the ultimate pleasures of the world; all but one, for that supreme pleasure of beholding the dear face of a beloved son was still out of his reach. Although sumptuous in every respect, the antapura was like a field of shara grass devoid of flowers and fruits. As the years went by taking his youth away, the king's grief over his childlessness became more and more intense. And his mind turned away from the pleasures of the senses. Surrounded by thousands of princes, the king was still lonely in his sorrow. He had eyes yet felt himself to be blind and lost. He who was the refuge of the whole world felt helpless in his despair.

Tarapida's queen was Vilasavathi, the first lady of the antapura, the wonder of all the three worlds and the mother of all loveliness and womanly charm. She adorned the king, like the crescent moon the tresses of Hara, like the kausthubha the chest of Madhusudana, like the creeper the tree it twined around.

He was spring and she the flowers bursting forth in bloom. He was the moon and she its lustre. He was the pond and she the lotus growing in it. He was the sky and she the clusters of shining stars.

One day, when the king came to visit her in the antapura, he found Vilasavathi in great distress. She was unadorned; her silk garments were damp with the tears that fell continuously; her hair was disarranged. She was sitting on a cushiond couch with her face resting on her left hand. Her maids-in-waiting

moved about sad and silent, their eyes brimming with anxiety.
The kanchukis standing close by did what they could, their
thoughtful, steady gaze resting on the queen. The elderly women
of the antapura were trying to comfort her. As she tried to rise
at the king's arrival, he pressed her back in the seat and he too
sat down on one side of it. Not knowing the cause of her tears
and a little worried, he wiped her tear-streaked cheeks with his
fingers and said:

'Devi! Why do you weep silently as though weighed down
with a great sorrow? Why do your eyelashes string the tear
drops like a necklace of pearls? Why, oh, slender one. Why have
you not adorned yourself? Why have you not applied the
morning-sun-bright alaktha to your lotus feet? Why have the
gem-inlaid anklets that tinkle like the call of the swans in the
lake of Manmatha been denied the touch of your lotus-feet?
Why is your waist silent in the absence of the *mekhala*? Like the
mark of the deer on the white moon, why are not your rounded
breasts decorated with the dark liquid of krishnaguru? Oh, noble
one! Oh, slender one! Why is your fair neck not adorned with a
hara even as the stream of the celestial Ganga adorns the
crescent moon in the tresses of Hara. Oh! Vilasavathi! Your
cheeks are bare, the tears having washed away the decoration
done in kumkum.

Why is your palm with its soft petal-like fingers decorating
your ear like a red lotus earring? Oh proud one! There is no
gorochana on your forehead and the disarranged locks are falling
on it. The unrelieved darkness of your abundant hair without
flowers hurts my eyes as twilight without the moon in the waning
fortnight. Devi! Please stop weeping and tell me the cause of
your distress. These long sighs of yours that disarrange your
breast-cloth make my heart tremble with love for you like a new
leaf. Have I done anything wrong? Or is it an offence committed
by one of our attendants? However hard I think I cannot see the

slightest fault on my part with regard to you. My kingdom and my very life are yours to command. Please tell me the reason for your sorrow, my beautiful one.' As his entreaties did not elicit any reply from his wife the king turned to one of the attendants for explanation.

Makarika, the carrier of the betel box and a constant companion of the queen answered the king. 'Deva!' she said. 'There is no question of the slightest offence on your part. And in your majesty's presence who would have had the temerity to cause offence to the queen? Not any of the attendants, nor any one else for that matter. But the queen has of late been constantly agonizing over her childlessness, that she is like a woman possessed by an evil spirit as her union with the king has borne no fruit. Her distress has indeed been a long-standing one. For many days now our lady has had to be coaxed somehow by us, her attendants into performing even her daily duties, like bathing, eating and sleeping, putting on her ornaments, and dressing, which she would somehow get through listlessly, all the time weighed down with sorrow. She never revealed her anguish to you for fear of causing your lordship distress. But today, being the fourteenth day of the lunar fortnight she had gone to pray at the temple of Mahakala; and there at an exposition of the Mahabharata she heard the following lines:

Not for the childless are the worlds of heavenly bliss,
For it is putra who saves you from the hell named pum.

Having heard this she returned home and disregarding the most humble entreaties of her attendants, she has refused to partake of any food or adorn herself with ornaments. She does not say anything but simply sheds ceaseless tears that cloud her face like a rainy day.' Having said this Makarika fell silent.

The king remained quiet for a while, then sighing deeply he addressed his queen: 'Devi! What could one do about such matters as are ordained by fate? Pray, do not distress yourself unduly. On the whole the gods have not been too kind to us. Perhaps in their reckoning our hearts do not merit the unparalleled joy of holding our own son in our arms. Or perhaps our record in our previous life has not been clean enough; it is only acts of merit performed in the earlier life that bring rewards in this. Even great sages cannot change what has been ordained by fate.

'So, I suggest you do what is humanly possible, and perhaps increase the intensity of whatever you have been doing so far. Increase your devotion to your teachers and the propitiation of the divinities. Pay greater attention to the honouring of the rishis, for their powers are far above those of the divinities; and if they are felicitated with sincere effort, they would grant whatever is wished for, even what is considered difficult of attainment. Surely you have heard how in days of yore, King Brihadratha of Magadha got a most mighty son, Jarasandha of incomparable prowess, a vanquisher of none other than Janardhana himself by pleasing that most quick tempered rishi of them all, Vishvamitra Kaushika. King Dasharatha of course, despite his advanced years was blessed with not one but four sons by the favour of Rishyashringa the son of Vibhandaka, four unconquerable sons like the four arms of Narayana, and uncontainable like the waters of the oceans. Indeed many a righteous king has had the pleasure of gazing at the face of the offspring as a result of venerating the ascetics. The service rendered to the sages is unfailingly fruitful.

'Devi! I too long to see you with child, listless with the burden, a little pale in the face like the night sky just before the rise of the moon. When will my servants in the joyful celebration of the birth of my son come to pull away my clothes and ornaments as their rightful gifts on the great occasion? When will my queen gladden my heart, clad in yellow garments with the child in her lap, glowing like the morning sky with the just risen young sun?

Oh, when will my little son, with his curly locks, tawny with the application of herbal mixture, drops of ghee mixed with white mustard and sacred ash on his palate, the knotted thread decorated with gorochana around his neck, lying on his back a toothless smile lighting up his face, fill my heart with delight? Oh when indeed would the little golden one, being passed from hand to hand among the women of the antapura remove like a lighted lamp, the darkness of sorrow from my eyes? When will he, his playful body covered with dust, with my heart and eyes following him in his rambles, adorn the courtyards of the palace? When will he beginning to crawl wander hither and thither like a lion cub, eager to catch hold of the young of the deer raised in the palace? When will he dart into the rooms of the palace chasing after the palace swans that would mill round the tinkling anklets of the women and tire out the wet nurses trying to keep track of him only by the sound of his mekhala? When will I see him strut about playing the part of a young excited elephant, delighted by the *dindima*-like gentle clucking of the wet nurse, his cheeks decorated with the rut fluid-dark krishnaguru, his body covered with sandalwood-powder-like dust that he has scattered on himself by his own raised hands, and shaking his head at the wet nurse who would try to restrain him with an admonitory forefinger curved like a goad? Eyes darting here and there with curiosity, when will I see him, fascinated with his own reflection in the polished stone floor, stumble after it? Eagerly beckoned with open arms by the thousands of princes, rolling his eyes in some distress in the glitter of the princely ornaments, when will a child of mine run around in my presence, in my court? In such longings do my nights pass! The sorrow of childlessness burns me too, day and night. I feel emptiness all around and ruling this kingdom too seems futile.

'Well, what fate has ordained cannot be reversed. Devi! Do give up this grieving. Learn to be brave and turn your mind to the carrying out of good deeds. Blessed are those who are in the constant company of the righteous'.

The king rose and fetched water himself with which he wiped her lovely, tear-stained face. He comforted her again and again with words of utmost tenderness and good advice, staying at her side for a long time.

Eventually, when the king left, Vilasavathi, somewhat consoled, set about her daily routine. From that day onwards she became very closely attentive to the propitiation of the gods, the honouring of the Brahmins and service to the elders. Whatever austerities she came to hear about she performed them all. She did not consider anything too arduous. After a bath, clad in white clothes she would fast in the shrine of Chandika, dark with the thick smoke from the continuous burning of *guggulu*. She further mortified her flesh by sleeping in a bed of axes arranged in lines and covered with freshly cut darba grass. She would have her bath in purified water from golden pots decorated with gems and the fresh leaves of the banyan and *pippala* trees sitting under cows of perfect physical qualities and decorated auspiciously by the senior women of the ranch. She would also bathe at the junction of roads on the fourteenth night of the waning moon, sitting in the centre of a *mandala* drawn by the chief occultist after propitiating the divinities in command of the directions. She worshipped at the shrines of the siddhas where the seeker would undertake vows to be fulfilled at the realization of their wishes. She visited the shrines of the divine mothers whose compassion was well known. She bathed in famous ponds where families of serpents lived. She circumambulated and venerated great trees like the pippala that were known to grant boons.

After a bath, holding in her hands, a silver vessel containing cooked white cereal mixed with curds she would herself feed the cows, her armlets shaking with the motion of her hands. She instituted a daily service for Durga with an abundance of flowers, incense and fragrant pastes.

She would herself fill the begging bowls of the oracular Jaina and Buddhist monks with her heart full of devotion and then ask them longingly whether she would ever be blessed with a child.

She diligently obeyed the commands of the female fortune-tellers; she eagerly consulted the interpreters of omens; she paid close attention to the exponents of bird signs.

She arranged for the chanting of the Vedas by the Brahmins who visited her. She herself listened with attention to devotional stories.

~12~

The days went by with Vilasavathi deeply engrossed in her propitiatory observances. Then the king had a dream. It was early morning; the night had already lost its intensity. A mere handful of pale stars lingered still in the sky that had turned a dusty grey, like the feathers of an old pigeon. The king saw Vilasavathi in his dream sitting on the terrace when the full moon entered her mouth, like a lotus stalk entering the mouth of a female elephant. He woke up. His eyes widening with joy and lighting up the palace, he summoned the revered Shukanasa that very moment and narrated his dream to him.

Overjoyed, the worthy minister replied: 'My lord! At last our ardent wishes and those of our subjects as well are going to find their fulfilment. Indeed in a very short while Your Highness will have the pleasure of gazing at the sweet face of your son. And I too had a dream last night. I saw a Brahmin of divine appearance, a personification of serenity itself, clad in clean white garments, place a white lily in full bloom, lustrous as the moon and of a thousand petals, with myriad filaments waving like tawny tresses and showering drops of honey, in the lap of my wife Manorama. Good omens foretell the coming of happy events. And what greater cause for happiness is there for us now? The dreams that occur when the night is drawing to a close come true without fail indeed. It is certain therefore that before long the queen is going to give you a fine son, a leader among the *rajarishis* like Mandhata who would be a source of joy to the whole world. The autumnal lotus plant pleases the rutting elephant by bringing forth a fresh bloom; the queen too will gladden you by giving you a new baby. Like the unceasing flow of the rut fluid of the elephants of the quarters your majesty is going to be blessed with an unbroken line of descendants all equal to the task of bearing the burden of ruling the earth.'

The king then took Shukanasa by his hand and led him into the inner apartments to share the good augury with Vilasavati.

In a few days, like the lunar reflection entering the waters of a pond, life entered Vilasavathi's womb. With the quickening of the womb, the queen glowed like Indra's Nandanvana with the *parijata* bursting into bloom, like the chest of Madhusudana with the kausthubha. In the guise of the foetus the queen carried the image of the king inside her like a shining mirror. Day by day the foetus grew and she, like the seawater-laden rain clouds moved about languidly. Yawning, her eyes squinting with sleep she sighed listlessly and turned away from food. Her nipples darkened like the dark days of the rainy season and her body turned pale like the ketaki. Her shrewd attendants who knew all the signs realised she was with child.

Now, the chief of the antapura attendants was a shudra woman named Kulavardhana. Having lived in the palace for a long time she was in command of all situations. She could hold her own even in the royal presence. On a chosen auspicious evening she went to the audience chamber where the king was holding court. A thousand lamps filled with fragrant oil had been lit and placed in the courtroom. In their midst the king shone like the full moon surrounded by the stars, like Narayana encircled by the thousand gems on the thousand-hooded Adisesha. The minister Shukanasa profound as the unplumbed depths of the ocean was with him, as well as some of the vassal princes. The king was engaged in a discussion of confidential matters with his minister. Kulavardhana went to him and whispered in his ear the happy news of Vilasavathi's pregnancy.

When those words, never heard before, words that carried tidings that the king never dared hope for, fell in his ears, he felt as if he was being showered all over with nectar. His body thrilled with the hair standing on edge and he was overcome with joy. A smile filled out his cheeks. The happiness that filled his heart overflowed in the brilliant rays from his teeth. With his eyes rolling and the eyelashes moist with unshed tears of joy the king glanced at Shukanasa.

Beholding the king in such unprecedented transports of joy and Kulavardhana's beaming face Shukanasa guessed the probable cause of their happiness. He knew under the circumstances only one particular piece of news would give rise to such intense joy in the king. He rose from his chair and going close to the king asked him in a low voice, 'Is this anything to do with that dream of yours? Kulavardhana is wide-eyed with joy! Your eyes too have stretched right up to your ears. Brimming with tears of joy, with rolling pupils they do reveal the cause of this happiness. But I long to hear the great news from you, so please tell me. What is it?'

The king smiled a little and said, 'If what Kulavardhana says is true then indeed it is my dream come true. But I hesitate to believe it though. Is it likely that such good fortune should be mine? Do I really deserve to hear such blessed words? I know

Kulavardhana would never utter an untruth, yet I do not quite believe her words! Come, let us go and find out from Devi herself if there is any truth in this.'

The king quickly dismissed the court. He then removed the ornaments from his body and handed them over to Kulavardhana as reward for having been the messenger of such wonderful news. His joy-filled heart driving him on, he sped to the antapura. His right eye throbbed like blue lily petals tossed in the wind, intensifying his happiness. The attendants carried the lamps ahead, and the flames, trembling in the wind dispelled the darkness of the interior as the king reached the antapura.

─13─

The queen's apartment had been made safe and secure for a pregnant woman by means of charms, incantations and medicinal herbs. It was freshly whitewashed and lit with brilliant, auspicious lamps. On either side of the entrance were placed, pots filled with water. Freshly painted propitiatory images of various deities brightened and beautified a part of the walls. A white canopy had been erected whose edges were hung with streamers of pearls.

A charmed circle had been drawn around the bed of the pregnant woman to ensure her safety. At the head of the bed was placed a silver pot, the *nidhra kalasha* to induce good sleep. Various medicinal herbs and roots as well as instruments like the plough were placed around the apartment. Various magical formulae had been drawn on the ground. Many rings rendered magically potent by incantations to the several manifestations of Shakthi were also drawn around Vilasavathi. White mustard seeds were scattered here and there. Bits of various metals and pippala leaves were strung on thin threads and hung. Tender green neem leaves were spread closely on the bed.

The cot, large like a rock surface of the Himalaya, just right for a woman with child stood on a high pedestal. A moonlight-white spread covered the bed.

Elderly women well versed in the right observances for the occasion were seen performing rites to exorcise all evil spirits. Some women were seen walking around Vilasavathi carrying gold pots filled with cooked watery rice with drops of curds on it and the lot strewn with various flowers. Yet another group carried a spread of fish with their faces intact mixed with fresh pieces of meat. Still others held lighted candles in small baskets. Some scattered white mustard seeds mixed with water and gorochana while others poured water in unceasing streams.

Her special attendants distinct in their white clothes, full of cheer, conversed mainly of auspicious things, as they waited upon Vilasavathi. The queen too was clad in a pair of silken white garments with the borders decorated with gorochana. In her pregnant condition Vilasavathi resembled, the earth with the *kulashaila*, the great mountains retracted inside it, the Mandakini with Iravatha submerged inside her waters, the mid-slopes of the Himalayas with all the lions gone inside the caves. In her lassitude, she was like daylight when rain-laden clouds curtained the sun.

When she saw her husband the queen tried hurriedly to rise laying a hand on her right knee, while her jewels tinkled as she leaned on the extended hands of her attendant. The king quickly pressed her back saying, 'Devi, please do not rise. There is no need for any ceremony'. He then sat down on the same couch along with her. Shukanasa sat on another nearby cot, with polished golden legs and a white spread on it.

His eyes on his pregnant wife, his mind in the euphoria of intense joy, the king asked her a little mischievously, 'Devi!

Shukanasa here wants to know if there is any truth to what Kulavardhana has told us.' A fleeting smile lit up Vilasavathi's eyes and coloured her cheeks and lips. The brilliance of her teeth serving as a veil to her face, she sat there with downcast eyes. Pressed again and again by the king she blurted out, 'Don't make me feel so bashful! I know nothing.' With her head still lowered she directed a sideward glance at her husband in mock indignation.

The moonlight of his smile suffusing his face in a gentle glow, the king said again, 'Oh beautiful one! If my words make you so shy then I must be silent. But what are you going to do about your own limbs that have already assumed the pale lustre of a newly opened champaka flower, and the white *kungkuma* paste applied on them could be inferred only by its fragrance? Or about your nipples that have turned dark as though there is smoke issuing out of them, even as that fire of longing for maternity is being put down by the nectar of your pregnancy? Indeed your nipples are blue lilies caught in the mouths of a *chakravaka* pair! Your breasts are a pair of golden pots whose mouths have been permanently decorated with *patralata* done in krishnaguru. Or, what would you do about your waist now suffering from the tightening of the girdle strings as it loses its leanness and the three lines on it disappear?'

As the king went on in this fashion Shukanasa concealing his smile admonished him. 'Deva! Why are you teasing Devi so? The very mention of her condition makes her bashful. There, that is enough said about the news brought to you by Kulavardhana.' They then spent a long time in lighthearted conversation until Shukanasa went home. The king stayed back to spend the night with his queen. In due course Shukanasa's wife Manorama too became pregnant with child.

Whatever cravings Vilasavathi developed due to her pregnant state were all duly satisfied which left her well pleased. After she completed her full term, Vilasavathi gave birth to a son on an auspicious day, at an excellent hour—the palace astrologers kept a vigilant eye on time with the help of an instrument that functioned on the measured flow of water while others out in the courtyard observed the falling shadows—like a cloud giving birth to lightning, gladdening the heart of the whole world.

After the baby was born, the palace became a scene of hectic and joyful activity. The footfalls of hundreds of servants running hither and thither shook the very earth. Innumerable kanchukis stumbled around looking for the king to impart to him the latest news about the little one. In the crush of people in the palace, the dwarfs, the hunchbacks and the *kiratas* were all trampled upon. As the crowd of women increased the charming tinkle of their ornaments was heard everywhere. The people scrambled for the *purnapathras*, the gift-filled vessels and got quite disarrayed in the process. The palace was like a city in excitement.

Then the drums began to sound. The kettledrums led with a rumble that might have been quite as deep as that which was heard from under the ocean when it was churned with the Mandara Mountain! Then all the softer instruments like the mridanga, conch, *kahala,* and *anaka* sounded. Then rose the sharp tone of the *pataha*. All the subjects along with the neighbouring vassal princes, all the women of the palace including the courtesans, all the royal officers, everyone young and old began to dance, as if intoxicated, with overwhelming joy. Like the ocean swelling up with the rising moon, the revelry over the birth of the prince rose in intensity.

Although the king was eager to see his son, he had to wait until the arrival of the auspicious hour determined by the astrologers. Then dismissing all his retinue and accompanied only by the worthy minister and close friend Shukanasa he went to the delivery room.

The lying-in chamber had been decorated auspiciously. Pots made of precious stones were placed on either side of the entrance to the room. Piles of various new shoots, a golden plough, a golden axe, garlands of loosely threaded white flowers interspersed with durva grass and a suspended tiger skin further adorned the doorway. A festoon of flowers with bells strung along its length was stretched across the threshold.

The chamber was filled with married women. They were all mothers who were good at organizing things to suit the various occasions. All of them were engrossed in decorating the chamber. One of them was making square platforms with cowdung on either side of the doorway. She pressed cowrie shells on them to give them an uneven surface. Then she decorated it by placing here and there variously coloured bits of *karpasa* flowers. And on this she drew a red swastika with the paste of the pollen of the *kusumbha* flowers.

A second woman was fashioning the figure of Shashti Devi draped in a turmeric-stained yellow garment. A third was putting together the figure of Kartikeya mounted on the back of a peacock with its feathers spread wide. A red flag fluttered and the god was holding aloft his fierce weapon called Shakthi. Still others were making artificial *kadamba* flowers. First they shaped the flowers in mud; they then stained them yellow with a thick paste of kungkuma. Then they scattered golden barley kernels on the surface to give them a raised appearance. Mustard seeds were then pressed on them and the balls now appeared as if smeared with molten gold. Finally they made garlands with these kadamba 'flowers'.

An old goat was tied close to the door and it was decorated with a variety of fragrant floral garlands.

The head of the cot was placed on a spread of various kinds of cereals. A powder made of snake moult and sheep horn was constantly burnt. Tender neem leaves were also burnt from which there rose a fragrant smoke protective and beneficent. The chanting Brahmins were sprinkling holy water everywhere. The godmothers were engrossed in their prayers to the mother-goddesses, who were protectors of children, and whose images had just been drawn on cloth. Sacrificial rites were being performed for the safety of the newborn, and a ceaseless chanting of the *sahasranama*, the thousand epithets of Vishnu was also in progress. The lamps fixed on golden pillars were lit, and the flames motionless as if praying intently for the welfare of the mother and child, lighted the room. With drawn swords the security men guarded the room. The king entered the lying-in chamber after touching water and fire.

There he saw his son lying in the lap of Vilasavathi who was pale with exhaustion after her labour. But the baby's glow outdid the lamps lighting the room. With the flush of the womb the little one resembled the rising sun with its pink aura; he resembled the setting moon with its red tint; he was like the tender leaves of the kalpataru, and the newly bloomed lotuses; he was like Mars come down to earth. His limbs seemed to have been fashioned out of tender shoots of coral, of bits of the red young morning sun, of the lustre of rubies. His molten gold-like lustre filled the apartment. He wore marks of greatness on his body, like jewels that he was born with.

He was like Mahasena with the other five faces unmanifested! Or could he be a son of Indra fallen on the earth having slipped from the hands of a celestial damsel.

The king was delighted at the sight of the little one. His eyelashes stilled, he gazed at him forgetting to blink. He wiped his eyes that brimmed again and again. His tenderly possessive eyes greedily drank in the sight of his son; his eyes spoke to the little one, caressed him, who was the fulfilment of all his heart's desires.

A well pleased Shukanasa scrutinizing the little one limb by tender limb said to the king, 'Deva! We cannot still see the full beauty of his limbs due to constriction in the womb, but we can already see the marks of greatness on him; the crescent-shaped forehead pink like evening twilight, the beautiful eyebrows as though made out of thin strands of fresh lotus stalks, the long lily-white eyes with curly lashes stretching almost up to the ears, lighting up the entire palace, as it were, as he keeps trying to open them, and the long high nose seemingly finished in gold that appears to be inhaling the natural lotus bud-fragrance of his own face. His lips too are auspiciously like lotus buds. On his lotus-red hands we see the signs of the conch and the discus, just like Vishnu. His feet soft as a kalpataru leaf bear the signs of a flag, a chariot, a horse, an umbrella and a lotus, and are thus fit to be kissed by thousands of crowned heads! And his cry resounds like the deep note of a dundubhi!'

As Shukanasa was talking, a messenger named Mangalaka hurried in, having pushed his way through the crowd of princes at the entrance and stood before the king in a state of excitement, with his face beaming with joy. He fell at the feet of the king and exclaimed, 'Deva! May you prosper! May your enemies be destroyed! May you live long and conquer the earth! By your blessings Arya Shukanasa's first wife Manorama, a Brahmini has given birth to a son as Renuka, the wife of Jamadagni gave birth to Parashurama. Oh king! Having heard this, command me!'

Mangaladasa's words fell like a shower of nectar in the ears of the king. He exclaimed, 'How wonderful! It is indeed true good and bad come in a series! In every way has fortune been dealing equally with you and me, both in sorrow and happiness.' Beaming with pleasure the king embraced his minister and laughingly pulled away Shukanasa's *utthariya* as he claimed the first gift from the minister in honour of the good news. He also ordered that Mangalaka the bringer of the good tidings be rewarded suitably. Then with the whole of the antapura following he hurried to the mansion of Shukanasa where he ordered the festivities be doubled in intensity.

There were wild demonstrations of joy, the people seemed crazed with happiness. They carried on as if they were possessed. They no longer bothered about what might be spoken and what might not. The women of the antapura were lost in an orgy of music and dance.

The sixth night vigil was observed. And on the tenth day after the birth of the child, at an auspicious hour the king donated cows and countless gold coins to the Brahmins. 'I saw the moon entering the mother's mouth in my dream' recollected the king and named his son, in accordance with the dream, Chandrapida.

The next day Shukanasa too performed all rituals as befitting a Brahmin, and with the king's consent named his son Vaishampayana, a name suitable for a Brahmin boy.

—14—

In course of time all necessary ceremonies beginning with tonsure were performed for the boys. The infancy of Chandrapida and Vaishampayana soon passed. It was now time to start their education.

In order to wean their mind away from childish pastimes, King Tarapida constructed a school for them outside the city on the banks of the Shipra. The building was half a *krosha* long and surrounded by tall, whitewashed ramparts that resembled the line of Himalayan peaks. There was a deep moat that ran round the structure close to the ramparts. The front doors were very strongly built. There was just a single opening to allow entry into the building. The building was equipped with a stable for the horses, a garage for the chariots, and a gymnasium for exercising in the basement. It was splendid like the abode of the devas. And the king took great efforts to gather the best possible teachers for the various disciplines.

It was here that Chandrapida was kept, like a lion cub in a cage. He was forbidden to go out of the complex. Apart from Vaishampayana his only other companions were the children of some of the noble families who had also come there to study, his teachers and of course, the attendants. All playful distractions having been removed, Chandrapida was delivered into the hands of his teachers on an auspicious day, along with Vaishampayana to embark on a course of study comprising all disciplines with single-minded concentration. Every day, early in the morning the king would go to the school with his wife to observe his son at study.

Thus placed in captivity, as it were, Chandrapida set about his studies with exemplary diligence and mastered in a very short time all that was imparted to him by his teachers; and they in turn were greatly enthused by the sharpness of intellect of their pupil and vied with each other in showing their own expertise in the various fields. As for Chandrapida all that was taught to him, all the arts and sciences entered his lucid mind like images falling on a clean mirror.

Soon he excelled in grammar, *Mimamsa, Nyaya, Dharmashastra* and *Rajaniti*. At the same time he acquired proficiency in the use of various weapons like the bow, the discus, the sword, and the club, the axe and the mace. He excelled in mounting elephants and horses and driving chariots, as well as in swimming, leaping and in the theory of making love as well.

His preceptors paid equal attention in training him in the fine arts too. Soon he became an accomplished player on the *veena* and the flute, the mridanga, cymbals and the *darduraputa* an instrument that sounded like the frog. He mastered as well the *Natyashastra* of Bharata and the *Gandharvaveda* of Narada. He gained expertise in all aspects of veterinary science, including the study of elephants and determining the age of horses.

On the lighter side he became skilled at the throw of dice and also delved into esoteric disciplines like magic, perfumery, interpretation of birdsong, astrology, and gemmology. His skills as a technician were developed as he learnt carpentry and ivory work and vastu techniques including the digging of underground passages. He learnt some practical medicine as well, which included the making of antidotes for poisons. The course was finally rounded up with painting, sculpture and the study of the various languages of the world with their scripts. In all these disciplines Chandrapida attained great proficiency.

Keeping pace with his remarkable intellectual progress was the extraordinary development of his physical prowess, thanks to the exercise he performed regularly that made him comparable to Bhima. Even in his childhood he had exhibited a stunning physical strength. He would playfully catch hold of the ears of a young elephant and the hapless animal could no more free himself from his grip than he could have from the claws of a young lion. With one strike of his sword he could fell the palm trees as though they were mere lotus stalks. His arrow could split asunder the very rocks on the mountains. He exercised with an iron staff that required ten people merely to lift it. Except for this extraordinary physical strength Vaishampayana proved his equal in every other respect.

Chandrapida held Vaishampayana in high regard both on account of his scholarly abilities and the fact that he was the son of the highly esteemed Shukanasa. Besides, having grown up together and played about with him in mud and dust,

Chandrapida had developed a great affection for Vaishampayana who became his close and trusted friend. Not even for a moment could he remain separated from his friend; and Vaishampayana too responded to the prince's affection in equal measure and followed Chandrapida around faithfully, like day following the hot-rayed one.

As Chandrapida's studies continued, there appeared on him in due course, the glow of early manhood, that enticed all the three worlds like the nectar rising from the ocean; it pleased the eyes and hearts of one and all, like the moon rising in the evening twilight. The first flush of manhood was capable of creating a kaleidoscope of variable feelings, like the changing colours of a rainbow in the rainy season; it was the weapon of Makaradvaja similar to the bursting forth of flowers on the parijata tree; it could create new sensibilities like the freshly appearing colours in a lotus field as the sun rises; it could make one capable of various blandishments. Like the flitting shades on the feathers of a dancing peacock it made him doubly beautiful.

Manmatha, the seductive god of love, was stealing near like a servant who had seized the opportunity to get close to the master. With increasing beauty his chest broadened; his thighs filled out, his waist thinned and his hips widened. The hair on the body grew along with his growing valour; the arms lengthened. As his mind as well as his moral sensibilities became refined his eyes shone brighter and clearer. As his authority grew his shoulders too broadened and swelled. With the deepening voice the heart too became profound.

Chandrapida had attained manhood and he had finished his studies successfully and to the great satisfaction of his teachers. It was now time to go home. On an auspicious day the king sent his senapati Balahaka with an army comprising the infantry and the cavalry, to bring his son home.

—15—

B alahaka arrived at the university with the army. Ushered in by the guards he approached Chandrapida and bowed deeply before him. He sat down for a moment at the appointed place, showing the prince the same deference that he would show to the king himself. Soon however, he got up and went near Chandrapida and said: 'Oh prince! The king speaks thus: "Our wishes are fulfilled. You have studied the sacred texts; you have mastered all the arts. You have gained great facility in wielding the weapons. Your teachers have therefore granted you permission to return home. Let the people now see you as you are, well educated, and accomplished in the arts. Released from a life of academic discipline let them see you come home like the young of the best of the scented elephants coming out of restraint, like the newly risen moon on *purnima*! Let the yearning eyes of the world get their reward after having been denied a sight of you for such a very long time.

The women in the antapura are eager to see you. It is ten years now since you entered the academy. You were six years old when you left home and now you are sixteen. Come home now and let your mothers who long to see you enjoy the sight of you. Pay your respects to your elders, and then free of all restraints, enjoy the comforts of your royal position and the sensual pleasures of youth. Bestow gifts on the royal officers, venerate the twice-born, take the subjects under your protection and gladden the hearts of your near and dear ones."'

The senapati, having delivered himself of the king's message now continued: 'And now, prince, there stands at the door a most magnificent horse, named Indrayudha, swift as garuda, fast as the wind, sent to you by the king. This splendid animal, not born of a womb but raised from the depths of the ocean, was gifted to your father by the king of Persia as a fitting mount for a great king. Experts on horseflesh have pronounced Indrayudha to be as excellent of limb as the divine Ucchaishravas himself. Please accept the gift by mounting it.

'And, here are the princes, the progeny of crowned kings, modest yet full of valour, handsome and well versed in the arts mounted on their steeds eagerly waiting to pay their respects to you.'

When Balahaka stopped speaking, Chandrapida, obeying his father's command with alacrity ordered, in a deeply resonant voice that sounded like the roar of a newly formed cloud, that Indrayudha be brought in.

In a moment the wondrous horse entered. There was a man on either side of the animal holding on to the golden ring of the bit of the bridle, straining at every step to pull the horse along. The horse was of such great height that a man standing next to him could reach up to the top of the back only by raising his own hand high. Indrayudha kept opening his mouth as if trying to drink away the entire stretch of the sky close to its mouth. His abdomen trembled with the effort, as he let out sharp neighs that filled the bowels of the earth, as though he were issuing challenges to the haughty Garuda's mythical claim to invincibility in speed. He snorted every now and then, as if expressing his swelling anger at being restrained. Or perhaps he was bringing out all the air he had swallowed while galloping at full speed. Undoubtedly speed was his essence. Now bending his head low, now raising it high, proud of his speed, he seemed to take the measure of the three worlds in order perhaps to leap over them all.

His coat was variegated and such a mixture of black, yellow, and pink that he looked like a young elephant with a multi coloured carpet thrown on its back. His long and lean face had a sculpted appearance. The tips of his ears were motionless; and the ears themselves, bathed in the brilliance of the rubies strung around his head were like red chamaras. The golden chain that bound him suffused him with its own lustre; a lacquer-red luxuriant mane cascaded down his neck, and one wondered if it might be the coral reefs of the ocean bed that had got caught around his neck when he wandered under the water. Yet another golden ornament embedded with gems and huge pearls tinkling at every step he took further decorated him; it gave the appearance of a cluster of stars seen in the midst of the russet hues of twilight.

His body was magnificent. His creator must have sculpted away at his legs, spread his chest out, polished away his face to make it radiant, raised his flanks in relief, and doubled the dimensions of the hind parts.

Being a very spirited animal, he chafed at being thus restrained and broke out into drops of sweat from every pore, which looked as if a mass of pearls had stuck to him when he was wandering under the ocean. He kept stamping the ground impatiently with his dark hoofs large like footstools of sapphire, producing an uneven sound, as though he were practising on his mridanga.

A competitor to the eagle in speed, a companion of the wind in roaming the three worlds, a fellow-student of the human mind in the study of speed. He was truly an incarnation of Indra's Ucchaishravas, and his stride was equal to that of Hari who stepped over the whole earth.

Chandrapida was wonderstruck at the sight of this horse, a true marvel, possessing all the benchmark qualities, and a stature more fit for the divine world than the human. He thought to himself, 'When the devas and asuras churned the ocean, pulling Vasuki hard to turn the Mandara mountain did they at all get anything of comparable value to this gem of a horse here? Nothing I am sure. Of what use is Indra's sovereignty over the three worlds if he has not ever mounted a horse such as this, with a back as broad as a rock surface of the Meru? I am sure

that Lord Narayana has not seen this horse as he is still riding
the Garuda. I am also sure that my father's sovereignity has
surpassed the authority of the devas as he could attain rare jewels
such as this horse here, the like of which is not seen in all the
three worlds, for his very own enjoyment. The extraordinary
splendour of this horse's physique and its great power make me
wonder if he might not be possessed by some divine spirit, and
I hesitate to mount him. For it is well known that even gods
sometimes become victims of the curses of ascetics and are made
to relinquish their own bodies to take refuge in such non-human
bodies as this horse here. The story goes that once a sage called
Sthulashiva cursed Rambha, the beautiful apsara, much admired
in all the three worlds. She left the heavenly abode and entered
the heart of a horse; she was then called Ashvahridaya and lived
for a long time in the mortal world in the service of a king called
Shatadhanvana in the kingdom of Mritthika. Surely Indrayudha
too is inhabited by a noble soul expiating a sage's curse. Deep
down in my heart I feel the divinity of this horse.'

Such thoughts held Chandrapida back although he was eager
to mount the horse. He rose from his seat and addressed the
horse silently: 'Oh great soul! Noble horse. Whoever may you
be I salute you. Please forgive me for the transgression of daring
to mount you. With their divinity unknown the gods become
the recipients of unpardonable insults.'

As though he appreciated Chandrapida's unspoken apology,
Indrayudha shook his head repeatedly; he narrowed his eyes as
his tawny mane struck them, and gave a sidelong glance at the
prince. He stamped the ground again and again with his right
foot and the dust rose and settled on his chest. He seemed to
invite Chandrapida to mount him as he snorted with flared
nostrils and neighed in a delightfully soft manner.

Assuming the horse had given him permission to mount,
Chandrapida climbed on his back. Once on his back

Chandrapida felt that the three worlds might indeed be contained within the span of the splayed thumb and the pointer. He came out of the school and there he saw the great mounted cavalry arrayed in front of him. The vast multitude of horses tapped its hooves furiously as though intent on pulverizing the very earth. It sounded like a rain of stones. The dust that rose almost choked the nostrils of the animals that they snorted furiously and neighed loudly rendering the entire creation deaf. The mounted princes stood with their spears raised and the unblemished spearheads glittered touched by the hot brilliant rays of the sun. The thousands of peacock feather umbrellas darkened the directions; but with the colours on them it seemed as if myriad rainbows were painting the rain clouds. The cavalry stretched as far as the eye could see; it was like the ocean in a swell as the horses moved restlessly, foaming at the mouth. The entire cavalry stirred in unison at the sight of Chandrapida, like the waters of the ocean at the rise of the moon. Soon the princes, hurriedly removing the umbrellas from over their heads, surrounded him, reining in their horses irritated by the crush. As Balahaka introduced them one by one to Chandrapida they bowed low, the rubies in the crowns on their heads sending out a flood of affection in the form of red rays.

Chandrapida returned their salute, and then, accompanied by Vaishampayana already seated on his mount, set out towards the city. A huge white umbrella with the royal insignia of a lion drawn on it and fixed on a great golden stem was held over his head to ward off the fierce heat of the sun. Streamers of huge pearls hung from the rim of the umbrella. In its whiteness and its wide expanse it was truly the *pundarika* flower, the white lily on which Rajyalakshmi was wont to rest. Verily it was the moon shining over the forest of white lilies that is the army of the vassal princes. His chamara-wielding attendants fanned him from both sides and his earrings danced in the wind as he rode on. Young gallants ran ahead of the procession. Thousands of attendants marching along raised benedictive slogans like 'victory to the prince', and 'long live the prince'. The bards sang panegyrics.

In due course Chandrapida reached the road leading to the city. Giving up whatever tasks they were engaged in the people of the city thronged to catch a glimpse of their prince returning home. To them he appeared no different from Ananga with his burnt body restored back to him once again. Their beaming faces reflected their happiness. Some said: 'There is no doubt that this is Kartikeya Himself of six lily-like faces, now masquerading as our own Kumara, our crown prince.' Others disagreed: 'No, this could be none other than Pundarikekshana, the Lord Vishnu Himself in the guise of Chandrapida.' But all agreed how fortunate they were, to be able to feast their eyes upon such a divinely beautiful figure. How their hearts brimmed with love for him. They joined their hands over their heads to offer their obeisance. Could there be any doubt now that they had indeed achieved the purpose of their lives, reaped the ultimate fruit of having been born?

All the doors and windows of all the houses all over the city were open. It seemed as if the city itself was gazing at Chandarapida with a thousand wide-open eyes.

The city women learning that Chandrapida was already on the way home from the academy abandoned their toilette and rushed up to the terrace in a frenzy of excitement, to catch a glimpse of him as he rode in. Some still held a mirror in their hands and looked like full moon nights with the moon shining in all its glory. With the alaktha on the feet of some still wet they looked like lotus plants whose blooms have just drunk the russet lustre of the young morning sun. The mekhalas of some slipped down as they rushed up, and fell around their feet making them stumble along like female elephants with feet bound in chains. With the pearl necklaces worn around their necks slipping down to rest in the hollow between their breasts some women exhibited the charm of a twilit evening, a time marked by the chakravaka pairs being separated by thin clear streams of water. There were some who held in their hands strands of huge pearls and resembled Rati wielding a crystal *akshamala* in grief over the destruction of Manmatha. Others rushed up having abandoned their half-empty wine goblets, their lips moist and shining, as though the wine were still dribbling from them. Still others with their faces pressed to the emerald trellis windows converted the skies into a moving lotus pond full of lotus buds.

In a moment there were women everywhere. The palaces seemed filled with them. Their alaktha-stained footprints seemed to cover the ground with fresh shoots. The splendour of their limbs flooded the city with loveliness. Their petal-soft hands held up to shield their faces from the sun turned the skies into a forest of lotuses. Their ornaments refracting the sun's rays turned all light into a series of rainbows. As they gazed at Chandrapida devouringly, his forms entered their hearts as if the hearts were mirrors, or were stretches of water, or were made of crystal.

In that instant a flood of conversation arose from among the women, teasing, confiding, expressing jealousy, coquetry, longing and desire.

'Hey, you hurrying woman! Won't you wait for me? And you! Mad for a glimpse of him aren't you? Catch hold of your utthariya will you? And why don't you gather up your tresses falling all over your face! Hey! You seem intoxicated with your own loveliness. Others are looking at you. Cover your breasts, you shameless one!

'Why don't you give me place too? And how long will you look? You are insatiable! Passion has blinded you, you don't spare a glance for your friends. You besotted one! You are pulling away my utthariya instead of your own. You wretched coquette! Don't tire your hips with such contortions. Hey you! So overwhelmed with curiosity that you seem to have forgotten to breathe. And you a model of chastity! By not looking at what has to be looked at you are merely cheating your own eyes. Get up now and gaze upon this prince who is none other than Manmatha himself, only without Rati and the *makaradvaja*.

'Hey look! He seems to be casting his eyes in my direction. Now he is sharing a joke with Vaishampayana, and his brilliant smile is lighting up the world. Just look at him, extending his hand with such slender fingers, to ask for tambula, so playfully. Lucky is the woman who would take his hand in wedlock. Blessed is Vilasavathi who bore him in her womb!'

The women chatted on in this fashion while their eyes drank in his appearance. The tinkle of their ornaments called out to him. The rays emanating from them sought to bind him as it were, like ropes. Their hearts followed him eager to gift him their youth. Already their arms had begun to waste away with unfulfilled desire for him. And their armlets were slipping down their arms.

In due course Chandrapida reached the gates of the palace. The entrance to the palace was crowded with elephants, which took turns on the stroke of the hour doing security duty. Their cheeks were constantly oozing with the ink-dark rut fluid and they looked like mountains made of collyrium. Their darkness made the day look cloudy. Thousands of white umbrellas were being held aloft. A crowd of envoys, having come from many distant countries waited at the gate for the prince. Chandrapida dismounted from the horse.

~16~

King Tarapida's palace gates were guarded by dwarapalas who held golden staffs in their hands. They wore white armour and had white turbans tied around their heads. Their clothes were white. Their topknots were decorated with white flowers. Their hands and legs were smeared with white unguents. They appeared as though they had come from the White Island. Of immense stature like the men of the Krita Yuga, they stood guard at the gates day and night, motionless, like figures painted or etched on the doorposts.

The palace complex consisted of many lofty, whitewashed mansions reaching up to the very clouds, as though competing with Kailasa in height and brilliance. The buildings had courtyards, *chandrashalas*, pigeon sanctuaries, pavilions and balconies. The women's ornaments, shining through the many trellised windows, seemed to drape the whole complex with a golden net.

The underground arsenal that housed a great collection of fearful weapons imitated the nether world crawling with poisonous snakes.

A small artificial hill had been created inside the complex for recreational purposes. This *kridaparvata* was laid with a mosaic of rubies, red like the alaktha on the feet of the delicate damsels. One could hear the shrill cries of the peacocks roosting on top of the hill.

Well-trained female elephants that would walk lengths to mark the passing hours, stood quietly in between the inner apartments, demure like well-brought-up women. They had brightly coloured spreads thrown over their golden saddles; the chamaras hanging on both sides of the head kissed their restless ears.

Seated near the tying post was a great male elephant called Gandhamadana, a scent elephant; his scent would drive the enemy elephants away. With his eyes three-fourths closed, and his trunk resting on the tip of the left tusk, his palm leaf ears stilled, he seemed to be lost in the music coming out of the inner apartments—the continuous soft beat of the mridangam accompanied by the delightful notes of the veena and the flute and the tinkle of the bells. He seemed to like the mahout's singing too, as his gentle grunts indicated his appreciation. A golden goad was hanging from one of his ears, imitating an earring. His temples decorated with the rut fluid set off the beauty of his ears. Attracted by the rut fluid swarms of bees were buzzing around his cheeks, appearing like a second pair of ears. The high fore parts and the low hind parts of his body created the illusion that he might just be climbing out of the netherworld.

In the stables were tethered, the horses, so beloved of the king. Their backs too were covered with silk spreads. Cute little bells tied around their necks tinkled gently as the horses moved their heads. Their manes were madder-red, like lion manes soaked in the blood of the forest elephants that they had killed. The stable keeper was perched on top of a huge pile of grass. The horses were being fed on mouthfuls of fodder mixed with jaggery. The sweet juice of the jaggery ran down from the sides of their mouths.

In the administrative offices of the palace complex the splendidly dressed *dharmadhikaris*, civil servants, personifications of probity were seated on high cane chairs befitting their high rank. The clerks in these offices, who knew the names of every village and every town, kept track of all the transactions in the entire world-kingdom. This they did with the remarkable ease of looking after just a single household. They also put down in writing the thousands of ordinances promulgated by the ruler. These offices were so thorough in their work that one wondered if they were in any way affiliated to Yama's capital where perfect records were maintained on each one of us.

Groups of attendants waited for their masters, the princes, who were in conference with the king over specific matters, having come from different parts of the kingdom. They carried night-sky-dark leather shields with golden half-moons and stars etched on them. They also had sharp and shining swords that glinted in the sun and worsened the heat and the glare. All of them wore just a single earring made of ivory. Their arms and thighs had designs drawn on them in white sandalwood paste. They were mostly of Andhra, Dravida, or Sinhala origin.

Many vassal princes were also gathered in the audience chamber diverting themselves in various ways, such as playing dice, or draughts, strumming the lute, or devising various kinds of literary games. Some even flirted with the courtesans. All of them seemed burdened with enormous crowns around which they had tied white turbans! Because of that they resembled the mountains whose winding stream-filled peaks were caught in the rays of the young sun.

The courtesans moved in and out with the golden-handled chamaras thrown over their shoulders. There were throngs of hunchbacks, diminutive kiratas, eunuchs and dwarfs; there were the deaf and the mute and those that belonged to the forest tribes.

As for the animals and birds there were the sheep, jungle fowls, ospreys, and the *chataka* birds; the quails were engaged in fighting with each other. The partridge, geese, pigeons and koels were calling loudly, the parrots and the mynas chattered incessantly. Dogs tied with golden chains sat on one side; musk deer wandered without fear lending their fragrance to the atmosphere. Lions caught in their mountain caves and kept in cages roared at the scent of elephant rut fluid. The deer caught recently in the forest and brought over to the palace seemed dazzled by the golden brilliance of their new surroundings; their speckled eyes rolled in the fear that they were in the midst of a forest fire. The peacocks were numerous, but their presence on the emerald floor could be discerned only by their raucous calls.

In the women's quarters the young girls played with balls and dolls or sat on the swings that swung ceaselessly as the bells fixed to the top of the swings rang on. The women were engrossed in enacting the life story of their great king Tarapida.

The kanchukis in charge of the inner apartments walked around in their white turbans and clean white, silk utthariya holding their golden canes in their hands. Of imposing stature and venerable age, they were incarnations of nobility and benediction. Like aged lions, they were still full of valour despite their years.

With fragrant smoke filling the air, the palace appeared cloudy all the time. Avenues of tamala trees darkened the palace, it seemed like night all the time. But the red ashoka cast a glow like the morning sun. Fountains sprayed incessantly; it was ever the rainy season around the palace.

The palace was like the arms of Ishana because just like the great serpents the *bhoginaha,* that twined around his wrists his *prakoshta*, the palace had great pleasure-loving people, the *bhogins*, moving around on the prakoshta, the verandas. The palace was like the Mahabharata because the *nara*, the people there, delighted in unceasing music, *ananta gita,* just as Krishna, that is *Ananta*, delighted Arjuna, or nara, with the *Gita* that he propounded. The palace was like the elephants of the quarters for there was uninterrupted flow of *dana*, or charity, in it just like the unceasing flow of the rut fluid, the dana, of the celestial elephants.*

Ushered in ceremoniously by Balahaka, Chandrapida entered the palace, hand in hand with Vaishampayana.

---

* This is yet another example of Bana's use of pun on words which have more than one meaning. Two different interpretations could be derived

-17-

A s Chandrapida entered the palace, the pratiharis came hurrying towards him. They saluted him and led him inside. All the vassal princes were assembled there ready to greet the prince. As the pratiharis introduced them one by one to Chandrapida, they bowed respectfully in salute, the glow from their moving crest jewels kissing the earth. Meanwhile, the senior ladies of the palace well-versed in traditional practices came out of the women's apartments, and performed rituals at every step in his progress in the palace complex, rituals appropriate for the occasion of the return of the prince, like scattering cereals and durva grass. Thus he passed through seven wings filled with countless varieties of creatures, each wing a world in itself, and arrived at the apartment of his father, the king.

The king was surrounded by his guards, hardy men with hands roughened and calloused by the constant wielding of weapons. They wore full metal armour, which left just their hands, feet and eyes free with the result they appeared like the posts for tying the elephants, around which would always hover dark bees in thick swarms drawn by the smell of the rut fluid. These guards were men descended from noble families and known for their immense stature, great well-muscled physical strength, hardihood, valour and loyalty. They were specially detailed for the personal security of the king. Chandrapida saw his father lying on a swan-white bed, like Iravatha on the white waters of the Mandakini bordered by white beaches, and fanned by beautiful women attendants.

from the use of the same words as it is done here in this passage. Bana compares the palace to such unlikely things as the arms of Ishana (Shiva), the Mahabharata and the elephants of the four directions because the words that he uses lend themselves to such a comparison.

'Here is your father,' said the pratiharis to Chandrapida who bowed his head deferentially from a distance. 'Come, come my son,' cried the king. Raising himself a little on the bed, the king spread both his arms in welcome; his eyes filled with tears of joy as he gazed at him, drinking in the sight of him. As Chandrapida drew near, the king embraced him hard and the hair all over his body stood on edge as though he wished to sew his son's body to his own, as though he wanted to make the two of them, into one.

When the king finally released him the bearer of the betel box hurriedly twisted her own utthariya to make a seat for the prince near the footstool of the king. However, Chandrapida pushed it away with his unshod feet and muttering softly under his breath 'take it away', sat on the ground. The king embraced Vaishampayana too with equal fondness, who then sat down on the seat prepared for the prince. The fan-bearing women forgot to wield their fans and stood still. Their long, slightly sloping eyes with speckled pupils, darted here and there like a line of blue lilies waving in the wind, as they cast sidelong glances full of desire at the prince, and drank in his beauty.

A little later the king said kindly, 'My son, go now. Give your respects to your fond mother and, gladden the hearts of all the ladies of the antapura who have been missing you all these days.'

Thus released, Chandrapida rose and dismissed all but a few of his servants. Accompanied by Vaishampayana and a handful of attendants who had permission to enter the antapura he made his way to his mother.

In the antapura the queen was surrounded by the white-clad kanchukis and looked like the goddess Lakshmi in the midst of the white waves of the milky ocean. Several highly respected elderly women ascetics of peaceful mien, of beautiful ears, dressed in dyed saffron garments like the sky clad in the hues of twilight, were entertaining the queen. They were engaged in the narration of ennobling stories of yore, reading of the epics and discussions about right conduct and observances.

There were eunuchs too in the service of the queen, who were all dressed like women and made-up rather fiercely. The maids in charge of the various items of toilet, like clothes, ornaments, flowers and so on sat around her ready to help. With a necklace of pearls that lay between her breasts, the queen was like the earth on which a stream of the Ganga flowed in the valley between two high peaks. The queen held a mirror in her hands and as her reflection fell on it she looked splendid like the sky in which the moon had entered the orb of the sun. Chandrapida went near and saluted her.

When she saw her son the queen got up excitedly and performed the welcoming rituals herself although her ladies-in-waiting were quite capable of carrying out her orders. In the fullness of love, Vilasavathi's breasts squirted milk; or perhaps it was her heart, melting with love for her child flowed out of her chest, as she mentally showered a thousand blessings on him. She kissed Chandrapida's forehead and held him close for a long time. Then she welcomed Vaishampayana too with great affection. She then sat down and pulled the unwilling Chandrapida on to her lap, as the latter was about to sit down on the ground.

Vaishampayana sat down on a cane chair hurriedly brought over by an attendant. Vilasavathi folded her son in her arms, stroked his forehead, chest and his shoulders over, over again and said, 'How very cruel of your father to have subjected this lovely body of yours, fit to be pampered in all the three worlds, to such a harsh regimen for so long a time. How did you put up with such a long stay under the control of the teachers? Such patience and courage, usually found only in maturity, in one so young. You are still of a very tender age, yet gone are the childish playfulness and mischief from your mind. And what extraordinary respect you have shown towards your teachers. Thanks to the great wisdom of your father I now see you thoroughly learned in all the arts and sciences. By the same father's grace I shall see you wedded to a suitable wife.'

Chandrapida sat with his head lowered a little and a shy smile lit his face as his mother kissed him on his cheeks. With his lustrous cheeks carrying the reflection of the mother's face, Chandrapida appeared as though he were wearing ear ornaments made of fresh lotus petals. The prince stayed a little while longer delighting all the residents of the antapura. Then he left, and mounting Indrayudha waiting at the gate he proceeded towards Shukanasa's residence to pay his respects to the minister.

Shukanasa's palace was as busy as the king's own and crowded with yama elephants, horses and people. There were those who had come to meet the minister for various business affairs. There were the wise men come from all over the country, men whose intellectual eyes had been opened by the collyrium of the shastras. There were the rag-clad Buddhist monks well advanced in the teachings of the Shakya Muni; there were the Pashupatas, the Brahmin devotees of Pashupati wrapped in their red garments. All of them waited on the minister day and night.

A great number of female elephants were gathered at Shukanasa's door. These belonged to the various princes who had come to consult the minister on matters of their own. The mahouts sat on the backs of these elephants with the twice folded over back spreads lying on their laps. As the princes had been gone a long time most of these men were asleep; while some of the elephants were restless others were quiet.

Chandrapida reached the gates of the Shukanasa residence and dismounted at the outer courtyard despite the pressing entreaties of the rushing pratiharis to ride right in. But Chandrapida left his horse outside and went in holding

Vaishampayana's hand, as the doorkeepers rushed ahead clearing the way. The crowd of princes gathered in the various outer wings for the purpose of offering their services to Shukanasa stood up and bowed, the edges of their crowns shaking in the act. The palace servants were frightened into silence by the angry growl of the hurrying pratiharis. Startled by the waving staffs of these officers the hundreds of waiting princes too began to move about and their footfalls shook the very ground of that wing. Observing all this Chandrapida entered the freshly painted residence of Shukanasa, the very replica of the palace of the king. There he saw Shukanasa, so like his own father and bowed low from a great distance.

Shukanasa got up immediately and so did the princes who were with him. He went towards Chandrapida in rapid strides; his widened eyes misted with tears of joy and he clasped both Chandrapida and Vaishampayana tightly to his chest. When released the prince sat down on the ground rejecting the seat brought over; Vaishampayana too did the same. At once all the other princes gathered there relinquished their own seats and sat down on the ground. Remaining silent for a minute or two, his body in the grip of gooseflesh, indicating his great joy, Shukanasa said, 'My child! It is only now, with the course of your studies all completed and you in the full bloom of youth that my lord Tarapida has attained the full fruit of his sovereignty over the earth. All the well wishes of the elders have come true today. And all the good deeds done over several births have found their reward today. The family deities are pleased. Sons like you, the wonder of the three worlds would never be born to the unworthy. How young you are and yet how divinely great your power and ability to grasp every aspect of knowledge, without exception. Blessed indeed are the subjects who have you, the very image of Bharata and Bhagiratha to protect them. What great deed did the Dame Earth do to win you as her husband. Like Vishnu who in the guise of the boar held the earth aloft in the wide circle of his teeth, may you along with your father, by the strength of your arms, protect the earth for several thousands of years.' Shukanasa then honoured the prince with jewels, clothes and flowers, along with unguents, and cosmetics and released him from his presence.

After paying his respects to Manorama, Shukanasa's wife, he mounted Indrayudha once again and made his way to the mansion built and furnished by his father for his use. The palace was exactly like the one in which his father lived. Welcoming *purnakumbhas*, shining metal pots filled with sanctified water were kept on either side of the main entrance. Auspicious flower garlands were tied across the threshold. Myriad flags had been hoisted. The air was filled with the beat of the auspicious *thuri* instrument. A profusion of lotus blooms was scattered on the floor. Fire sacrifice had just been completed. The different groups of servants were ready for him dressed in fine clothes. After performing the various rites enjoined for entry into a new house Chandrapida went into his palace.

First he spent some time in the beautifully done-up audience chamber with the attendant princes. Then he had a bath and partook of a meal with the princes. He also saw to it that a place was set aside for Indrayudha right inside his own bedchamber.

─18─

The day then came to an end. Looking like the red ruby anklets of the descending goddess of the day the lustre-filled orb of the sun fell throwing his rays upward. The brightness of the day flowed like a flood of water behind the chariot wheels of the day maker into the west. In the clear pond that was the sky, the lotus-red twilight bloomed. The rays of the descending sun, resembling a rosy palm the colour of new shoots, were the hands as it were, with which the darkening day completely wiped away the redness of the lotus. The bees swarmed in drawn by the fragrance of the lotus, but finding the blooms closed, circled around the neck of the chakravaka birds; and the birds, as though pulled apart by the string of bees like the rope of Yama, separated.

Presently, the faces of the quarters darkened as though painted with a thick paste of dark sandalwood. As a field of blue lilies, with swarms of hovering bees would overshadow the red lotuses in the pond, the spreading darkness wiped out the redness of the evening. Serried rows of dark bees, like so many hands of the darkness closing in, entered into the heart of the still open red lotuses, as though desirous of pulling out the sun's lustre drunk in by the flowers the whole day, from inside the blooms.

The pigeons were already huddled in the interstices of the palace windows. The dense darkness at the top of the peacock poles created the illusion that the birds were actually there perched on them, even though there weren't any. In the cages hung on the branches of the mango trees in the courtyards the parrots and the mynas had become quiet.

The swings stopped moving as the young women had left them; the golden seats remained still and the bells hung on them fell silent. The music in the women's quarters ended and the veenas were put away. The swans in the palace became quiet, as the women's anklets had stopped sounding.

The lights were lit in the stables of the horses that the king was so fond of. The elephants of the first three-hour watch had already made their appearance. The priests were on their way home, having performed the evening rites for the well being of the palace residents. The palace apartments, emptied of most of the attendants and the vassal princes, looked enormous. Countless lamps had been lit and their flames, as their reflection fell on it, seemed to kiss the polished stone floor; it also created the illusion that myriad champaka petals were scattered on the floor.

In the wells the glow of the lamps took the guise of morning sunlight for the pining lotus plants. In the cages the lions had become drowsy with sleep.

Kamadeva, like a night watchman, had already entered the women's quarters with his bow raised. In order to excite erotic feelings towards their lovers, messengers of love were whispering words of passion in the women's ears. But the pining hearts of those separated from their lovers were on fire as though the flames from the *suryakanta* stones had passed on to them.

It was at this evening hour that Chandrapida went walking to his father's palace surrounded all the way by glowing lamps. He spent some time with his father and mother and then returned home. Like Hrishikesha lying under the expanded bejewelled hood of the king of the cobras Chandrapida too lay down in his bed.

Getting up early the next morning, Chandrapida, having already obtained his father's permission the previous evening, mounted Indrayudha and set out eagerly on his first hunt, well before the sun had risen. A great army of elephants, horses and footmen accompanied him.

Huge hunting dogs, the size of donkeys ran ahead, held on golden leashes by the dog-keepers. These men wore tunics made of old tiger skins and their hair was tied up by means of strips of coloured silk cloth. They had a luxuriant growth of facial hair and wore a golden earring just on one ear. A single piece of cloth was wound tightly around their waist. Their thighs were sturdy with continuous exercise. They carried a bow in their hands and ran ahead. Their enthusiastic cries raised the pitch of Chandrapida's excitement.

While the deity of the forest looked on with eyes half closed in fear, Chandrapida, pulling the bow string right up to his ear released the half-moon-shaped arrows, with the lustre of blue lily leaves, arrows powerful enough to break the foreheads of frenzied elephants. He felled countless wild boars, lions, and deer of various kinds. With great courage and valour he also captured alive many other animals that were now shaking with fear.

When it was midday it was time to go home. Indrayudha was bathed in sweat. As he had gnashed at the bit, foam mixed with blood dribbled out of the corners of his mouth now slack with fatigue; it had splashed as far as the binding strip of the saddle. Leaves and flowers stuck on his head and around the ears showed that he had been inside the forest.

Chandrapida was seated on the back of Indrayudha and his armour was thoroughly splashed with animal blood. He too looked flushed and therefore twice as handsome. In the heat of the chase the umbrella handle had broken off, so now a makeshift one made of fresh leaves protected Chandrapida from the sun. Covered with the pollen dust of a variety of flowers he appeared like a personification of spring. Clear streaks of sweat appeared on his forehead grainy with the dust raised by the horses' hooves. Those who followed the hunting party on foot were now left far behind, and the path ahead too looked empty. Only a few princes who had fleet-footed horses that could keep pace with Indrayudha were now with Chandrapida. And the talk among them was still about the hunt that had taken place. Describing and analysing the way the various animals, such as the lion, the boar, the bison and deer had been killed, Chandrapida came home.

He dismounted from the horse and sat down on a seat brought over quickly by one of the attendants. First he removed his armour and then the rest of his riding attire. He rested there a while being fanned by his servants. Then he got up and made his way to the bathing apartment furnished with a golden stool and several water pots made of silver, gold and precious stones. After the bath he wiped his body with a clean towel and tied a fresh silk cloth around his head. He then dressed and said his

prayers and then proceeded to the anointing chamber. There all
the female attendants of the palace under the chief pratihari as
well as all those serving Vilasavathi including Kulavardhana met
him. They had been sent by the king with boxes of varieties of
garments, ornaments, garlands of flowers and unguents, which
they now placed before him. Chandrapida himself applied the
unguents first on Vaishampayana and then on his own body.
Then he gave away the clothes and ornaments to the princes
sitting with him according to what suited them. Then they moved
on to the huge dining room furnished with a variety of bejewelled
vessels containing food.

A carpet folded twice over was made into a seat for
Chandrapida to sit on. While Vaishampayana who sat next to
him extolled the prince's great qualities, Chandrapida solicitously
hospitable, took care that the princes were served properly. And
the princes fully charmed by him became eager to serve him.

The meal over, he washed his hands and accepted tambula
and then went over to Indrayudha. He expatiated to the princes
on the wonderful qualities of the horse, such as his leanness,
his speed and his instinctive understanding of what the rider
wanted. Although the stable hands were eager to do his bidding
Chandrapida who had lost his heart to the noble qualities of the
horse himself spread the fodder before him. Then he went to pay
his respects to his father and then to his own home for the night.

-19-

The next day as soon as it was dawn, Chandrapida had
visitors; Kailasa, the kanchuki who was in charge of all the
women's apartments and a trusted officer of the king, had brought
with him a beautiful young girl.

The girl appeared quite at ease with the royal ways, yet she had not abandoned her natural modesty. Just out of childhood, she wore a pink veil, the colour of *shakragopa*, which made her appear like the eastern skies doused in the rays of the young morning sun. The freshly ground *Manashila* lustre of her body just flowed out of her like a river and filled the mansion.

She was moonlight taken refuge on the earth, having fled the moon perhaps out of fear of being swallowed by Rahu.

She was the patron goddess of the royal family come in human form.

Her lotus-feet were adorned with dulcet sounding anklets; truly she was a lotus plant crowded upon by indistinctly cooing swans.

She wore an expensive golden mekhala around her hips. Her young breasts were still not full. Her lips were betel-darkened, her nose straight and high, and a little rounded at the top. As she swung her hands gently while walking, the brilliance of her nails released steady streams of loveliness. Her eyes were like white lily blooms. Her cheeks were lit by the brilliance of her gem-inlaid eardrops. On her forehead the sandalwood tilaka put on the previous day had become dry and pale. Her body was soft and tender like a creeper. She was slim-waisted, rather like a *vedi*, and she was of exceedingly noble appearance.

The kanchuki stepped forward and placing his right hand on the ground in salute, spoke with deference: 'Prince! Mahadevi Vilasavathi commands thus: "This girl here is Patralekha, the daughter of the king of Kulutha. Your father, the king conquered the Kuluthas sometime ago and brought this girl along with the bards and left her in the antapura in the midst of the maids. I felt drawn to her, perhaps because she was a king's child and I brought her up as my own daughter. She is now of an age to be your tambula karankavahini, your

betel box bearer. I am therefore sending her to you; please do
not treat her as an attendant but cherish her like a child, treat
her like a student, nay, look upon her like your own friend
sharing every confidence with her. As I have brought her up all
these years my heart is bound to her as if she were my own
child. I am indeed very fond of her. As she is of a noble lineage,
this position of tambula karankavahini is right for her. She is
very disciplined in her ways and I am sure she shall win you
over quickly. Please treat her in such a way that she will serve
you faithfully for a long time."

Having delivered this message the kanchuki fell silent.
Patralekha paid her respects to the prince. Chandrapida looked
at her contemplatively for a while. Then he said to the kanchuki
'I would do as my mother commands me to'. Then he discharged
the palace officer from his presence.

From that moment onwards, Patralekha, having developed
an instant eagerness to serve the prince, followed him like a
shadow. She was with him day and night, never leaving his side
awake or asleep. Chandrapida too had liked her at first sight,
and found this liking growing every minute to transmute into
great affection for her. As the days went by he treated her with
more and more graciousness and favour and began to repose
the utmost trust in her as though she and he were indeed one,
her heart no different from his own.

─ 20 ─

After a few days had passed in this fashion, King Tarapida
decided the time had come to appoint his young son the
crown prince of the realm. It was on one of those days just
before the investiture ceremony that the minister Shukanasa,

desirous of making the young prince even more refined than he was already gave him wide-ranging advice on many things, in order to groom him for his future responsibilities.

Shukanasa Speaks . . .

My child, Chandrapida! You know already all that is to be known, you have mastered all the branches of knowledge; it would seem that there was indeed very little that could be proffered to you as advice. Yet we know that the dense darkness of confusion born of youthful passions by its very nature is not easily removed; not by the light of a lamp, nor by the brilliant lustre of the gems; it cannot be broken even by the light of the sun. Then there is the terrible arrogance of wealth, which does not mellow down even when one is past one's prime. Incurable indeed is the blindness caused by the pride of wealth and is of far greater virulence than the curable blindness of the eye. The fever induced by pride cannot be brought down by any cooling treatment. The obsessive enjoyment of the poison of sensual pleasures brings on an unconsciousness to which neither medicinal roots, nor incantations could ever provide an antidote. The encrusted filth of sensual indulgence cannot be washed away by a daily bath or other cleaning procedures. The sleep induced by the comforts of a royal life is horrible, as it finds no termination in a dawn that brings wakefulness. It is for these reasons that I am talking to you at length.

To be endowed with the power of wealth right from birth, to be in possession of young manhood with incomparable beauty of appearance and a prowess that borders on the divine—these are indeed a series of disasters. Any one of these endowments could harbour any number of pitfalls, so what could one say about a combination of all these?

At the first flush of youth the intellect, although washed clean with the waters of erudition can and does get muddied. Just as a dry leaf swirling around in the dusty churning wind is blown far away, the young man, his youthful nature in a whirl in the swell of passions, is carried far astray, without any resistance. Just as the deer thirsting for water chases after a mirage and meets with its destruction, the youth too with his senses aflame runs after the irresistible mirage of the sweet pleasures of the senses, and courts destruction. The young minds tortured by desires and passions find indulgence pleasurable; no wonder really, for tongues with a bitter taste on them would find even unsweetened water sweet.

Only people like you are ready for good counsel; with minds cleaned of all dirt, the teachings would enter them easily like the rays of the moon entering the crystal beads. Should any mental turbidity born of weaknesses in character still linger, the advice of the preceptor would remove it just as the same rays of the moon light up the pitch darkness of the evening after the sun is set. This is indeed the right time to counsel you, when you have not yet tasted the pleasures of the senses. Once the arrows of Kama have pierced the heart, advice would be like water running through a sieve.

The advice of elders cleans one of all impurities; it is truly a bath without water. It leads to mental maturity, which is old age without its physical disfigurements. It adds to one's weight without adding to one's flesh. It is a fine ear ornament that is not made of gold; it is light without flames, it gives alertness without anxiety, especially for the kings.

There are indeed few true preceptors around; most echo the rulers' words out of fear. And should there be one who dares to give advice, the ruler hardly listens, his swollen pride having closed his ears completely. Or having heard the advice he disregards it completely and insults the teacher as well in the process. It is in the nature of kings to become afflicted with the raging fever of inordinate pride, leading to the darkness of delusion and delirium. Wealth gives rise to false pride; sovereignty is the lassitude inducing poison administered by Rajyalakshmi.

Thou of noble resolve, observe Lakshmi to begin with. Lakshmi is one who wanders among the forest of swords held by valiant warriors even as a bee roams in the midst of lotuses. Her passionate nature partakes of the glowing hues of the parijata; in addition she has inherited crookedness from the crescent moon, restlessness from Ucchaishravas, hypnotizing powers from *kalakuta*, the ability to intoxicate, from wine, and harshness from kaustubha; having lived a long time in the company of these under the milky ocean, she clasped these qualities of her companions to her bosom when she came out of the ocean, as though to mitigate the sorrow of actual separation from them.

There is none else in this world quite like this vile female who treats the bonds of friendship with such contempt. Even if you attain her she can be held only with very great difficulty. Bind her with the ropes of diplomacy and war and still she disappears. Or put her in a cage made of the raised swords of a thousand brave soldiers, yet she absconds, probably to the enemy side. Guarded by a mass of rain-cloud-dark elephants, she still runs away. She shows no respect for a lineage that has celebrated her for generations; she cares nothing for the virtues of a ruler.

She has no understanding of truth and is never moved by charity; erudition means nothing to her; righteousness does not control her. She is ephemeral; one may see her, like a phantom, in a play of light. She reels as though still giddy from having been whirled around by the churning Mandara Mountain. As if she has been pricked by thorns while wandering in the lotus field of the turbid lakes, she does not bear to plant her feet in one place and remain still. Even when held within the palace of a great king she stumbles into the wrong path as though drunk with the rut fluid of the scent elephants. To teach cruelty she ever dwells on the sharp edge of the sword. She is so fickle that she would, all of a sudden desert a king who has fully prospered, like the full blown lotus at day's end, and seek the company of a worthless king like a creeper twining around the thin branch of a tree.

She never favours those blessed by Saraswati, out of sheer jealousy.

She does not honour the magnanimous, considering them inauspicious.

She does not touch the virtuous as being impure! The good, she avoids as being of no consequence.

The well-born, she skips over, as though they were snakes. The valorous she moves away from, as one would from thorns.

The generous are forgotten as bad dreams, the noble are laughed at as deranged.

Like a magician she puts together mutually contradictory principles. As she kindles the fire of longing, for wealth, she gives rise to the coldness of indifference, to right and wrong; she holds out high status to the low-minded.

Herself born out of water she gives rise to the thirst of greed in people. This fickle-minded goddess, in whatever fashion she chooses to shine, brings out only unclean soot.

For the long sleep of delusion she is the bed of sensuality. For the ghosts of the pride of wealth, she is the old attic of the house.

If the sense enjoyments were the liquor, then she is the drinking den.

If the poisonous serpents were the pleasures of the senses then she is their cave home.

If there is a play staged of underhand intrigues she is the prologue to it.

To the vision gained with the shastras she is the onset of eye disease.

If the swans were the virtues she is the untimely rain that hides them from view.

Even as a painted picture she would disappear!

As a mere figurine she would indulge in magic!

As just a carving she could deceive!

The kings caught by such a deceiving one become weak and slaves to all sorts of unseemly habits. The corruption process starts right at the time of coronation. With the anointing pots of water all generosity gets washed away. The smoke of the sacrificial fire darkens the heart, and all forgiveness is swept away when the priest waves the kusha grass. When the turban is tied all thoughts of approaching old age get shrouded and the royal umbrella removes the hereafter from sight. Loud slogans of 'Long live the king' drown the quiet words of the wise and the well meaning.

Some kings become greedy for wealth, which is as shaky as the trembling necks of exhausted birds, as fleeting as the momentary twinkle of the firefly. The acquisition of just a little wealth fills them with pride and they forget the circumstances of their birth. As they get into the grip of kama and krodha they are laid low, just as the body weakens when the blood is polluted with maladies. Ever hungry for sensual gratification, they are exhausted as though driven not by a mere five but by a thousand different senses. Naturally of a vacillating nature, and now with the availability of a variety of indulgences, the one mind splits into a thousand as it were and renders them totally in a dither.

Like men on the verge of death, such kings do not recognize even their close relations. Like men with eye disease who cannot bear to look at bright objects, these kings cannot look at men of valour, out of jealousy. Just as those bitten by a virulently poisonous snake cannot be brought back to consciousness by any amount of incantations, any amount of counselling would be unable to enlighten them.

Like ornaments made of lacquer they cannot bear the proximity of fiery valour. They do bring down princes of noble lineages however, but from afar, by the use of unwarranted force and aggression, just like bringing down fruits from high up on the tree by wielding a long stick.

Then there are princes who fall victim to wicked courtiers who are out only to advance their own selfish prospects, vultures that come after the flesh of wealth. They are like ducks in a lotus pond that conceal themselves among the petals of the lotus only to pounce upon the unwary small fish. They give wicked advice to the king; they would say that dice is fun, seducing another man's wife is skill, hunting is exercise, drinking is enjoyment, arrogance is valour, to abandon one's own wife is detachment, disregarding the advice of elders is a show of independence, indulging in dance, music, and the company of the courtesans is being artistic, putting up with the insults of others is forgiveness, the flattery of one's own bards is fame, flitting from one interest to another is enthusiasm, undiscriminating behaviour is impartiality.

By presenting failings as virtues they corrupt the mind, all the while laughing at the king in their own heart of hearts. They are such adepts at deceit that with fulsome praise not really suitable for mere human beings they lead the prince astray. The princes for their part, arrogant with wealth, believe all the false praise as true and begin to think of themselves as divine rather than human, and begin to act accordingly, inviting derisive laughter from the people.

They become so convinced of their divinity that losing all their rationality they come to believe that they have two more hands concealed beneath the two that are visible, in the fashion of the deities. They suspect that they have a third eye too on their forehead hidden under the skin. They think that merely showing themselves to the people is benediction; just glancing at them is serving them. They believe their commands are boons and their mere touch is sanctifying. Full of this unreal greatness, they do not worship the true deities, they do not honour the Brahmins; they do not give respect where respect is due. They have the temerity to laugh at the erudite that the latter have merely wasted their energy in the unnecessary pursuit of knowledge, energy that could have more profitably been used in the enjoyment of sensual pleasures. They dismiss the advice of the elders as the confused prattle of old age.

It is only these sycophants who sing their praises day and night with hands folded in supplication and treat them like divinities heaping unwarranted greatness on them that the princes always favour, regard them as their friends, keep them always at their side, showering them with gifts and reposing all their confidence in them. These princes rely entirely on the extremely cruel and merciless Kautilya Shastra for their governance. Their priests too are of the pitiless kind who would organize terrible rites to bring about the destruction of others. The only ministers whose advice they accept are those that are experts in the art of deception.

Dear prince, statecraft is fraught with a thousand pitfalls, full of difficult manoeuvres. That is on the one hand; on the other is youth blinded with the impaired perception born of ignorance and confusion. Therefore, my child, conduct yourself in such a way that the people do not laugh at you, and the virtuous do not censure you. See to it that your preceptors do not get displeased with you, that your good friends do not disown you. Behave in such a way that the debauched would never treat you with familiarity. Be on your guard that the dishonest do not feed off you, that your servants do not plunder you. Never allow the devious to cheat you nor be enticed by the coquetry of women. Do not lose your balance to Kamadeva.

Chandrapida! You are by nature strong and your father has, by a great effort, groomed you into a very fine young man. It is only the weak-hearted and the untutored intellects that fall a prey to the allures of wealth. It is really my pleasure over your great qualities that has made me talk in this strain. There is only this that I would keep telling you again and again, namely that the most learned, the wisest, the strongest, the best born, the most valiant, and the most hard working, all can be led astray by that mischievous, wayward, wicked Lakshmi.

May you enjoy your investiture as the crown prince, being planned auspiciously by your father. The burden of ruling borne so far by your father is now for you, the latest in the line to bear. After the crowning go on a victorious march, conquer the earth, already subdued by your father, once again. This is the time for you to establish your power; only the commands of a king who makes his power felt would bear unfailing fruit, like the commands of an omniscient yogi.

~

Having talked at length Shukanasa fell silent.

Chandrapida, after listening to those clear words of advice, felt as if he had been washed clean and purified. He believed his eyes had been opened, his angularities smoothed and softened; he felt he had been polished and made to shine; he felt ennobled. Happy at heart, he stayed with Shukanasa for a while and then took his leave.

―21―

Sometime later King Tarapida appointed his son the crown prince of the realm with due ceremony. A favourable day was chosen. The priests performed all the auspicious rites demanded of the occasion. Then the king himself lifted the pot containing water collected from every sea, every river, and every sacred spot, and mixed with every herb, every fruit and every kind of mud on the earth and precious stones of all kinds and purified with sacred chants, and adding finally his own copious tears of joy to it, bathed his son ceremoniously. Shukanasa was with him as well as innumerable princes. Rajyalakshmi at once, like a creeper leaving its own tree and going over to twine around another, at once abandoned Tarapida and went over to his son whose body was still wet with the anointing water.

Vilasavathi surrounded by her women, her heart tender with love, herself applied the fragrant sandalwood paste, cool and moonlight-white, on her son's body right down to his feet. His head was decorated with a garland of fresh white blooms. His limbs were stained with gorochana; his ears were adorned with the very tender shoots of durva. Chandrapida then wrapped himself in two pieces of brand new moon-white silk cloth with straight ten-inch long tassels at either end. The priest then tied a sacred string around his wrist. A necklace of pearls, like a new lotus stalk, so to speak, in the pond that was Rajyalakshmi, a necklace that looked like strung saptarshis, the constellation of seven stars and made one wonder if those sages had come down to watch the coronation, embraced his chest. White floral garlands that went under the arms and hung down to his knees covered his body completely.

With the white garments and the white flowers, Chandrapida was splendid, like Mount Kailasa with the rivers flowing crisscross on it, like Iravatha wrapped in a net of lotus stalks in the Mandakini, like Narasimha sporting the great mane. Picking up the cane staff the father led the way to the court, where Chandrapida mounted the golden throne like the moon ascending the Meru mountain.

The crown prince then duly gave away gifts to the entire assembly of vassal princes. Then it was time to set out on the victory march. A deep reverberating boom was now heard, like how the thunder must have rumbled at the time of the final dissolution of the *yuga*; like how the milky ocean being assaulted by the churning Mandara Mountain must have groaned; like how the surface of the earth hit by the violent winds at the end of the yuga must have howled; like how the bowels of the earth must have roared when set upon by the snout of Adivaraha. It was the dundubhi, struck with golden sticks announcing the departure of the prince on the victory march.

The sound filled, roused, separated, extended and went round the spaces of the universe. The grid of the directions seemed to be rent asunder. And the echoes reverberated. It was as if Nandi, believing it to be a new kind of *attahasa* of his own lord, one he had never heard before, was responding to it with his own happy *hunkaras* on top of the Kailasa. It was as if the elephants of the quarters raising their tusks again and again were calling out to the directions imagining the sound of the dundubhi to be the roar of the enemy elephants. The echoes circled around as if the sun's horses struck with fear started going round and round with reduced speed. In the world of Yama, the *mahisha* of the god of death startled by this sound never heard before, bent its horned head aslant as if bowing to it in supplication. Travelling all around, the beat of the dundubhi distressed the ears of the guardians of all the three worlds.

When they heard the dundubhi everyone shouted 'hail' to Chandrapida, who got up from the throne and came out of the audience chamber. The waiting circle of vassals saluted him with great respect; rows upon rows of crowns on the bowing heads shook; their thousands-strong elephant forces turned restless; countless princely umbrellas were crushed one against another. As Chandrapida came out of the palace a mahout led an auspiciously decorated female elephant to the prince. Patralekha, the carrier of the betel box was already seated on it, occupying the middle seat. Chandrapida mounted the elephant after all the rites of departure were performed, and sat under a huge white umbrella of a thousand spokes that was indeed like the mighty white whirl caused by the fast turning Mandara mountain in the milky ocean. Gandhamadana, the scent elephant followed him with his forehead decorated with sindur. A huge pearl ornament hanging from a banner on the elephant fell almost to the ground. With a garland of white flowers adorning the head, the elephant appeared like a peak of the Meru made gritty with a collection of stars.

Resplendent with gold jewellery that looked like handprints in vermilion on his body, Indrayudha was led ahead of the prince. The procession went slowly in the direction of Indra, the east. The forest of white umbrellas placed on all the elephants swayed to the gait of the elephants. The slowly marching army seemed to inundate the earth, just as the swelling waters of the ocean would flood the land. The commotion created by the army was truly amazing.

Meanwhile Vaishampayana, anointed with white orpiment and clad in silk garments and looking like a second crown prince, rode a swift-stepping female elephant and came over to join Chandrapida; he had been seen off with due ceremony and was accompanied by several princes.

Soon shouts of 'the prince is leaving' were heard from here and there. And then the entire army moved shaking the very earth.

All at once the surface of the earth appeared as if made solely of horses, the circle of the directions solely of elephants, the mid

regions of the heavens of umbrellas and umbrellas alone and
the vault of the skies, of only flag posts. The wind was of the
fragrance of the elephant rut fluid alone and all creation consisted
as it were, only of kings. And shouts of victory seemed the only
stuff of which the three worlds were made.

Columns of dust rose from the earth looking like smoking
comets. The moving elephants the size of mountains, trumpeted
with the harsh deep sounds of a violent whirlwind. Rank upon
rank of horses gallopped on like the agitated waves of the ocean.
The quarters darkened and showers of elephant rut fluid turned
it into a stormy day. Shattered by the weight of the army and
stamped upon by the feet of the elephants, the earth rumbled
fearfully. It appeared as if the end of the world was imminent.

As the army moved the noise became truly deafening. The
commotion created by those who rode in front, the long shrill
sound of the *kahala*, the stamping of the horses' hoofs mixed
with the neighing, the shrill trumpeting of the elephants combined
with the constant flapping of their ears, the uneven clanging of
the bells tied around the neck of the animals as they moved at
different paces, the blowing of the conch, the beating of the
pataha, and the sounding of the dindima here and there, all
these contributed to the general roar which not merely deafened
the people but even reduced them to unconsciousness.

As the army picked up speed the dust rose, and in as many
varied hues as the earth's surface was of different shades. It was
smoky grey like the under part of an old fish, or it was the colour
of the camel's mane; it was dark like the fur of an aged deer, or
it had the whiteness of the threads of washed silk cloth. It could
be yellowish brown as the hair on an old monkey, or it could be
another kind of white like the foam from the ruminating mouth
of Nandi.

The dust shut one's eyes—like laughter. It drank up the rut
fluid of the elephants as though thirsty. It flew up into the sky as

though it had wings. It kissed the rut-soaked cheeks of the elephants like the bees. It caught hold of the flags, like the victorious in battle. It was old age turning the hair white. It settled on the honey drops on the flowers worn on the ear as though enjoying the fragrance. It entered the elephant ears as though scared by their constant flapping. It flew up like sandalwood powder when the wood was sawed. Swallowing the sun and its rays completely like Rahu, the dust rose spreading thick like the untimely onset of dark clouds.

It came from everywhere, even from the very skies. It came out of the moving feet to be sure, but it seemed to come out of the eyes too. Did the wind blow it out of itself? Did the sun's rays create it? It caused sleep in people without taking away their consciousness. It caused darkness without the sun setting! It created underground dwellings although it was not summer. It brought on a monsoon-like atmosphere although there was no rain. It fashioned a nether world without serpents. Grown huge like the feet of Hari, the dust enveloped all the three worlds. The universe seemed to be made of one element alone—dust.

The elephants burning with their own heat were squirting a whitish liquid from the tips of their trunks; the flapping ears spread the oozing rut fluid everywhere; the neighing horses showered around the saliva from their mouths. With this wetness the dust seemed to settle somewhat and the quarters regained their brightness. It was then that the army could be seen as though risen out of the waters of the ocean. Vaishampayana, struck with its immeasurable size, spoke thus to Chandrapida: 'Oh prince! Is there anything that has not been conquered by the great king Tarapida that you can now conquer? Which quarter, not yet brought under control, is now left for you to bring under control? What forts still unconquered that you can take over now? What divisions of the earth, not yet made his, would you now make your own? What gems still not acquired, would you now acquire?

'Who are the rulers that do not bow to the great king's authority, and who indeed that do not join their hands, lotus bud-like in supplication? Are there any princes still left whose golden bands worn around their foreheads do not make the court floor shine with constant rubbing? Are there any indeed whose crest jewels have not grazed against the footstool of the king? Are there any left still, who have not wielded the cane staff in the manner of the palace guards, or raised the chamaras, or have not sung victory slogans for the king?

'There are princes, arrogant because their forces have accomplished the difficult feat of going across the four oceans, princes who are no doubt made in the image of Dasharatha, Bhagiratha, Bharata, Dileepa, Alarka, and Mandhathri. They are proud of their lineage, they have performed the soma sacrifice and have partaken of the soma juice. Even those kings, lords of the earth bear the dust of your feet on their crowned heads purified with the water of coronation, as though it were sanctified *vibhuti*.

'Then there are kings who, like the hoary mountains, have been holding up the earth with their forces that practically flood all the space between the ten directions; they too are now eager to serve you. Just look! Wherever you turn your eyes you see the forces, as though the nether world has thrown them up; as though the quarters have poured them out; as though the earth is spawning them; as though the very skies have rained them down. I do believe that the earth is so burdened today with the weight of these forces that she must be remembering the tumult of the Mahabharata war of ancient times. Like rivers springing up into the skies out of fear of the earth being shaken with the weight of the forces, the rows upon rows of moon-white tongues of flags completely shroud the circle of the ten directions. It is indeed a wonder that the joints of the earth, held together by the great mountains, have still not come apart nor the earth herself broken into a thousand bits, nor that the hoods of the great serpent, exhausted by bearing the burden of the earth with all these armies, are all in a tremble.'

As Vaishampayana chatted on excitedly they reached a travellers' inn that was ready to receive the prince and his retinue. Festoons had been put up at the entrance. Around a grassy quadrangle there were several houses; and several tents of white cloth had also been pitched all over the place.

Dismounting, Chandrapida performed all duties exactly as his father would have done. He spent the day meeting with all the kings and their ministers in the retinue and discussing many things with them. As night fell the prince lay down to rest not too far away from Vaishampayana. Patralekha too lay down on a rug spread out on the ground quite close to the prince. Most of the night was however spent in talking about his father and mother and Arya Shukanasa.

In the morning they rose at dawn and set out again on their march. At every setting out they were joined by more allies and the army swelled. The earth was shattered and tormented, the mountains were shaken, the waters of the rivers were made to spill out leaving them almost dry, the ponds were emptied, the forests were pulverized, and the undulations on the ground were flattened out; all obstacles on the way were destroyed. Thus did the armies march on.

And they marched on freely. The rebellious on the way were subdued; the submissive were rewarded. Those who sought refuge were given protection. The treacherous were rooted out. Young vassal princes were crowned. Chandrapida earned much wealth by accepting the tribute offered by the vassals and by collecting taxes.

He tightened his control over his vast kingdom. He issued commands in accordance with the laws of the land; he erected pillars as symbols of his authority; he proclaimed his victory by issuing edicts.

He generated goodwill among the people by honouring the elders, by venerating the sages and protecting their hermitages. He instilled awe among his subjects by demonstrating his valour, courage and heroism. He won the admiration of all by his virtues and good conduct. Destroying the forests on the shores of the ocean, he traversed the earth with his army rendering even the waters of the oceans dusty.

First the east, then the south described as the tilaka on the forehead of Trishanku, then the west under the rule of Varuna and finally the north, marked by the presence of the seven starry sages were duly conquered. In three years the entire earth came under his authority. Chandarapida then wandered over his earth-kingdom at will, a kingdom which had the oceans themselves as a moat around it.

Almost at the end of his march around the earth, Chandrapida conquered a city called Suvarnapuri not too far away from the eastern ocean, a city belonging to the Kiratas, natives of Hemakuta, a mountain range close to Kailasa. He established his camp there in order to give his armies the much-needed rest.

─22─

Mounting Indrayudha one day Chandrapida went out to hunt. Roaming the forest, he chanced upon a *kinnara* pair, animals with the head of a horse on a human body, coming down a peak. Having never seen such creatures before, Chandarapida was overcome with curiosity, and a desire to capture them. He drove his horse close to them, when the kinnara pair, for their part having never set eyes upon humans took fright and fled. The prince kicked Indrayudha on his side to increase his speed and went after the fleeing kinnara pair in hot pursuit. In a very short time he had left his troops far behind.

Inducing Indrayudha to make that extra effort and telling himself 'Now I have caught them. There, now they are within my grasp.' he traversed, in no time at all, more than a hundred miles from where he had left the army. Keeping his eyes on the kinnara pair the pursuer followed it up one of the very tall peaks that loomed ahead.

Still climbing Chandrapida suddenly realized that the horse had lost speed due to the steepness of the rocky flanks of the peak; reluctantly removing his eyes from the speedily climbing kinnara pair he looked at his horse as well as at himself, both bathed in sweat due to the excessive exertion. He laughed a little ruefully and chided himself. 'How like a child I have behaved and unnecessarily exhausted this creature in this futile pursuit. Did it matter whether I caught this pair or not? How very stupid I have been. I have wasted such a lot of time and effort in this pointless endeavour, while so much work remains still to be done. The digvijaya remains incomplete; my father's work is as yet unfinished. Framing laws for the domains of the friendly princes started by me has not as yet been completed. Like one possessed, I have come so far away from my troops. When I try to analyse how I could have committed such a folly, my own mind as if it were something other than me, begins to laugh at me. I do not know what distance actually separates me from my army. I was not paying any attention to the route on my way up. For one thing, Indrayudha was very fast, and secondly my eyes were fixed on the kinnara pair. Further all along there was a dense growth of trees and the branches were thickly entwined with creepers. The forest ground was covered with the dry leaves fallen from the tree. It is therefore impossible to retrace the path by which I reached here. However hard I may search the region it is highly unlikely that I would meet another human being from whom I can find out the way back to Suvarnapuri. I have also heard it said that human settlements come to an end north

of Suvarnapuri beyond which there is only jungle up to Kailasa
with no human habitation. There is Kailasa ahead of me. The
only course left for me is to take the route due south and go
along playing it by the ear. One has to pay for one's own follies.'
Pulling the reins with his left hand Chandrapida turned the
horse around.

Then he thought again. 'The sun god is now shining with
intensified heat and brilliance, right in the middle of the sky,
like a brilliant gem in the girdle of the goddess Day. Indrayudha
here is exhausted. Let me feed him some mouthfuls of tender
durva grass and lead him to a lake or water fall or perhaps a
river where I can give him a wash and a drink of water. I too can
quench my thirst. Then we will rest a while under a tree and
then start on our way down.'

Scanning the mountain slopes for water his eyes soon fell on
what could only be the tracks left recently by a herd of mountain
elephants on their way back from sporting in a lotus lake. He
saw the slush left by the elephants' feet; he saw the path strewn
colourfully with lotus and lily plants pulled out by the roots
with blooms and buds, that must have slipped from the animals'
trunks. There were uprooted white lily plants with clumps of
earth clinging to the roots. He also saw wet, tender, dark *shaivala*
grass in the upper reaches of the path. The bees were hovering
over the pulled out flowers. The track was wet with the
tamala-dark rut fluid redolent of fresh floral blooms.

Chandrapida guessed that some considerable water body
must be present not too far away. He followed the track in the
opposite direction from that taken by the returning elephants
and soon reached the foothills of the Kailasa, a densely wooded
area with *sarala*, *sala*, and *sallaki* trees, so tall that one had to
look up to see their tops, which were circular like umbrellas.
Although dense they gave the impression of sparseness because
they had no branches. The ground was covered with yellowish

shingles. Grass and creepers were sparse due to the rocky terrain. Red arsenic dust was in the air making everything tawny, the mineral having been ground to a powder by the wild elephants. The scattered blossoms of the *pashanabhangini* had made curved tattoo-like designs on the rock surfaces.

The rocks had become sticky with the constantly oozing gum from the gum trees. The bitumen leaking from the peak had made the stones even more slippery. The chisel-like hoofs of the horses had pounded yellow orpiment into powder and the dust permeated everything. There was also gold dust, the gold having been dug out of the ground by the rats. He saw the deep hoof marks of the deer on the sand, as well as the fur shed by the *ranku* and the *rallaka* deer. A *chakora* pair was perched on a rugged rock.

Going along the foothills of Kailasa pungent with the smell of sulphur and dense with cane and bamboo groves, for some distance, he saw yet another thick grove of trees to the north-east of the Kailasa peak, dark as a night of the waning fortnight of the moon, appearing truly like an array of rain-laden clouds. A cool moist breeze bearing the sweet smell of pollen wafted out of the grove, and embraced Chandrapida like a shower of cool sandalwood water. The distant calls of the swans excited with the nectar of the lotus called out to him. Chandrapida entered the grove.

There, right in the middle of the grove, was the most delightfully beautiful lake he had ever seen. It was surely the gem-mirror of Lakshmi, the goddess of all the three worlds, or the crystal-floored chamber of the goddess of the earth. Had the quarters melted, or have the skies themselves come down to turn into the pristine waters of this lake? Had Kailasa melted or all of the Himalayas themselves? Had all the white clouds of autumn come together to become the water of this lake? Could it be the mirror mansion of the god Varuna? Had moonlight taken this watery form? It must surely be the lucid mind of the ascetics, or the chaste qualities of the virtuous that had transformed into water; how could the water be so pure otherwise? The transparent lucidity of it enabled one to see right down to the bottom so clearly that one was immediately struck with doubt, if there was any water there at all. The doubt cleared only when the breeze lifted up the water in waves and the sprays broke into rainbow colours. It then appeared as though Indra were wielding a thousand bows to protect everything around the lake. The lake was very deep and the tamala forest that fringed it was reflected darkly in the waters; it was as if one could see right down to the gates of patala, the nether world.

Khandaparashu, the great Mahadeva Himself must have come down from the neighbouring Kailasa hundreds of times to bathe in the lake; as he plunged into the waters repeatedly the crescent moon on his head would have shaken and oozed nectar, competing with the lustre that flowed from the water-washed cheeks of Parvathi on the left side of Mahadeva, and mixed with the waters of the lake.

Brahma, it was said, would often fill his kamandalu with the waters of this lake and purify them in the process. It was to this lake that the *balakilyas*—ascetics of exceedingly small stature— would come in groups to perform their morning, noon and afternoon worship. Many indeed were the times when the Seven Sages had bathed here and had, by that act sanctified the water, as did the women of the Siddhas clad in the bark of the parijata tree. The very deep and circular navels of the women of Kubera, round like the fully drawn bow of Makarakethu, would drink in the water whenever they came here to bathe.

Here on the lake Varuna's swans must have drunk the nectar from the lotus field. Yonder where the faded lotus stalks lay broken in pieces the elephants of the directions must have plunged into the water! And surely these stone chips on the shore here must have been pulverized by the horns of Triambaka's bull.

At the very sight of this beautiful lake, whose name he later learnt was Acchoda, Chandrapida's weariness fled. And he thought: 'My failure to capture the horse-faced kinnara pair is more than compensated by the sight of this lake. My eyes have now attained their highest reward in their quest for beauty. For I have seen the ultimate manifestation of it. I have reached the very bounds of the pleasurable. I have gazed at the supreme form of mind-captivating charm. Those that are responsible for creating things to delight the senses have now put before me their entire stock. Brahma merely repeated himself in creating amrita after he made this lake. Umapati does not leave Kailasa only because of the splendour of the lake. As for Lord Vishnu, how could he still seek to satisfy his craving for water by lying in the midst of the salty ocean, disregarding this lake here?

These waters delight all the senses, like amrita. They gladden the eye by their clarity; their coolness comforts the sense of touch. The fragrance of the lotuses gratifies the sense of smell, the sweetness of the waters satisfies the sense of taste. The calling of the swans thrills the ears.'

Enchanted with the lake, Chandrapida reached the southern shore. On the shingled shore he saw lingams made of sand that bore the marks of the worship of the vidyadharas in the form of scattered lotus plants with blooms on them. The red lotus offering must be the one placed by Arundhati to Divakara, the maker of the day. Those must be the footprints of the divine mothers like Brahmi who doubtless came down to the lake to bathe, as it was so close to Kailasa. The scattered sacred ash surely indicated that the *pramathaganas* had pounded the *bhasma* there. And the lion of Katyayani must have left these huge pugmarks when it came to the lake to assuage its thirst.

─23─

Chandrapida dismounted from Indrayudha and removed the saddle from his back. The horse sat down at once and rolled on the ground and then stood up again. After feeding him some *yava* grass Chandrapida led him to the lake where the horse drank the water to his heart's content. Then Chandrapida washed the horse in an unhurried manner. He removed the bit and the reins and led him to the shade of a tree nearby where he tied the horse's feet to a low branch with a golden chain. He cut some durva grass growing on the shores and placed it in front of the horse.

Then he too stepped into the water. Washing his hands first he drank water like the chataka bird. He then ate bits of lotus stalk like the chakravaka bird. He placed the lotus stalks on his chest like one struck with the arrows of Ananga. He delighted in the cool breeze like Adisesha. Then he got out of the water. He made a bed of freshly plucked cool lotus leaves dripping with water on a rock surface under a bower of creepers. With his own utthariya rolled into a pillow he lay down and rested for a while.

It was Indrayudha who heard them first, the faint strains of music coming from the northern shores of the lake. The horse let the half-chewed grass slip from his mouth, and his ears became still. His face turned towards the north, and with his neck raised he listened intently. Exceedingly melodious, the feminine voice floated in mixed with the sound of the veena strings; the music sounded divine in its sweetness.

When he heard the music Chandrapida was filled with curiosity. 'Where can such music come from in this wilderness devoid of any human habitation?' he wondered. Rising from the lotus-leaf bed he peered in the direction from where the music seemed to be coming. Hard as he strained his eyes he could see nothing, the source of the music seemed to be very far indeed.

Impelled by curiosity Chandarapida decided to investigate the matter. He saddled the horse once again. This time he was shown the way by the forest deer that went ahead although he never asked for their help. He rode along the western shores of the lake fringed by dark woods of *saptachada* and *bakula* trees, cardamom and lavanga plants and lavali creepers swaying in the wind. The buzz of the bees filled the ears.

As he proceeded a pleasant breeze blew bringing with it the sweet fragrance of flowers. It was cool and moist with a spray of water from the clear mountain streams. It loosened the barks of the *bhurja* trees. It moved the nutmeg trees and shook the pollen out of the rudraksha flowers. It kissed the top of the head of Shanmukha's peacock and had the audacity to swing the tender shoots on the ears of Ambika. It delighted in swinging the ear ornaments of the women of Uttara Kuru. It was pure and it brought with it joy, this breeze blowing from Kailasa.

Enjoying the breeze Chandrapida rode on and reached a spot on the western side of the lake that shone with a sort of white lustre-like the rays of the moon. Situated at the foothills of Kailasa it was suitably named Chandraprabha. On the western shores of the lake he saw a lonely shrine of Shulapani; it was a *siddhayathana,* a shrine where one could attain fulfilment of one's desires through penance.

The spot was surrounded on all sides by a verdant growth. It resonated with the charmingly melodious call of the harita bird. The cuckoos lived there and ate mouthfuls of the tender shoots of the mango trees. The maddeningly noisy honey bees buzzed around the opening buds of the mango trees. The circling *bhringaraja* birds were crushing the full-grown hardened buds with their claws. The peaceful chakora birds feeling at home in the area pecked at the fresh pepper with the tip of their beaks. The chataka birds drenched in the yellow pollen dust of the champaka were pecking at the fruits of the pippala trees. The sparrows had hatched their young ones in the nests built on the pomegranate bushes laden with fruits. The beating wings of the scuffling young ones of the pigeons were creating a shower of flowers. The *sarikas* mottled with the pollen dust were on the top of the trees. The ground was strewn with the fruit bits minced by the beaks and claws of a thousand parrots. The disappointed cries of the water-obsessed chataka birds floated over from the dark tamala groves mistaken by the birds for water-laden clouds.

The plantain leaves waved gently in the wind. In the coconut grove the trees were bent as they were laden with coconuts. There were areca nut trees with slender fronds as well as an abundance of *karpura* and *aguru* trees.

Chandrapida entered the shrine and at once became completely covered with the pollen dust of the ketaki blown about in the wind, as if someone first smeared sacred ash on him before letting him enter the presence of Mahadeva. Perhaps it was spiritual merit that covered him, merit that had already gone to his account by this visit to the shrine. Inside he saw the four-faced idol of Triambaka, the lord of all creation, worshipped in all the three worlds, fashioned out of white marble. The idol was placed in a small crystal pavilion standing on four pillars; it had just been worshipped as indicated by the presence of freshly picked white lilies from the Mandakini, the water still dripping from the top edges of the petals. They looked like the moon broken at the top and oozing nectar. Looking like siblings of *panchajanya*, the conch of Vishnu, as they lay scattered they also created the illusion that they might be phases of the brilliant laughter, the attahasa of Shiva.

Seated on the southern side of the idol in the yogic posture and facing it was a strangely beautiful woman. She seemed ethereal and not of this world. There was an astonishing lustre to her body, which seemed to swell and spread over all the quarters. It was like the white waters of the milky ocean flooding over at the end of the Yuga; it was like the diffusion everywhere of ascetic power gained over years of penance; it was like the three streams of the celestial white Ganga coming together in the gaps between the trees and flowing. The lustre drenched the mountains and the forests like splendorous moonlight. Her fairness even whitened Kailasa in a different way. Hers was the lustre that would travel through the eyes of those who gazed at her, deep into their bodies to whiten their very hearts as it were, and to gladden them.

Enveloped in that white splendour she appeared as though she had been enshrined in crystal, as if she had been immersed in milky water, or shrouded in fine white silk from China, or hidden inside a mass of white autumnal clouds. In this haze her limbs appeared indistinct. Had she been fashioned out of the quality of whiteness alone, shunning the use of all the five gross elements and all other qualities?

Was it Rati covering herself thickly in sacred ash come to pray to Hara for the restoration of Kama's body? Was it the goddess of the milky ocean come to meet the crescent moon on Shiva's head, once her own companion under the milky waters? Was it the moon himself come in the guise of this woman seeking refuge from the fearful Rahu at the feet of the three-eyed god?

Was it the brilliance of Mahadadeva's laughter having issued out of his southern face, taken a seat outside? Had the shining purity of Gauri's heart taken a human form? Had the powers of Brahma's penance descended to the earth? Or had His splendid fame resulting from the creation of the first yugas, tired of having wandered over all the seven worlds come here to rest?

Had the three Vedas disgusted by the loss of dharma in the Kaliyuga taken to life in the forest? Or had the seed of the future Krita Yuga taken the form of this woman?

When Kailasa shook at the extermination of the Ten-Headed One, did a bit of its radiance fall down here?

Had all the swans of the world shared their whiteness with her? Had she been carved out of seashells? Did she rise out of a mother of pearl? Were her limbs made out of lotus stalks? Or ivory pieces? Was she stroked with a brush made of moon rays? Was she painted white, or plated with silver, or bathed in mercury, or carved out of the moon?

She was the epitome of whiteness.

Her hair falling down her back had the radiance of the first rays of the young sun just climbing over Udayagiri. It had a lightning-like russet lustre. As she had just had a bath drops of water still remained on her hair. On her head, tied with strands of her hair, there reposed a pair of sculpted feet made of precious stones and inscribed with name of the Lord. She wore sacred ash on her forehead, ash that shone like star clusters powdered by the hoofs of the sun's horses. Her white lily glances expressing her matchless devotion were surely another garland on Bhutanatha.

She wore around her neck a rosary of huge, gooseberry-sized pearls, so pure and clear that they were like the meaning of the Vedas taken right from the mouth of Brahma Himself. Or could they be the syllables of the Gayatri mantra strung together. Perhaps they were the Seven Sages who had come down in their starry form just to be sanctified by her touch.

Her well-rounded breasts were like the lustrous golden pots placed on either side of the entrance to Brahmaloka. She wore a tawny utthariya that appeared as if made of the mane of the lion of Gauri. It was actually made of the bark of the *mandara* tree and was knotted in between her breasts. She wore a sacred thread, which sanctified her body. The thread seemed woven with the rays of the crescent moon on the head of the One with the unmatched eyes, and given to her as a favour. The fine silk cloth that she wore around her waist reaching down to her feet was naturally white; yet it had taken on a pinkish hue in the lustre of her upturned feet in *padmasana*.

Her youthfulness devoid of all unruly passions, served her with the humility of a servant. Hers was a chaste beauty; her loveliness was that of an innocent temple deer. She was doe-eyed but her eyes had no coquetry in them. She carried a veena decorated with ivory in her lap as if it were her own child. She was playing the instrument with the fingers of her bhasma-whitened right hand holding the ivory stick. She also wore a bracelet of shells around her wrist. She was truly gandharva vidya in a human form.

Her form was reflected on the freshly washed wet idol, as if she had entered right into the heart of the Lord because of her extraordinary devotion! She was singing and accompanying herself on the veena. She sang with discipline, yet her music was filled with passion. The notes of the various ragas and raginis coursed out of her; notes, soft, loud and long whirled about. The forest animals, the deer, the boar, the monkey, the elephant and even the lion had gathered around and listened in utter stillness to the harmonious blending of the veena and the voice.

She seemed perfect like the language of the *dikshita* at the sacrifice; like an uncompounded word she seemed to have no apprehension of duality, no awareness of heat or cold, joy or sorrow, comfort or discomfort. Like the waters of the unchurned ocean she seemed to be of a clear mind. Like one who had already partaken of ambrosia she seemed to thirst for nothing. Like the earth held on all sides by water, she too was sustained only by water. She evinced no sense of possession, no envy and no pride. She was of divine appearance and because of that it was difficult to tell her age. But she seemed no more than eighteen years of age.

Chandrapida dismounted from the horse and tied it to the branch of a tree. He then approached the idol of Lord Trilochana and bowed his head in worship. Then he gazed at the divine looking young woman without moving his eyes as though to make sure that she was really there. Her serene beauty created a feeling of wonder in his heart. He mused: 'How the unexpected happens in this world. There I was engrossed in the chase and without reason I started following the horse-faced pair. It was only because of that I could see this extraordinarily beautiful place meant only for the divine and out of reach for human beings. Then looking for water I came upon this magical lake whose waters have been used by the holy and the godly. Resting on the shores I heard the distant divine music. Following the music, here I am gazing at this young woman surely not of this world. That she is of divine origin I have no doubt; her very form is proof of that. Besides where could one come across such a voice, such notes, and such music among the mortals. If she does not disappear when she opens her eyes and looks at me or climb away to Kailasa, or rise up to the heavens, then I am going to draw near and ask her questions as to who she is, her name and why she is doing this tough and rigorous penance. This indeed is a moment of wonder.' Chandrapida sat down a little away near another pillar and waited.

—24—

The music ended, the veena fell silent. The young woman rose, circumambulated the idol and prostrated before the Deity. Then her naturally clear gaze, full of the confident serenity born of intense control of the body and mind fell on him. It reassured him; it washed over him like the sanctified waters of a sacred spot; it purified him, rendered him sinless as it were by the power of penance; it seemed ready to grant him boons.

Then she spoke: 'Welcome indeed to the guest. How did his Excellency find his way here? But please do rise and accept the rites of hospitality.' Feeling blessed by these words of hers, Chandrapida rose and saluted her with great respect and followed her with the deference of a pupil towards the teacher.

As he followed her, he made a decision. 'Good! She did not disappear at the sight of me. I am now seized with great curiosity. Rare indeed is such beauty among those who take on such rigorous austerities. Her extraordinary graciousness towards me indicates her nobility. I do believe that should I ask she would tell me her story.'

Cogitating thus, hardly had he taken a hundred steps when he beheld a cave. In the dense growth of the tamala trees the entrance to the cave was dark; it was like night even during the day. The area around it was abuzz with bees hovering over the flowers in the bowers of creepers. There were many waterfalls around the cave that fell from great heights, with the water bursting into foam when it hit the white rock surface. The tips of the jutting rocks shattered the water rushing down creating a great noise. The water broke into cool sprays covering the place with a fine mist. The streams on either side of the cave were like garlands of snow, nay, like moving chamaras.

A collection of kamandalus made of precious stones was kept inside the cave. On one side hung the strip of cloth to be worn at the time of practising yogic postures. Suspended from the forked top of a stump was a loop of rope to which was tied a pair of clean footwear made of coconut fibre. There was a bed made of bark, somewhat dusty with the bhasma that must have fallen from her body. A sculpted begging bowl of shell with the brilliance of the moon and a gourd for storing bhasma were also visible.

As he sat down on a flat rocky surface just at the cave entrance, she placed the veena on one side of the bark cloth covered bed. Then she went to the stream and fetched water in a leaf cup for performing the rites of welcome to the guest. He protested: 'Please do not take so much trouble. My lady! There is no need to show all this deference to me. Just the sight of you is enough to destroy all sins and purify everything, like the *Aghamarshana suktha*. Please do sit down.' But she stopped his protests and duly performed all rites of welcome, which he accepted, his head deeply bowed, in great humility.

Then she too sat down on the rocky surface and after a moment's silence asked about him. Chandrapida told her everything about himself, from his setting out from his kingdom on a digvijaya, and losing his way in the chase after the horse-faced pair, until the moment he found himself in her presence. Having heard his story she got up again and picked up the begging bowl and walked under the trees of the shrine. Soon the bowl filled with fruits that fell of their own accord from the trees. She brought them to Chandrapida and gently insisted that he eat them.

Chandrapida thought: 'There is indeed nothing impossible for the power of tapas to accomplish. Even insentient creation behaves as if endowed with consciousness. These trees offer their fruits to her and attain their own fulfilment. What an amazing phenomenon this is, never seen by me before.' His wonderment increased a thousand fold.

He got up and fetched Indrayudha over, unsaddled him and tied him close by. He then repaired to the stream and bathed after which he partook of the fruits offered by the young woman, fruits that tasted like nectar to him and drank the icy cold water of the stream. Then he rested. By this time the young woman too had finished her meal of fruits and roots. Having performed all the evening rites she too sat down on the stone seat. It was then that Chandrapida approached her and sat down on the same stone seat a little away from her and said with humble politeness: 'Revered lady! Your graciousness has kindled my all too human curiosity; it has also emboldened the flippant in me to ask questions, even if I, in mature consideration should not wish it. A small favour from a great soul would make even a timid individual bold of speech. Further, being thrown together even for a short while gives rise to a certain familiarity. A little polite hospitality leads to a projection of friendship. I make bold to request you to extend further the favour already shown to me by telling me about yourself, if the recounting of it would not cause you too much trouble. My curiosity has indeed been great ever since I set eyes on you.

'Of what descent are you? Which deva, rishi, gandharva, or apsara lineage has had the honour of your birth? Why have you assumed this life of terrible austerities? You are so young and this penance is so rigorous. Your form is so very lovely and here you are subduing your senses. It strikes me as truly strange. And even if such a course were necessary for you, why have you set aside the beautiful hermitages of heaven full of siddhas and *sadhyas* and taken refuge here in this lonely uninhabited forest? How come your body presumably made like every one else's out of the five great elements is so white? We have never seen or heard of anyone like you. Please do satisfy my curiosity by telling me all about yourself.'

When the young woman heard these words she sat silent for a while as though in deep thought. The she sighed and began to weep quietly. Huge teardrops rolled down her clear cheeks one following the other, like pearls from a broken necklace. Perhaps it was the innocent purity of her heart, or the utter blemishlessness of her senses, or the essence of her rigorous penance, or even her unusual fairness, that might have melted to fall as tears. They moistened the top of her breasts bound by bark cloth.

When Chandrapida saw her tears he thought, 'Misfortunes are unavoidable indeed! They affect even such unassailable natures. No one bearing a body is exempt from suffering. The hold of dualities—like joy and sorrow, heat and cold—is very strong in this world. As for me, my curiosity has only been made all the greater by her tears. People of this stature would not bend before a slight misfortune. A light wind does not shake the earth.'

Although his eagerness to know the story had increased several fold, he was also aware that he had been the one who had reminded her of her misfortunes, whatever they might have been. Chandrapida got up and brought water from the stream to wash her tear-stained face. The tears that were falling uncontrollably now stopped with Chandrapida's solicitous entreaties. She washed her slightly reddened eyes, wiped her face with the end of her bark garment and sighing deeply and long, replied slowly. 'Oh prince! Of what use would it be to listen to the joyless story of this pitiless wretched woman, a story of sorrow right from birth, a story not fit to be recited or heard. Yet, if you are eager to know I shall tell you everything.'

Mahashveta Speaks

25

It is generally known to people who devote themselves to the welfare of the entire world, that in the realm of the immortals are the apsaras, girls who remain unmarried. Now, there are fourteen lineages of apsaras, one of which has originated from the mind of Kamalayoni Himself, the lotus-born Brahma. Some of the others were born of the Vedas, of Agni, Vayu and out of the churned amrita. Still others originated from water, and from the rays of the sun and the moon. Some were born of the earth and others of the lightning. Even Death was the progenitor of some lineages and there were others descended from Kama. Among the many daughters of Daksha Prajapati, the two named Muni and Arishta gave birth to two more lineages, when they came together with the gandharvas. These two lineages are now counted among the gandharvas.

Muni bore sixteen children; and of the sixteen the last child Chitraratha has been outstanding. His valour has been famous in all the three worlds. His glory acquired an added sheen when Aakhandala at whose lotus feet all the other devas place their heads in veneration, accepted him as a friend. Whilst still young, he gained supremacy over all the gandharvas with the might of his hands, hands that appeared dark in the presence of the brilliance of the sword he wielded. Chitraratha lives not too far from here in the land of the *kimpurushas*, immediately to the north of Bharatvarsha, on the mountain called Hemakuta, which forms the boundary of his land. Several thousand gandharvas live here under the protection of his powerful arms. It was he who created these woods called Chaitraratham; it was he who had this huge lake, Acchoda dug; and it was he who built this shrine for Mahadeva.

Arishta's children are six in number one of whom is Tumburu. The eldest is Hamsa, well known in the world. He was crowned king of the second lineage of the Gandharvas whilst still a child by none other than Chitraratha himself. He too lives on the same Hemakuta surrounded by his immeasurable gandharva forces.

In the apsara lineage descended from the rays of the moon was born Gauri, as beautiful indeed as the other Gauri, the goddess, and a delight to the eyes of all, in all the three worlds. She seemed made of moon rays, with the combined loveliness of all the crescents of the moon. Her complexion was of the fairness and glow of moonlight. Hamsa, the lord of the second line of the gandharvas took her as his beloved just as the Ocean took as his lover, the celestial Mandakini. Having united with Hamsa, a lover suitable to her in every respect, like Rati with the all-powerful Manmatha, like the lotus with autumn, Gauri ascended the peak of happiness. She attained the position of the mistress of the entire royal antapura as well. It was to these great people that I was born, as their only daughter—devoid of all marks of auspiciousness, abode of all the sorrows of the world.

Having long remained childless, my father rejoiced in my birth and celebrated the event even more grandly than he would have the birth of a son. On the tenth day, having duly performed all the rites, they named me Mahashveta, a name suitable to my fair appearance. As a sweetly lisping child, I was passed, like a veena, from lap to lap among the doting gandharvas. I had indeed a delightful childhood, taking all that love for granted, with no knowledge of friendship and no understanding of sorrow or fatigue. In due course as I came of age, loveliness and the bloom of youth burst upon my body—like the new growth in spring, of flowers on the new growth, of bees on the flowers.

It was spring and the forest was in full bloom. The mango trees became covered with new buds, and heightened the sense of longing for love. In the gentle breeze that had set in, the flags hung up in honour of Ananga fluttered. The bakula tree burst forth with blooms as though it were thrilling with the mouthfuls of wine spat on it by the beautiful women in their intoxication. The sound of myriad gem-embedded anklets resounded in the forest as the women kicked the ashoka to make it bloom. The forest floor turned a sandy white with the increased shower of pollen. As the excited koels sitting hidden among the new shoots of the lavali swung on the branches a shower of honey fell like rain. Manmatha's ceaseless arrows swished around deafening the quarters. Seized with desire even during the day, crowds of roused women were hurrying to their assignations. The ocean of love had broken its banks and was flooding over.

One such heart-thrilling day in spring I had gone with my mother to the Acchoda Lake that truly sparkled with the riotous blooming of white and blue lilies and the red lotuses, to have a bath. At first I paid my respects to the images of Triambaka drawn on a rock surface near the lake no doubt by Parvathi on a day when she came down to bathe in the lake.

There was a charming bower of creepers the filaments of whose flowers were bent with the weight of a swarm of bees. An avenue of sandalwood trees was full of wildly dancing peacocks; the snakes had all slithered away in fear of these birds.

Bunches of flowers strewn on the ground showed that the forest nymphs had been swinging away on the creepers. The carpet of pollen under the trees on the shore had the footprints of swans on it. Captivated by the endearing beauty of the place and greedy to see more of it I wandered around with my companions.

All of a sudden there came, borne by the breeze, a strange fragrance submerging the scents of all the abundantly blooming flowers of the forest. It spread quickly and its extraordinary sweetness washed over one like a liquid; it filled the nostrils as if seeking to satisfy the utmost cravings of the sense of smell. The bees went wild with this fragrance never experienced before, a fragrance not really of this world. 'Where is this divine smell coming from?' I wondered, and unable to contain my curiosity and attracted by it like the bees themselves, I took a few quick steps towards it like a swan attracted by the sound of anklets, and soon saw this amazingly handsome young ascetic accompanied by another who was engaged in collecting flowers for worship. Obviously both had come to the lake for bathing.

26

My mind was in a whirl. Was it Spring taken to austerities in grief over Madana having been reduced to ashes by the fire from Hara's third eye? Had the crescent moon on the head of Ishana decided to do penance to regain his fullness? Could it be Kama himself in the guise of an austere ascetic intent on winning over the god of uneven eyes?

Such was the young man's lustre that he appeared imprisoned in a sparkling lightning cage. He seemed to have entered right into the heart of the summer sun. He seemed to stand in the midst of raging fires. The incandescent glow issuing out of his body, yellow like the flame of a lamp, lit up the forest turning everything around him golden.

His locks a soft yellow, the colour of the thread tied around the wrist at the time of one's wedding, had been conditioned with gorochana water. On his forehead were drawn three lines in sacred ash, like the banner of blessedness. His eyebrows met in an arch. His eyes were large and so beautiful as if all the deer of the world had shared with him the loveliness of their own eyes. His nose was long and high. His ascetic heart had never allowed the entry of youthful passions into it; these passions had therefore to be content with merely colouring his lips red. His youthful face had no hair on it and was like a tender lotus bloom, as yet with no bees circling over it! He wore a *Yagnopavita* that looked like the pulled string on the bow of Manmatha; no, surely it would be more appropriate to say it was like the lotus stalk growing on the pond that was the tapas done by him. He carried a kamandalu that had a handle and was shaped like a bakula fruit. The other hand held a rosary made of crystal beads that looked like the teardrops of Rati weeping for her destroyed husband. His navel was a whirlpool at the junction of several streams of knowledge. A thin growth of hair on his abdomen, like lines drawn in dark kohl, could have been the footprints left by the darkness of delusion when it fled away from the erudition within him.

He had tied a rope of *munja* grass around his hips; subduing the sun by his own lustre had he brought down the sun's corona to tie around his hips. He was dressed in *mandara* bark garments pink in colour like the eyes of an aged chakora bird, and washed clean in the waters of the celestial Ganga.

He was an adornment to *brahmacharya;* he was Dharma in His youth; he was the pleasure of Saraswati, and the chosen husband of all vidyas; he was the meeting ground of all the Vedas.

As I gazed at the youth, I saw a stalk of flowers on his ears; they were flowers I had never seen before. They were like the brilliant smile of the goddess of the forest overjoyed at the arrival of Spring. They were like the *lajanjali*, the welcoming shower of puffed rice that Spring would give to the southerly wind from the Malaya Mountains bringing with it the fragrance of sandalwood. They were like the drops of perspiration on Rati in the exhaustion after love. The flowers oozed ambrosia.

Inexhaustible indeed is Brahma's stock of material for creating things of extraordinary beauty. He had already created the beautiful one with the flower arrows. Still he had the wherewithal to create this one here of even greater beauty, this other Kama in the guise of an ascetic. When Brahma made the moon and the lotus for Lakshmi to sit on, it must have been only by way of practice or training, for acquiring the skill to produce a face like this one here. It is wrong to believe that the sun with his special ray called sushumna drinks up all the brilliance of the moon in the waning fortnight; I am sure all those rays of the moon enter into the body of this ascetic one here. How else does he retain such beauty in a life of such emaciating penance and abstinence?' I was completely smitten; the god of the floral weapon who ignored considerations of compatibility and was ever partial to physical beauty and youth had completely bewitched me, like the nectar of the flowers enthralled the bees.

I sighed deeply; I narrowed my eyes while my pupils darted about wildly. I managed to look at him out of the corner of my right eye, and I looked at him as though I wanted to drink him up entirely. My gaze seemed to declare, 'I am under your power'; there was pleading in it; it seemed to place my heart before him. My entire being seemed to want to enter his heart in order to become one with him. I wanted to surrender to him, crying out 'I am overpowered by Kama. Please save me! Please give me place in your heart!'

I did realize, at the same time, how improper, how exceedingly shameful and unfitting it was for one born of such a noble family as mine, to do what I was setting out to do. But I had no power over my senses. I stood still, like a painted picture, like a sculpted statue; I was motionless like one chained, like one fallen into a trance, like one possessed. My limbs felt paralysed. But an untaught expertise, I do not know how I came by it, helped me out. Was it his extraordinary beauty or my own mind, was it the doing of Kama or my own burgeoning youth, I cannot truly say which of these, or something totally different that proved preceptor, but the fact was that I managed to gaze at him for a very long time.

My senses seemed to lift me and bear me towards that young ascetic. My heart pulled me forward and the god with the floral arrow pushed me from behind. But I held myself back somehow, although quite unconscious of having made the effort. My breath came rapidly; my nipples began to throb as though wishing to speak out my heart's desire for him. My bashfulness trickled away along with the lines of perspiration. My body trembled; my limbs longed to embrace him. The hair on my body stood on end.

Even in that state there was a glimmer of reason and I thought 'Is not Kamadeva starting something totally ignoble by throwing me at this unworldly young man who has decided to keep away from all physical passion? Foolish indeed is woman's heart, and incapable of judging whether it is proper or not to fall in love with someone. Where is this splendid ascetic, a veritable storehouse of penance, and where the love sport enjoyed by the unrefined and the common? Surely he would laugh at me, tricked as I am by Makaraketu. How strange it is that although I understand perfectly the unsuitability of the situation I am unable to rein in my feelings. How is it that a mere momentary glance at his outward form has affected me so much as to enslave my heart so completely? It is surely the handiwork of Spring. It is qualities like beauty that make Kamadeva invincible. As long as

I still have my wits around me, the best thing to do would be to leave this place before he became aware of my love-struck state. Who knows, my unsolicited passion may kindle his anger and he may then subject me to some terrible curse. The ascetic type is really quick to anger.'

I wanted now to go away from that spot. But I also thought that it would be quite all right to pay my respects to him before I left, as indeed the whole world bows to the ascetics. I removed my eyes from his face and without still being aware even of the ground I stood on, with stilled eyelashes, my earrings swinging slightly away from my cheeks and touching the top of my shoulders, and quite conscious of the fact that my flowers must look really fetching in the slightly disarranged hair, I bowed before him.

Can the will of Manmatha be transgressed? The headiness of the spring season, the excessive loveliness of the spot, the unruly nature of the senses, the innate fickleness of the human mind, the wildness of youth, all contributed to it. Perhaps destiny too. What more can I say. Due to my dire misfortune or evil-mindedness if you would, or because of things preordained to come to this terrible pass, he noticed my passion; having noticed it, his steadiness was undermined, and he too became tremulous like a flame in the wind, thanks to the workings of Ananga.

His body too thrilled with the hair standing on edge. His heart seemed to hurry towards me, being shown the way by his rapid breath that came ahead. The rosary held in his trembling hand shook as though with the fear of vows being broken. Lines of cold sweat adorned his cheeks. His eyes widened with delight at the sight of me. My passion intensified several-fold observing the visible changes in him. At that moment I experienced an emotional state that was truly indescribable. Is it not quite obvious that it is Makaraketu himself who teaches the victim varieties of blandishments, steps in coquetry and dalliance?

Otherwise how could this young man who had never so far in his life given a thought to the affairs of the heart, in which various emotions and sensitivities come into play, send me a glance dripping sexual feelings like nectar. Eyes now contracted with love, now languid as though heavy with sleep, now the pupils roving in an ecstasy of joy with the eyebrows dancing. Where did he get this expertise from, to communicate his heart's desire wordlessly, with just his glance?

—27—

Encouraged by his interest I approached his companion, the other young ascetic, saluted him and enquired, 'Bhagavan! What is the name of this youth here, which sage's son is he? What is the name of the tree whose flowers he is wearing on his ears? Their extraordinary fragrance, never experienced so far by me, excites my curiosity.' He laughed a little and answered me, 'Why do you want to know? But you are curious and I shall satisfy your curiosity.'

The Young Ascetic's Companion Speaks . . .

There lives in the world of the devas a great ascetic named Shvetaketu, of sublime austerities, whose fame has spread to all the three worlds, and who is held in great reverence by all the celestials. When young he was extraordinarily handsome; both the deva and asura women delighted in his beauty which surpassed even that of Nalakubara.

Once, this ascetic entered the white waters of the Mandakini speckled with the rut fluid drops from the temples of Iravatha, to gather lotus flowers for worship. Seated as usual on the white lily of a thousand petals amidst the forest of lotuses, was the goddess Lakshmi who saw the handsome young ascetic entering the water. As she looked at him she fell in love with him. She drank in his appearance with eyes narrowed in passion and streaming with tears of joy, the pupils rolling as the tears welled up. She rested her languid face on her hand and gave herself up to her lust for him. Her desire was satisfied right there seated on the thousand-petalled white lily merely by gazing at him.

There was a son born to her right then and there. She picked him up from her lap and brought him over to Shvetaketu and said, 'Bhagavan! Accept this child, your son.' She handed over the baby to the ascetic. Shvetaketu accepted the child and performed all the rites prescribed for infants and named him Pundarika, as he was born on a white lily. As the child grew up the ascetic completed other prescribed rites such as Yagnyopavita and taught him all the arts as well as instructed him on all the other branches of learning,—such as the Vedas, Dharmashastras and the philosophies. This young man here is that Pundarika.

And now about the flower. When the suras and the asuras churned the milky ocean there arose from it along with many other things, a tree called parijata. These are the flowers of the parijata tree. I shall also tell you how they came to rest on the ears of Pundarika here, as such adornments are forbidden to those who have undertaken vows of penance. As today happens to be *chaturdashi*, he and I set out to go to Kailasa to worship Ambikapati. As we approached Nandanvana, the garden of Indra, the presiding goddess of the garden came out leaning on the soft hands of the Spirit of Spring. Her girdle was of bakula flowers; the garlands of parijata flowers that she wore around her neck and which came right down to her knees covered her entire form. Her earrings were of the new mango blossoms. She was drunk with the nectar of the flowers.

She held in her hands more parijata blooms; she approached Pundarika, saluted him and said: 'Bhagavan! These parijata flowers are just right for someone of your physical beauty, which delights the eyes of all in all the three worlds. Please accept these flowers; they are not available to anyone else. Place them on your ears and let the parijata attain the fruit of its existence today.' However, this one, embarrassed by such full-blown praise of his physical form walked on with downcast eyes paying no attention to the goddess of the garden. But then I saw that she was following him and said to him 'Come now, there is nothing wrong in accepting what she is giving you as a token of her affection and regard.' I took the flowers and put them on his ears although he did not want them at all. And that is the whole of it, who he is, who his father is and who the mother, and how the flowers found their way to the top of his ears. There, I have now told you everything.

Mahashveta Continues . . .

At this Pundarika smiled a little and said, 'Curious one! How many questions you do ask. If you like the fragrance so much, then here they are. You take the flowers.' He came towards me and removing the flowers from his ears put them around mine. The sweet indistinct murmur of the bees hovering over the flowers seemed like a whispered prologue to his love play. My body thrilled at the touch of his hands. As for him, his fingers trembled when they brushed against my cheek; he seemed unaware of the rosary slipping from his trembling fingers. I caught the rosary before it fell to the ground and playfully put that rare pearl necklace-like rosary around my own neck, feeling as if his arms were going around me.

While this intimate exchange was going on my umbrella carrier came and admonished me, 'Princess! Your mother's bath is over. It is almost time to go home. You should have your bath now.' When I heard her words I turned to go, unwillingly, like a newly caught elephant at the first prod of the goad. Only with effort was I able to withdraw my eyes, caught in the beauty of his face, like feet caught in slush. I pulled my gaze away with great difficulty as if it had got entangled in the net of hair on his thrilling cheeks, as if the arrows of Kamadeva had pinned it down, as if threads of blessedness had stitched it on to him, and proceeded for my bath.

As soon as I turned to go, the second young ascetic observing his shaken companion chided him with gentle anger. 'My friend Pundarika. This does not become you. This is the path of small men. Unshakeable steadfastness is the wealth of the sages. Like a spiritual rustic you fail to take hold of your weakening mind. Why this sudden agitation of the senses never seen before in you? What happened to the steadiness of your mind, your control over your senses, your detachment, your tranquillity, and above all your brahmacharya, which is the hallmark of your lineage? I see a total failure of intelligence. The study of the scriptures and ethics carries no merit, it appears; the grooming of the mind too can be rendered powerless. The discrimination born of the teachers' instructions does not help. Vain is the understanding of truth. Why? Because even people like you can be sullied by the attraction of sensual pleasures; they too can be overpowered by faulty judgment. How could you have been so carried away that you were not even aware of the *akshamala* slipping from your hand. She is taking it away. How amazing it is to forget oneself so. The akshamala is already gone; at least take hold of your heart that is also being stolen away by this unworthy girl.'

Scolded thus, young Pundarika looked a little shamefaced and replied. 'Kapinjala! You misconstrue me. I shall certainly not allow this impudent girl to take away my akshamala.' Pretending to an anger that he really did not feel, trying hard to look forbidding by knitting his eyebrows, the lips trembling more with a desire to kiss me than in displeasure, he said to me; 'Flighty

one! Without returning the akshamala to me I shall not allow
you to take even a step from here.'

Only half aware of my actions I removed what I thought was
the akshmala from around my neck and placed it in his extended
hand. As his eyes were fixed on me reflecting the longing in his
heart, he never looked at the mala offered to him. I had become
bathed in sweat; still I went to the lake to bathe yet again.

After I finished my bath I returned home with my mother,
led forcibly by my attendants, like reversing the course of a river.
All the while, however, I thought of him. I entered the antapura
but I was really lost to the world, stricken with longing for him.
My mind was in complete confusion. Have I returned home or
am I still standing there? Am I alone or surrounded by people?
Am I silent or am I saying something? Is this wakefulness or
sleep? Is this joy or sorrow? Is this longing or is it some kind of
disease? Is this a calamity or a cause for celebration? I knew
nothing, I was aware of nothing. Not having ever known the
pangs of love I had no idea what to do. In whom could I confide?
And what could be the remedy for this malady?

I climbed up to the unmarried girls' apartment and dismissed
all the attending women. I also ordered that no servant be allowed
to enter the chamber. Putting an end to all my usual activities I
remained with my face pressed to the window grill of precious
stones and gazed into the same direction where I had left him.
That direction seemed especially adorned because of his presence
there. It seemed to bloom with special flowers, it seemed rich
with a special wealth of treasures; it seemed especially splendid
with a full moon shining upon it. The ocean of divine nectar
seemed to flood it; it pleased my eyes.

I wanted to question the wind blowing from that direction
for news of him; I wanted to question the forest fragrance wafting
in, and the birds whose calls were heard in that direction.

Love had made me partial to him in every way. It seemed to

me the hermit way of life was good because he had taken it up; youth was attractive because it resided in him; the parijata flowers were captivating because some of them adorned his ears; Suraloka could be a pleasant place because he dwelt there. Although he was far away, I turned my face towards him, like the lotus looking up to the distant sun, like the ocean tides rising towards the moon, like the peacocks raising their faces to the rain clouds.

I realized that I had given Pundarika my pearl necklace instead of his akshamala, which still lay around my neck. It now acted as a charm protecting my life which otherwise would have left my body due to the intense pangs of separation. The parijata blooms that he had given me were still on my ears whispering secrets about him. My cheeks still thrilling with the memory of his fingers touching them bloomed like kadamba flowers. I stood motionless at the window.

—28—

I have a maid named Taralika who is in charge of the tambula box. She had come with me to the lake, but had taken longer getting back. Taralika now came to me and said softly, 'Princess! Of the two divine-looking young men that we met near the Acchoda Lake, the one that put the flowers of that tree in heaven on your highness' ear, stole away from his companion and caught up with me in a dark part of the woods, dense with creepers and flowers. He addressed me from behind seeking information about your highness. He asked me: 'Child, who is this young girl? Whose daughter is she? What is her name? Where has she gone now?' I replied that you, Mahashveta, were the daughter of Gauri, the apsara of the lunar lineage and Hamsa the lord of the gandharvas whose wealth is so great that the goddess Lakshmi herself would be willing to make her lotus hands serve as his foot stool; and that you had now gone to the abode of the gandharvas on the Hemakuta Mountain. After he had heard me out he remained quiet for a while as though lost in thought. He then looked at me steadily for a long time appearing as if he were about to beg a favour of me, and spoke again. 'You are of such a noble form that there is no doubt that you are endowed with fine qualities and strength of mind although you are barely out of childhood. Would you be kind enough to do me a favour, I beg of you.'

To this I replied in all humility with my hands folded in respect, 'Who am I that you talk to me with such deference? Great men like you are worthy of respect in all the three worlds. Without spiritual merit even a glance which itself is purifying, from one such as you does not come our way, how much more rare a command? Please order me as to what has to be done without demur, honour me by doing so.' The young man then looked at me gratefully as if I had already helped him, as if I had been a friend who had saved his life. He went and brought a leaf from a tamala tree and crushed it on a rock surface. Then he tore off a strip from his utthariya made of bark. With the tamala juice serving as ink and using the tip of the nail of his little finger as a quill he wrote something on the strip and handed it over to me saying, 'When she is alone, please give this to her without any one else's knowledge.' Taralika pulled the strip from inside the tambula box and gave it to me.

Whatever Taralika said about Pundarika were words and therefore, mere sounds. Yet they seemed to touch me physically. The sounds seemed to spread all over my body thrilling all my limbs. Under a sort of spell cast by this talk of Pundarika I took the bark strip from Taralika's hand and read the verse.

Even like a *hamsa* of the Manasa Lake
Is led so far, tempted by the white lily stalk
You, with your lily-stalk-like neck take
My passion far, to unbearable heights.

The verse only served to worsen my condition, like a traveller who had lost his way losing his sense of direction as well, like the onset of delirium in one naturally incoherent, like inebriation for one who was mad. I became as agitated as a river in spate. Taralika appeared blessed in my eyes, for had she not seen him a second time? In my eyes she had become transformed, as one who had enjoyed life in heaven, as one crowned the ruler of all the three worlds, as one who had partaken of nectar. I saw her seated on top of all the worlds although she was right there with me. Extremely familiar though she was she still looked a wonder.

I fondly touched her curls falling on her cheeks. Our roles now seemed reversed, she the mistress and I, the servant. I begged her, 'Taralike! Please tell me, won't you? How did he appear to you? What did he say to you? How long did you tarry there? How far did he follow you here?' Questioning her thus repeatedly I spent the entire day, with just Taralika for company.

Soon it was evening. The sun that had turned red as though he was sharing the passion in my heart now hung suspended at the edge of the sky. Daylight entered the caves of the Meru that echoed with the gleeful neighs of the sun's horses happy to be going home. The red lotus closed its eyes by gathering up its petals and the bees caught inside symbolized the darkness in the heart of the flower due to separation from the sun. The chakravaka pair held a single stalk by their beaks communing through the hollow while the falling night separated them physically.

The umbrella carrier came to me and said, 'Princess! One of the two *munikumaras* is here at the door. He says he has come to

beg for the akshamala'. At the mention of the word munikumara
my heart leapt up in the hope that it could be Pundarika who
had come. I ordered the kanchuki to bring the visitor in. In a
short while I saw, not Pundarika but Kapinjala, his dear friend—
like youth is the friend of beauty, like Kama the friend of youth,
like spring the friend of Kama and the southerly wind that of
spring—enter behind the aged, greying kanchuki, a young sun
following the paling light of the moon. As he drew near I saw
that he looked confused and depressed, desolate and dejected.

I rose and saluted him. I washed and then wiped his feet
with the end of my utthariya, although he seemed reluctant to
receive such honours of welcome. Then I sat down on the ground
near his seat. He made as if to say something but stopped and
looked at Taralika sitting next to me. Reading his thoughts I
said at once 'Bhagavan! She and I are indeed one. You can speak
your mind without fear.

Kapinjala then spoke. 'Princess! What can I say! A sense of
shame makes it difficult for me to give expression to what I
have to say. Where is the ascetic, living peacefully on roots and
fruits and where, this worldly existence of sensual indulgence
and desire, ruled mainly by passion, and quite unfit for men of
tranquillity. You see how fate has set in motion this sequence of
improprieties. Effortlessly indeed does God make man an object
of mockery. I do not know if all this bears any relation to bark
garments, or *jata* or penance! How could this be a part of the
dharma one has been taught?

'This cruel play of fate is without a precedent. But the story
has to be told. There is no other way out, no other antidote.
There is no one else who can help; to say nothing about it is
bound to end in a great calamity. A friend's life has to be saved at
all costs, even at the sacrifice of one's own. You saw that I spoke
to him harshly then in your presence. Then I went away in anger
abandoning even the flowers gathered for worship.

'After you went away I began to wonder what Pundarika might be up to, alone. And so I came back and concealing myself behind a tree I looked for him. When I did not see him I reasoned that he must have followed you a little distance in his state of infatuation. Coming to his senses once you were out of sight he was probably avoiding me feeling a little ashamed of his behaviour. Perhaps he was even a little angry with me; or perhaps he was looking for me elsewhere. Weighing all these possibilities I waited a while longer.

'Then I found myself getting anxious. Right from Pundarika's birth he and I had been together. We had been inseparable. I was unused to his absence even for a short time. Then an awful thought struck me. Ashamed of his loss of control over himself, would he try to do something to himself? He ought not to be left to his own devices. I decided to go in search of him.'

—29—

Kapinjala Continues . . .

I searched for him for a very long time, my heart going out to him in his distress; I imagined all kinds of calamities as having befallen him. I looked for him everywhere, in the dense woods overgrown with creepers, in the avenues of sandalwood, in the bowers on the shores of the lake, my alert eyes darting all around.

Finally I saw him, in a very beautiful spot close to the lake, full of flowers, koels, bees and peacocks, a spot that could truly be called the birthplace of spring. There he was lying motionless, like a painted picture, like a sculpted statue. It was impossible to say whether he was merely stunned or already dead, whether he was merely sleeping or had gone deep into meditation. He was absolutely still physically, yet he was moving away from his ordained path; he was alone but Madana was with him; he was silent yet eloquent about his erotic longing.

His absolute stillness made one wonder if his senses had abandoned their posts; had they entered right into his heart to see his beloved enshrined there, or unable to bear the heat of love had they gone and hidden themselves elsewhere, or altogether left him angered by the unsteadiness of his mind? Streams of tears flowed ceaselessly from his closed eyes through the eyelashes as though the smoke from the fire of desire inside was smarting the eyes. His red lips were like the leaping flames of that fire raging in his heart; his hot sighs shook the filaments of the flowers close to him.

He lay there with his cheek resting on the palm of his left hand. The bees buzzing around the parijata flowers on his ear attracted by the fragrance still left in the flowers seemed to be teaching him incantations to win over Manmatha. The raging fever had made the hair on his body stand on end; it looked as if every pore of his body bore the tip of Madana's arrows. With his right hand he held the brilliant pearl necklace on his chest, the necklace that seemed a symbol of the flagrant transgression of all the rules. The trees around assaulted him with a shower of pollen as though it were a kind of love potion for seduction. The forest goddess poured on him the honey of the fresh flowers as though she were crowning him king of the land of love.

Showers of golden champaka buds with the hovering bees drinking in their sweet fragrance struck him; they were like the smoking tips of the heated arrows of Madana. The south wind seemed to threaten him with a roar by carrying over the loud buzz of several swarms of bees heavily drunk with the heady fragrance of the forest. The spring season filled with the riotous calling of the mating cuckoos distressed him.

He was pale like the moon at dawn and diminished like the waters of the Ganga in summer. He had withered like the branch of a sandalwood tree on fire. He looked unfamiliar, unrecognizable, as though he had taken another birth, another life, another form. He was like one possessed by an evil spirit, as he saw nothing, heard nothing, uttered nothing. He looked like one who had been cheated out of everything. Only desire filled him, he seemed to have reached the ultimate state of love. He was not anything like the Pundarika that I knew.

I stared at him for a long time; my heart trembled with pity. I wondered, 'Is the power of Makaraketu so potent that in such a short time Pundarika has been reduced to this state of hopelessness with no remedy in sight. How at one stroke, all the knowledge that he commands has been set at nought. His conduct has been so steady and unshakeable right from his childhood that he has been held as a great example to be emulated by me as well as by the sons of the other sages. Now with his knowledge overpowered, the greatness of his penance set aside and his profound nature uprooted, Manmatha has reduced him to the stupefaction of the ignorant. It is indeed difficult to remain steady in one's youth.'

I went to him and sat down on one side of the same rock, touched his shoulder and whispered, 'My friend, Pundarika! What is the matter? Please speak to me.' He opened his eyes with great effort; as though the eyelids had become stuck and had to be forced open having remained shut for such a long time, indeed as if it pained him to open them, like one stricken with an eye disease. The eyes were red with weeping, and were still flooded with tears. They were like lotuses seen through a curtain of fine white muslin cloth. He looked at me dully for a long time sighed deeply and spoke hesitantly apparently overcome with shame. 'My friend Kapinjala! Why do you ask me questions? You know very well what is wrong with me.'

When I heard this I realized that he was beyond any cure, at any rate by mere words. Still one ought, to the best of one's

ability, try to prevent a good friend from rushing into the path
of destruction. Therefore I said, 'Pundarika! My friend, yes I do
know what is ailing you. I would like to ask you something
though. This love affair that you have now started, where did
you learn all the tricks? From your preceptors? Did you perhaps
study them in the Dharmashastras? A new method of earning
moral merit? Another kind of tapas, a new way to attain
salvation? Or is this a secret vow that would lead to release, a
new set of observances? Does it behove you even to think of
matters of the flesh, leave alone look at women with such
thoughts? Tell me, how could you, like one steeped in ignorance
allow yourself to be made an object of ridicule by that knave
Manmatha and yet be unaware of it? What pleasure have you
found in this affair despised by the wise but celebrated by the
worldly and the uneducated? You are watering piously a garden
of poisonous creepers; you are clasping a sword believing it is a
garland of flowers; you are hugging the black snake thinking it
is the curling smoke from the incense; you are touching a burning
ember in the delusion it is a gemstone; you are trying to pull out
the tusks of a rogue elephant believing them to be lotus stalks. It
is a fool who projects a sense of pleasure on activities that would
lead to a series of misfortunes, one following the other.

You are well aware of the real nature of sensual pleasures;
you know they are devoid of power, like the light of the firefly, yet
you hold on to them. Why? Why have you not reined in your
senses rushing in the wrong path like a river breaking its banks
and getting muddied in the process? Who is this Kama anyway?
Come, gather your strength and threaten the rogue away.'

Pundarika heard me out, wiping his tear-filled eyes with the
palm of his hand; he then grasped my hand and said 'Friend!
What is the point of speaking at length? You are in good
condition. You have not come in the trajectory of those lethal
floral arrows with the virulence of the poison of the asp.

Therefore you feel free to sermonize others. In any case, only he is fit for advice that has still his senses intact, his mind and heart under control, who sees and hears and can analyse what he has been taught, who has the ability to discriminate between good and bad. As for me, I have left all these amenities far behind indeed. Good conduct, wisdom, steadiness and discrimination between right and wrong, these qualities of mine have all disappeared. My life forces still hold on although no effort is being made on my part to save them. The time for advice is long past; the scope for stability is no longer present.

'Who else can advise me at this juncture, apart from you? Who else but you can save me from going down the path of destruction? Whose words other than yours can I accept and follow? There is none else in this world who is my friend and well-wisher. But if I cannot control myself what do I do? You see the terrible state I am in. I only ask one favour of you. As long as I live please do something to alleviate this heat of Madana, which is burning me like the twelve suns at the time of dissolution. My limbs are being cooked, my heart is being consumed, my eyes burn, and my whole body seems to be on fire. Please do what is necessary in this situation.' Then he fell silent.

However I did not at once give up hopes of getting him back to his senses. I tried again and again by talking at length on the principles expounded in the Dharmashastras with clear examples; I tried, with instances from the epics to make him see reason. I spoke with affection and understanding. But all my effort was in vain; he did not seem to be even listening to my words. I realized that he had indeed gone too far to be brought back, to be redeemed. All that I could now do was to try and somehow save his life.

So I got up and went to the lake. I pulled out sap-filled lotus stalks and cool lotus leaves moist with the water drops on them. I also plucked blue and white lilies pungently fragrant with the pollen inside them. With these I prepared a bed on the rock surface in the bower of creepers. Pundarika lay down on it. Then I plucked some leaves from the sandalwood trees growing nearby and crushed them and applied the sweet smelling and dew-cool juice all over his body from his forehead down to his feet. I powdered the camphor in the withered barks of the trees growing near by and applied it on him to offset the perspiration. With clean plantain leaves dripping with water I then set about fanning him. On his chest lay the utthariya valkala wet with the sandalwood water applied by me.

At frequent intervals I brought fresh lotus leaves to refresh his bed. I applied fresh sandalwood paste again and again on his body, similarly with the application of camphor to dry the perspiration. I was struck with wonder at the power of Manmatha that could bring together individuals as incompatible from every point of view as these two, this innocent boy living like a deer in the forest, and the gandharva princess Mahashveta, full of grace, dalliance, elegance and charm. But soon wonderment gave place to anxiety as I sought a way out. 'There is nothing beyond the power of Manmatha who has reduced Pundarika, an unfathomable ocean of spiritual depths to this state of feathery lightness. What great penance he has done and what state he is in now. There seems to be no way out of this calamity. What should I do now? How should I act? Which way to go? Whose help do I seek? What plan of action would save his life? What skill, what ruse, what measures would make him live?'

Slowly some kind of clarity appeared in my dejected mind. I said to myself, 'What is the point of such fruitless thinking at length? His life has to be saved, that is the main thing, by whatever means possible, auspicious or inauspicious. And there is only one way of doing it and that is to bring them, Mahashveta and Pundarika, together. He is very young and inexperienced in the ways of the world. He is also ashamed of having fallen in love with Mahashveta and considers his condition contrary to all rules of penance, unsuitable to his chosen way of life and laughable in the extreme. Even if he were to be left with just one more breath of life in him, he would not, of his own accord, go and seek union with her. Therefore, there is no more time to be lost. The sages do realize that great wrongdoing may be justified for the sake of saving a friend's life. Shameful as it may be it is now necessary to bring the two together. I shall go to her and explain his condition to her.

Having thus made up my mind I left Pundarika without informing him where I was going lest in his shyness and his sense of shame, he might try to dissuade me from coming to you. I merely invented an errand and here I am. In this situation it is up to you to decide what to do, to consider what is appropriate for a love of such a nature and what would be the right thing for you to do.

—30—

Mahashveta Resumes . . .

Kapinjala fell silent and looked at me expectantly for my response.

When I heard this account, I felt as if I had plunged into a lake of pleasure, as though I had descended into an ocean of sensuality. I found myself at the pinnacle of joy, at the peak of fulfilment of all my hopes and desires, at the ultimate state of celebration. At the same time I became bashful too and lowered my face a little, so the tears of joy, when they came, fell without touching the centre of my cheeks. The tears fell without coming into contact with the lashes, one huge drop after the other as if they were being strung into a garland. The clear drops revealed the joy filling my heart. I thought, 'Kama has really been favourable to me. If Pundarika finds himself in this condition how could one say that Kama has not arranged matters well. Surely no untruth can come out of the mouth of the serene Kapinjala. Now the question is what do I do? Should I go and talk to him myself or should I send a messenger?' As I was trying to think coherently the pratihari entered in great agitation and cried, 'Your mother is here to see you, having learnt from the attendants that you are not feeling too well!'

Kapinjala got up at once wanting to avoid the crowd of people accompanying the queen. He said to me. 'This is going to cause a lot of delay. The day-maker, the crest jewel of the three worlds is about to set. Therefore I shall now take my leave. As *dakshina* from me to you for saving the life of my beloved friend I join my hands in salute for this happens to be my greatest wealth.'

As he made to go without waiting for my reply, my mother entered, being shown in by the pratiharis wielding their golden canes and the kanchukis holding the tambula, flowers and the perfumed powder and waving the deer-fur fans. Dwarfs, hunchbacks, deaf-mutes and eunuchs also crowded in with the queen; blocking Kapinjala's path. But somehow he found his way out. My mother sat with me for a long time before she returned to her own palace. I was in my own world and quite oblivious of what she said or did all the time she was with me.

As night fell, as the god with the dark horses, the lord of the red lotus, and the bringer of happiness to the chakravaka pairs set, as the western sky reddened and the lotus fields darkened, as the eastern direction turned blue and the world was about to be engulfed in darkness I found myself in a state of great confusion; I simply did not know what to do.

I went to Taralika and lamented. 'Oh Taralike! How is it you do not see the terrible anxiety in my heart and the agitation of my senses, as I am utterly unable to decide what course of action to take? Please advise me as to what would be the right thing to do. Kapinjala told me the whole story in your presence. Should I, like a common girl giving up my modesty and bashfulness, with no thought to the public scandal it would cause if I crossed the bounds of good conduct, with scant regard for the good name of the lineage, without the sanction of my father, without the joyous blessings of my mother, go to him and make him take my hand in marriage? Or should I simply bow down to the rules and put an end to my life? But even that course would not be without blame. In the first place I would be setting aside the request of that sainted soul Kapinjala who came to me of his own accord, in good faith and out of his deep friendship for Pundarika. Secondly should anything happen to Pundarika due to the shattering of his dreams as a result of my action, then that great sin of causing the death of a sage would come upon me.' While I lamented thus, the eastern sky, the province of Indra had faintly brightened with the imminent rise of the moon, like the pollen-lightened avenues of trees in spring. The sky appeared as if sandalwood powder had fallen on it off the breasts of the Siddha beauties residing on Udayagiri, as if the sand on the shores of the ocean had flown up in the wind rising amidst the waves of the ocean.

As the glow of the rising moon slowly lit up the sky and moonlight fell on the earth, it appeared as if Lady Night was breaking into a slow but dazzling smile at the approach of her lover. In due course the moon, the delight of the whole world, the beloved of sensuous women, the friend of Kamadeva, the god of eternal youth whose light kindled passion in men and women and who was singularly suitable for the enjoyment of love-making, rose higher and the night was transformed into a thing of beauty.

I looked at the newly risen moon slightly tinged with red as though the coral reefs in the eastern ocean had cast their brilliance

on him, as though he had been stained by the alaktha on the feet
of Rohini angry with her lover. Although there was inside me
this raging fire of love, my heart was in darkness. My body was
lying in Taralika's lap but it was under the control of Kama. My
eyes were directed towards Chandra but in reality I was looking
at death. I thought, 'On one side are the enchantments of spring
like the cool breeze blowing from the Malaya mountains; on
the other is this villainous killer Chandra. It is impossible to
bear the combination. My heart is in great distress with unbearable
longing for love. Chandra's rise is like a shower of burning embers
in the heat of fever, a rain of dew while in the grip of severe cold,
the bite of a black snake on one already full of poison with the
bursting of a toxic tumour.'

While my mind was struggling with these thoughts my eyes
closed as the lotus blooms close at moonrise and I lost
consciousness. Taralika brought me round quickly, by the
application of cool sandalwood paste and by fanning me with a
palm leaf fan. As I opened my eyes I saw her a personification of
anxiety, with tears clouding her face, applying the oozing
chandrakanta stick to my forehead. When she saw that I had
woken up she touched my feet and folded her hands wet with
sandalwood water and beseeched me: 'Princess! Why are you
worried about shame or about the approval of your parents?
Please do send me, I shall go and fetch him, your beloved, over
here. Or you get up and go there yourself. I cannot bear to see
your agony increasing with the appearance of the moon, like
the swelling of the waves of the ocean.'

I said to her, 'You silly girl! What can Kama do alone? But
this friend of the kumuda flower has indeed arrived to take
me either to Pundarika or to Yama himself. He has offset all
arguments by gradually taking me beyond endurance. He has
rendered all antidotes useless. He has quelled all doubts regarding
the propriety of the affair; he has removed all shame and has

effectively covered up the indignity of a girl going after her lover. So get up now, somehow I shall go to him and as long as I keep breathing I shall serve this troublesome loved one.'

Leaning on Taralika, I pulled my limbs up, languid with unfulfilled love and drenched in perspiration. As I set out, my right eye throbbed, indeed an ill omen. My heart became troubled and I feared the worst.

The moon had climbed a little higher in the sky. The white rays came down like streams of sandalwood water, like myriad waterfalls of the white celestial Ganga as though the ocean of nectar was flooding over, and filled all the crevices of the earth. The white lilies were beginning to bloom in every pond and well, with the bees hovering over them. The world was immersed in an ocean of delight; it was brimming with sensuality, love and a sense of celebration. The cry of the peacocks frolicking in the water running from the chandrakanta stones was delirious with joy and filled the late evening.

I climbed down from the terrace of the palace. The akshamala was still around my neck; the parijata flowers were still kissing the top of my ear. The sandalwood paste applied on my forehead by Taralika when I fell unconscious had become dried and made the disarranged forelocks somewhat dusty. I had covered my head with a ruby red veil. I saw to it I was not noticed by any of my close attendants. Only Taralika came with me carrying various flowers and betel leaves, orpiment and incense powder.

─ 31 ─

I came down from the terrace and left by the side door of the garden, with just Taralika at my side. The bees that came to the parijata I had on my ear, abandoning the garden and the white lily fields, surrounded me like a dark veil. 'For someone on her way to meet her lover of what use would ordinary attendants be?' I thought to myself. 'There are others unseen, who seem to have taken over that role. There is Kusumayudha who follows with his bow raised and the flower arrows at the ready. There is the moon that pulls me by my hand with his extended rays. Passion holds me up at every step as though afraid that I might stumble. The heart carries all the senses with it and races ahead pushing shame out of the way. The intensity of longing leads on creating its own certainty.'

Aloud I said, 'How I wish this wretched Chandra had caught him too, like he has caught me, by his locks and brought him over to me.' Taralika laughed and said, 'Princess! You are so innocent. This Chandra behaves as if he is himself in love with you. In the guise of reflection in a drop of perspiration he kisses your cheeks, and falls on your beautiful full breasts. With trembling ray hands he touches the gems on your girdle. Reflecting himself on your shining toenails he falls at your feet. Chandra himself seems to be in the heat of passion as he now has the whiteness of dried sandalwood paste, and the pallor of the lotus stalk; he falls on the cool stone floor in the guise of his rays, and dives into the lily pond in the guise of a reflection.' Bantering in this fashion, we reached the place where Pundarika was supposed to be.

As we washed the pollen off our feet in the streams running down the chandrakanta stone surfaces on the Kailasa Mountains, we heard the lamentation of a man; it seemed to come from the very place where Pundarika was supposed to be, on the western side of the lake. The words were unclear because of the distance. The throbbing right eye had already caused me disquiet; now completely shaken I cried out 'Taralike! What could this mean?' and hurried towards the source of the cry with a heavy heart, fearing the worst and my body trembling all over.

As we drew near, in the stillness of the night I could make out the distressed voice of Kapinjala. 'My God! I am done for.

I am burnt out. What a terrible thing has come to pass. You rascal Madana! You devil! You sinner! What horror have you perpetrated? And you sinful woman. Mahashvete. What harm did he do to you? And you cad Chandra! Chandala! Are you now satisfied? And you merciless one, the south wind! Is your desire now fulfilled? Blow on to your heart's content.

Hey Bhagavan Shvetaketu! You loving father! You do not know that you have been robbed. Oh Righteousness! There is none now to be your ward. Oh Penance! You have no refuge left. Ah Saraswati! You have been widowed. Oh Truth! You are orphaned.

My dear friend! Do wait for me. I too shall follow you. I cannot for a moment live without you. How could you go away like this leaving me alone here, as though you do not know me, as though you have never seen me? Life has lost its meaning. Tapas is futile, there is no pleasure in the world any more. With whom shall I wander and with whom shall I share my thoughts? Get up now. Answer me. What happened to your smiling chatter and your love for me?'

When I heard this outcry my heart almost stopped. I let out a loud cry and rushed on stumbling at every step, as the land was unfamiliar to me; my utthariya tore getting caught in the plants growing on the banks of the lake. Somehow I reached the spot as though dragged on by someone, and I saw him whose life had just flown. I saw Kapinjala embracing his neck and sobbing 'He cannot die, he cannot die', with the tears streaming down his face.

There he lay on a chadrakanta rock close to the shores of the lake with cool drops of water on its surface, on a bed of flowers—lilies and lotuses and lotus stalks and various other forest blooms—a veritable arsenal of Kama. He was so motionless that I imagined that he was listening keenly for my footsteps. As the passion raging within had been put out, he seemed merely to be sleeping comfortably. Or could he be doing pranayama as atonement for the agitation of his mind? He had turned his back to the moon's rays as though he hated them. His lustrous lips seemed to say to me 'It is for you that I have reached this state.' Had his life left him in anger because he had now found someone dearer to him than itself?

The sandalwood paste applied on his forehead served as the *tripundraka;* fresh, juicy lotus stalks filled in for his yagnopavitha. My single-stranded necklace was the akshamala round his neck; the thickly applied powdered camphor was his sacred ash. The lotus stalk bracelet was the beautiful protective amulet. Having taken a vow to serve Kama and being thus suitably attired for that was he even now mastering incantations for union with me? With his eyes narrowed in pain from the arrows of Kamadeva he seemed to be complaining 'Hard-hearted one! Will you not favour me, who am in love with you, with at least another glimpse of you?' His left hand rested on his chest as though trying to restrain me who was enshrined there in his heart, saying 'You are as dear to me as life itself, hold on please, don't you go away too along with the departing life forces.'

When Kapinjala saw me his sorrow swelled and he cried out throwing up his hands This is not right. He cannot die now.' At once the darkness of unconsciousness came over me. I seemed to fall deep into an abyss. Then I knew nothing, where I was, or what I said or did. And I could not understand why my life forces did not leave my body that very moment. Was it because my deluded heart was that hard, was it because my wretched body was capable of bearing a thousand sorrows? Or was it simply because I was destined to undergo a long period of misery as punishment for whatever ill deeds I might have done in my previous life. I could not really figure out the reason. All I knew once I regained consciousness after a long time was that I was lying on the ground motionless; I was conscious of an unbearable agony as though I had fallen into fire. Not quite believing that he was dead while I still lived I sprang up and lamented loudly, 'What calamity is this that has befallen me. Oh mother! Oh my father! My dear friends! And my lord! The only reason for my existence. Tell me, where have you gone leaving me all alone here? Ask Taralika, what I have suffered on your account. What I have gone through this single day would equal the miseries of a thousand epochs. Please look at me a little. Will you not talk to me at least once? Will you not take pity on one who is devoted to you? Have you no fear of the ill fame that comes of abandoning your faithful servant? I am in agony, I love you, I have none to protect me, and I have no way out. I have lost everything—you, my father, my mother, my family, my honour and the future world as well.

'How could I have been so hard-hearted as to leave you in this state and go home. Of what importance is one's home, one's mother, father, relations or attendants?

'But whose help do I seek now? Oh Fates! Show mercy on me. I beg you, please be compassionate and give back the life of my lover. Protect this destitute girl. Goddesses of the forest. Please give his life forces back to him. Oh Mother Earth! The Mother of all Grace! Why have you not taken pity on me? Oh Father! The Lord of Kailasa! I fall at your feet. Have pity on me.'

I was wild with grief. I raved and ranted like one who had completely lost her mind. A flood of tears, stream upon stream of them flowed down from my eyes in which I seemed to be dissolving away. My very body seemed to turn into water. If only he would live, I was ready to die for it. He was dead, yet how desperately did I long to enter his heart. With my hands I stroked his cheeks and forehead, where the sandalwood paste had dried and whitened the roots of his hair, his shoulders on which lay the wet, cool, juicy lotus stalks and his chest covered with lotus leaves with the marks of the sandalwood water drops still on them.

I chided him: 'Pundarika! I lament so much, yet you are indifferent to me.' Then I tried to placate him. I kissed him again and again; I put my arms around his neck and wept. I railed against the single strand of pearl necklace still lying on his chest, 'You wicked one! Could you not keep him alive until I returned?' Then I fell at Kapinjala's feet and beseeched him 'Hey Bhagavan! Take pity on me.' I clasped Taralika in my arms over and over again and wept.

Even today I do not understand how those thousand poignant terms of endearment unknown to me till then, having never read them myself or been taught by anyone, came pouring out of me. I had never lamented like that ever before; nor had I wept so grievously, so piteously. The tears came rushing out with the force of ocean waves; words of lamentation pushed themselves out like fresh growth from the ground; sorrow rose up like a thousand mountain peaks.

~

Reliving thus the sad sequence of past events in the narration of them, Mahashveta fainted away, overwhelmed by the intensity of remembered grief. As she was about to fall on the rock a tearful Chandrapida who had been greatly moved by her story rushed to her side and held her with his outstretched hands. He fanned her with the ends of her utthariya drenched with her own tears until she regained consciousness. With his own cheeks wet with tears and filled with pity Chandrapida said 'My lady! Forgive me. It was my fault that you had to experience your sorrow all over again. Please do stop the narration. I too cannot bear to hear anymore. Besides it is not right that your life forces holding on somehow with great difficulty should be used again and again as fuel to the fire of remembered agony.'

Mahashveta sighed deeply and replied tearfully, 'These hardened life forces of mine did not abandon me that terrible night. It is unlikely that they would now. The god of death too seems to be avoiding me as being too wretchedly sinful, having brought about the untimely death of a Brahmin. Sorrow? How could there be sorrow in one so hard hearted? It is all pretence on the part of this wicked heart of mine. Having abandoned all sense of shame I stand first among the most shameless women of the world. With adamantine hardness have I been able to bear the pangs of love, so what could happen with the mere telling of it? Further, I have already told you the worst; there is nothing more terrible left to narrate. Now I want to tell you about that wonderful phenomenon that took place after the terrible thunderbolt had struck; it is that mysterious event that is extending to me the mirage-like hope that makes me hold on to this wretched body that is dead for all practical purposes, and a useless burden.'

Mahashveta Narrates . . .

On that terrible night, I had decided that death was the only way out of the horrible situation. I cried out to Taralika, 'Get up you hard-hearted one. How long are you going to cry? Go and collect firewood and arrange a pyre for me. I shall follow in the footsteps of the lord of my life.'

It was then that a fantastic thing happened. No sooner had I spoken than a great being came out of the orb of the moon and descended to the earth pulling around him the foamy white utthariya that had flown up in the wind and had got caught on the edge of his armlet. The ruby kundalas on his ears cast their red brilliance on his cheeks. A very long necklace of huge pearls, like stars strung together adorned his chest. His turban was of soft white silk. His abundant curly locks, dark like a swarm of bees were tied up on the crown of his head. He wore white lily blooms on his ears. There were marks on his shoulders left by the kumkum from the breasts of his women. He was fair like the lily and of immense stature. He carried all the marks of a superior being; indeed he appeared divine. As he descended, the lustre of his body seemed to wash over the quarters like crystal clear water. A shower of cool, fragrant, nectar drops, like dew, issued out of him making one shiver as if with cold. There was a glow everywhere. With his long hands resembling the trunk of Iravatha and fingers soft and cool to the touch he picked up the dead body and spoke in a kindly voice that sounded deep like the dundubhi, 'My child Mahashvete! Do not give up your life. You will reunite with him in due course.' Bearing Pundarika in his arms he rose up into the sky and disappeared.

Frightened, wonderstruck and curious as well I asked Kapinjala what this could mean. But Kapinjala's attention was elsewhere; he never answered me. Instead he shouted at the retreating figure of the divine being, 'You rascal, where are you taking my friend?' He tied his utthariya quickly around his waist and sprang into the sky following that mysterious individual. Very soon, even as we were watching all of them entered among the stars.

As for me the disappearance of Kapinjala was like losing my beloved all over again. My grief doubled and rent my heart. Not knowing what to do I approached Taralika and asked her if she could make anything out of all this. Poor Taralika, she too was shaken by all the strange events; she was grief stricken and trembled with fear for my life. Overcome with dejection and pity she said, 'Princess, sinner that I am I do not understand anything. But I do know this is a most wonderful happening. That person, he was undoubtedly of divine appearance. He was full of compassion and he consoled you like a father before he went away. Generally divine beings such as this one would never, even in their dreams utter a falsehood. So it seems to me that at least for the time being you should give up your decision to end your life. Further, it is clear that Kapinjala has gone after him. Who this individual is, where he is from, why he has taken away the dead body and above all why he has given you this impossible promise of reunion with Pundarika—all this we can learn from Kapinjala once he gets back. The decision to die is not difficult to make and it can be made later. As long as Kapinjala is alive he will not remain without getting in touch with you. Do stay alive until he comes back.' Having said this Taralika fell at my feet

I accepted her advice; I decided to live. The whole world finds it difficult to overcome the love of life. Or perhaps it is in woman's nature to be quintessentially mean. Perhaps I was eager to see Kapinjala again. Or more likely it could have been the mirage-like hope contained in the words of that divine individual. Whatever might have been the reason I decided that what Taralika suggested was the right thing to do. I spent the night right there on the shores of the lake, that night of terror that felt like the night of pralaya. I tossed about on the ground; my dishevelled hair became dusty and stuck to my cheeks wet with tears. The night dragged on for a thousand years. It was a night of sheer agony, of grief, of hell fire. My throat was sore with my ceaseless piteous weeping. Only Taralika was there with me in my misery.

In the morning I got up and bathed in the lake. I took Pundarika's kamandalu for my own use and also put on the bark garments he had left behind. All of a sudden this earthly life had become worthless. I understood the extent of my misfortune. I came face to face with the enormity of the calamity that had befallen me; I knew my sorrow had no antidote to it. I understood the utter indifference of fate to my condition. I sensed poignancy in every attachment; and it came to me that all existence in this world was transient, and all pleasures evanescent.

I gave up all my family—my mother and father and all my attendants. I withdrew my mind from the pleasures of this world; I controlled my senses and took a vow of chastity. And I took refuge in this shrine of Sthanu, the Lord of all the three worlds.

Having come to know the whole story, my father and mother came down to see me with several members of the family. They lamented over my fate. They also importuned me to abandon the course of action that I had set my mind upon. They gave me much advice, calmed me in various ways and tried their best to take me home. Even when they understood at last that my mind was irrevocably made up they were unwilling to leave because of their love for me, their child. They lingered on for several days, but went home eventually, with grieving hearts.

From that day onwards I have lived here in this cave with just Taralika for company. I have lived here in great grief showing my constancy to Pundarika in the ceaseless tears that I shed. This body of mine is much reduced as I pine for him; this shameless, inauspicious abode of debilitating cares has been subjected to a thousand penances, of the greatest rigour. I live on the fruits and roots of the forest. In the guise of prayers I enumerate his virtues. I bathe in this lake three times a day and I worship the Lord Triambaka. Indeed for a long time now I have led this existence.

So here I am a sinner, devoid of all felicity, a shameless, cruel, friendless woman, fit to be condemned in all ways, a woman who has been brought into the world for no purpose, who is continuing to live without being of any use, with none to protect her, none to lean on and with no happiness. What can your lordship do, having seen and heard the story of this terrible sinner, the one who has committed the vile crime of bringing about the death of a Brahmin?

— 32 —

Covering her face with the end of her white bark garment, like autumnal clouds shrouding the moon, Mahashveta sobbed for a long time unable to control the welling tears.

Chandrapida had already developed a great respect for Mahashveta; her beauty, modesty and kindness, her gentle way of talking, her humility and detachment, her serenity, purity and nobility of bearing had made a great impression on him. Her goodness and constancy revealed in the narration of her story now captivated him completely, creating in his heart, a fondness for her. Moved by her predicament he now spoke slowly.

Chandrapida Speaks . . .

Madam! It is only the ingrates and the faint-hearted, attached to their pleasures and afraid of the rigours of observances for the welfare of the beloved, who seek to show their love merely by shedding useless tears. But you madam, you have expressed all your grief in action. What indeed have you left undone for the sake of love that you cry? You have given up the dearest of your relations as though they were but mere strangers. You have turned away with contempt from the comforts of life although they are near at hand; you have spurned the pleasures of a wealth that surpasses Indra's. Your body already slender as the lotus stalk has been reduced to extreme thinness as a result of unkind mortification. You have assumed celibacy. You have driven yourself to do great yogic penance. Above all you have taken upon yourself to live in the forest, a course of action extremely difficult for women.

It is easy for those afflicted with sorrow to end their lives; it requires much greater effort to throw oneself into a life of abnegation. This act of women dying with the dead husband is a most futile act. It is a path treaded by the uneducated and the ignorant. It reveals a narrowness of vision; it is an act of violence and madness. If one's life forces do not leave on their own at the death of a dear one, a father or a brother, a friend or a husband then it is not right to put an end to them violently.

If one analyses this practice of following a dear one in death, it becomes clear that it is done for selfish reasons, to save oneself from an agony to which there is no other antidote. This act surely does not benefit the dead in any manner. Does it bring the dead back to life? No. Does it enhance one's spiritual merit? No indeed! It does not earn higher worlds, it does not insure against one's falling into hell. It is certainly not the way to see the beloved again, to unite with him again. Any person who takes his own life simply gets caught in the web of his own karma and is taken accordingly to the suitable world, the suicide merely adding to his other sins. The one who lives on helps both his soul as well as that of the departed by performing all the prescribed rites.

Do you not remember Rati, the beloved wife, the only wife of Manmatha, did not give up her life when her husband, the joy of women's hearts was burnt to cinders by the fire of Hara's third eye? Pritha too of the Vrishnis, the daughter of Shurasena, did not give up her life when her husband Pandu, who had conquered the world effortlessly, fell a victim to the fire of the curse of the sage Kiminda. Utthara the young daughter of Virata lived on when her husband Abhimanyu, a delight to the eyes like the young moon, modest and valorous, fell in battle. Dusshala, the only daughter of Dhritarashtra, and the darling of all the hundred brothers did not follow her husband, the exceedingly handsome Sindhuraja Jayadhrita, who had been blessed to greatness by Hara, in death when Arjuna felled him in battle. And indeed there are many other women, apart from these, the daughters of devas, asuras, humans, siddhas and gandharvas, who have continued to live after the death of their husbands.

If there has been any doubt about the future union with Pundarika then perhaps there is a case for giving up your life. But your ladyship has heard with her own ears, words that promised certain union. What uncertainty can yet remain? How could such a great being of such extraordinary appearance utter a falsehood? There is no doubt that it is only out of compassion for you that the celestial being has taken the body away to the heavenly regions to be revived at the proper time. The powers of such beings are beyond one's imagination. Astonishingly varied are the manifestations of this phenomenal world; strange are the ways of fate; passing strange are the powers of penance.

A careful analysis of the phenomenon described by you makes it clear that the reason for the removal of the body of Pundarika could only be for restoring him back to life. Her ladyship should not conclude that such a thing is impossible; this has indeed been a well-trodden path. Pramadvara born to the gandharva king Vishvavasu and the apsara Menaka, died of snake bite in the ashrama of Sthulakesha; a young sage Ruru the grandson of the Bhargava, Chayana then joined half of his own life to hers. Arjuna died at the hands of his own son Babhruvahana while chasing after the ashvamedha horse; the Naga woman Ulupi, the mother of Babhruvahana, then infused fresh life into her husband. Then there was Parikshit, the son of Abhimanyu. Scorched by the heat of the missiles of Ashvatthama, Parikshit was still born; taking pity on the lamenting mother Utthara, Bhagvan Vasudeva revived the baby, and what a wonderful phenomenon that was. In the case of Pundarika too, something similar is bound to happen.

In any case we are completely in the hands of hard-hearted Fate without whose consent we cannot even breathe; sly, pitiless Fate does not tolerate for long, love that is innocent and heart-warming. Happiness is by nature fragile and short-lived; sorrows last longer. Lovers come together in one life only to be separated in the next thousand.

Please do not blame yourself, for you are indeed blameless. Such things do happen to those who have entered upon the arduous and dangerous path of samsara; only the steady manage to get over the perils.

~

Chandrapida consoled her thus with his gentle words. He brought fresh water from the stream and made her wash her face once again.

As though saddened by the story of Mahashveta the sun too lowered his head. As the day withered, the descending orb of the sun became reddish yellow in colour like the pollen of the full-blown blooms of the *priangu* creeper. The red evening light, soft like silk stained with kusumbha juice, left all the quarters, one after the other. The sky, no longer blue became suffused with a russet lustre, similar to the glow of the eyes of the chakora bird. The koel-eye red-yellow glow of twilight spread over the whole world. Soon sight-stealing darkness, the colour of forest bison, swallowing vast expanses of the sky spread the blackness of night all around. The woods appeared denser with their greenness blanketed by the thick darkness. The breeze began to blow through the dense trees and creepers, cool with the nocturnal dew, and carrying with it the fragrance of a hundred forest flowers. The birds fell silent with sleep.

At this evening hour, Mahashveta got up slowly and worshipped the goddess of the western twilight. She washed her feet with water from the kamandalu and sat on the bark-cloth covered bed with a troubled heart, sighing deeply. Chandrapida too got up and performed the evening worship with flowers and water from the spring. On the second rock surface he made for himself a bed with shoots and flowers. As he sat on the bed his mind kept returning to the sad story of Mahashveta. He thought,

'The frenzy induced by the one with the flower arrows is indeed impossible to bear. Even great men are unable to hold their own against the love god; they lose their grit and give up their lives. So I bow down to Makaraketu whose writ runs in all the three worlds.'

—33—

Having prepared his bed, Chandrapida asked Mahashveta again, 'My lady! Where is that friend of yours Taralika who is sharing with you the travails of living in the forest and who too has taken a vow of celibacy?'

Mahashveta replied. 'Noble One! I assume you remember what I told you about the apsara lineage that sprang up from amrita. Madira of the intoxicating eyes who was born in that lineage married Chitraratha the great gandharva king. Captivated by her great qualities the king enthroned Madira as the first lady of the antapura; she was honoured with a golden plank to sit upon as well as with other insignia of high position such as the umbrella, the staff and the chamara and the title of *Mahadevi*.

'As they were engrossed in their growing love for each other, and delighting in the pleasures of youth, a daughter of extraordinary beauty and virtue was born to them, cherished as their very life not only by the parents, and the gandharva lineage, but by the entire world. Her name, rightly enough, is Kadambari for she is of intoxicating beauty. She is a beloved friend, a second heart of mine as it were; a close confidante, we have been inseparable from her birth, having eaten, drunk and slept together. Together we learnt the arts, music and dance; and together we played as children, to our hearts' content.

'Saddened by the unfortunate turn of events in my life, this dear friend of mine has now sworn in the presence of friends that as long as I remain in such distress she too will not wed anyone; she has further sworn that should she be given in marriage to anyone against her wishes, she would put an end to herself, by starvation or by fire, by hanging or by poison. The news of this vow undertaken by his daughter eventually reached the ears of the king through the antapura grapevine. Looking at Kadambari in the first flush of youth, the king's distress knows no bounds. He is indeed powerless to say anything; she is his only daughter, his only child, and very close to his heart.

'Unable to find a way out of the situation the gandharva king sent his kanchuki Ksheeroda just this morning, after consulting his wife Madira, with this message. "My child, Mahashvete! We are already greatly troubled by your condition; added to that we now have the problem of Kadambari's vow. We need your help in making Kadambari change her mind". I have great respect for my elders and I love Kadambari very much indeed. I have therefore sent Taralika back with Ksheeroda with the following message. "Dear friend Kadambari, why do you cause more pain to people who are already unhappy? If you want me to live, please do what your parents wish". Taralika left just a few minutes before your highness arrived here.'

Having said this Mahashveta fell silent.

Soon Chandra, the lord of the stars, the crest jewel on the tresses of Shiva, rose in the sky. The dark blemish on his body seemed to symbolize Mahashveta's heart burnt by the fire of sorrow; or could it be the mark of the terrible sin of causing the death of the son of a sage?

Chandrapida slowly sat down on his bed. He saw that Mahashveta was already asleep. He suddenly wondered what Vaishampayana might be thinking about him now, or Patralekha, or for that matter, all the accompanying princes. Then he too fell asleep. When dawn broke Chandrapida woke up to see Mahashveta already seated on the rock chanting the sacred Aghamarshana. He too got up and performed the morning rites.

In the meantime Taralika had already arrived accompanied by a sixteen-year-old gandharva youth, strongly built, who moved with the heavy tread of an elephant languid with the flow of the rut fluid. His thighs were dusty with the dried sandalwood powder applied the previous day. He wore a single garment around his waist secured tightly by a series of golden chains. The end of the garment that escaped the girdle was flying in the wind. His waist was slender and his stomach flat. He had a broad chest and long tapering hands. He wore a bracelet of precious stones on his left wrist. The lustre of the earring on one ear fell on that shoulder like an utthariya. Constant chewing of betel leaves had coloured his lips to the shade of tender mango shoots. He had long brilliant eyes. His forehead was broad and shone as if made of gold. His straight hair was dark like a swarm of bees. He was full of poise and self-confidence. His name was Keyuraka.

Taralika kept sending curious glances at Chandrapida as she approached Mahashveta, bowed to her and sat down. Keyuraka, too, came forward and saluted Mahashveta with great deference. Then he went and sat down on a rock slightly away, but within sight of Mahashveta. He, too, was struck with wonder at Chandrapida's extraordinary beauty, easily surpassing that of Manmatha and several other classes of celestial beings; he had never seen anyone so handsome before.

Having finished her prayers Mahashveta asked Taralika, 'Did you see my dear friend Kadambari? Is she well? Will she follow my advice?' Taralika replied in a very sweet voice, 'Princess! I saw the princess Kadambari and she is very well. She enquired about you. When she heard your message however, she wept, shedding huge tears; and she has sent her reply with Keyuraka here, who is her veena carrier.'

Then Keyuraka said, 'Princess Mahashvete, Devi Kadambari hugs you closely and asks: "This message that you have sent with Taralika, tell me, is it out of consideration for my parents, or is this some sort of test of my intentions? Or are you subtly censuring me because I still live at home? Or do you want to put an end to our friendship? Is this just a ruse to get rid of me, who am devoted to you? Or are you angry with me? You know my heart is filled with spontaneous love for you, yet you send a message like this. Are you not ashamed? You used to be so sweet spoken; who has now taught you to use these unloving harsh words? Even if one were at peace, how could one, a person of discrimination direct the mind to such a trivial and ill boding an act? How would such a thing be possible for me who am so distressed by your condition? How can there be any inclination towards pleasure in a mind that is in grief over a friend's misfortune? Would I ever willingly fulfil the desires of that poisonous evil-doer Kama, who has brought this terrible suffering on my friend?

"Even the chakravaka pair separates at night, giving up the pleasure of being together and sharing in the misery of the lotus plant at the absence of her lover the sun. When, my very dear friend, mourning for her lost lover has given up contact with other men, how can I allow a man to enter my heart? When my dear friend is subjecting her limbs to excruciating austerities and denials how can I go after pleasures and take a husband, affecting indifference to her agonies? And even if I did would I be able to get any happiness?

"In this matter, out of love for you I have gone against all rules of conduct prescribed for young women; I have asserted an unseemly independence and laid myself open to censure. I have disregarded the advice of the elders and discounted the ill fame that might be heaped on me. I have thrown away modesty that is the natural ornament of a woman.

Therefore, I join my hands in prayer, I bow to you, and I hold your feet. Be kind to me. Remember, when you went away to the forest you took my life too with you. Do not entertain such thoughts even in your dreams."' Keyuraka gave this message and fell silent.

Mahashveta was lost in thought for a while. Then as if she had come to a decision she said to Keyuraka, 'Very well, Keyuraka, you go back now. I shall go to Hemakuta myself and do what is necessary.' After Keyuraka left, she turned to Chandrapida. 'Prince! The Hemakuta Mountains are beautiful; and the kingdom of Chitraratha is full of varied wonders. The kimpurusha land too is full of curiosities. The gandharvas are beautiful and Kadambari is open-hearted and generous. If you reckon the travel would not incommode you unduly, if it would not come in the way of important business, if you are by nature curious about things you have never seen before, and if you believe I am worthy of your friendship, then my request should not be refused and this is what I suggest. You come with me to the beautiful Hemakuta and meet Kadambari who is no different from me. Help me put some sense into her and spend a day there in relaxation. Tomorrow you can return.

'You have become a dear friend now, I have been drawn to you from the time I met you. My mind had remained pressed down with the weight of dark sorrow for such a long time; I feel infused with new life after I shared my sad story with you. Even the grief seems bearable now. Good people lighten the minds burdened with unhappiness.'

Chandrapida replied, 'From the moment I met you I too have felt myself under your command. Employ me in whatever way you think fit.'

─34─

Mahashveta and Chandrapida set out and in due course reached the palace of the gandharva king on Hemakuta. They passed through the arched golden doorways of the seven wings and arrived at the entrance to the antapura of unmarried girls. The pratiharis saw that Mahashveta had come for a visit and hurried over to salute her. Wielding their golden staffs they quickly led the visitors inside.

It appeared to Chandrapida that the whole palace was filled with women. It could have been another world altogether composed only of women. Or, had Brahma brought all the women of all the three worlds together to take a census perhaps. Or it could be another time altogether, a different Yuga, the fifth one perhaps, a Yuga solely for women, created possibly by another Brahma who hated men. Is this Brahma's factory where he makes an infinite variety of women to be used in the various Yugas? Chandrapida thought it was a place made of romance, of beauty. It was crowded with the gods of pleasure, filled with the floral arrows of Kama. It was of the stuff of softness and sweetness, it was a place of wonder.

It appeared to Chandrapida as if it were raining moons in the antapura, with so many beautiful faces all seen together. And so many sideward glances converted the palace into a field of waving lilies. So many arched eyebrows created the illusion of a thousand moving bows of Manmatha. The mass of dark tresses seemed like the weaving together of a million twilights of the waning fortnight of the moon. The lustre of so many cheeks glittered like a thousand mirrors made of gems. The brilliance of all their smiles seemed to create an ambience of spring bursting with white flowers. The delicate pink of so many palms was truly a shower of lotus petals over the whole world. The rays shooting out of their nails were a thousand arrows of

Manmatha covering all the directions. A thousand peacocks raised in the palace were dancing surely because they were excited by the rainbow-like flashes of the jewels.

The girls went about their daily activities but to Chandrapida every one of their actions appeared to be an exotic lesson on love play. Merely holding each other's hands transformed into learning how to grasp the lover's hands. Playing the flute transmuted into lessons in kissing and plucking the veena strings was surely practice for leaving nail marks on the lover. While playing with the ball could become a lesson in stroking, what could holding the water pot by its neck be but practising to put the arms around the lover. As they whirled about in play, he saw them as swinging their hips and breasts in allurement. As they merely bit on the tambula he fancied them training to bite the lover in love play.

The women were in need of no external cosmetic aids to their beauty. Their own lustre streaming down their cheeks washed their faces. The long lily-eyes that stretched up to their very ears did duty as earrings. The brilliance of their laughter served as the anointing liquid; and their own breaths were sufficient unto perfuming their body. Their own slender, fair shoulders were the garlands of champaka blooms. While the redness of their lips surely served as the kungkuma unguent, the transparently lustrous breasts did more than hold their own as mirrors. And the soft flush of their toes was itself the alaktha. Their sweet chatter was the strumming of the veena. The lustre of their own bodies was the veil.

The women were so delicate that the alaktha on their feet could have been a burden. The mekhala of bakula flowers could impede their gait. The weight of the anointing liquid might lead to gasping for breath and the weight of their fine garments could cause weariness. The auspicious thread around the wrist was sufficient to cause the hand to tremble. The weight of an earring could tire them and to be blown by the wings of the bees hovering around the flowers on their ears, could well have been exhausting.

To rise to greet a friend without leaning on someone's hand was an act of daring. Bearing the weight of the pearl necklace showed the firmness of the breasts. When collecting flowers for worship it would not do for the delicate damsels, having plucked one flower, to take the second. And stringing flowers was an act altogether too harsh for them. And it would have caused no great wonder at all to see womanly waists broken while bowing down in worship.

The visiting party took a few steps into the apartment and heard the sweet voices of Kadambari's close attendants giving such delightfully exotic orders to each other. 'Lavalike! Make a bund around the lavali creeper with the pollen dust of the ketaki. Sagarike! Scatter the sand of gems in the golden well of fragrant water. Mrinalike! Colour the toy chakravaka pair in the pond of artificial lotuses with kumkum. Rajanike! Put the lights in the avenue of tamala trees. Nalinike! Feed the swans with the pollen juice of the lotus. Kadalike! Take the peacocks to the shower room. Mayurike! Send the kinnara pair into the music chamber. Harinike! Teach the parrots and the mynas in the cage.

Listening to the talk of the women, the group led by Mahashveta approached Kadambari's apartments. Chandrapida saw a path flanked on both sides by gardens; the path appeared sandy with the pollen dust falling on it from the blooms in the gardens. With the koels cutting into the mango fruits with their claws it seemed to rain mango juice on the path. It was misty as the wind sprayed the mouthfuls of wine spat out by the beautiful women on the bakula trees in order to make them flower. With a scatter of the blooms of the champa the path was like an island of gold. The bees hovering over the flowers made the path appear like a dense wood of dark ashoka trees. The women who were waiting on either side to serve Kadambari seemed to make a rampart of beauty at the entrance to the path. Chandrapida saw, coming from the interiors of the path towards him, like a river flowing in a straight plait-like course, the collected lustre of all the jewels of all the women inside the apartments. Going against that flow he soon saw the entrance to a pavilion of exotic beauty.

There was a couch of medium size covered with a blue spread placed right in the centre of the pavilion on which sat Kadambari surrounded by glitteringly bejewelled young women, constituting as it were a bower of *kalpalata,* a dense growth of the wish-fulfilling creeper. She sat at the head of the couch covered with a dark silken cloth and leaned her elbow on a white pillow. The lustre that spread from her body was the water in which the chamara wielders swung about their arms that were the whirling oars as they fanned her. She was of such remarkable beauty that her own attendants often gazed upon her unblinkingly. Had the ideals of beauty themselves, roused to passion come and possessed her limbs unable to resist her? She was just out of her childhood but already had the glow of young womanhood on her, as though Yauvana, in love with her beauty had taken impetuous possession of her, without her parents having given her away.

The red lustre of her feet seemed to flow in streams, like liquid beauty that was stained with alaktha. The streams appeared as if they were the hanging tassels of the red garment she was wearing, nay, the red rays of her ruby anklets. So tender and so full of colour were the toes that sometimes it appeared as if a stream of blood was flowing out of the gap between the nail and the flesh. The nails were like a circle of earthly stars while the feet themselves were a flowing river of the essence of coral.

Were the upward shooting rays from the gems of her anklets lending a helping hand to the thighs distressed with the burden of supporting her wide hips by holding them up? When Prajapati fashioned her slender waist he must have pressed it hard and the loveliness that spurted out must have hit the firm surface of her hips and divided into the two streams that became her thighs. She wore a golden chain round her hips whose sparkling brilliance cast a protective net over them; would it have been an act of jealousy on the part of the jewel, to prevent men from gazing at them?

Her waist was so small that one wondered if it were not wasting away being deprived of a glimpse of her lovely face hidden by the high breasts. Her deep navel could well be the finger mark of Prajapati left on her extraordinarily soft body when he fashioned her. It looked like a small whirlpool in the waters of a river. The line of hair above the navel was surely a panegyric written by none other than Manmatha himself, on her beauty, which helped him conquer all the three worlds. The flowers that she wore on her ears cast their reflection on her large lustrous breasts. It looked as if her chest pressed down by the weight of her breasts, veritable footstools of Kama's, was trying to push them up with its own hands. Her arms were like the long downward rays of her earrings, nay, slender lotus stalks growing in the waters of pure beauty. As for her nails, their lustre dripped as though perspiration poured down her arms distressed with the burden of the armlets.

Her face was a little bent no doubt with the weight of her breasts; the rays coming up from her pearl necklace seemed to hold it up by pushing up her chin. Her coral reef-red lips were like waves rising, whipped up by the gust of youth, from the ocean of passion. Her cheeks shone with a pale pink fresh brilliance like wine-filled oyster shells. Her nose was like the charming gem stick used to play the *parivadini,* the seven-stringed veena of Rati. Her long eyes were slightly red at the corners; her eyebrows were like the twin streaks of the rut fluid on the elephant that was inflamed with adolescence. Her forehead shone with a bindi done in a paste of *manashila* and one wondered if it could have been the impassioned heart of Kamadeva himself imprinted there.

She wore charming golden *talipattas* on her beautiful ears; it created the illusion of honey dropping from the flowers on her ear. Suspended from them were kundalas of rubies encased in golden clasps done in a crocodile design. Her forehead acquired a lustrous flush from the shining *chudamani*, which kissed her hairline and seemed to wash her long hair too with a brilliant wine-pink colour.

If Gauri had become arrogant that Hara had pervaded half her body then what of Kadambari whose entire body had been pervaded by Manmatha, enhancing her beauty and grace. If Hara had become proud of having placed a single moon on his own head, what about Kadambari who scattered a thousand moons every time her face lit up with her sensuous smile. If Hara in his anger could burn one Manmatha mercilessly Kadambari could create a thousand Manmathas in every single heart. If Narayana had become too proud of carrying one Lakshmi on his chest what of Kadambari who could create a thousand of them with her own image reflected on a thousand surfaces?

And how kind she was by nature! She would make her attendants create a sandy shore with lotus pollen for the separated distressed chakravaka pair in the artificial river in her palace, so that they could sleep at night. If the sound of the anklets of the attendants had excited her beloved pair of swans, she would immediately have them brought over to her. If the young one of the palace deer tried to eat the emerald jewellery of the women confused by the green lustre, Kadambari would at once remove the barley sprout from the ear of her women and herself feed it to the young animal. And she would give away all the ornaments she wore to the gardener who came to offer her the first flowers of a creeper that she grew herself.

The *shabari* looking after the kridaparvatha would bring various forest flowers and fruits bound with leaves; Kadambari innocently playful, would keep drawing the woman into conversation just to hear her quaint unclear speech. The pearl inlaid *chandralekhika* ornament fashioned like the crescents of the moon that the betel-box bearer wore would cast its reflection on her breasts; Kadambari would pretend they were the sweat-drop-filled nail marks of her lover and playfully throw coloured powder on them. The reflection of her gem-inlaid kundalas would fall on the chamara wielder's cheeks and Kadambari would pretend that they were the fresh nail marks of the attendant's lover and would hasten playfully to hide it with the flowers removed from her own ear.

But she sent away the fine princes who came wooing her and was content with just the pleasures of fragrance and flowers.

Now as she was seated on the couch she was impatiently enquiring of Keyuraka sitting in front of her, 'Who is he? Whose son is he? What does he look like? And what is his age? How did he get to know Mahashveta? Is he coming here now?' It was at this moment that Chandrapida cast his eyes for the first time on Kadambari.

—35—

Chandrapida looked at Kadambari's lovely face shining with the lustre of the moon and his heart swelled with delight just like the waters of the ocean. He thought, 'How I wish I could have Brahma change all my senses into sight alone. How fortunate my eyes are to have the uninterrupted pleasure of gazing at this girl. Where, I wonder, did Brahma come upon the matter for creating this extraordinarily lovely form? I am quite sure that all the fragrant flowers of the world, the lilies and the lotuses came into existence out of the tear drops falling from the eyes of this beautiful form when she wept with distress at the touch of Brahma's hands when he fashioned her.'

As his thoughts raced on in this excited fashion his eyes fastened on hers. Kadambari realized this was the person Keyuraka had talked about; her face lit up with a smile when she saw his extraordinary beauty and her eyes lingered on him for a long time. First her body thrilled with the hair standing on edge, then one heard the tinkle of the ornaments, then Kadambari rose.

At once Kamadeva took possession of her. It was he who made her break out in perspiration, but the hurried getting up was made the excuse. He it was who impeded her gait by making her thighs tremble, but it was the *hamsa* pair that followed her footsteps at the sound of the anklets that drew her censure. The sighs that broke out of her disarranged her utthariya but the blame went to the chamara wielder. It was her great joy that brought the tears to her eyes, but the pollen from the shaken flowers on the ears was made the ostensible cause. It was the trembling of her body that caused the hand to shake but the pretence was that she merely shook away the hand of the pratihari extended to hold her.

Manmatha who had already entered Kadambari made a double of himself as it were and set foot into Chandrapida's heart along with her. The prince fancied that the brilliance of her jewels was only the screen separating them who were about to be wedded. Nay, Kadambari's mere entry into his heart was his true wedding with her; the tinkle of their ornaments was their love talk, the mingling of their body-lustre their physical union.

Kadambari took a few steps as though with difficulty and embraced Mahashveta whom she had not seen for a long time, with a lot of affection. Mahashveta too held her closely and said, 'Dear friend Kadambari, there is in the land of Bharata a great king called Tarapida whose victorious horses have left their hoof marks all over the world right up to the four oceans. He protects his subjects from all evils. This is his son named Chandrapida who, with the strength of his own pillar-like arms bears the burden of the earth with ease; he bears it like a garland on his head, and gives her comfort. The prince is here in the course of his digvijaya.

The moment I set eyes on him I felt an inexplicable selfless affection for him. Although I have hardened myself and given up all my attachments, this prince here with his openness and great qualities has captivated my mind. Rarely does one meet such charming people who give their friendship freely and who are kind without any reservations. I persuaded him to come here with me for I felt that you too like me, would find him a wonderful example of the creator's great genius. His beauty is unrivalled; he is indeed an example of this mortal world outdoing the divine in every way. He is the cynosure of all eyes; he is one in whom all the arts, all felicity, all wealth and all that is civilized in human beings have come together. I have told him a lot about you. So do not be bashful because you have never seen him before. Do not be wary that he is a stranger and do not entertain any doubts about his good conduct. Please treat him as you treat me for he is your friend too.' When Mahashveta introduced him thus to Kadambari, Chandrapida bowed to her in salutation.

As she looked at the bowing Chandrapida out of the corners of her long eyes, those eyes shed copious tears of joy; her moonlight brilliant smile spread and lit up everything; one of her eyebrows arched up as if instructing her head to reward the dear man by returning the salute. Her hand went up to her languid face to cover the beginning of a sensuous yawn. The emeralds on her rings cast a dark green shadow on her fingers so it appeared as if she were merely carrying the tambula to her mouth. Chandrapida's image fell all over her body awash with perspiration. As she scratched the ground with her toenail the anklets sounded softly as if calling out to Chandrapida; and when his reflection fell on her shining toenails it appeared as if he had responded to that call. One could see his image in between her breasts as if her heart eager to see him had rushed out and brought him over close to itself. All the women present were stealing a look at him out of the corners of their eyes; the pupils of their eager eyes rolled like the roving bees on the flowers on their ears, as though they wished to slip out of the corners altogether, such was the force of their unbridled curiosity.

Kadambari returned Chandrapida's salute in a flurry and then went and sat down on the divan next to Mahashveta. In the meantime the attendants had hurriedly brought over a gold-legged seat covered with a white silk spread and placed it near the head of the divan for Chandrapida to sit on. After he sat down, at a hint from Mahashveta who guessed her friend's mind, the pratiharis silently signalled the musicians to stop playing their instruments; at once the veena, the flute and the singing bards, all fell silent. In the meantime the attendants had brought water with which Kadambari herself washed Mahashveta's feet and wiped them. Kadambari's very dear and trusted friend Madalekha, her equal in everything, insisted on washing Chandrapida's feet despite the prince's protests.

Mahashveta turned to Kadambari sitting next to her on the divan. She lovingly rearranged the flowers on Kadambari's ears and tidied the front locks disturbed by the breeze from the chamara. She then laid an affectionate hand on her shoulder and enquired after her health. Kadambari admitted rather reluctantly it seemed, to her well being as though she had feelings of guilt for living at home in comfort while her dear friend was going through the rigours of life in the forest. Her eyes regarded Mahashveta with sadness over her plight. Yet every now and then those eyes with their speckled pupils, as though pulled away forcibly by the one with the floral arrows would rest on the prince and find it difficult to move away from him. The tears of joy welling up in her eyes blurred his figure and therefore made her sad.

After a while when Kadambari sought to offer tambula to her Mahashveta advised her: 'Dear friend, the right thing for all of us to do now is to extend a proper welcome to our guest Chandrapida who has come for the first time. Do please offer him tambula.' But Kadambari with her head bent and her face averted a little said slowly and indistinctly, 'Dear friend, I feel bashful as I'm not used to such civilities. Here take this tambula and offer it to him yourself.' But Mahashveta demurred insisting that it was up to Kadambari to perform the rites of welcome. However, it was a while before she took herself in hand sufficiently to do her duty as the hostess, somewhat with reluctance, as though she were a rustic unused to such social graces. Her eyes were still fixed on Mahashveta; her body trembled, her eyes showed distress and her chest heaved with deep sighs. She seemed afraid that she would drown in her own perspiration. She was on the point of swooning, hit by Manmatha's arrows. The hand extended to give the prince the tambula seemed to beg for support; in the fear of losing her balance she seemed to want to cling to him.

Chandrapida held out his naturally pink palm that had now become calloused with the marks of the bowstrings, to receive the tambula. As he extended his hand that longed to touch the hand of Kadambari, all his five senses as well, like yet another set of five fingers driven by passion sought to reach her. As for Kadambari all sorts of erotic feelings invaded her as though impelled by curiosity to see her newly but effortlessly attained blandishments. Her blindly outstretched hand holding the tambula seemed to seek Chandrapida's hand; as it trembled and the armlet tinkled it appeared as if the hand by itself, were carrying on a conversation with him. As perspiration flowed out of her she seemed to be giving herself away to him using her own perspiration as water to sanctify the gift. She seemed to say, 'Please accept this servant offered to you by Manmatha'. When she finally gave the *tambula* to him she seemed to give away her very life to him. She seemed to say: 'From now onwards I am in your hands.' Her gem-inlaid bangle slipped down when she drew her hand back, but she was unaware of it. She picked up another plate of tambula and offered it to Mahashveta.

All of a sudden a myna appeared from somewhere. Her feet were yellow like the filament of the white lily, her face was the shape of a champa bud and her dark blue feathers were the colour of the petals of a blue lily. She seemed to have been put together with flowers. A slow-footed parrot followed her; his neck was a three-toned circular rainbow. He had a coral red beak and emerald green feathers. The myna approached Kadambari and blurted out in anger. 'Oh princess Kadambari! Why do you allow this wretched bird, this arrogant false lover to pester me? He is harassing me so. If you continue to disregard my plea then I swear on your lotus feet I shall put an end to myself.' Kadambari smiled; not knowing the story behind it, Mahashveta asked Madalekha, 'What is the myna saying?'

Madalekha replied. 'This myna is Kalindi and she belongs to Princess Kadambari. The princess got her married to this parrot called Parihasa and so now this myna is his wife. But this morning the myna saw the parrot chatting away with Tamalika, Princess Kadambari's *tambulakarankhavahini* when she was alone. Since then the myna is angry and jealous. She does not go near the parrot, does not talk to him, does not touch him, and does not even glance at him. Although we have tried our best to pacify her she has so far refused to relent.'

Chandrapida's cheeks twitched in amusement. He laughed softly and said, 'Indeed this story is making the rounds everywhere. Inside the palace it is spreading from ear to ear

with all the servants talking about it. And people outside too
are at it. In all the directions everybody is discussing only this
matter. We too have heard that ever since this parrot Parihasa
got infatuated with Devi Kadambari's tambula holder Tamalika,
he has become unaware of even the passing of days. Let this
scoundrel abandon his own wife and cling to that shameless
woman. But is it proper on the part of Devi Kadambari not to
make this flirtatious evil-minded attendant mend her ways? For
having given away poor Kalindi to such a wicked bird Devi
Kadambari may justifiably be accused of having no affection at
all for the myna. What can poor Kalindi do, now that she has
been made to share her husband with another? This has always
been the prime cause of a woman's anger and estrangement and
the greatest insult imaginable. But one thing is clear and that is
this myna is of a very strong mind. In spite of this great misfortune
leading to such terrible disenchantment she has not swallowed
poison, nor walked into fire, nor is she fasting unto death. In
spite of having been so grievously wronged she seems willing to
be wooed by him, she seems ready to make up with him. But
that is enough talk about her now. She has to be avoided. Who
will talk to her now. Who will condescend to call her by name.
And who will even look at her.' The palace women were in splits
of laughter when they heard this banter from Chandrapida.
Kadambari too laughed.

Hearing Chandrapida's witty speech at the expense of the
birds, the parrot Parihasa got very angry indeed. He said hotly,
'You villainous prince! This myna here is very intelligent. Neither
you nor anyone else for that matter can deceive her, thinking
she is just a scatter-brained female. She is shrewd having lived in
the palace all these days. Do not think you can make her the
butt of your teasing remarks, your twisted puns. Stop trying to
put one over this one. It does not become you. This myna here
who can talk so sweetly, knows whom to get angry with, whom

to be gracious to; she knows the time, the place and the occasion for anger and propitiation.'

At this juncture the kanchuki came in and addressed Mahashveta, 'May you be blessed with long life. King Chitraratha and queen Madira would like to see you.' Mahashveta, getting up to go to them, turned to Kadambari and asked, 'Friend! Where shall Chandrapida stay?' Kadambari thought to herself laughingly, 'Are not the hearts of all these women spacious enough for him to stay?' Aloud she replied, 'Dear friend Mahashvete! Why do you ask? Don't you know that from the time I saw him he has conquered me body and soul. Of what significance then are this palace, this wealth and these attendants, all of which are his to command. Let him stay where his fancy takes him, or where you wish him to be.' Mahashveta replied, 'In that case he can stay in the pavilion made of precious stones on the kridaparvatha right inside the antapura garden, close to your palace.' Then she left to meet the gandharva king and queen. Chandrapida too then took his leave. Accompanied by musicians, poets, dice players, painters and the women detailed by Kadambari to take care of his needs he went to the pavilion on the kridaparvatha with Keyuraka showing the way.

As for the gandharva princess, she dismissed most of her women and went up to the top of the palace with her confidential attendants who stood discreetly away from her and tried to divert her as she flung herself on her couch. She felt as if she had just recovered from a loss of consciousness. And she became aware of an acute sense of shame.

Her natural bashfulness chided her. 'What have you got involved with now?' Her sense of modesty censured her. 'Oh gandharva princess! Does this behove you?' Her budding adolescence however mocked, 'Where has your innate childish nature gone now?' The sense of her own greatness and exalted position condemned her. 'This is not the path that well-born girls take.' Her sense of propriety threatened her. 'Ill-behaved one! Uphold decency and decorum. You have been laid low by Madana.' The tradition of the high-born cried out to her in anguish, 'You have abandoned me.'

Kadambari's mind was in turmoil. 'What have I gone and done now, exhibiting such weak-mindedness in the delusion of love. Did I pause to consider that he is totally unknown to me? Did it even occur to me that the world might think me frivolous? So shameless have I been. I was ever so stupid that I never found out his mind on this matter. Whether he liked my appearance or not, I never ascertained. I have simply rushed headlong into it with hardly a demur over possible repudiation, undeterred by possible scandal and with no thought spared for Mahashveta's suffering. I was so stupid and so totally unaware of my surroundings that I failed to realize that my friends and the attending women standing close to me would notice my condition. Even a thick-headed person would have noticed such gross misconduct; can there be any doubt that Mahashveta, experienced in the ways of love and my friends, all worldly wise and full of insight, did. Even the servants in the women's apartments are all so very shrewd that they too would have missed nothing.

Is it not better for me to die rather than live on in shame? What would my parents say when they come to hear of this shameful episode? Or the rest of the gandharva world? Oh what shall I do now? By what ruse shall I cover up this slip of mine? To whom shall I reveal this infatuation brought on by my senses? What happens to the vow that I first took in front of Mahashveta herself and later reiterated in my message sent through Keyuraka? I do not know what has brought this trickster Chandrapida to me, my bad deeds or contrary Fate, or the wicked god of death or something else. All I know is some stranger never seen before, nor thought of, never even conceived in imagination has come here to ruin me. At first sight I have been bundled up and donated to him by my senses. Manmatha has imprisoned me in a cage made of his arrows and offered it to him. Love has made me a slave to him. My own heart, for the price of his virtues has sold me over to him, making me a commodity as it were.'

At this point Kadambari's defences collapsed completely. Possessed by a frenzy of love she sprang up and rushed to the window from where she kept gazing at the kridaparvatha. It would be more accurate to say that she saw with her memory rather than with her eyes because her eyes had once again become curtained with tears of joy. She drew his picture in her mind for fear that the perspiration dropping out of her fingertips would mar the likeness painted with a brush. She embraced Chandrapida with her heart rather than with her chest lest the hair standing on its edge on her body came between them. Her own heart became a messenger of love to him for she would not brook the delay of engaging an attendant with the mission.

⟶36⟵

Chandrapida entered the house made of gems with the same ease and facility as he had entered Kadambari's heart. There he threw himself on a stone divan covered with a carpet and piled high with cushions on either side. Keyuraka placed the prince's feet on his own lap as the young women who had accompanied him sat down in their appointed places. Chandrapida's restless mind went back to his meeting with Kadambari. He wondered. 'All those captivating blandishments of the gandharva princess, are they merely natural to her, traits that she had been born with perhaps? Or have they been produced unsolicited, by Makaraketu for my sake? Was it under his influence that she directed sidelong glances full of love at me, with narrowed eyes as though the pollen from the floral arrows troubled her? When I looked at her she bashfully covered herself with the lustre of a smile, like a piece of white silken cloth. And she kept her face slightly averted from me as though eager to have my reflection fall on her mirror-clear cheeks. And I saw how her hands trembled when she extended the tambula to me.'

But then he reasoned. 'How often do we see the human mind fall easy prey to a thousand fancies that have no basis in reality. Youthful ardour devoid of all discrimination deceives. A mild interest shown is exaggerated. A diseased eye magnifies a mere speck of dirt into something big. A mere drop of oil falling into the water spreads widely. Like a poet giving free rein to his imagination there is no knowing what fancies an ardent youthful mind would weave around the object of its fascination. The mind of a young man under the influence of Manmatha is like a paintbrush in the hands of an expert painter; there is nothing that it cannot draw. Like a dream, the desires of the young take forms that are not real. Like the feather brush of the magician the young mind creates impossible apparitions of hope.'

All at once he seemed to come to a decision. 'Why do I torture myself unnecessarily? If the bright-eyed one has really fallen for me, that very same Manmatha who gives his favours without being asked, would soon reveal this too and remove all doubts in the matter.'

Then he mingled with the women present; he played dice, made music on the veena and *panava,* discussed various points regarding the different notes and narrated pleasant tales. After a little while eager to see the garden he came out of the mansion and climbed to the top of the kridaparvatha.

Kadambari, still at the window saw him go up to the top of the hill. She left the window at once and under the pretext of looking out for Mahashveta, who had still not returned, went up to the terrace of her palace, her heart all in a flutter. There on the terrace she stood under a moon-white, golden-handled umbrella, which protected her from the rays of the sun. Four of her attendants fanned her with foamy deer hair fans. Kadambari would every now and then, playfully grasp the tops of the fans, or clutch the stem of the umbrella. She would place her hands on Tamalika's shoulders or embrace Madalekha. She would pirouette and her upper garment would fly up revealing the three lines on her abdomen. She would every now and then rest her cheek on top of the pratihari's staff. Or she would strike her attendants playfully with the lotus that had slipped off her ear; and if they tried to run away she would give them chase laughing all the while. Or she would place the tambula on her lips with a steady hand. All the time she kept shooting glances at Chandrapida and he too looked back at her. Much time was spent in this fashion and Kadambari was quite unaware of its passing.

Then the pratihari came and announced the return of Mahashveta and Kadambari descended from the terrace. Although she had lost interest in her toilette, due to the insistence of Mahashveta she went about her daily routine. Chandrapida too had his bath with the assistance of Kadambari's attendants, performed his daily worship on a clean stone surface and had his food right there in the pavilion on the kridaparvatha.

— 37 —

There was on the eastern part of the kridaparvatha an emerald slab green like the harita bird, moist with the spray from the foaming mouths of the ruminating deer and darkly lustrous like the still waters of the river Yamuna; bowers of creepers surrounded it. Close to it was a music pavilion where the peacocks danced. After finishing his meal Chandrapida came out and sat on the slab and looked around.

All of a sudden a splendid white lustre seemed to pour fluidly over the brightness of the day. It was as though sunlight was being drunk away by a ring of lotus stalks. The earth seemed to be flooding over with the waters of the milky ocean. Liquid sandalwood seemed to shower over the quarters. It was as though the heavens were being smeared with nectar. Chandrapida was wonderstruck. 'Has the lord of the herbs, the moon risen betimes? Or is it merely the fountain houses throwing a thousand streams of white water all around? Could it be on the other hand the wind-scattered white spray of the celestial river descending to the earth?'

In the meantime Madalekha was making her way to the kridaparvatha in the company of several women. One of them held a white umbrella over her head; two others fanned her from either side. Kadambari's pratihari was with them carrying in her left hand, in addition to her usual cane staff the circular shell inside a coconut containing sandalwood paste and covered with a piece of wet cloth. Her right hand was given to Madalekha. Keyuraka at the head of the procession bore in his hands two pieces of extraordinarily fine silken cloth, made of kalpalata; they were of such fine texture that they could have been blown away by the breath of a person; and they were pure like the moulted skin of a snake. Tamalika followed Madalekha carrying a garland of *malati* flowers.

Taralika, walking close to Madalekha, held a box covered with a piece of white cloth. There lay within the box a necklace, slender like the stalk of the lotus growing from the navel of Narayana. Did the milky ocean owe its whiteness to this necklace? It was as white as the foaming nectar thrown around by the whirling Mandara. Was it really a gathering together of the broken phases of the moon? Or had the reflections of the star clusters been picked up from the waters of the ocean and strung together? Had it been fashioned out of bits of autumnal clouds, or out of the sages' hearts surrendered to the beauty of Kadambari? It seemed like the very life force of moonlight yet it was a rival to the moon. It shimmered like the water drops slipping from the petals of the lotus. Its rays lit up the cloudless skies like the autumnal moon. Like the streams of the Mandakini it was redolent of the fragrance of the breasts of celestial women. It poured lustre all around.

Chandrapida realized later that it was this necklace, whose brilliance had surpassed the splendour of the moon and the lustre of the day that had been the cause of the sudden brightening he had observed. He immediately rose from his seat and welcomed the approaching Madalekha courteously. Madalekha sat down on the emerald slab for a minute and then rose and herself applied the sandalwood paste held by the pratihari, on Chandrapida's body. She then draped around him the fine pair of white garments carried by Keyuraka. She decorated his hair with the garland of malati flowers. Finally she took the necklace in her hand and addressed Chandrapida thus: 'Prince! Who can withstand the charm of your beauty, which sets at naught all varieties of beauty. It is however, your modesty that encourages those thus charmed by you to approach you. Is there even one whose heart you do not command by this magnificent form of yours? Is there at all anyone in whom your sweet ways have not generated feelings of friendship? Who indeed would not be comforted by your innately gentle qualities and manners?

'Prince! In a way your benevolence deserves censure because it emboldens us and at the very first encounter inspires confidence. But then if it were not for that all dealings with people of your greatness would appear improper. Mere conversation would be an insult; praise would seem a display of one's talents in composing. To show affection would reveal a lack of wisdom, as friendship is possible only among equals. Even entreaty would appear as presumption and the giving of gifts would look like an insult.

'Indeed, prince, what can one give to someone who has taken away your very heart? What does one give to the lord of one's very life? What can be done in return for the mighty favour of your visit here? The sight of you has granted us life's fulfilment; what favour equalling that can we do in return?

'By offering a gift such as this Kadambari only shows her friendship to you, she does not flaunt her wealth. For is it not an accepted fact that the wealth of the virtuous belongs to all? So there need be no discussion on the matter.

'Let us leave wealth alone for the time being. What Kadambari wants to convey to you is that by becoming the servant of someone like you she does not run the risk of reproach. By giving herself to you she does not get cheated. And she has no regrets even after offering her very life to you. The greatness of the wise rests in being generous to those who have genuine affection for them and accept their offerings. The giver of gifts feels more bashful than those that ask for them. Truly does Kadambari feel as if she were causing you an offence by sending this hara to you.

'This necklace is called *sesha* for the simple reason it was the one left over from all the brilliant gems and jewels that came out of the ocean when it was churned for nectar. Cherished by the lord of the ocean for this very reason, it was given by him to Varuna who in turn gave it to Chitraratha the gandharva king. The king gave it to Kadambari. And she, being of the mind that only your splendid body is fit to be adorned by this jewel, has sent it to you.

'Although men like you adorned by their own great qualities do not generally care to bear the weight of the jewels held in value by others, the affection of Kadambari should be a good reason for you to wear this. Did not the Lord Sharngapani accept that piece of stone kaustubha as it too had come out of the ocean along with Lakshmi, like a brother being born out of the same womb? But let me emphasize, Narayana does not surpass you, nor does the kaustubha excel even slightly this sesha nor for that matter can Lakshmi be even a close second to Kadambari as far as beauty is concerned. She certainly deserves the honour of your wearing the jewel. Nor is she unfit to receive your affection. Should you repudiate her affection, there is no doubt Kadambari would take Mahashveta to task with a thousand words of censure for having formed a friendship with one so cruel and then give up her life. Mahashveta herself understanding the importance of this gift has sent her own friend Taralika to bear the necklace to you along with this message. You should not even entertain the thought of repudiating Kadambari's first affectionate overture.' Madalekha then took the necklace and placed it around his chest where it looked like the stars encircling the golden mountain.

Overwhelmed Chandrapida replied. 'Madalekhe! What can I say? You are the expert. You know how to make people accept gifts. You grant no opportunity for a reply. You are indeed peerless in using words. You silly girl! I am no longer my own man really. It is no longer up to me to accept or reject anything. My freedom has disappeared. Your kindness has made me your servant and you are free to employ me in any fashion you choose, to make me do what I like or what I do not like. Devi Kadambari is so warm and gracious that there can be none, including the most discourteous, who would remain impervious to her charm.' Chandrapida continued to talk about Kadambari and her qualities, and it was only after a very long time that he bade farewell to Madalekha.

~38~

Madalekha had not gone too far on her way back when Kadambari, eager to see Chandrapida who had returned to the kridaparvatha, like the moon rising over Udayagiri, climbed up again to the terrace of her palace. The prince looked quite splendid with the sandalwood paste, the new silk utthariya and of course the brilliant necklace on his chest. She had dismissed all her attendants and had dispensed with all the insignia of her position as the gandharva princess, such as the staff, the umbrella and the chamara. Only Tamalika accompanied her. Once on the terrace, she charmed Chandrapida with her various graceful amorous gestures.

Now she would place her left hand on her hip, and stretch out the right hand as though to catch hold of the utthariya flying in the wind. She would stand still in that pose with her gaze fixed and unmoving. Now she would yawn and would quickly raise her hand to cover her mouth as though afraid, the name Chandrapida would slip out. When the wind took the utthariya away she would fold her arms over her breasts; was it to cover herself or was she giving him the signal that she was eager to embrace him? She would remove the flowers from her hair, hold them in both her hands and raise them to her face; was she smelling the flowers or saluting him with folded hands? Again and again would she trip over the flowers spread on the ground for decoration and her trembling hand would seem to tell him her agony of being the object of Kama's arrows. The golden girdle would slip down and fall around her feet impeding her tread, as though Manmatha had chained her to be delivered to Chandrapida. Her fine silk utthariya would very often trail the ground having slipped with the movement of her thighs and then she would try, with just one side of it to cover her breasts. Her tresses coming undone would fall on her shoulders and she would gather them up again and again with hands that would soon tire with the effort. Her shy smile brightened her cheeks. Several emotions played on her face as she shot sidelong glances at him.

In the meantime, with the sun drawing in his rays, the day was coming to an end. Pushan, the life-giver of the lotus, the emperor of all the worlds, turned red, with red-hot passion for the lotus enshrined in his heart. The skies turned russet-hued as though the anger-reddened eyes of the women waiting for the lovers who did not turn up at the end of the day cast their redness on them. The lotuses closed and the lotus field dimmed. While the white lily fields brightened, the skies reddened and the face of the night darkened.

Soon the sun set in a blaze of red rays that revealed his passion for the beauteous day and his longing for reunion with her. Or was it the ocean of love in Kadambari's heart flooding over and drenching the world of men in russet twilight? Soon night spread with the dark lustre of the tamala, like smoke issuing out of a thousand womanly hearts set on fire by Manmatha mixed with their own tears of longing. When it became so dark that one could not see the other, Kadambari descended from the terrace and Chandrapida too climbed down the kridaparvatha.

Very soon, as if propitiated by the blooming white lilies that caught at his ray-feet, the moon rose. There was a red lustre that accompanied his rise; surely it was the alakhta on Rohini's feet that had stained him when she kicked him in love sport. The young moon carefully stole around the sleeping lotuses in the fear of waking them. Loved by one and all, the delight of all eyes, the moon spread blessedness all around. Once this white umbrella of Manmatha's sovereignty, this ivory earring of Dame Night had risen, the world itself appeared as if carved out of ivory. Chandrapida lay down on a translucent pearl-like stone seat, cool, as it had been washed with white sandalwood water, and decorated with white *sinduvara* flowers. Nearby was a pond, whose white waters appeared in the white moonlight as if made of white lilies. On the wave-washed white steps of the pond a swan pair was asleep in the gentle breeze, while elsewhere on the banks the separated chakravaka pair was calling out to each other.

As he rested, Keyuraka appeared and said, 'Devi Kadmbari has come to see your lordship'. Chandrapida got up in a hurry and saw Kadambari approaching. She had done away with all her royal insignia and most of her jewellery. She merely wore a single strand of pearls around her neck. Her slender creeper-like body was white with the application of sandalwood essence. On just one ear she wore a leaf-like ivory ornament, while both ears were adorned with white lily petals. Her moon-white silken garments were of the fibre of the *kalpa* tree. In her charming apparel suitable for the hour she appeared as a goddess noble enough to command the moon. Love had made her soft, tender and delicate. When she came near him she sat down on the ground as an ordinary woman. Immediately Chandrapida followed her example and sat down on the ground, despite Madalekha's entreaties that he remain seated on the stone slab.

When everyone was seated Chandrapida thought for a while and said, 'Devi! When I have been won over by a mere glance from you and when I am ready to be your servant with no need even for conversation what can I say about this great honour now? However minutely I scan myself I do not see even a small glimmer of merit that might justify in some measure, this graciousness on your part. You are so artless and charming and so utterly devoid of arrogance that your benevolence and courteousness extend even to newly recruited servants like me. Does Devi Kadambari think that I'm so awkward that I can be won over only by such a great show of courtesy and politeness? In fact I consider your attendants fortunate because you command them. Why do you show me such respect? This body of mine is for service to others; this life is insignificant. I feel ashamed to offer this body and this life to you who have come here to me. Still, here they are. This body, this life and these senses of mine, out of these please accept what you consider the noblest or the best and by so doing, confer honour on it.'

At this speech Madalekha protested. 'Prince! You are distressing Kadambari with all these fancy sentiments. What is the use of saying all this? She has accepted all this without your having to utter them. Why go on again and again, which does not serve any purpose but only causes doubts in her mind.'

She then changed the subject and asked about Chandrapida's family, his father and mother and Arya Shukanasa as well. What kind of a city was Ujjayini and how far was it from Hemakuta? Was Bharatavarsha, the world of the mortals, beautiful? The visitors stayed on for a very long time talking of many things. Before retiring for the night Kadambari ordered Keyuraka to sleep next to Chandrapida; she appointed some attendants to look after his needs. Then she left to go up to the terrace of her palace where she lay down on her bed placed under a white silk awning.

Chandrapida too lay down on that stone slab. His mind dwelt on Kadambari's loveliness, her complete lack of arrogance and her enigmatic personality. He thought of Mahashveta's spontaneous affection for him, Madalekha's goodness, the nobility of all the attendants in general, and the prosperity of the world of the gandharvas. His mind dwelt with pleasure on the unsurpassed loveliness of the world of the kimpurushas. With Keyuraka pressing his feet the night seemed to pass in a minute for Chandrapida.

~39~

The moon, the lord of the stars, having remained awake the whole night gazing at the sleeping form of Kadambari, was now overcome with sleep, and began to descend from the sky, through the tala and the tamala trees and the groves of *kadali* in the woods along the shores of the ocean, cooled by the gentle breeze blowing over the waves. The moonlight faded, as if the hot sighs of the women who had to leave their lovers at the approach of day, had dulled its rays. Lakshmi, who had spent the night in the interior of the white lily, now sprang into the lotus, as if she too, in the grip of Madana, had become eager to see Chandrapida.

The night was almost over; the lamps in the homes grew pale and faint as though in yearning memory of the sensuous women waving the lilies on their ears to beat the flames out in bashfulness during the night of love. A light early morning breeze like the tired breath of Kama exhausted with having discharged his arrows all night long, started blowing, wafting the fragrance of the flowers. The stars losing their lustre took refuge in the bowers of Mandaragiri out of fear as it were, of the impending calamity that awaited them at the first light of the sun. In due course the sun rose, appearing like a red globe. Chandrapida got up from the stone slab and performed his morning rites. Having taken tambula he said to Keyuraka, 'Please go and see if Devi Kadambari is up and if she is then find out where she is.'

Keyuraka returned with the information that Kadambari was with Mahashveta in the courtyard of a palace called Mandara. Chandrapida at once hurried over to see the gandharva princess. He found them both in the midst of women ascetics of various persuasions. There were those with the mark of the sacred ash on their foreheads whose hands were moving the rosary, ascetics, who had taken the Pashupatha vows and were clad in garments dyed red with some mineral. There were others who wore garments the colour of the mature bark of the tala tree and were Buddhist sanyasinis. There were ascetics clad in white clothes, whose breasts were tightly bound and who wielded a white cloth as a fan. Some women had piled up their hair in a topknot and wore a girdle of munja grass; they had with them the skin of black buck, bark garments and a stick. All of them with marks of celibacy on them were chanting praises to Triambaka, Ambika, Kartikeya, Vishnu, Vasudeva, the Buddha, Mahavira and Prajapati.

Mahashveta was seen honouring the respected ladies of the antapura and the gandharva king's senior kinswomen who had come to see her. She greeted them, bowed to them and talked to them sweetly after making them sit next to her. While the kinnara pair played a delectable *tana* on the flute, the sweet-voiced daughter of Narada read that most blessed of scriptures, the *Mahabharata,* with Kadambari listening attentively.

Chandrapida approached them and bowed and sat down on a seat on the platform. He looked at Mahashveta for a while and smiled slightly with tremulous cheeks. Mahashveta, understanding at once what Chandrapida had in mind, smiled in return and said to Kadambari, 'My friend, Chandrapida is so moved by your qualities, like the chandrakanta stone melting in the moonlight, that he cannot speak out what is in his mind. No doubt the prince wants to leave as he has left behind his vassal princes who must be worried about him, not knowing where he might be. The bond between you two will surely thrive till the end of time, even though distance may separate you, like the lotus and the sun, the *kumuda* and the moon. So allow him now to take your leave.'

Kadambari replied, 'The prince is the master of me as well as mine including all my attendants. The question of giving permission does not arise at all.' Then she turned to the gandharva boys and ordered them to accompany Chandrapida to his own land. Chandrapida rose and first saluted Mahashveta and then spoke to Kadambari. Captivated by her eyes full of love for him he said with feeling, 'Devi! What do I say? Those who say a lot are usually not believed. I shall only say that when you are dealing with your servants remember me too.' Then he left the antapura. All the women, who had been thoroughly charmed by his great qualities, went with him as far as the outer gate to see him off. Only Kadambari stayed back.

—40—

As soon as the women turned away Chandrapida mounted his horse brought over by Keyuraka and accompanied by the gandharva youths set out from Hemakuta. As he rode on, the daughter of Chitraratha filled his mind and became the object of his most ardent desires. He saw her everywhere, in all the directions. He saw her behind him, coming after him, her heart filled with unbearable agony over their separation. He saw her in front of him, blocking his way; he saw her up in the sky as though flung there by the force of the longing in her heart; he saw her, the doe-eyed one, on his own chest where she had come to sit, no doubt, to be better able to see his face.

Chandrapida soon reached the hermitage of Mahashveta where he saw his army camped on the banks of the Acchoda Lake, having found its way there by following the hoof marks of Indrayudha. He bade good-bye to all the young gandharvas who had ridden with him. Welcomed with warmth, joy and wonder by his army Chandrapida greeted all his vassals with the respect due to them. He spent the rest of the day in the company of Vaishampayana and Patralekha talking ceaselessly about his new friends Mahashveta, and Kadambari, of Madalekha, Taralika and Keyuraka.

Intense longing for the bright-eyed one filled Chandrapida and kept sleep away the whole night. The next morning when he entered the courtroom, his mind still dwelling on Kadambari, whom should he see but Keyuraka, being led in by the pratihari. Chandrapida cried out in joy 'welcome, welcome!' and embraced the gandharva youth, first with his affectionate glance, and only then with his outstretched arms as he ran towards him. He made Keyuraka sit close to him and eagerly asked after all his friends in Hemakuta. 'Is Devi Kadambari well with all her friends? Is the respected Mahashveta well?' His smile expressing his great love for all of them washed over Keyuraka, and anointed him as it were; Keyuraka felt his travel weariness disappearing with that smile of Chandrapida.

He bowed and replied. 'She is well now, she of whom you ask.' Then he took out a parcel wrapped with lotus leaves and tied with a thread of lotus stalk. Sandalwood paste was smeared over the parcel and a royal seal of rings made of very tender lotus stalks was fixed on it. A piece of wet cloth covered the whole parcel. Opening the seal Chandrapida saw yet another token of love sent by Kadambari.

In the parcel were juicy areca fruits with sprouts, emerald green in colour with their skin removed, betel leaves the colour of myna's cheeks, and camphor the size of the crescent moon on Hara's head and sandalwood paste outdoing musk in delightful fragrance.

Keyuraka then related his message. 'Red lustre showering through the gaps between her tender fingers, Kadambari touches her crest jewel with her hands joined over her head as she bows to you. Mahashveta enquires after you with a tight embrace. Madalekha bows to you with the moonlight lustre of her swinging crest jewel suffusing her forehead. With the tips of their *makarikas* rubbing the ground all the womenfolk bow to you. Tamalika touches the dust on your feet. Mahashveta addresses you thus. 'Those who have not met you, they are indeed fortunate. For those of us who have experienced your dew-cool moonlight like qualities, in your absence, the world seems to be made only of the hot rays of the sun. The people here do ardently wish for that day again, the one that has just gone by, a day comparable to the one when nectar appeared. With you gone away the city of the gandharvas is feeling low, like the day after a great festival. You know that I have given up everything, yet my heart has developed such an inexplicable affection for you that it wishes to see you again. Kadambari is far from well; she thinks only of your beautiful face, so like Manmatha's. She deserves to be honoured by your coming here again, for the respect shown by great people raises one's own esteem. You should bear with the inconveniences arising out of your acquaintance with people like us. It is only your good nature that emboldened me to send this improper message to you. We are sending this *seshahara* you had left behind in your bed.'

Having delivered himself of this message from Mahashveta, Keyuraka untied one end of his utthariya and took out the hara whose rays had all the while been escaping through the fine weave of the cloth, and was about to hand it to the chamara wielder.

'I have worshipped at the feet of Mahashveta and it is due to her blessing that Devi Kadambari bestows such great tokens of remembrance and grace on me who is but her humble servant,' said Chandrapida and he accepted the parcel and the hara himself and first placed them on his head. He then took the delightfully scented cool orpiment and applied it on himself; had the orpiment been made of the flow of loveliness from Kadambari's cheeks, out of the essence of her glowing smile, or out of her heart that had melted with love? He then put the hara around his neck. Accepting the tambula he placed his left hand on Keyuraka's

shoulder and walked towards the elephant called
Gandhamadana. There he himself picked up handfuls of dried
grass and threw them before the elephant. And as he made his
way towards the stables of his beloved horses he cast meaningful
glances at the attendants standing around him.

The pratiharis realized that the prince wanted to be left alone
with the visitor. They quickly dismissed all the servants and
prevented them from following him. Chandrapida, accompanied
by Keyuraka entered the stables. The stable-hands with their
eyes showing fear that they might be beaten up by the stable
guards hurriedly bowed and scrambled out. Chandrapida went
up to Indrayudha, rearranged the cloth on its back that had
slipped a little to one side and lifted and tucked away the
kungkuma-brown mane falling on his narrowed eyes, obstructing
the vision. Placing a foot on the wooden plank meant for
Indrayudha to rest his hoofs on and leaning on a wooden pillar
he asked Keyuraka eagerly, 'Keyuraka! Tell me all that happened
at the palace of the gandharva king after I left. How did the
gandharva princess spend the day? And Mahashveta? What did
Madalekha say? What was the talk among the attendants? And
what have you been doing? Did anything happen relating
to me?'

— 41 —

Keyuraka then related everything. 'Deva! Please listen. As
soon as you left, the antapura resounded with the tinkle
of the anklets of the young women who rushed behind you,
like drums announcing the departure of a thousand hearts going
along with you. Kadambari then climbed to the terrace with
her women and stood there gazing at your retreating figure, in
the dust thrown up by the speeding horses' hoofs. When you

disappeared from sight she rested her face on Madalekha's shoulders and brimming with love for you, flooded, as it were, the direction you took with the brilliance of her gaze. She remained on the terrace for a long time and then came down unhappily; she stopped for a while in her apartment, but restless she got up again and stepped out. Seeing her shaken state the bees hovering over the flowers spread on the ground seemed to buzz their warning to her to watch her step lest she trip. The cawing of the excited palace peacocks looking up at the stream of lustre flowing from her nails which they mistook for rain, annoyed her; and as she stretched her hand in irritation her bangles slipped down the birds' necks as though she were trying to silence them. Her hands held the palace creepers full of white blooms for support; but her mind sought strength by holding on to your innumerable virtues. By and by she made her way to that same kridaparvatha where your lordship had spent the day.

'"Here in this bower of creepers watered by this emerald fountain made in the shape of a crocodile, was where he rested, on this cool seat; it was on this spread of rocks, rough to the touch with the swarms of bees stuck to the surface drawn by the fragrance of the bath water, that he bathed; here on the pollen strewn shores of this mountain stream was where he worshipped the Lord, the trident wielder. It was yonder on that crystal seat that put the moon to shame that he had his food. And here on this pearl-like stone bench with marks left by sandalwood water was where he slept." As the attendants thus pointed out one by one your favourite spots, she kept gazing at the marks left by your stay.

'At the end of the day, coaxed by Mahashveta she partook of some food right there in the crystal pavilion, although she had no desire to eat. Then the sun set and the moon rose, and she still stayed there her body bathed in sweat, as though melting

away like the chandrakanta stone in the rays of the moon. Her
hands resting on her cheeks and her eyes narrowed she remained
for a while lost in thought. Then she rose and stepping heavily
as though she walked with difficulty she reached her bedroom.
There she threw herself on the bed. At once she began to toss
about with a severe headache. A fever too raged accompanied
by a terrible thirst. Seized with an indescribable longing she never
did close her eyes even for a moment; but remained awake and
spent the night in utter misery in the company of the night lamps,
the white lilies and the chakravaka pairs. In the morning she
called me and chided me for not having gone to find out if her
specially revered guest had reached safely.'

When Chandrapida heard this story he became impatient to
go to Hemakuta and calling out for his horse he left the camp.
Indrayudha was brought by the stable hands, all saddled and
ready to go. Chandrapida mounted his steed with Patralekha
climbing up behind him. He appointed Vaishampayana in charge
of the army camp and accompanied by Keyuraka riding a horse
of his own set out for Hemakuta. Arriving at Kadambari's mansion
he dismounted. Leaving the horse with the guards he entered
the palace with Patralekha, who was eager for her first glimpse
of Kadambari. As he hurried through the palace he learnt from
a eunuch that Kadambari was in the cool house at the foot of
the kridaparvatha, crowded with excited peacocks, near a well
in which lotuses grew thickly.

With Keyuraka showing the way he went through the palace
garden and came upon a lush emerald-green plantain grove, the
greenness of which seemed to turn the very rays of the sun the
colour of fresh grass, and with it the day itself a vivid green. In
the centre of this grove he saw the cool house blanketed with
closely strewn lotus leaves.

Chandrapida saw the women skilled in creating cool
conditions to relieve the fever of Kadambari come out of the

cool house. Their dripping clothes clung to them and they seemed clad only in the waters of the Acchoda. The lotus stalks that they carried in their arms, like ornaments rendered their limbs fair; on one ear they wore an ornament made of the interior petals of the ketaki more beautiful than ivory; tilakas of sandalwood decorated their foreheads and their faces thus made beautiful seemed to proclaim their conjugal bliss! They wore sandalwood tilakas on their cheeks as well. They had covered their breasts, slightly whitened with camphor powder mixed with drops of sandalwood water and decorated with a bakula garland, with lotus leaves. They carried fans in their hands, whitened by the constant contact with the sandalwood paste, with handles made of lotus stalks and the fan itself woven with threads drawn out of the stalks. For mitigating the heat they held umbrellas made out of bunches of long-stalked tender lotuses, white and blue lilies, lotus and plantain leaves. These women appeared to be made of the essence of coolness; they milled around like a gathering of water goddesses, like a community of autumnal seasons, like an assemblage of myriad ponds.

When they saw Chandrapida they fell at his feet and quickly led him into the cool chamber.

—42—

When led into the cool house Chandrapida stood on the threshold over which hung a *torana* of plantain leaves, and cast his eyes around. He saw platforms plastered with sandalwood paste, and fans made of strings of sinduvara flowers. Huge buds of mallika flowers had been made into garlands and hung. There were smaller garlands of clove shoots and sandalwood flowers. Flags made of strung white lilies were waving in the air. The pratiharis held lotus stalks in place of cane staffs and wore attractive floral ornaments; standing guard at the entrance they were like images of the spring season.

There were artificial rivulets flowing with sandalwood water. Pollen dust had been scattered on either side of these rivulets to give the appearance of sandy banks. Tamala shoots were planted thickly on the banks to create the impression of forests along the 'rivers'. On one side he saw crystal chambers whose walls were so transparent that their presence could be inferred only by touch. The crystal walls were awash with cardamom-scented water. On another side were the couches spread with red lotus blooms placed on platforms of red lead under moistened canopies fitted with red reed fans.

Filaments of the *shirisha* flowers had been used to create a meadow on which stood a fountain chamber of lotus roots. It had on top of it toy peacocks drenched with water sprays. Elsewhere one saw thatched cottages whose interiors were covered with the tender shoots of the jamun tree soaked in the sap of the mango tree. In yet another spot there was the tableau of a toy elephant herd stamping on golden lotuses.

There was a gold-plated platform, on which stood a well, filled with scented water; there was a water wheel on this well whose spokes were made of stout lotus stalks and the water pots it carried were fashioned with artificial ketaki leaves and strung together with threads drawn out of blue lily stalks. Fountains in the form of a ring of crystal ducks were spouting water; and there were paintings of rainbows and clouds done so realistically that the clouds actually seemed to be floating around. There were mechanical trees in beds made of powdered pearls and whose branches rained water drops ceaselessly. There were rows of revolving mechanical birds made of leaves, which shook their feathers periodically giving rise to a fine spray of water, like dew.

There were golden pots whose mouths were concealed by the leaves of the lotus plants growing from within. Garments

woven with lotus fibre were being scented with the hand-crushed
juice of the tender camphor shoots. On one side there were
women making umbrellas with the trunks of the plantain trees
and bunches of flowers tied to the top. A stone vessel was filled
with the cool juice of a medicinal herb and attendants were fanning
it with a fan made of lotus leaves to create a cool breeze. It was a
magically cool atmosphere created by the ingenuity of Kadambari's
attendants with cleverly invented devices to reduce her heat.

The central part of the cool house was therefore like the very
heart of Himavan. It was verily Varuna's pavilion for water sports.
It was like the ancestral abode of the divinities of the sandalwood
forest. It was the home of all the nights of the month of Magha,
wintry, dark and cool. It was the trysting spot of all the showers
of rain! This was the spot for the rivers to flow in to remove the
heat from their waters in summer. This was indeed the place for
the oceans of the world to repair to in order to shed the heat of
the *vadava* fire burning within. This was surely where all the
clouds congregated to heal the burns caused by the streaks of
lightning. Dinakara, the sun stayed away from the spot fearful
of being touched by the thousand cool sprays shot out by the
water mills. The wind tossed the plantain trees surrounding the
himagriha and it seemed as though they too trembled in the
cold. The buzzing of the swarms of bees excited by the fragrance
of all the flowers sounded as though teeth were chattering in the
cold. The creepers thickly surrounded by the bees seemed as if
they were covering themselves with dark blankets.

The excessive coolness both inside and outside the cool house,
that seemed to smear him in its almost solid intensity, affected
Chandrapida tangibly. It caused a momentary confusion in him
that his own mind might have been made of the stuff of the
moon, his senses of the stuff of the white lilies, his limbs of
moonlight, and his intellect of the stuff of the lotus stalks. The
sun's rays appeared as pearl garlands, sunlight as sandalwood,

the breeze as though made of camphor; time itself seemed as if made of the stuff of water and the three worlds of mist and spray.

— 43 —

Chandrapida saw Kadambari inside the chamber surrounded by all her friends, like Ganga encircled by all her tributary rivers in a cave on the side of Himavan. There was a small pavilion made of lotus stalks around which flowed an artificial 'river' of camphor water. Kadambari lay on a bed of flowers under the pavilion.

Her necklace, armlets, bangles, girdles, and anklets were all of lotus stalk, and seemed to keep her bound, as if at the command of a jealous Manmatha. And all the other gods too seemed to conspire to possess her, part by part, and thwart her union with her beloved. The sandalwood-whitened forehead seemed to reveal the mark of Chandra's touch. The ceaseless rain of tears was surely Varuna kissing her eyes. And it must be Vayu biting her lips as she panted and sighed. And who else could it be but Surya running riot over her hot-fevered limbs. Agni had seized her heart burning with passion.

A weakness had come over her as though her limbs were trying to run away from her to her lover following her heart. Her agitated breaths shook her body; the utthariya kept slipping away from her high breasts and it appeared as though her very beauty, afraid of being burnt in the fever was trying to flee. The reflection of the chamaras being swung on both sides fell on her lustrous breasts and created the illusion that they had grown wings to fly away to the lover. And as Kadambari placed her hands on her breasts it appeared as though she was trying to restrain them.

The fever raged and she would, over and over again put her creeper-slender arms around a cool stone figure; over and over again would she place a camphor doll against her burning cheeks and rub her feet against the coolness of an effigy made of sandalwood paste, as antidote to her torment.

The tender shoots adorning her ears fell on her luminous cheeks in the guise of a reflection and appeared to be kissing her with longing. The pearls on the necklace spread their rays all over her as though embracing her.

As her attendants watched Chandrapida's arrival they, one by one, duly reported his progress to their mistress. As for her, she looked at them with rolling eyes and cried out, 'Tell me, is he really here? Have you actually seen him? How far away is he still? Oh! Where on earth is he?' She uttered his name over and over again as she directed her questions to each and every one of her attendants present.

When her eyes, opened wide in her eagerness, caught sight of him still at a distance, the beautiful Kadambari tried to rise from her flower-strewn bed. But alas! Like a newly caught elephant tied to the post, Kadambari's stunned thighs restrained her and she found herself unable to move; then it was the bees swarming there on the flowers, seeing her difficulties, that seemed to pull her up. Her body trembled with the effort. Her upper garment slipped and she sought to clasp the rays from her pearl necklace instead, to her bosom. She placed her left hand on the polished stone floor as though to beg her own reflection for help. As she tried to get up her hair came undone and the effort of gathering it soaked her in perspiration. Her eyes were shedding tears of joy. She seemed to want to wash her cheeks of the pollen that had fallen on them from the flowers on her ears so that her lover's reflection might fall on them. With her head slightly lowered she rose from the bed. Her pupils pressing against the corners of her eyes locked themselves on to his face. The long gaze tried to pull him over to herself.

Chandrapida drew near and as before paid his respects first to Mahashveta and then bowed to Kadambari. She returned his salute and sat down again on the flower-scattered bed. In the meantime the pratihari had brought over a seat of gold with shining gem-inlaid legs. But Chandrapida kicked it aside and sat down on the ground. Then Keyuraka introduced Patralekha to Kadambari. 'Devi! This is Patralekha the trusted friend of Deva Chandrapida, and the carrier of his betel box.' Kadambari looked at her and mused, 'Prajapati has indeed a special love for the women of the human race.' As Patralekha bowed to Kadambari she called her to her side with affection and made her sit next to herself, while all her attendants stared at Patralekha with unabashed curiosity. Having taken an instant liking to Patralekha, Kadambari kept stroking her with great affection.

Chandrapida having accepted all the rites of hospitality from his hosts saw the state of distress the daughter of Chitraratha was in. Yet he was assailed with doubts. He thought to himself, 'I am so untaught in these matters that even now I am not confident that I am really the object of her love. Well, let me try to clear my doubts by skilful conversation.'

Aloud he said, 'Devi! I do know that it is passion that has brought on this intense and unrelenting fever and sickness. Oh beautiful one! I do know this for sure that this fever that is upon you cannot distress you as much as it distresses me. If I could relieve you of your agony by giving my body to you I would do so. I tremble merely at the sight of you trembling. As the floral arrows fell you, my heart too is felled. Your wasted arms are shorn of armlets and your eyes are lotus-red with the raging fever. Seeing you suffer thus your attendants too weep, and they too have removed their ornaments. Do put on your ornaments;

the young creeper looks lovely only when it is with flowers with the bees hovering over them.'

Young and innocent as she was, Kadambari, now under the tutelage of Manmatha did understand the full import of his words; yet unable to comprehend that her dearest wishes had found such complete fulfilment she merely adopted a humble position and overwhelmed with shyness remained silent. And not merely silent, but distracted by the bees hovering around and darkening the face of Chandrapida, she smiled as well.

Then it was Madalekha who replied. 'Prince! What shall I say. This fever is virulent beyond description. Her body is exceedingly delicate as it is in the first bloom of youth. There is nothing that does not cause her distress. The cool tender stalks of the lotus plants burn like fire. Moonlight feels like the hot rays of the sun. And don't you see the pain produced in her mind by the breeze of the fan made of tender palm fronds? Her fortitude alone keeps her alive.' Kadambari mentally endorsed all that Madalekha uttered.

But Chandrapida was greatly confused with Madalekha's words. Madalekha had used the term *kumarabhavopetaya*; was Kadambari's condition due to her newly bloomed youth, her *kumarabhava* or to her feelings, *bhava* for him, the prince, *kumara*? Did Madalekha say 'Oh *Dhira,* the valiant one. *Tvameva,* you alone, are the cause of her being alive', or did she mean that it was her *dhiratvam,* her strength of mind, that kept her alive? He became unsure of himself and turned to Mahashveta and spent a long time in amiable conversation with her alone. Then he forced himself to bid farewell and left Kadambari's palace to return to the camp.

He was about to mount his horse when Keyuraka, who had followed him out, said, 'Deva! Madalekha requests you to leave Patralekha behind as Kadambari has taken a great liking to her

from the first sight of her, if you do not mind.' Chandrapida
replied somewhat bitterly: 'Fortunate indeed is Patralekha. She
is to be envied for having become the recipient of Devi's grace,
which is very difficult to come by. Please do take her in.'

Leaving Patralekha behind Chandrapida arrived at the army
camp.

—44—

As Chandrapida entered the army encampment his eyes
alighted first on the very familiar face of the confidential
royal messenger from Ujjayini. He reined in his horse immediately
and called out to him with pleasure. 'Anga! Are they all fine
back home, my father and my mother and all their attendants in
the palace?' The messenger Anga came forward bowed and said,
'My lord! Everybody is indeed well' and handed over the two
letters that he had brought over from the palace. The prince
placed them first respectfully on his head and then opening them
himself, read them one by one.

He read first, the one from his father. It said: 'May you prosper!
Tarapida of Ujjayini, the great king, the supreme lord of great
kings, a great devotee of Maheshvara, kisses the head of
Chandrapida, the abode of all wealth and whose forehead is
being kissed by the lustre rising from his crest jewel, and rejoices
in him. The subjects are all well. A long time has elapsed since
we saw you. Our heart longs for you. The queen and all the
ladies of the antapura are mightily saddened by this separation.
As soon as you finish reading this letter fix the time of your
return to the capital.'

The second letter was from Shukanasa giving expression to
the same sentiments. Vaishampayana too had received two similar
letters, which he at that very moment brought over to show to

Chandrapida. 'I shall do as my father orders,' stated Chandrapida. He mounted his horse immediately and gave orders to sound the drums of departure. Then he turned to Meghanada, the son of Balahaka, the commander of the great cavalry, who was standing at his side, with this order. 'You tarry a while and return with Patralekha. I am sure Keyuraka will escort her down to the army camp. Then you send the following message to Devi Kadambari through him. 'Human nature, incorrigible, incomprehensible and unresponsive to friendship, deserves to be condemned in all the three worlds. Falling prey to inconsistency, it fails to honour unselfish love. My going away now has seemingly reduced my friendship to something insincere and unreal. My protestations of love now appear as just clever figures of speech, my surrender to you a sweet ceremony devoid of sincerity. It seems to reveal a dichotomy between my words and my intent. Devi too, by giving her affections to an undeserving mortal,— she deserves only the divine,—has made herself open to censure. The graciousness shown to the undeserving not only does not bear any fruit; it ultimately gives rise to a sense of embarrassment.

As for me, my heart is not quite as heavy with shame with regard to Devi Kadambari as it is with regard to Mahashveta for having exposed her to Devi's displeasure. It is certain that Devi Kadambari will repeatedly chide Mahashveta for having favoured an unworthy person and heaped praises on him for his non-existent virtues.

But, what other course is open to me? Mighty as the command of my father is, it has power only over my body; the heart longing to stay in Hemakuta has already signed a document of surrender to Devi valid for thousands of janmas. Just as the army commander holds the movements of the forest tribal under his control, Devi's graciousness restrains me, but go I must to Ujjayini in obedience to my father's order. Whenever stories of cads are related, the rascal Chandrapida would be remembered. But you should never believe that Chandrapida, should he survive, could continue to live without the pleasure of serving at Devi's feet.

My respectful salutations to Mahashveta. I bow to Madalekha and give her a tight embrace, and to Tamalika as well. And greetings to all the attendants of Devi Kadambari. My salutation and farewell to Bhagvan Hemakuta.'

He then turned to Vaishampayana and appointed him the head of the army and advised him to lead the forces back by stages, without unduly straining the allies as well as the men. Then he mounted his steed followed by the officers of his cavalry who held up a forest of lances in readiness. The young horses neighed with excitement at the prospect of a march, a sound that shook Kailasa and the stamping hoofs almost rent the earth. His heart desolate at the separation from Kadambari, Chandrapida set his horse at a trot as he enquired of the king's messenger of the happenings at Ujjayini.

―45―

On his way back to Ujjayini Chandrapida traversed a huge desolate forest with trees of enormous girth. The path through the forest often skirted around piles of trees felled by the wild elephants. One came across huge heaps of grass, leaves and sticks put together, no doubt by the brave travellers to conceal themselves from the wild animals; it is however certain that many of them would have met their end, all the same, attacked by the fierce creatures. Carved figures of the goddess Durga found under the trees seemed to be guarding the forest.

Wells dug long ago, no doubt for the convenience of the travellers had not much water left in them now; and what little water was there, was muddy, discoloured and rancid smelling with rotting leaves. The ground around them was carpeted with the pollen of the *karanja* blossoms. The robbers infesting the

forest had tied rags around the branches of the trees growing
near the wells like flags marking their territory. Due to the
unavailability of good drinking water the route through this
area was never a favourite with the travellers.

There were of course mountain streams but they too had very
little water in them; their sandy shores were a dusky white with
drops of honey from the sinduvara. The travellers had dug wells
on the sandy soil no doubt in the hope of finding fresh water but
the scanty water found in these wells was equally muddy. These
wells and the dried riverbeds merely made the ground uneven in
the forest. From the crowing of the cock and the barking of the
dogs one could infer the presence of small meagre villages in the
midst of the densely growing trees on the shores of these streams.

Chandrapida rode through this forest for a whole day and at
sunset, when sunlight was the colour of the *bimba* fruit, arrived
at a place that had an abundance of tall trees such as the
kadamba, shalmoli, and palasha; all their branches had been
lopped off, and they were left standing with just a single cluster
of leaves growing right at the top, like umbrellas. The ground
was thickly plaited with the roots of such tree stumps. There
was also a cultivated field of ripened millet around which had
been built a fence of mature yellow bamboo. A scarecrow made
of grass was guarding the place from animals. It was in this
cultivated area separated from the forest that Chandrapida saw
from a distance, tied to the top of an ancient *rakthachandana*
tree, a pole on which were attached red tongues of banners;
freshly stained with rakthachandana and alakhta they resembled
juicy meat and new blood. It was also hung with shiny human
hair-like blackbuck tails for decoration. All this together looked
like freshly killed game. Above this a golden trishul, hung with
a sharp sounding bell on a chain of iron from one of its tips, and
from the other a chamara of the appearance of the mane of a
lion, was etched against the sky. The whole ensemble seemed to
be lying in wait for the flesh of the unwary traveller.

Chandrapida rode towards the flag and soon saw a shrine with the image of Chandika inside. The door to the shrine was made of ivory and appeared like a mass of ketaki shoots. Across the doorway there hung a torana, consisting of iron discs that looked like mirrors; they were framed in deer tails and had the appearance of a row of dark shabara faces with tawny hair. Facing the door was a collyrium-black stone platform on which stood the figure of an iron buffalo, which bore the hand marks of the devotees in red sandalwood paste. Had Yama been driving the buffalo himself with his blood-stained hands? The jackals thirsting for blood were often tricked into licking the red eyes of the buffalo thinking it was blood. There were floral offerings— red lotus, like the eyes of the buffalo, agasthya and kimshuka buds like the claws of the lion and the tiger stained with blood. There were also offerings that spoke of cruelty—a heap of curved deer horns 'sprouting' on one side, moist bits of tongue, like fresh shoots on the other; thousands of bloody eyes like blooms on one side, and a heap of severed heads, like fruits on the other, all indicating animal sacrifice.

In the courtyard grew a red ashoka tree on whose branches the red roosters had taken a permanent abode, in fear of the wild dogs, and made the tree appear in untimely bloom. The palm trees had dropped their head-like fruits as offering to the goddess; they were like goblins that had come thirsting for the blood of the sacrificed animals. All around in the dense groves, the plantains waving in the wind, seemed to sway, with feverish fear over their own safety having watched the blood sacrifices; the branch of the date trees too swung up like hair flying up in sheer fright; and the thorn on the *bilva* trees seemed like goose pimples appearing in the thrill of distress.

The courtyard, filled with the effluents of slaughter, reflected the russet evening sun and gave the impression that the sun might have fainted and fallen with the sight of all the killings.

Across the double interior doors was hung a garland of peacock necks tied with a cloth, stained by the smoking hanging lamps. A closely strung line of bells whitened with rice flour was also hung over the doorway. Lion's faces made of lead were fixed on both the doors the centres of which were implanted with huge iron spikes. The latch was of ivory.

Inside the shrine there was a platform on which rested the feet of the image of Devi. This platform was fully covered with a piece of cloth dyed in red alakhta juice. It seemed as if the life forces of all the creatures sacrificed there had fallen at the goddess' feet in surrender in the form of that red cloth. The place was sombre perhaps rendered so by the dark lustre of the instruments of slaughter, which seemed permanently to carry on themselves the aura of the killed blackbucks and the dark sheen of the hair of all the beheaded animals. The goddess seemed to be living in the nether world.

She was of terrible appearance; she was covered with the blood-red kadamba flowers offered for worship, which made her appear as if she were thrilling to the harsh beat of the drums that accompanied the bleat of the animals. Bilva patra and *sripala* stained in rakthachandana and strung alternately into a garland—it looked like a garland of infant heads—adorned her. She wore a gold diadem around her head. The shabara women had applied a tilaka in red sindur on her forehead. She had red pomegranate flowers on her ears which lent a flush to her cheeks. Her lips were reddened by the blood-red betel juice. The eyes were brown framed by anger-arched eyebrows. Her slender body was draped in safflower-stained silk cloth. She appeared as if she were ready to keep her tryst with Mahakala.

In the shrine there were goats with long beards, taking on the aspect of ascetics observing vows for the goddess; there were rats whose trembling mouths appeared to be intently uttering prayers; and there were black snakes—like ascetics clothed in blackbuck skins; with the brilliant red jewel on their heads they seemed to worship the goddess with lamps held on their heads. All around the raucous crows cawed as though they too were engrossed in singing the Devi's praises.

An old repulsive looking Dravida priest administered this shrine of Chandika. A mesh of twisted and knotted veins stood out prominently on his withered body giving the impression of a dried tree stump to which clung lizards and chameleons. Indeed he seemed to be the abode of all unloveliness; his body was entirely covered with pockmarks.

His matted locks wound round his ears and fell over his chest like a rudrakshamala. There was a growing tumour-like swelling in the middle of his dark forehead, a result of falling constantly on his face at the feet of Ambika. He had lost one eye by the application of medicated eyeliner, a bitter potion, given by some quack. His teeth protruded and every day he tried to push them back by brushing it hard with the juice of the bitter gourd. One arm had withered after he hit himself in the wrong place with a hot sacrificial brick to cure himself of some malady. His toes were raw with the constant rubbing of the silk cocoon, which he used to cover his feet with in order to protect them from the prickly kusha grass. By the ingestion of drugs and elixirs not prepared according to rules he had brought on himself fevers that attacked him periodically.

He wore a tilaka made of herbs with supposedly occult properties on his forehead in the hope of winning great wealth for himself, having been advised to do so, no doubt, by some ill educated *shramana*. He had in his possession a palm leaf manuscript, the characters written with smoked alakhta juice; it contained incantations for black magic. The Dravida priest was seized with the disease of greed, which at times gave rise to obsession with alchemy, the so-called technique of conversion of base metals like iron or copper into gold.

The priest had a fascination for gandharva girls it was said; it was also said that he was completely caught in the outlandish desire of learning incantations that could make him invisible. All the same he was arrogant, proud that he belonged to the Shaiva faith.

He had pretensions to music as well. He had with him a veena made of gourd that he would often play tunelessly, ill taught as he was. He would thus distress and eventually drive away the travellers. The whole day he would be humming some tune or the other sounding so much like the drone of the mosquitoes, shaking his head all the while. He would dance too at times, to a prayer song composed in his mother tongue in praise of Bhagirathi.

His brahmacharya was of the equestrian variety forced on him merely by the unavailability of women. He would therefore try to entice old women *sannyasins* come from other parts of the country by throwing love powders on their bodies.

He was generally hostile towards travellers and would do his best to prevent them from staying at the shrine; in the fight that ensued it was he who would get beaten on his back Mischievous children often teased him and when trying to drive them away he would stumble and fall on his face. He could not tolerate wise men from other parts of the country being honoured by the local people.

All the same he was a pitiable figure. Due to lack of education he spent his time in frivolous acts. He limped because he was lame; he could see only during the day as he had night blindness and he was hard of hearing and could converse only by means of signs. But he had a great appetite and ate a lot.

The numerous monkeys living in the forest around the temple, angered by the Dharmika's constant shaking of the trees for the fruits had scratched his nose so viciously that it was full of holes. As he went around gathering flowers for the shrine the disturbed bees in their thousands would attack his body quite mercilessly. Many were the times when the vicious black snake had bitten him as he slept in the unswept unclean temple. And as many were the times when he had fallen from the top of the bilva tree and had almost broken his head to pieces.

All his fasting and penance at the various shrines had borne him no fruit. Placed in such miserable circumstances he seemed to foster the various diseases that he had as if they were his own family. The follies that his manifold addictions had given rise to, he showed off like so many of his own offspring.

His possessions were few; a basket woven out of dried forest creepers for collecting the flowers, a hook fixed to a bamboo pole for plucking the flowers and a piece of black woollen cloth that served as his muffler which he was never seen without.

―46―

When Chandrapida came upon the shrine he decided he would spend the night at that very spot. He dismounted from his horse and entered the shrine and prayed to the goddess with devotion. He circumambulated the shrine, bowed again and then set about to explore the peaceful surroundings when he heard a loud voice shouting at him in anger.

As he looked around he caught sight of our Dravidian priest; in spite of his mental agony over Kadambari, Chandrapida burst out laughing. His men too were greatly amused at the sight of the priest and were about to start teasing him when Chandrapida quickly signed them to silence. Then he pacified the irate priest with sweet words who, mollified, at once shot questions at the prince wanting to know his place of birth, his caste, the nature of his education, his marital status and if he had any children, the size of his wealth, his age and the reason for his travel. In turn, when asked about himself he became extremely voluble and spoke at length, of his great valour, his great looks and his great wealth. Chandrapida was quite captivated by his volubility; it was a welcome diversion to his tormented mind. The priest was friendly and offered tambula to Chandrapida.

When night fell the princes in the retinue settled themselves under the trees. The bridles of the horses were removed and hung on the branches of the trees. Rolling on the ground and shaking the dust out of their manes the horses seemed to regain their spirits. Then they were washed; with water splashed on their backs their fatigue disappeared. They were fed and then tied to the lances planted on the ground.

Close to where the horses were tied, grass beds were prepared for the men. The timekeepers who were weary with all the travel and wanted to sleep changed their duty hours with others, who then took over the night watch. Several fires were lit in the encampment and their glow swallowed up the darkness; the night was almost like day. Chandrapida's bed had been prepared close to the place where Indrayudha was tied. He lay down on his bed and at once all his torment returned. He had no desire for conversation even with his very close friends and sent them all away. But sleep eluded him. His mind went again and again to the land of the kimpurushas. He thought of Hemakuta to the exclusion of everything else dwelling on the selfless affection of Mahashveta and yearning desperately for a sight of Kadambari whom he considered the only reason and reward of his existence. He longed for a discourse with Madalekha, a discourse that would be as delightful as it was free of arrogance. He wanted to see Tamalika again and daydreamed that Keyuraka had returned. He saw the himagriha in his mind's eye. Hot sighs escaped him. He fondled the sheshahara with intensified love. 'How lucky for Patralekha to have stayed back.' he thought.

Chandrapida spent a few days at that extremely lovely spot and then left for Ujjayini after donating a lot of wealth to the aged priest thus fulfilling abundantly all the lifelong yearnings and dreams of that old man.

—47—

Chandrapida entered Ujjayini unannounced and took the people of the city by surprise. Excited and overjoyed by the unexpected arrival of their prince the subjects joined their hands over their heads in obeisance and welcome, their folded hands appearing as a thousand lotus blooms offered in worship. Chandrapida acknowledged their greeting and rode into the city.

As he neared the palace, the servants having sighted him vied with each other to be the first to convey the good news to the king. They called out to their king, 'Deva! Deva! Chandrapida has returned!' When the father heard the cry he rose at once. In the fullness of his joy he moved slowly pulling along his trailing utthariya, like the turning Mandara Mountain swirling the water of the milky ocean along with it; shedding copious tears of joy the king appeared like a parijata tree showering streams of pearls. All the vassals of King Tarapida followed him. They were all of mature years, white haired, and smeared with sandalwood paste; they were clad in uncut and unbleached silk cloth, and wore armlets, turbans, and crowns. Their hair was decorated with flowers. They had their own sword, staff, umbrella, flag and the chamara. With this retinue behind him the king walked up to receive his son.

When he saw his father coming up to receive him, Chandrapida dismounted from the horse and saluted him, his head, adorned by the brilliant chudamani, touching the ground. The father opened his arms to the long lost son and clasped him to his bosom. He held the prince in close embrace for a long time. When he was finally released, Chandrapida saluted all the other venerable rulers present. King Tarapida then took his son by his hand and led him to the palace of Vilasavathi. There too Chandrapida was received with great joy and all the rituals of welcome were duly performed. He remained there for a while with his mother and father recounting the tales of his digvijaya. Then he proceeded to pay his respects to Arya Shukanasa and informed the venerable minister that Vaishampayana was well and in command of the forces. After paying his respects to Manorama he returned to his mother's palace where he performed his ablutions as though he were in a dream, unaware of his own actions, like a puppet being moved by an outside agency. In the afternoon he went home to his own palace. There alone, his longing for Kadambari became unbearable; not merely his palace or the city of Ujjayini, but the entire world appeared desolate in the absence of Kadambari. So desperate was he for news of the gandharva princess that he now eagerly awaited the return of Patralekha, an event that all of a sudden, swelled in importance, like the attainment of a longed for boon, or a cause for great celebration, or a great event like the appearance of nectar in the milky ocean.

A few days later Meghanada arrived bringing Patralekha with him. Chandrapida's face brightened with a smile. Patralekha was already dear to him, and now that she had become the recipient of Kadambari's good wishes and affection she had become doubly dear to him. He embraced her with great affection; when Meghanada bowed to him he patted him on his back affectionately. When they all sat down he asked, 'Patralekhe, tell me! Are they all fine, their ladyships Mahashveta and Madalekha and her highness Kadambari? And all the attendants including Tamalika and Keyuraka?'

She replied, 'Lord, yes, they are all well. Devi Kadambari bows to you, with her hands joined over her head, along with all her friends and attendants.' When he heard this Chandrapida quickly took her inside the palace after dismissing all the attendant princes. His excitement now knew no bounds and he was no longer able to contain his eagerness. He drew Patralekha first to the centre of an umbrella made of the huge stalks and leaves of land lotuses grown in the palace. There was a swan pair sleeping peacefully on the floor of yet another emerald green bower of leaves. Chandrapida kicked them awake and chased the birds away. He then sat down there and questioned Patralekha. 'Now tell me Patralekhe! How were you after I came away? Was Devi affectionate to you? Do tell me all that happened there. Who remembered me the most? Whose affection for me was the strongest and the deepest?'

Patralekha replied, 'Listen to me carefully, when I tell you how I fared, how Devi treated me, what things transpired, who remembered you most, and whose affection for you was the deepest.'

— 48 —

Patralekha Speaks . . .

As soon as you, my lord, left with Keyuraka, I went back and sat down near the flower-strewn bed on which Devi Kadambari was resting and became at once the recipient of her wonderful kindness. What more can I say than that her eyes were in mine, her body was where mine was, her hand in mine, and her voice in the enunciation of my name and her heart in her love for me. That was how that first day was.

The next day leaning on me she left the cool chamber and walked around and we wandered into a new garden that she was very fond of and which was out of bounds for the attendants.

There was a whitewashed platform with a series of emerald steps, like a garland of waves in the Kalindhi, which she climbed. There she stood holding a pillar of polished gemstone apparently lost in intense thought; it appeared as if she were making up her mind to say something, as she fixed her unwavering, unblinking gaze on me for a long time. All of a sudden her body became drenched in perspiration. Weakened by that flood as it were she trembled; then grief caught hold of her—as though afraid she might fall.

I looked at her steadily and earnestly and said, 'Please command me.' Her own shaking limbs seemed to say 'no, no' to her speaking out; she rubbed the polished stone floor with her toes as though she wanted to erase her reflection on it to prevent her own image from hearing her secret. The swans came clustering around her feet drawn by the tinkle of her anklets as she rubbed the floor. She kicked them away impatiently. Her face was hot and when she fanned it with her utthariya the bees hovering over the flowers were blown away. She now peered around as though it struck her all of a sudden that the forest sprites might be listening to her words. Her extreme bashfulness made her tongue-tied and although she was eager to talk she could not utter anything.

In spite of great efforts the words never came out of her mouth; as if they had been reduced to ashes by the flaming fire of Madana; or washed away by her flood of tears; or broken to pieces by the falling arrows of Manmatha; or blown away by her rising sighs; or caught up in the myriad thoughts jostling in her mind. Only the teardrops rained down—not touching her cheeks as she had bent her face a little—like a broken akshamala to count the thousand miseries in her heart.

Seeing her in that condition I enquired, 'Devi, what is the matter?' Kadambari merely rubbed her tear-reddened eyes. She picked up a flower garland as if with it she would like to put an end to herself; with one eyebrow raised she seemed to peep into the world of the dead. As for me I understood her suffering and I pressed her again and again to speak out her mind. But she, tied down by extreme shyness scratched the ketaki leaf with the tip of her nails as if to say she would rather write than speak what was in her mind although her lips trembled with the urge to speak. Thus she remained quiet for a long time with her eyes fixed on the ground.

After a while she raised her eyes to me and made once again an effort to speak.

She looked at me with eyes that filled again and again with tears; as they fell the tears seemed intended to wash the words sullied by the smoke from the fire of Kama raging within. The rays threading out from her teeth as she smiled sadly seemed meant for tying up the words she intended to speak, for fear that they might otherwise escape her memory. She said: 'Patralekhe! You have come to dominate my affections as they have not so far been, by my parents or by Mahashveta, or Madalekha; in fact you have become dearer to me than my own life, and that in the very short time since I met you. I do not know why indeed, setting aside all my dear friends, my heart reposes confidence in you. Apart from you there is none to whom I can reveal, this disgrace of mine; there is no one else with whom I can share my distress. I shall now lay before you this unbearable burden of sorrow and then give up my life. I am ashamed to face my own heart that knows of this disgrace of mine, how can I then face others when they come to know about it?

'I have besmirched a lineage as pure as the rays of the moon by giving rise to scandal. I have abandoned my traditional maidenly reserve and indulged in wantonness. Here is Kadambari not betrothed by her father, not given away by her mother, nor blessed with the approval of the elders in the family to act in the matter. As such she is not sending messages, or tokens of love, or revealing the changes wrought by love. Yet that arrogant prince

Chandrapida treating her like an over eager wanton, like a lowborn woman, a woman with no one to protect her, has made her deserve serious censure.

Tell me, does this conduct of his behove the noble? Is this how one rewards true friendship, by treading upon my heart soft as the new lotus stalk? It is not proper on the part of young men to cause distress to young maidens.

It is bashfulness that first falls victim to the fire of love, only then the heart. First it is qualities like modesty that Kama's floral arrows break to pieces, only then the vitals. So here I am to bid farewell to you so that I may be with you in the next birth. Believe me there is no one dearer to me than you. I shall wash away the stains of my behaviour by sacrificing my life as atonement.' Kadambari then fell silent.

As for me I had no idea what this was all about, and I felt at a loss as to what to do, and was quite troubled, ashamed and bewildered. I spoke with distress. 'Devi! Please enlighten me on this matter. What did my lord Chandrapida do? What misdemeanour is he guilty of? What rude act of his has hurt the lily-soft heart of Devi that deserves never to be upset at all. Once I know I shall first put an end to myself and then Devi can take her own life.'

Kadambari said, 'All right, listen carefully to what I have to say. Every night he keeps appearing in my dreams. The expert villain that he is he sends the parrot and the myna in the cage as secret messengers. While I sleep, his unfulfilled desire infatuating his mind, he writes down secret places of tryst on the inside of my ivory ear ornament. He sends charming love messages expressing his obsessive desire for consummation, while the eyeliner-stained teardrops that fall in a row tell the story of his distress. He stains my feet forcibly with alakhta as though he were in truth colouring them with the intensity of his passion. I am alone in the garden and I run in fear of being caught by him but alas my utthariya gets caught in the creepers and they, the creepers, that have been my dear friends, hold me back and hand me over to him. I turn away from him but that fake valiant tries to embrace me from behind. Crooked as he is, he draws the picture of a winding, twisting creeper on my breasts no doubt to teach me deviousness, me who am naturally straight, open and innocent. That sweet-tongued scoundrel with his cool breath, like a breeze rising from the waves of his own longing for me, blows away the drops of sweat on my cheeks.

When I am watering my very dear young bakula sapling, this impudent fellow tries forcibly to feed me with his own mouthfuls of wine again and again by holding me by my hair. As I kick the ashoka tree to make it flower, this evil-minded prince intercepts my kicks with his head. Oh Patralekhe! Tell me, how does one ward off a love-befuddled fool devoid of intelligence. To him my rejection is just a show of jealousy, my anger is mere pretence, my silence is dignity, my criticism is just a ruse to enable me to keep uttering his name, and my insults are only a show of informal friendship; and scandal, he looks upon as fame.'

Listening to Kadambari going on in this fashion I was filled with joy and I thought to myself, 'She has indeed been led a long way by Manmatha in her love for Chandrapida. If the favour of the love god has really fallen upon Chandrapida with respect to Kadambari then Chandrapida too has helped the god in his efforts in manifold ways, by means of all his great qualities, both natural, and nurtured; his fame that lights up the very quarters, his young manhood, that in the form of waves rains gems in the ocean of love, his prankish nature and geniality that enhance his own beauty, and his loveliness that rains down a nectar of delight like the phases of the moon. After a long time indeed, the south wind, 'malayanila' has found a worthy opportunity to fan the flames of love. The moon has found a good cause for rising, and the abundant blooming of the spring flowers, its just reward.'

I laughed and said, 'Devi! Please do not be angry. Cool down. You should not blame the prince for the faults of Kama. These are the illusions created by that rogue, the prince is at no fault at all.'

Then Kadambari asked eagerly, 'Tell me then if this is really Kama or someone else. What are his various forms?'

I replied, 'Devi! What form? He has no form at all. He is formless fire. With lightless flame he creates heat; with invisible smoke he causes tears; the hidden heap of ashes brings on the pallor. There is none in the three worlds that has so far escaped the pain of his arrows, none can escape them now nor will anyone in the future. With the floral bow in his hands he pierces the mightiest with his arrows. Under his influence when the smitten women mentally dwell on the beloved, whole expanses of the skies become crowded with a thousand images of the lover's face. If they set about to draw the likeness of their lover they would find the whole earth not place enough for the exercise. If they seek to count the qualities of the beloved they run out of numbers. When they wish to hear the fame of the loved one they find even Saraswati's speech inadequate. Daydreams of reunion with the lover always seem to end too quickly for the dreamer.'

Kadambari remained lost in thought for some time. She then said, 'Patralekhe! It is just as you say. The one with the five arrows has made me entirely the prince's. All his manifestations that you describe are found plentifully in me. You are so close to my heart, I request you, please advise me. I am so ignorant about such affairs. The only thing I know is that I have behaved in a way that would draw my parents' censure and I am ashamed of it. So it is better to die than continue to live in disgrace.'

I chided her again. 'Devi! Why do you go on and on about putting an end to yourself, unnecessarily, when Bhagvan Kamadeva of the floral arrows has, without having been importuned by you, of his own accord, conferred this blessing on you? And why should your parents censure you? Manmatha decides like the father, rejoices like the mother, gives away the bride like the brother, induces longing like a friend, and like a foster mother, teaches the fine blandishments of love making. So many women have chosen their own husbands. If none ever did, would not the rules found in the scriptures for *svayamvara* be entirely meaningless? Therefore my dear lady, enough of this death talk. I touch your lotus feet and swear, write your message and send me with it, and I shall bring your beloved to you.'

Kadambari looked at me eagerly with her eyes wet with tears of joy. Her bashfulness broken through at last by the myriad arrows of Kama, she was now eager to talk about her lover. She spoke slowly, still somewhat shy, having been so right from birth as most girls are, although her heart was brimming over with happiness. 'I know your deep love for me. Whence would women, soft as the tender shirisha flower, get confidence and boldness, especially those who are barely out of their childhood? Bold indeed are those who would send messages or approach the beloved on their own. As for me I feel shy to send a message of my own, as I am so young.

'And what message shall I send? If I say, "You are very dear to me" it is mere repetition. "Do you love me?" is a stupid question. "I cannot live without you." goes against the facts of experience. "I am deeply in love with you." is a statement only a courtesan is fit to utter. "I have been handed over to you by Manobhava" sounds like a ruse to get close to him. "You must come to me" smacks of arrogance in love. "You will know about the extent of my love once I die" is a futile statement.'

'And listen to this as well', continued Kadambari. 'Even if you do bring him here my bashfulness would make me tremble; and the fact that I tremble would make me even more shy, with the result I would not be able to look at him. The loss of beauty caused by the love fever will not let me go in front of him. Ignorance and shyness would cause stupefaction, a dullness that would prevent me from moving towards him. That I have brought him here by force would never let me be at ease in his presence.

Therefore for some reason—it could be the embarrassment of informing his parents of this affair, or the pressure of his princely duties, or the reluctance to forgo the pleasure of being with his childhood friends from whom he had had a long separation, or just the wish to avoid the strain of such a long journey, or the simple desire of staying in his own country—you are unable to bring him here, in spite of great efforts on your part such as falling at his feet, that you may be compelled to make out of your excessive love for me, then indeed it is just as well. As a matter of fact, has anything really happened that is in excess of what is permitted? How is the situation now different from before?

There is the himagriha, the refuge of the smitten women where their distress at the separation from their lovers is only intensified by the piteous calls of the separated chakravaka; where the one with the flower weapon, expertly removes the inhibitions of the high-born women already excited by the fragrance of the blooms; where at twilight when the moon rises it sports a redness reminiscent of womanly cheeks flushed with the grazing of the kundalas and wine; where the sparkling white rays of the rising moon envelop everything in a shower of moonlight. The lotus pond with a vast field of flowers close to the himagriha scatters the fragrance far and wide. The chandrakanta stone peaks on the kridaparvatha melt in the moonlight and form rustling brooks on the slopes; soothing sprays of mist are everywhere. Yet the himagriha could only cool the bodily heat. It was in this himagriha crowded with women that I was leaning on a floral bed; that was the Kadambari that the prince saw. These are the same eyes that then saw him and never became sated with seeing him again and again; this is the same mind lacking in wit that could not hold him who was already in my heart; this is the same body of mine that then remained so indifferent although it was so close to him; this is the same hand that under the pretence of waiting for the approval of the elders did not then allow itself to be grasped by him. He too is the same Chandrapida who, unwilling to cause inconvenience to others came here twice and went away. As for the god with the five arrows who seems to have spent his entire arsenal on me and is now powerless elsewhere, he too is the same, just as you described him.

I gave my word to Mahashveta; I swore, 'When you remain in sorrow I shall not give my hand in marriage to anyone.' But she warned me, 'Devi! Please do not take such a decision. This Makaraketu is exceedingly cruel and villainous. He can even take a life away with the intense longing he produces in one who is separated from the beloved.' But as you see that is not true as far as I am concerned as I have this strange thing happening to me, and I have no idea why. Is it the doing of Kama again or of the Fates? Is it my separation from my lover that is causing it all, or my love, or my passion for him? I only know that something has conspired to create an image of the prince that haunts me ceaselessly. In the presence of others, like some magician, he is invisible to others but always shows himself to me. Unlike the real Kumara who abandoned me and went away, this one never leaves me. In truth he is the one who is pining for me. He is not concerned with wealth or power, day or night; he is not the lord of the earth. He is not drawn to Lakshmi day and night; he does not desire Saraswati. Nor does he spread his own fame. I see him day and night, while sitting and standing, while rolling in the bed, awake or with the eyes closed, or dreaming. I see him in the women's pavilion, in the ponds, in the gardens, in the wells dug for sport. I see him everywhere; his only intention seems to be to deceive ignorant people like me. But then I have already told you all this, so that is enough talk about bringing him here.'

Having said this, Kadambari, like one momentarily losing consciousness, closed her eyes; the tears collected at the tips of her eyelashes ran down. The agony inside her seemed to grip her, to melt her away with its virulence. Placing her flushed lotus-face on her creeper-slender arms she fell silent and remained motionless like a carved figure.

I fell into thought not without irony: 'How fortunate indeed to have this life support and distraction in the form of the imaginary lover for the pining well-born women, especially for the young girls. With such a lover there is no need to fall at the feet of a friend to act as a messenger. Every moment there could be a thousand unions with the beloved. One can go after the lover with no restraint of time or place. The lovemaking too is with no loss of virginity. The embrace does not crush the breasts. There are no nail or teeth marks left on the body to cause embarrassment in the presence of the elders. The hair is never disarranged when held by the imaginary sweetheart. The union is silent without the tinkle of the ornaments. Above all this, an imaginary lover in not hidden by darkness, nor stalled by rain, nor shrouded in mist.'

By this time it had become evening and I suddenly realized that the skies had turned russet, as though they too had become immersed in the emotions of the love story. The reddened sun seemed to be running away, struck with shyness, like the heart of Kadambari that had revealed its love. Very soon young girls carrying lighted lamps filled with scented oil that diffused fragrance, came in to stand in a circle. These flames were reflected on the flawlessly beautiful skin of Kadambari like so many flaming arrows of Manmatha. I requested her again, 'Devi! Please do not distress yourself. You do not deserve to be unhappy. Control your agitation. I am here to help you. I will go and bring Chandrapida here.' At the mention of your name she woke up immediately as one would from poison induced sleep at the sound of the mantra; she looked at me eagerly and sat down on the emerald seat. Then she said to me, 'I am not saying this merely to please you. I hold on to my life only by being with you. If you have confidence in this matter then you act as it suits your wish and convenience.' She then offered me clothes, ornaments and tambula and bade me farewell with great affection.

Patralekha was silent for a while with her head lowered. Then she spoke again hesitantly. 'Deva! Having just experienced the extraordinary kindness of Devi and also saddened by her plight I feel emboldened to importune you further. Does it behove the Deva known for his kindness towards those seeking refuge in him, to spurn Devi Kadambari in her state of distress?'

Patralekha's accusing words found their mark. Chandrapida thought of all that Kadambari had said. Her words had been expressive of deep affection and longing sprinkled with mockery. They were importuning words touched with pride and a little contempt as well, words that conveyed her agony, her love, her anger and her desire for total surrender, her goodness and her misery. Words that were so sweet yet so harsh to the ear, full of melting sentiments yet capable of drying up one's heart, soft words yet harsh in their import, words at once humble and haughty, endearing and egoistic. Unable to bear the sorrow brought on by dwelling again and again on Kadambari's words his lash-stilled eyes filled with tears and losing all his natural steadiness and firmness Chandrapida became deeply troubled.

Along with her words, all of Kadambari's symptoms of distress too seemed to have travelled all that way to take possession of Chandrapida. His heart was seized with an agonized rage; his life forces seemed to press up against his throat. His lips trembled, the tip of his nose twitched, and his eyes filled with tears. As the tears ran down he cried out: 'Patralekhe! What shall I do? I have behaved like a villain practised in evil ways, arrogant about his knowledge, who considers himself an expert in everything, but whose pretensions to steadfastness amount to nothing. I was so stupid that I allowed my mind to be distracted by a thousand misconceptions. Although the god Manmatha, the preceptor of the dance of love, had seized control of the poor child so completely as to make her reveal all her feelings towards me, I, foolish as I was and having never met anyone like her before, merely assumed that such blandishments were only natural behaviour on the part of one so beautiful and of divine lineage. Her show of extraordinary friendship towards me I suspected might be nothing more than a natural trait in her. I never believed that her actions were specially meant for me. Being swung about between doubt and misunderstanding, I have become the cause of Kadambari's great distress and the object of your displeasure.

'Perhaps it was a curse that was clouding my mind. Otherwise in a matter that should give rise to no doubts whatsoever even in an unawakened intellect, with the symptoms of love so openly displayed how could my mind have been in such delusion? Well let us grant that the gestures were too subtle for me; the smiling glance, the artful words, the pretending to a bashfulness not really felt, all these acts could be misunderstood. But she removed her necklace that had adorned her for so long and had it placed around my luckless neck. How could one misinterpret that gesture which revealed everything.

'And you saw what happened in the himagriha. Devi never uttered a word that was improper even out of anger born of love! It is entirely my fault, all this misunderstanding. I am now ready to put my very life on the line to prove my love, so that Devi would not think of me as so extremely cold hearted.'

Before Chandrapida finished speaking the pratihari came in without announcing his arrival, wielding his cane staff, bowed before the prince and conveyed the following message from Devi Vilasavathi. 'I hear from the servants that Patralekha who had stayed back has now returned. I brought her up and so far as my affections are concerned, there is no difference between you and she. As for you I have not seen you for such a very long time; it has become very difficult indeed to see your face, a face that has fulfilled a thousand wishes of mine. So both of you come over to see me.'

— 50 —

When Chandrapida heard his mother's message he fell into confusion. 'Oh my god,' he said to himself. 'My life seems to be hanging in uncertainty. On the one hand is my dear mother who grieves every moment she spends away from me. But here is Patralekha with Kadambari's artlessly loving command to go to her. Strong indeed is mother's love, experienced since birth. But the heart is subject to all kinds of desires. One cannot give up the pleasure of serving one's mother and father. But the villainous Manmatha drives one mad. You are drawn to your parents because they make much of you. But the longing for the beloved is unbearable. Love of one's own family cannot be given up but I am eager to respond to the new love. The kings of good lineage always look up to the commands of those in authority. But the only reward of my life is to look at my beloved's face. The subjects hold me in great affection, it is true, but deep is the love of the gandharva princess. I cannot easily give up my own land. But Kadambari has to be honoured. My heart cannot bear the delay but Hemakuta is so far away from the Vindhyas.' His mind in a whirl Chandrapida held Patralekha's hand and came to his mother's apartments. There with his mother's solicitous attentions he forgot for a while the agony of his own heart.

Night fell, darkening the directions, just as Chandrapida's agony darkened his heart. He lay in bed wide awake. The diversion of sleep escaped him. He recollected and dwelt on every inch of Kadambari. He fancied he was already in Hemakuta fallen at Kadambari's feet to recover from the fatigue of travel as it were. His mind then climbed over her legs and attached itself to her tightly packed thighs; it inscribed itself on her broad hips; it sank into the depths of her navel; it thrilled in the hair on her body; it climbed over the three folds of her midriff; it established itself on her large, high breasts; it abandoned itself in her arms; it held on to her hands; it twined around her neck, it entered her cheeks, it embedded itself on her lips, it strung itself on the line of her nose. It bloomed along with her eyes; it lingered on her forehead and got caught in the darkness of her hair. It immersed itself thus in the flood of her beauty that inundated the quarters. Chandrapida spent the night dwelling on the beauty of Kadambari, the abode of Kama.

From that day onwards Chandrapida lived in a fever of love. In his reveries he would see Manmatha draw his bow and aim his floral arrows at Kadambari; Chandrapida would immediately interpose himself between the god and Kadambari in order to protect her. All day long his tear-filled rolling eyes would seem to chide Kama, 'Are you not ashamed to strike so pitilessly at one whose body is soft as the malati bloom?' Sometimes he would imagine her fall into a swoon; he would then hold her in his arms to bring her back to consciousness. His own body would then break into perspiration as if to sprinkle her awake, with beads of his own sweat; he would sigh deeply as though to fan her. The hair on his body would become erect with the fancied thrill of having made Kadambari come back to life.

Was he mentally asking Kadambari if her agony was bearable? For he would often become silent as though straining to listen to her reply. With her ever-present form in front of his eyes, he seemed blind to everything else. With his ears filled with her talk he heard nothing else, neither the notes of the veena nor the chants. The talk of his friends was harsh to his ears; the chatter of his family was no pleasure. Afraid of others finding out the state he was in he avoided meeting anyone, so unlike him before he fell a victim to love.

But he did not take refuge in a bed of fresh lotuses although the ceaseless flames of passion were consuming him; he did not seek the freshness of the lotus stalks to cool his burning limbs, lest his parents got to know about his condition. He did not go anywhere near the fountain chamber clouded with chilled sprays of water. He refrained from taking shelter in the cool bower of creepers in the palace gardens where there was a constant shower of pollen. He did not roll on the polished stone floor made wet with sandalwood scented water.

Nevertheless Chandrapida suffered day and night with no respite from the heat of passion. It set him on fire, but did not burn him. The fuel of love fed the fire but did not spend itself out in the process. Chandrapida's tortured body shrivelled. Stalked by the whimsical Manmatha, Chandrapida yet managed to conceal his love from the public eye with great effort.

His deep love for Kadambari rested on her beauty and virtues and they were pulling him towards her. But his great respect for his parents and his strong ties to them held him back. The waters of the ocean rise pulled by the rays of the distant moon, but they stop when the limit is reached. Likewise Chandrapida too controlled himself. All the same, the few days that he spent like this dragged on like a thousand days for him.

—51—

One day, seeking some respite from the turmoil in his heart, Chandrapida left the city and walked down to the banks of the Shipra where the air was cool and moist, laden with water particles from the river. The sandy shores too were moist and soft and reverberated with the calling of the swans and the chakravaka pairs. He walked along the river at a quick pace and reached the temple of the son of Rudra, situated on the banks.

It was then that he saw the horses, still some distance away. They were galloping so fast that at times they seemed welded together, while at other times they appeared scattered. Now spirited, now slowing down, they would at times break their formation and stumble along and even fall down. Yet they were goaded on by the riders to greater speed. The horses exhibited the exhaustion of having traversed a long distance at a great speed indicating the serious nature of the riders' errand that had brought them here.

Chandrapida was instantly curious and sent a man to find out who the horsemen were and where they had come from. He got out of the knee-deep water in which he had been walking and went into the Kartikeya temple to wait for the return of the messenger with information regarding the visitors on horseback.

As he stared at the group of horses in the distance, he suddenly pulled Patralekha, who was standing at his side, by her hand and exclaimed, 'Patralekhe! Look! The rider in the front, his face is not clearly visible because it is hidden by the umbrella with the long hanging peacock feathers; but I am sure he is Keyuraka.' Even as he was watching, the horseman dismounted and seemed to enquire of the messenger sent by the prince where Chandrapida was.

As the rider made his way to him Chandrapida saw that it was indeed Keyuraka who was however, of changed appearance; much the worse for the long travel, his body was dark with dust not having had time during the journey without any break to attend to his toilet. With his saddened face and unhappy eyes that indicated the burden of sorrow that he carried within himself, he seemed to convey wordlessly that all was not well with Kadambari even without being asked about it. He looked a different man altogether.

At once Chandrapida cried out, 'Welcome! Welcome!' As Keyuraka bowed and then hurried forward Chandrapida opened his arms wide and enveloped him in a close embrace. When released Keyuraka fell at his feet and Chandrapida raised him and enquired after his health, including the other horsemen as well in his enquiry as his kind glance swept over them repeatedly.

Then he said, 'Keyuraka, your very arrival here tells me that all is well with Kadambari and her friends. After having rested and are settled in comfort you shall tell me the reason for your visit.' A female elephant had, in the meantime been hurriedly brought over for the prince and his guest. It was waiting on its knees ready for mounting. Chandrapida climbed up first asking both Patralekha and Keyuraka to follow suit even as Keyuraka muttered to himself 'Comfort! Where do I get comfort from!' Thus they proceeded to the palace. When the day's duties were done and his guests' needs were attended to, the prince repaired to his favourite garden with Keyuraka and Patralekha. Dismissing all his servants and with just Patralekha by his side, he said to Keyuraka, 'Keyuraka, tell me now, what is the message from Kadambari, Madalekha and Mahashveta?'

Keyuraka sat down respectfully in front of Chandrapida and gave his reply.

Keyuraka Speaks . . .

Deva, what shall I say? I have not the least little message from any of them, not from Kadambari, nor from Madalekha, nor from Mahashveta. When I returned to Hemakuta after entrusting Patralekha to the care of Meghnada, I informed Mahashveta about your return to Ujjayini. She listened to my story, raised her eyes heavenward, sighed deeply with sadness and muttered to herself 'that is that' and returned to her ashrama to continue with her austerities.

As for Kadambari when she heard the news it was as if she was hit in her heart by a mace; it was as if she was struck on the head by a bolt from the blue. She remained with her eyes half closed as one who had lost her consciousness. She felt bereft, deceived, humiliated, and stunned. She was unaware even of Mahashveta's return to her ashrama.

Then she opened her eyes and as though recollecting something that she had forgotten, and told me a little cuttingly to inform Mahashveta about Chandrapida's departure. Then she turned to Madalekha and smiled mirthlessly and asked her somewhat rhetorically, 'Madalekhe, do you think anyone else has ever done or would do in the future what the prince has done?' She then got up and dismissed all her attendants and fell on her bed, covered her head with her utthariya and remained in that position the whole day. Sunk in unrelenting misery, she said not a word even to Madalekha.

The next day when I approached her in the morning she looked at me accusingly as if to say 'You are all thriving in your strong bodies while I am in this state.' She seemed to reproach us with unspoken words. 'Why do you stand in front of me' she seemed to say angrily. Then with tear-filled eyes she looked at me for a long time. I decided, although she never said it, she wanted me to go to you. So here I am; I did not tell her that I was going to you. I only want to save the life of a person whose only refuge is you. So please listen to me with attention and bestow your kindness on her.

When you first came to Hemakuta you swept all the women up there off their feet even as the southerly wind sways and shakes the trees and the creepers. When Devi Kadambari first saw you, the captivator of all the three worlds, she fell in love with you and Makaraketu took possession of her even as spring takes possession of the *rakthashoka*. Soundless, driven by no wind, leaving no ashes, spewing no smoke, the fire of Manmatha has been burning ever since and she gets no relief from the ministrations of her attendants. But how very strange indeed, the more the fire of Manmatha burns the more flawlessly brilliant her beauty becomes, like the cloth purified by fire.

Even such a tender nature as Kadambari's can harden, like soft water attaining hardness as pearl, with the eagerness to unite with the beloved. So strong is that desire to come together with the lover that even with an agony that debilitates the vital forces, life holds on. Now how shall I describe that agony of hers? With what figures of speech? How do I show you the intensity of it? With what other great suffering do I compare it, this intense longing that she is experiencing? With her body wasting away every minute it is not just her *kankanam* that she has to hold from slipping down; her tender hands seem again and again to be steadying her shaking heart as well. Her body seems to wither even with the touch of her attendants' hands, cool and moist though they are, like the garland of artificial lotuses that shower water.

It is with her feet that she now holds her girdle, it having slipped down from her waist; the broad hips have now become waist-like. The hope of union with you holds her heart even as her heart holds you. Her life forces are held at the throat and her lotus hands hold her cheeks. The talk of you holds in the tears. Her forehead holds the cooling sandalwood paste even as her shoulder holds the single plait of hair.

Like her friends touching her to find out the state of her fever, loss of consciousness too seems to touch her. Like her maids raise her up in bed, her own love frenzy too makes her spring up. Like her attendants hurrying hither and thither her own limbs too toss about in sheer agony.

She would wander only in that part of the garden where the creepers were dense with leaves as though she might be tempted to put an end to herself were she to see a leafless, rope-like creeper. Often would she get in to the lotus pond in the garden for relief; as her tear-reddened eyes found their reflection in the water it would appear as if the lotus blooms, afraid of being cut and spread on Kadambari's bed were trying to hide themselves under the water. She would rise from the pond and seek the avenue of tamala trees. There she would stand with her eyes closed holding a high branch with her raised hands; thus would she paint the picture of one trying to put an end to herself with a garland of champa flowers.

Then she would go to the music room; but there the rhythms of the *nritya* accompanied by the mridanga would only increase her agitation like that of the peacocks. So she would rush into the fountain chamber with its continuous showers. Her body would thrill with the hair standing on edge like a *kadamba* bud, having been hit with the cool water sprays; all atremble, she would make her way to the lotus pond in the women's apartments. However, unable to bear the cackle of the antapura swans she would be on the move again; but she would first remove her anklets ostensibly to ward off the birds, but in reality as if she were showing by means of an expert dance gesture that she had indeed become too weak to dance ever again. At times Kadambari would sing to express her intense yearning for her beloved; at this the koels living on the mango trees in the courtyard as if angered at being outdone in sweetness of voice would at once set up their own calling, no doubt to harass her. Thus do the days pass for her, in unrelenting distress.

It is a different story at night. As the darkness flees at the rise of the moon Kadambari's courage too flees as though it too is made of the stuff of darkness. Lotus-like her heart wilts, as the white lily splendour of Madana spreads. Her eyes, as though made of Chandrakanta stone begin to water. Her sighs rise higher and higher like the waves in the ocean. Like one in the grip of fever, she runs her trembling fingers on the reflection of the moon on the polished stone floor, as though she is wordlessly recounting the distress caused by him.

When the music begins with the beat of the mridanga, Kadambari thinks it the cackling of the peacocks and rushes to cover the mouths of the emerald birds in the shower room. When night falls as though to outwit the impending separation she brings together the chakravaka pairs drawn on the walls with lotus stalk fibre. Dreaming about her imminent lovemaking, she puts out the night lamp by waving her lotus petal ear ornament; in her letters expressing her yearning she writes about imaginary incidents taking place when she and the lover have been together, or chide Chandrapida about some act of his conjured in her fantasies.

Like the beauty of summer time declining as the days go by, Kadambari too wastes away a little every day. Everything is going down. Not just her limbs but the aids to sustain her too are getting depleted by the relentless succession of days, such as the lotuses and their stalks due to the incessant making of the garlands, the flowers in the palace garden with the making of her bed, and the words and advice at the command of her friends. What more needs to be said. All her friends have your name on their lips, all the whispered secrets concern you, all the efforts of the attendants are devoted to getting news about you and all questions asked, concern your story. All diversions have you as the subject; all painting is the painting of your likeness, all lyrics that the minstrels sing scold you. All her dreams consist of seeing you again. When she chatters in her love-induced feverish state she mocks you for the most part; yet your name is the only antidote to her delirium of passion.

—52—

Hearing all this Chandrapida whispered, 'Please do stop now, I cannot hear anymore' and fell into a swoon that came upon him as if taking pity on his agony over hearing Keyuraka's account. It prevented Keyuraka, at least for the time being, from continuing with the heart-rending story although the story itself was far from being finished.

As he fell, Keyuraka held him and Patralekha fanned him. Chandrapida regained consciousness, no doubt due to their ministrations, but also because of what fortune held in store for him. Once conscious, he was struck with fear over the terrible offence he had committed, and ashamed and dismayed. He addressed the silent Keyuraka haltingly in a voice choked with the pressure of unshed tears. 'Keyuraka, Patralekha has told me everything, how Kadambari finding me indifferent to her overtures and concluding that I did not reciprocate her love, has abandoned all hopes of my return ever, which was why she never ordered you to go to me. And this is again the reason why Mahashveta has not sent any message for me, and why

Madalekha, too has decided not to take advantage of her affection for me to reprimand me through you.

Devi Kadambari does not fully understand herself, nor does she realize that she too has a role to perform. Maybe it is her high birth, or her overwhelming generosity, or her stoic attitude towards joy and sorrow, or her extreme gentleness that has led to this passive attitude. The chandrakanta stone can only melt with the lustre of the moon, it cannot pull the rays to itself. Those who are deeply in love are like the bees; intensely desirous of honey, the bees can only hover close, while it is up to the buds to open and allow the bees to drink. All that the sun-withered lily bud can do is to raise its head; it is up to the moonlight-happy night to make it bloom. The trees may be full of sap, yet without the onset of spring how can they bring out their fresh red shoots?

There I stood, her servant, waiting merely for her lips to move. But she acted not and allowed herself to be dictated to by that crippling, limb-paralyzing bashfulness that ever kills all pleasure and produces only sorrow and renders one insensitive to the pain of others. It is this that has now reduced her to such a condition that her very life hangs in suspense. How could she otherwise have had any confusion with regard to her conduct towards me her servant? Although unwilling, she appeared to have been forced into inaction by this womanly rule of bashfulness. What kind of shyness was this anyway that was directed towards me who was at her feet? How can there be any question of respect or obedience with regard to me? Or was it lack of trust in me? What is only all too clear is that she who is as gentle as the shirisha flower has brought on herself this terrible agony and at the same time has thwarted my most ardent desires as well. Perhaps this hiding of the emotions is natural to women, especially those who are barely out of their childhood, and whose sexuality is not fully roused.

It is perhaps understandable that Kadambari was unable on her own to get rid of her shyness towards me. But Madalekha?

She is her second heart. She saw how that consummate rascal Kama before whom even ascetics with a wealth of self control find themselves defenceless, was distressing Devi, yet she never said anything to me, never even whispered anything in my ears. Now I do know everything. But of what use is it? What can I do now? I am so many days' travel away from her. So tender is Devi's body that it can hardly bear the impact of a flower falling from a creeper shaken by the mountain wind. And the arrows of Kama are such that even those with iron in their hearts can hardly withstand them. Anything can happen any moment. I am sure Kadambari too realizes it.

I see the cruel hand of Fate in all this; Fate, the giver of sorrows, the expert in creating unbearable situations, quick to anger and to anger without reason. I also see all this as just the beginning, for Fate is not going to stop with this. He is leading on relentlessly to some horrible denouement. Otherwise why should I chase the horse-faced pair into areas unknown to humans? Is it not strange that I should come upon the Acchoda Lake, that I should hear strains of divine music, that I should meet Mahashveta? If you and Taralika had not come down at that precise moment my going to Hemakuta would not have happened at all. Why the meeting between Kadambari and me and why the sprouting of love for me in Kadambari? And why should my father's orders for me to return immediately arrive just at that moment with my love still unfulfilled? Is it not very clear indeed that Fate took us up to very great heights only to throw us down? Fate contrives to bring about all sorts of calamities by the force of our own deeds, itself remaining unseen all the while. Yet I shall endeavour to save Devi.'

As Chandrapida went on in this fashion giving expression to his agony, the sun, seemingly moved to pity for the pining prince and deciding as it were, not to add to his distress by his heat and lustre as well, gathered in his myriad sparkling rays of molten gold spread over all the directions like the open flying tresses of the dancing Shiva. Following the setting sun, the day too moved away, pulling along the bits of russet light still clinging to the top of the trees. In compassion, twilight spread her own moist colours like a piece of wet cloth over everything, soon to be followed by night who erected a pavilion of dark cloth, unwilling as it were to let the world see a dear friend in the throes of separation from his beloved. The lotus, fearing that Chandrapida might take to a lotus petal bed unable to bear the drying heat, promptly closed its petals. The compassionate white lilies on the other hand, vied with each other to open quickly so that a cool moist bed might be laid out if necessary for the agonized lover. The moon rose, a silver pot of nectar, a single umbrella over the whole world, a beauty spot on the face of the maiden of the eastern direction, as though wishing to touch Chandrapida with his nectar-anointed ray-hands, to soak him in the rain of moonlight in order to revive him.

The seat made of chandrakanta stone in that beautiful enchanting garden had broken into beads of moisture at the touch of the moon rays. Chandrapida flung himself on it and Keyuraka hurried over to press his legs. Craving reassurance Chandrapida spoke again. 'Keyuraka, do tell me please. Do you think Kadambari will live until I get there? Can Madalekha keep her distracted till then? Would Mahashveta go back to console her? Will I ever get to see Kadambari's smiling face again with her long timorous eyes like those of a frightened young deer?'

Keyuraka answered: 'Deva, take heart and prepare for the journey. Let us not worry about her attendants and friends. It is her desire to see you again that has completely taken control of her and does not allow her freedom even to blink her eyes. It is that which fills her heart; the hair on her body stands constantly on edge; her eyes remain filled with tears day and night.

Sleeplessness keeps its watchful eyes on her the entire night. Her life is hanging by a thread.'

Ordering Keyuraka to go to bed, Chandrapida fell into musing about his journey. 'If I go away without informing my parents, without receiving their blessings and affectionate farewells, if I steal away as it were, what indeed would be the state of my mind? Would I be happy, would my wishes bear fruit? Or let us leave this worry aside that is in the future. How do I run away in the first place? Father has now freed his own arms of the burden of ruling—arms that have been the bridge across the ocean of war, arms that could grant every boon to the subjects like a veritable kalpavriksha, arms that have been the latch on the door preventing the fame and valour of the enemy from issuing forth, arms that are the supporting beams of the dwelling that is the entire world— and has laid it on me. With the result, if I even take a step without informing my intention, the entire circle of princes with all their forces would follow causing a great commotion, looking for me in all the eight directions right up to the ocean, disregarding their fatigue and hunger. And it will not be just the princes alone; every prosperous citizen of the country, out of love for my father would start looking for me, abandoning his wife and children. I am sure of that.

And who else is there on whom my father could transfer the love he has for me and tell himself, 'Let him go! It would make no difference whether he stays or goes,' and harden his heart by taking refuge in anger at my wilful ways? Who else is there whose face my mother can gaze upon fondly so that she would not lament at my absence? Now she would only trouble my father to bring me back somehow. If my father himself sets out after me then indeed the entire world of eighteen islands would set out after me. In that case where would I go? Where would I hide myself? If they catch up with me and ask me why I have run away what answer shall I give them?

Let us for the sake of argument assume that by a stroke of luck I do manage to get away; would it not be a great sin, by so doing, to plunge my father in this great distress which he deserves not at all? Or to push my mother, who has never known a moment's sorrow in all her life, loved and cherished as she has been by my father, into this deep ocean of despair?

On the other hand, suppose I decide to inform my parents and leave only with their blessings. In that case what would I tell them? That the gandharva princess Kadambari who is in love with me suffers greatly by her separation from me being subjected to the unrelenting cruelty of Manmatha? Or that my own love for her is so intense that I cannot live without her? Or that Mahashveta who feels responsible for my life as well as Kadambari's has ordered me to return to wed the princess? Or that Keyuraka unable to bear the agony of Kadambari has come of his own accord to fetch me back to her? I cannot fabricate a story for going back. I have just returned after three years of victorious march over the whole world. And my army that has been away for so long and exhausted by the long effort has not even come back yet.

This matter needs a confidante and I am caught in this alone. Vaishampayana is not here with me, and so whom will I consult? Who will help me decide whether I should go or not? And if I decide to go, whether I should inform my parents or not? I have no other friend like Vaishampayana who is happy in my happiness, and sorrowful in my sorrow. There is no one else on whom I can thrust the burden of deciding what has to be done and obtain some relief. There is no one who can make my angry parents understand the situation and take me away.'

The night that seemed endless in its misery at last came to an end. Early in the morning he heard the news that the armies had arrived at Dashapura. His heart lightened a little. He felt that at last the Fates had decided to be a little kind to him. 'No sooner did I think of Vaishampayana, my second heart really, than he has come back to me.' he exulted. He cried out to Keyuraka 'Keyuraka! Our problems are solved. Vaishampayana is here.'

~53~

Keyuraka was perturbed by the delay likely to be caused in the projected journey by the arrival of Vaishampayana. Yet he replied politely that this piece of good news, namely the return of Vaishampayana, would doubtless relieve the prince's mind of worries. After Chandrapida tactfully dismissed the servants however, Keyuraka spoke more openly.

'The spreading brilliance of the lightning indicates the definite advent of the clouds; the darkening clouds augur the sure arrival of the rain as the paling of the east heralds the imminent rise of the moon, and the fragrant southerly wind, the unfailing setting in of spring, while the opening of the kasha flowers guarantees the onset of autumn. So are the indications that your Highness would definitely undertake the journey.

My lord will have to attain Kadambari. Has anyone ever seen the moon without the moonlight? Or the lotus pond without the lotuses? Can there be a garden with no creepers? Spring has no splendour without the mango blossom. Has anyone ever seen the face of the lord of the elephant herd without the beautiful marks left by the rut fluid?

But of course, when Vaishampayana gets back you would have to discuss your journey with him and that is going to take time. On the other hand, as I have already told you the physical state of Kadambari is such that it does not brook any delay. Her life hangs by a thin thread of hope. If this hope of seeing you again disappears, then by what consolation would her heart sustain itself? The news of you that I take back with me will no doubt convince her of the necessity to live on despite the great agonies she has to endure. Mentally your highness has really flown ahead, and physically too you would make haste. What purpose is served therefore by my lingering here now? My heart, made proud by your love and graciousness now desires your permission to leave for Hemakuta with the message of your early arrival.'

Chandrapida's dark-eyed glance resembling a dense garland of blue lilies, expressing the joy in his heart, rested on Keyuraka with benevolence. He replied: 'What can I say? Who, other than you would ever, in order to share the agonies of my heart, have disregarded the comforts of his own body? Who else could have shown such practical sense, such disinterested attachment to me? Go my friend and save Kadambari's life. Let Patralekha too go with you so that Devi would be reassured of my arrival; Patralekha too has been a recipient of Devi's kindness, and she in turn is devoted to her.' Having said this he turned and looked at Patralekha sitting behind him as if seeking her assent to his proposal. She replied, with her head lowered a little, 'Let my lord command me.'

With the matter of Patralekha's travel settled Chandrapida sent the pratihari to fetch Meghanada, who appeared immediately and bowed before his prince. Chandrapida himself instructed him first. 'I want you now to accompany Patralekha and Keyuraka to that very same place where I had left you earlier, in order for you to fetch Patralekha back to the capital. After meeting Vaishampayana who has returned I too would follow you quickly with the cavalry.'

Thus ordered Meghanada left immediately to prepare for their departure. Keyuraka rose and bowed in farewell not wishing to delay the return any longer. Chandrapida embraced him again and again with the hair on his body standing on edge and gazed at him with tear-filled eyes full of affection. He removed from his ears his colourful earrings and put them on Keyuraka's and said in an emotionally charged voice, 'Keyuraka, you did not bring any message for me from Devi. Should I pay her back in her own coin and not send any message either? Or perhaps I should ask her whether I too should now trouble her by assuming the burden of a shyness not really felt? Anyway Patralekha is going with you and she will ask her the question.'

As for Patralekha, she was overcome by this impending unforeseen separation from Chandrapida and was quite unable to control the rush of tears, although she knew they were inauspicious; her swimming eyes not fixing on any object she was about to fall at his feet when Chandrapida looked at her directly and said, 'Patraleke, this is what I want to submit to Devi with folded hands and bowed head. Out of all the ill-bred actions of mine, the worst was that I left without bidding farewell to Devi who with her naturally affectionate heart had taken such an immediate liking for me and treated me with such extraordinary favour and kindness. What did I do by way of return to all that kindness? I just allowed my sensitivity to turn to dullness, my wisdom to stupidity, steadiness to wavering, friendliness to harshness, my profundity to frivolousness, my natural gentleness to cruelty, my compassion to indifference, my candour to clever turns of phrases, my modesty to brazenness, my sense of appreciation to fault finding. What other quality do I have left, with which I may now commend myself to her? For what virtue of mine would Devi now accept me?

'Have I not deceived her heart by a false show of surrender to her? Have I not stolen her guileless heart and absconded? Have I not disregarded her life-threatening illness? Am I not responsible for her present condition? But despite all these faults and misdeeds I did serve her for sometime. That is why, although I am lacking in all good qualities now, Devi's virtues sustain me. It is her natural compassion and her candour that protect me from the fire of Madana although I am far away from her. Her love calls out to me again and again. Her constancy takes me close to her. Her generosity attracts me and her affection conquers me. I am sure that her soft-heartedness would restrain her from rebuking me and her magnanimity would raise me up and honour me. If I can still be audacious enough to go to her and look her in the face, it is only due to her graciousness, characterized by innocence, generosity and decorum, qualities, that, with just a few moments' acquaintance, forge a lifelong attachment. And they constantly remind you of the worthiness of Kadambari for service. They teach you the nuances of serving. They show you the methods of pleasing. "Be clever! Be resourceful!" they admonish you incessantly. They appease my irritation at people who approach me at all times for favours. They make me pull forward those who lag behind bashfully.

'These qualities may never be given up because they are so honour-worthy. One leans upon them because of their weightiness; one cannot leap over them because of their vastness; one cannot avoid them because of their power. It is these qualities that now draw me to her compellingly even without an expressed order from her. That my journey may not be in vain, that the world may not turn empty for me, Devi should make an effort to hold on to her life.'

To Patralekha he now said, 'Patralekhe, while travelling you should not allow this separation from me to upset you. Please do not neglect the care of your body. You should eat at the proper times. Do not take unknown routes or stop over in all sorts of places without first ascertaining their suitability. Do not divulge your errand to unknown people. Never, never neglect your safety. What shall I do? My concern for Kadambari's life outweighs my concern for your welfare. And that is why I am sending you all by yourself to save her life; my life too rests in your hands. So please do take care of yourself.'

Then he embraced Keyuraka and pressed upon him to take
care of Patralekha. He also insisted that both Keyuraka and
Patralekha should come down to Mahashveta's ashrama to meet
him when he arrives and take him to Kadambari. Then he bade
them farewell.

— 54 —

Feeling somewhat dejected after Keyuraka and Patralekha
had left, Chandrapida sent a messenger for news of the
army that was camping at Dashapura. His mind however dwelt
on the travelling pair: will they reach quickly or will there be
delay on the way, and how many days will they take to reach
their destination? These questions occupied his mind when he
made his way to his father to get leave from him to go and
welcome Vaishampayana whom he had not seen for a long time.
With the servants scattering away as he approached, the way to
the king was wide open. Chandrapida bowed to his father from
afar, with his right hand and knee touching the polished stone
floor on which fell his reflection, and the length of his tresses
appeared doubled.

King Tarapida called out to his son, 'Come along, come along',
in an affection-filled voice that sounded like the deep rumble of a
water-laden cloud. Chandrapida hurried over and paid his respects
to Shukanasa and was about to sit down on the ground when his
father pulled him over and sat him on the footstool and gazed at
him for a while with eager affection. He then fondly stroked his
son's handsome limbs splendid in the first flush of youth and
observed to Shukanasa: 'Shukanasa, do you see the beginning of
hair growth on our prince? Does it not bring to mind the luminous
dark rock of the golden-peaked mountain, the streaks of rut fluid
that lend a shine to the cheeks of the young scent elephant, the

blemish on the moon that casts a shadow on its brilliance, the paint brush dipped in black that would bring out the beauty of the painting, the darkness of the newly formed water-laden cloud, the lines of smoke on the flaming lamps of love, smoke issuing out of the fire of valour? He has arrived at the right age for getting married. So, Arya Shukanasa, consult Devi Vilasavathi and fix an alliance with a princess suitable to him in every way. So busy is he that rarely do we get to see him. Let us at least rejoice in the company of our daughter-in-law.'

Shukanasa replied, 'My lord is right indeed. Our noble prince has established all learning in his heart. He has mastered all arts; he has won over all the subjects; the maidens of all the directions have been espoused; Rajyalakshmi has settled down with him like a housewife losing all her fickleness; and Dame Earth in her four-ocean girdle has accepted him as her lord. What else is left to be accomplished that he does not marry?'

Chandrapida was overcome with shyness at this talk of marriage. But at the same time the talk pleased him and he thought to himself with downcast eyes, 'How wonderful! At a time when I am thinking of how to get united with Kadambari, the idea of my marriage has occurred to my father too. It is like light appearing to one floundering in the dark. Having lost one's way in the forest it is like coming upon one who knows the way. When struggling in the waters of the wide-open seas it is like chancing upon a craft of some sort. It is like a shower of amrita on one who is about to die. Meeting Vaishampayana is the only thing that stands between me and Kadambari.'

The king rose and placing an arm on his son's respectfully bent shoulder made his way to his wife's apartments followed by Shukanasa. While Vilasavathi bustled about to do the honours of welcome, the king called out without even bothering to sit. 'Devi, look at our son. Nature seems to be chiding you for your lack of interest in acquiring a daughter-in-law and has taken the matter in hand. Look at the line of hair on his face. It seems to tell us that our own days of youthful dalliance are clearly all over. What do you think? I am asking you this important question and you are turning your face away in shyness. You are now the mother of an eligible bachelor. I know, you do not love Chandrapida at all, that is why you show no interest in this important matter.' Bantering in this pleasant fashion the king stayed with his wife and son for a long time.

In the meantime Chandrapida had obtained permission from Shukanasa to go and meet Vaishampayana; he spent the rest of the day at his mother's residence, making the necessary arrangements for receiving his friend.

When night fell Chandrapida went to bed but could get no sleep at all, with the excitement of seeing Vaishampayana again. The moon rose and its brilliant rays exchanged the darkness of the night for light. They stole the greenness of the woods; they drove the darkness from under the trees; they entered into the caves on the sides of the mountains and pulled the night out impatiently as it were. They whitened further the whiteness of the whitewashed palaces. The stars and the planets appeared attenuated while the sandy shores of the rivers looked vast. The rays were scattered around on the peaks of the mountains; they were gathered up on the terraces of palaces and pressed together at the entrance to highways; they rode the crest of the waves in the river and became merged with the swans. Following each other in quick succession, scattering far and wide, the rays rained down a flood of moonlight. Chandrapida could no longer remain in bed; he rose and gave orders for the conch of departure to be sounded.

At once the long shrill sound of the conch swelled up into the vault of the quarters. It circled around inside the cloud-touching towers of the city. It roamed in the interiors of the palaces it bloomed out in the squares of the city, it spread on the highways, and it wound through the crowded interiors of the houses and penetrated the dense flower gardens. The cranes living in the lotus ponds of the palace came awake and accompanied the conch with their own long, shrill calls that were punctuated by the indistinct cackling of the swans.

At once the horses were readied and assembled. Soon they filled all the roads making the large city look small and crowded. All ears were filled with the neighing of the horses and the sound of the stamping of their hooves. The entrance to the palace of the prince became awash with the foam from the horses' mouths. The very rays of the moon became metamorphosed, as it were, into the lustre of the equestrian ornaments.

In a very short time Chandrapida, fitted out for travel, mounted Indrayudha already waiting for him in the courtyard. The auspicious white umbrella named Hamsadhaman, a veritable second moon in splendour, was carried ahead, signalling departure. The vassal princes all mounted on their steeds, moved around saluting the prince, as and when they met his eye. The roads were largely free of crowds since the people of the city were still asleep, but with the cavalry pressing around Chandrapida had to pick his way with difficulty. Somehow he managed to get out of the city.

After riding a short distance he reached the river Shipra. In the flood of moonlight, the pure waters of the river were hardly visible. One could only infer their close presence by the very cool breeze wafting from the river. It was only by their agitated cackling that the travellers became aware of the white swans flying about excitedly in the water of the river. In the moonlight the river and the shore became one, as it were. Chandrapida crossed the river and took the road to Dashapura. The already broad road appeared broader still in the moonlight. The empty road increasing his enthusiasm Chandrapida sped on.

The horses galloped fast, seemingly carried along by the rushing moonlight that flowed like a river in flood from all directions. And Indrayudha whose speed kept pace with Chandrapida's heart that raced ahead in its eagerness to meet Vaishampayana, pulled along the other horses by the force of the wind raised by its speeding knees. Before the second half of the night got over they had covered a distance of three *yojanas*.

The delightful morning breeze soon started blowing as though wishing to remove the travel weariness of Chandrapida and his retinue. Cool and moist with dew, it fanned the dust-wilted tender shoots of the forest into freshness. And it was redolent of the sweet scent of the blooming white lilies. The paling moon whose lustre seemed to have been drunk away by fields upon fields of white lilies all through the night from the time of evening twilight, was kissing the virgin goddess of the western direction. The star clusters disappeared as though they were mere water bubbles that came up when the flood of moonlight poured into the western ocean. Washed in the falling dew the skies lost their powdered pearl-like moon lustre. As though rising from the waters the trees and creepers regained their natural greenness. Soon the redness of dawn appeared like a red flag on the chariot of the sun. As the red rays of the sun lit up the insides of the canopies of the trees making it appear as if there was a forest fire, the chirping flocks of birds took wing, leaving their tree abodes.

The still sleepy deer got up and stretched their stiff limbs and left their salt beds. The wild boars having freely dug out the *musta* grass growing on the banks of small ponds all night, now made their way towards the dense forests. Herds of cattle moving out early in the morning appeared like white dots on the meadows bordering the villages. The roads slowly came into view and the villages as well as though they were just being born. The quarters moved apart to take their proper places, the forests receded, the village boundaries widened, and the mountain ranges separated.

It was the time of early dawn when one's eyes could just pick out the objects in front. All at once Chandrapida saw the army that had travelled a krosha during the night, in front of him, as though the netherworld had thrown it up out of fear of a quake, as though the earth had scattered it unable to bear the weight of it, as though the very quarters had pushed it together in the fear that they had not space enough for it. It was like an eighth ocean deep but waterless and filled with creatures. The vast army seemed to extend wherever the sun shone. However hard one tried and strained one's eyes one could still not see the end of it. Protected by innumerable vassal kings it seemed like yet another world on the move. A cloud of dust covered it; and things were not clearly visible. All that one could see was that white flags were being hoisted everywhere; one could also see the elephants moving around. Presumably the horses, elephants and men were hurrying around to find their stables and tents.

Chandrapida decided he would go unannounced and meet Vaishampayana. He therefore discarded all the royal insignia, and set out leaving behind all the vassal princes and taking with him just a few horsemen with fleet-footed horses. Chandrapida covered his head with the utthariya and reached the encampment quite unrecognized by the men and women going about their business.

After entering the camp he went to the various tents and enquired where Vaishampayana's dwelling was. The women not recognizing him because of his altered appearance continued going about their business while their eyes filled with unshed tears. They merely chided him. 'Sir why are you asking this? As if Vaishampayana is here.'

Chandrapida lashed out at them: 'You wretches. Why do you spout rubbish like this.' Yet not knowing what to do he escaped from the women without asking them anything more. Like the hunted young one of the deer, like a young elephant who had lost his way, like a young calf with his ear raised in fear, having been separated from his mother, Chandrapida, completely distraught, oblivious to everything, his mind in a whirl rushed to the centre of the camp, neither seeing, nor hearing, nor uttering anything, like one who had become blind, deaf and dumb.

In the meantime the news that the prince had come spread, the men having recognized Indrayudha and the few princes who had followed him. There was at once great commotion in the camp. They all came running in agitation, all the princes who had been left with Vaishampayana, their utthariyas flying, their eyes brimming with tears and bowed all together before Chandrapida. Without any preamble Chandrapida asked them, 'Where is Vaishampayana?'

—55—

The assembled people quickly consulted each other and spoke all together. 'Let Deva dismount under this tree and we will explain everything.' At these ominous words more cruel in their implication than a blunt statement of fact, Chandrapida felt as if he had been struck in the heart by an arrow. And his heart came close to breaking. Thankfully unconsciousness always a friend in such circumstances, came to his rescue and he fell into a swoon. How he dismounted, and how he was held and helped on to a carpet by several of the crowned kings present there equal in age, valour and dignity to his own father, he knew not.

When he regained consciousness he fell into even greater confusion at not seeing Vaishampayana in the camp; he was completely disoriented as to who he was, where he was and what he was doing, even as an ascetic would be at the moment of realization of divine truth. His senses seemed to fail him and he was unable to comprehend anything except that the army was back and that Vaishampayana was not with it. And because of that absence his mind imagined the most terrible possibilities, leaving him completely at a loss as to what to do.

'What should I do, lament, or steadying my heart, stay silent? Should I strike at myself and simply separate my body from the soul? Should I renounce everything and just go away somewhere all by myself?' he raged within himself. The beautiful world no longer delighted him; the earth so full of people seemed suddenly empty to him; although well-born and well brought up he felt he had been cheated of the fruits of his life's labour. He felt weak with despair. His mind was in turmoil. 'Why should I continue to live, or Kadambari for that matter? Where shall I go now looking for Vaishampayana? Who will now give me another friend such as Vaishampayana? How can I meet Uncle Shukanasa without Vaishampayana beside me? How can I console grief-stricken Amba Manorama?' Perhaps, Chandrapida reasoned, he has gone to conquer some part of the world not yet brought under control; perhaps there remained a king not yet subdued and he had gone to subdue him; or there might still be some branch of knowledge left unmastered and he had stayed back to master it.

Torturing himself with unanswerable questions and unprovable suppositions, and ashamed that he was still not dead and condemning himself as a villain because of that, he remained with his head bent and his face hidden. Then slowly speaking with difficulty he questioned his vassals. 'After I left, was there any fighting? Or was there an outbreak of some fatal illness that this bolt from the blue has fallen upon us?'

At this all of them, covering their ears with their hands, cried out in unison 'God forbid! May Vaishampayana live for another hundred years like the gods.' When he heard this Chandrapida felt like a dead man brought back to life. Shedding tears of joy he embraced them all and cried out, 'I could not imagine a Vaishampayana alive and well, yet staying away; that was why I had to ask all those questions. Now I understand that he is alive and well. So tell me what has held him back? Where is he now? Why have you left him there all alone and come away? I am impatient to know why you were not able to bring him back by force?'

'Deva,' said the vassals, 'after you left having ordered us to follow you slowly under Vaishampayana's command a day went in preparations for the long journey ahead, gathering provisions, grass and fuel for the army. The next day when the drums of departure were sounded and everything was ready Vaishampayana said to us early in the morning, "I have heard it said in the *Puranas* that the Acchoda Lake is one of great sanctity. I would like therefore to bathe in the lake and worship Bhavanipati, Lord Maheshwara with a bit of Shashanka on his head residing right there on the shores of the lake at the Siddhayatana, after which we can depart. After all how many have ever chanced upon a spot such as this frequented by the devas themselves; for most of us it may not happen even in the dream." Vaishampayana then walked up to the shores of the lake where he wandered around taking in the beauty of the surroundings.

'And then he saw this bower of creepers whose fresh shoots were splendid enough to adorn the ears of divine women. They were gently moving in the wind blowing in from the Acchoda Lake. Swarms of bees were buzzing around the dense clusters of flowers on the creepers greedy for the honey. As the flowers danced in the wind and the bees buzzed the bower seemed to be beckoning to the travellers. The vivid emerald of the creepers seemed to colour the entire atmosphere green. The bower was so dense that the sun's rays hardly ever penetrated it; it was night inside the bower even during the day. Appearing like a formation of rain clouds it deluded even the peacocks roosting right there and familiar with it; they were constantly stretching their necks up in the expectation of rain and calling out. The bower was the very home of the rainy season; it was cold's permanent abode and the antithesis of all that was hot. It was a place where a pining Rati might have found solace. And it was the ultimate resort of all kinds of beauty.

'There was a stone seat inside the bower served by the gentle fragrant wind rising from the lake. When Vaishampayana saw the bower with the stone seat in it, he stared at it as if he were looking at a long-lost brother, or a son, or a friend; he had no eyes for anything else. He stood there motionless, like a painted picture, a carved figure; and then as suddenly, as though powerless to carry his own limbs, as though about to lose consciousness, having been abandoned by all his senses, he sat down on the ground and became lost in thought. It was apparent that some deep memories had been stirred; he now appeared to be keenly concentrating on something. His face was expressionless but the tears were coursing down his face.

'When we saw him thus we thought, "Even men of much worldly experience and mature intellect, especially if they are of a sensitive nature, do get overwhelmed at times by certain things. How much easier and how natural for the heart of someone so young and so full of youthful ardour to be simply overpowered by the sight of all this beauty." So we gave him sometime to recover and then spoke to him. "You have seen here beauty in its ultimate form. But you have to get up now and perform your bathing duties. It is getting late. All preparations for the journey are over. The army is ready to depart and is waiting for you. One should not delay now." But he sat there still and silent, as if he never heard our words. He said nothing in reply, like one who had lost the power of all his senses, like one who had been struck dumb, like one who never learned how to talk. He continued to gaze at the bower of creepers with tear-filled eyes that were so still as if they had been painted on him.

'As we continued to press him to get ready for departure Vaishampayana with his eyes still fixed on the bower of creepers replied in a harsh tone that brooked no argument. "I cannot leave this place. You go taking the army with you. As Chandrapida has gone back it is not proper at all for you to linger here with this immense army, without his protection and control."

'We realized that something in that area had cast a spell on him, making him lose interest in everything. We tried our best to reason with him. Failing in our effort and upset by this inexplicable behaviour we even used harsh words to make him come out of the spell. "Yes indeed, it is not proper for us to tarry here. But what of you? You are the son of Arya Shukanasa, such a close friend of the king that they appear like one entity. Devi Vilasavathi has cherished you in her lap. And you grew up a close and trusted friend of Chandrapida and shared the tough scholastic years with him. Does it now behove you, when that friend, elder brother, the loved one, your lord, the lord of the world, that noble individual has entrusted you with everything, to abandon all your responsibility and stay back here? You and the prince are the same to us; we make no difference between the two of you. With the love and respect that we have for you how can we leave you here alone in this deserted country and go back? And if we did how would we justify our behaviour to the moonlight-gentle Chandrapida? So please get rid of this confusion and make up your mind to start the return journey."

'Vaishampayana smiled at us without joy. He said, "Am I so lacking in understanding that you have to advise me? It has never been possible for me to be away from Chandrapida even for a

minute. I should have had the strongest urge to leave from here.
Yet what shall I do? All my control over myself seems to have
slipped away that very minute when my eyes fell on the bower.
Groping towards some deep memory my mind refuses to think of
anything else. The eyes seem to see something here and refuse to
turn anywhere else. The heart is attached to some spot here but
knows not where it is. My feet feel chained and are unable to take
even a step. My body feels impaled to this ground and I am unable
to move from here. You may want to take me by force but in that
case I do not think I shall live. As I stand here, that unknown
something that is going round in my mind is holding me back,
but it is also that alone which, I believe, is still keeping me alive.
Please do not press me to leave. You go. May you enjoy the
presence of Chandrapida for as long as you live. Unlucky as I am,
fate has now wrested that boon from my hand."

'As we continued to importune him he said with finality, "I am
ashamed to be saying all this. I swear on Chandrapida I do not
know why I am unable to move away from this place. You have
seen all this happen. So please go back." Then he fell silent.

'In a short while he got up and wandered around the
beautiful woods, in the bowers of creepers, and on the shores of
the lake and in the temple near by as though he was looking for
something he had lost. After a while distressed at heart he sighed
deeply and sat down again in the bower. We too stayed close to
the bower in the hope he might come out of his delusion. A little
later we urged him to perform the day's ablutions and have
something to eat to which he replied, "My dear friend the prince,
loves these life forces of mine even more than his own. If they try
to leave me then I have to take steps to hold them back. I long to
see Chandrapida not death." He got up and had his bath and
then a repast of fruits and roots like an ascetic. Three days and
nights went by with Vaishampayana still remaining in that
wonderstruck bewildered state of mind. It soon became clear to

us that neither would he return of his own accord, nor would it be possible to bring him back by force. So we left him there with his attendants and the necessary provisions and turned back. We did not send a messenger after you because he could not have caught up with you; and we did not despatch any one to the capital because we did not want to trouble you with having to start again on a journey so soon after getting home after such a long absence.'

-56-

When Chandrapida heard the story of Vaishampayana—a sequence of events he could not have imagined even in his wildest fancies and dreams—he was struck at once with amazement and dismay.

'What could have been the reason for this sudden renunciation of the world on the part of Vaishampayana? What has made him turn into a forest recluse shunning all attachment?' he wondered. 'I do not see any wrongdoing on my part' he thought, trying to analyse the situation logically. 'Thanks to my father's grace all the other princes too accord him the same respect that they show me. They do not treat him differently. In the abundant store of enjoyments his share is no less than mine. He has as much power to confer bounties as I; his writ runs wherever mine does; the guilty fear him as much as they fear me. The world envies him as much as it envies me. Should he come back now would he not be welcomed with the same degree of parental affection by my father and mother as by Arya Shukanasa and Amba Manorama? Is it possible that my father or Arya Shukanasa would have wounded him with words of admonition perhaps wishing for greater obedience?

'But I have never known Vaishampayana to be the unloving kind lacking in affection and reverential attachment towards his elders. He has never been of unsteady mind, or guilty of irresponsible action. He has never shown any wilfulness as the first-born or the only child of his parents. Considerate and helpful always, would he now show anger against his parents and stop obeying their authority?

'And he is not at an age right for renunciation; he has not even entered the stage of the householder, as befits a well-educated man; he has not therefore paid back his dues to the gods and to his ancestral spirits and to his fellowmen. Bound by these dues where can he go now? He has no experience at all of women and consequently of samsara. He has not therefore attained any of the *purusharthas* of life, namely dharma, artha and kama. He has not even rendered personal service to his parents to ensure their comfort. He has not helped his loving relations, nor endowed his dear friends with wealth, nor honoured the wise. He has not shared his wealth with his dependants nor fulfilled the desires of those begging for favours.

'He has not founded his lineage by begetting sons and grandsons. Nor has he performed any great sacrificial rituals. He has not given generous gifts nor fulfilled his obligations of hospitality. He has not done his duty by this world. He has not adorned the earth with dams, wells and water distributing centres, with palaces, ponds and groves. Above all he has not still spread his fame far and wide which alone would live on till the end of the world.'

~

Chandrapida stood for a long time under the tree, desolated, his agitated mind trying to fathom the reason behind this inexplicable behaviour of Vaishampayana. With a troubled heart he dismissed all the accompanying princes after having conferred suitable rewards on them, and entered the royal tent put up for him that very instant.

Chandrapida went directly into his own chambers, made ready for him just then but resembling, all the same, a fully equipped palace. Removing all his travel clothes and the extra ornaments he fell on the bed. An attendant gently fanned him with a palm leaf fan; another massaged him. Slowly his travel weariness disappeared. But he could not fall asleep although he had been on the roads practically the whole night. Unhappy thoughts and doubts assailed his already troubled mind. 'If I now leave right from here without the permission of my parents, without comforting Arya Shukanasa and Amba Manorama I will have behaved in the same way as Vaishampayana has. On the other hand, if I return to the capital to seek my parents' permission to go in search of Vaishampayana I fear very much that permission might be denied. What do I do now? Perhaps I am wrong in assuming that I would not be allowed to go. In a way my good friend by abandoning me in this fashion has helped me; he has created a pretext for me to travel to Kadambari. On further thinking, I do feel that no one, neither my parents nor Arya Shukanasa would stop me from going in search of Vaishampayana. I shall first reach the lake, meet my friend and then proceed further with Vaishampayana by my side.'

Having made up his mind with regard to the future course of action he felt that the present distress regarding Vaishampayana was merely a bitter medicine, which would eventually lead to his well-being, in the form of happy union with Kadambari. His mind quietened, he rested until the conch sounded the peaceful passing of the third half yama of the night and then rose to perform his ablutions. Taking heart in the fact that both Vaishampayana and Kadambari, the two most dear to him in the whole world, were in the same place he had something to eat and set about the day's duties.

While a fire raged within Chandrapida thanks to Madana and the absence of Vaishampayana, an equal fire raged outside with the sun up in the middle of the sky spreading his massed rays in all the directions. He seemed to gloat, 'I can cause distress effortlessly.' The rays seemed to spew forth molten silver. The sun's fiery embers seemed to shoot through the body. The animals were crowding under the shade of the trees. The glare was blinding, the very directions seemed ablaze. The ground was hot and the water stations were crowded with the hot and thirsty travellers while the roads were empty. The birds huddled in their nests as their own hot breath bothered them. The buffaloes wallowed in small ponds. Young women's cheeks were flushed a lotus red, and drops of perspiration on them shone like broken pearls. People dreamed of cool moonlight; they sang the praises of frost; they yearned for the rainy season. At the very least they wished that particular day would come to an end.

Chandrapida now made his way to the water pavilion, built near a lake. Perennially flooded with streams of water, there was no heat at all inside the pavilion. There were brook-like channels supplied with water from showers falling with force. All the pillars in the pavilion were wound around with streamers of flowers, tender leaves and creepers. A thick wet smear of sandalwood paste made for further coolness. The whole ground was covered with emerald-green lotus leaves, on which were spread piles of fresh, moist sweet-scented lotus blooms.

For Chandrapida, however, the sheer beauty of the cool pavilion only served to intensify the thousand yearnings caused by Manmatha. And the coolness of the showers kindled a fiery longing for the dear missing friend. Somehow, alone, he managed to cross that limitless, unfathomable ocean of a day by the craft of his own steadiness. As day reddened into evening, he got out of the water pavilion and went into the courtyard paved dark with cow dung. A gentle evening breeze blew about the white flowers on the ground. Chandrapida tarried a while in the reception tent close by to meet the princes and discuss the problem of Vaishampayana with them. Then he gave orders for departure at the stroke of the second watch, dismissed the princes and returned to his own chamber.

The army impatient to be back in the capital city it had not seen for so many days was ready to leave even without performing the ceremonies of departure. Chandrapida too, unable to get sleep set out earlier than he had planned, taking with him a small princely force of cavalry and elephant riders. As he travelled, the night spent itself out and early in the morning Chandrapida and his small army had arrived at the capital.

As he approached Ujjayini he could see at a distance, people who had walked out of the city, gathered in groups, some seated, some taking a few uncertain steps and some even turning back. As he drew close, Chandrapida could see that most had tears in their eyes, their faces pale with distress. Some were heard to murmur 'Ah! ah! What agony,' while others were silent with the weight of their sorrow. Even the sages and the saints, the detached and the desireless as well as the generally indifferent were now overcome with emotion. What Chandrapida heard all around him was the agonized discussion, questioning and answering, and guessing at what might have happened to Vaishampayana.

He felt shaken. 'If this is the condition of the people at large, how much more terrible would be the state of those who brought him up on their laps and who delighted in his childish pranks. It is going to be very difficult to face Arya Shukanasa and Amba Manorama.'

Focussing his brimming eyes on the tip of his nose he entered the city without glancing at the happenings around him. Dismounting at the entrance to the palace he learned that his parents were with Shukanasa. Chandrapida too made his way there. As he neared the palace he could hear the loud and heart-rending lamentation of Manorama. 'Ah my child Vaishampayana, you are still a child to me, to be taken on my lap. How can you stay all alone in the lonely forest filled with hundreds of thousands of cruel wild animals? Who will protect you from them? Who is there to make a comfortable bed for you? When you are hungry, or sleepy, or thirsty who is there who would feel your pain? You have now left my lap, but you have not gained a wife who will share your pleasure and pain. I had hoped that when you returned, with your father's permission, I would be blessed with a daughter-in-law. It seems that wish is not to be fulfilled. But in addition I seem to have lost you too. Wherever you wish to live, you take me too, with your father's permission; I cannot live without seeing you. You have never disobeyed me, not even in your childhood. How could you, all of a sudden turn so harsh and unfeeling? I have never seen you angry, how could you get so angry with me now all of a sudden? Have you lost your love for us having seen other countries? You could not stay for a moment away from Chandrapida; have you now lost your love for him too? Please come back. The parents should be kept happy at all times; but you have caused them so much unhappiness. I do not know what you mean to gain by acting this way.' Manorama went on in this strain shaken by the absence of her son while Devi Vilasavathi was trying to comfort her and steady her.

Chandrapida was moved beyond description by the piteous cries of the devastated mother; reeling under the intensity of that sorrow he walked on as if in sleep. Almost on the point of falling unconscious he collected himself with his innate strength and went in. His father was sitting motionless like the stilled waters of the ocean after the churning stopped; Shukanasa too was absolutely still with no movement of his limbs, like the Mandara Mountain at rest. Ashamed to look his father in the eye he bowed to him with lowered head and sat down at a distance.

His father looked at him for a while and spoke in a voice that shook with the effort of controlling the welling tears, and sounded like the rumble of rain filled clouds. 'My son Chandrapida, I know that you love your brother Vaishampayana even dearer than your own life. That a loved one who should be the source only of happiness has become, unbelievably enough, the cause of great sorrow, makes it all the more unbearable. This conduct on the part of your friend is so uncharacteristic of him; it goes against the nobility of his birth, his affectionate nature, his habitual good conduct, his natural willingness to learn and his invariable respect towards his elders. I therefore suspect that some mistake of yours might have had something to do with it.'

─57─

When Arya Shukanasa heard King Tarapida rebuking Chandrapida, his face darkened with sorrow and anger and with trembling lips he spoke emotionally.

'My lord! If the moonlight were to start giving heat, if one were to find coldness in fire, if the sun with his garland of rays were to begin to create darkness, if the oceans were to run dry, if Adisesha were to lay down the burden of the earth, if the saintly were to stop living for others, then perhaps the prince too would become guilty of misdemeanour. Chandrapida is more virtuous than you, my lord, and deserves to have been born in the Krita Yuga. How can you suspect such a one without any investigation, of involvement in the doings of that ill-born wretch, that villain, a traitor to his king and his own friend, that unloving son, that destroyer of parents, that ingrate, that sinner, that perpetrator of evil deeds. There is nothing that should be more abhorrent to a man of sterling virtues than that people should ever suspect him of a misdeed; how much more intense ought that abhorrence to be if one's own father should turn accuser? This son of mine brought up on your knees and Devi Vilasavathi's lap has proved to be uncontrollable like the wind; what could Chandrapida have done to rein him in?

'Creatures like my son do appear on their own, huge insects, born of flesh and the abode of all sins; they are like terrible diseases full of poison within. They are vicious and cause destruction, like great calamities do. They slither along like serpents full of darkness, and are crooked in their ways. Their souls are stained and they are traitors to their own lineages. There is no tenderness in them; they are shameless, insensitive and bestial. Like swords that get sharpened with the application of soft grease they become sharp and cruel in the presence of affection. Like the cheek of the elephant that gets dark with the flow of dana, the rut fluid, their nature gets darkened in the presence of generosity, dana. Devoid of all virtue they push themselves forward riding on the strength of their friends; it is the force of the wings on the arrows that carries them far when released from a bow.

'They return harshness for affection, crookedness for honesty, and wickedness for goodness. They are disobedient to the master, treacherous to friends, destructive to the trusting, cruel to the servants, harsh to the weak. They show their strength only to women. They return hate for love. Their meagre intellect is directed towards deceiving others and not for gaining knowledge; their learning is used for fraud and trickery and not for bringing about amity. Their valour is directed towards causing distress to people and not for helping them.

'Everything gets topsy-turvy in their perception. The weighty is seen as trivial, the degraded as noble, the unapproachable as within reach; unfairness is seen as fairness, the improper as the proper, frailty as firmness, arrogance as modesty, and falsehood as truth.

'This fellow Vaishampayana too is one such wretched being; it did not occur to him that he was letting down his friend Chandrapida. He did not pause to consider whether such conduct would not anger Tarapida, ever a stickler for propriety. Did he think of his mother who lives solely for him? Does he not realize that his father has brought him into the world for serving the ancestral spirits, thereby ensuring the continuity of the line? How could he give up everything without his father's consent? What could one do with a man floundering in the darkness of ignorance, a man who has eyes but does not see? Your lordship has instructed him over and over again, as one would a parrot; even the birds become attached to their benefactor and become faithful to him. They certainly show affection to their progenitors unlike this wretched sinner who has lost both this world and the next and has brought everything to ruin. For what he has done let his soul fall in the midst of animals or birds, for it is clear that he has not been born for keeping us happy. He has in fact pushed us into an ocean of grief.

'All clear-headed people work towards their own as well as others' welfare. But this wretch has only plunged us in sorrow by doing something that is neither to his own good nor to that of others. I fail to understand, try as much as I can, why he has gone down this path to destruction. He was born only to cause us grief.' As he spoke Shukanasa's eyes became like autumnal lotus blooms, filling with tears; his lips trembled with the effort to contain the volcanic rage within.

King Tarapida looked at his friend and spoke gently. 'Does the lamp enhance the brightness of fire? Do the drops of water from the clouds swell the oceans? Does the breeze from the fans augment the force of the wind? Any advice that I give you would in like fashion pale into insignificance. Yet even a wise man, a learned man, a man of great courage, strength and steadiness of mind may allow, in the presence of great sorrow, his normally lucid mind to become clouded, as one sees the clear waters of a lake becoming turbid with rain. Once the mind loses its clarity all knowledge and wisdom perish. It loses the very power of thinking. The intellect fails to understand; the powers of discrimination disappear. That is why I would like to say something now, though you know the ways of the world much more than I.

'Is there anyone in the world who has been able to get over the wild impulses of youth without getting scathed in the process? The closeness to the parents vanishes with the end of childhood. New attachments begin with the growing years. As the chest broadens, the desires too widen. As the strength increases, youthful ardour too intensifies. With the swelling arms the intellect too swells. But, with the thinning waistline studiousness too thins. As the thighs gain power the heart too acquires a certain heady arrogance. With the sprouting of facial hair depravity-causing confusion makes its appearance. Thus the passions of the heart keep pace with the increasing beauty of the body. The eyes are clear, yet full of desire; they are long yet they do not possess far-sightedness. The ears are good, as the hearing is acute, but the advice of the elders does not enter. There is obsession with women and the heart does not recognize any other subject to study.

'The passions rise because of enhanced sensitivity that, like excessive rain, soaks everything. Day becomes the mere harbinger of the night to be filled with pleasures, and as for night, it is just the provider of darkness to offset all light of reason. The mind reels and falters, and when the mind trips all sense of shame vanishes. Once stripped of the protective cover of a sense of shame, the god of the floral bow, so difficult to ward off, the cause of all unrestrained conduct makes his entry into the heart.

'Once Kama sets foot in the heart, a thousand vulnerabilities appear and all energy and strength dissipate. What would good conduct hold on to then? From what would humility and respectfulness draw their strength? How does one preserve one's steadiness? How does one rein in the senses? How do you move away from conduct that brings ill fame? By what light can one remove the darkness of ignorance that blinds the eye and binds one to tainted ways? What indeed can a youth perceive in the absence of maturity of vision?

'But maturity of vision does not come even with age, and so how could it appear in youth? Only some fortunate ones have purity of conduct keeping pace with the whitening of hair. Vicious like the poison of the great snake that causes unconsciousness, befuddling like the fluid-secreting rut of the elephant, and an abode of all sensual pleasures, the state of young manhood exercises the tyranny of the scoundrel on the victim. In this state all who stray into the extremely uneven path of sensual gratification are bound to lose their footing. Why then this anger on the part of Arya for a child who has to be cherished, protected? Why utter such harsh words full of rage so unbecoming of a father's love for the child? It is said that words of curse or blessing directed at their children, uttered by parents even in their sleep come true without fail. Parents are like gods to the children. While blessings from them take the form of boons, words uttered in rage turn into curses. When Arya speaks in such anger against Vaishampayana my mind is greatly distressed. One gets attached even to a tree that one has planted and nourished; how much more should one love one's children born out of one's own loins. Enough of this torrent of rage against Vaishampayana. He would not have done anything that goes against his nature.

Without finding out the cause of his renunciation why should we ascribe bad motives to him? Sometimes such disobedient acts too result in some untoward good. Bring him home now. Then we would know more about this impetuosity that is so out of character for him; then we would decide what to do about it.'

Shukanasa however insisted, 'You are too kind, my lord. Your great affection for Vaishampayana makes you command thus. Can any conduct be worse than abandoning the prince and staying on by himself wilfully?'

─58─

Chandrapida had sat silent all this while. His father's words expressing his suspicion that he might have had a hand in Vaishampayana behaving in such a fashion lashed at his heart like a whip. Now he got up and approached Shukanasa and spoke to him.

'Although I know without a doubt that it is no fault of mine that Vaishampayana has not returned, still, such a suspicion may arise in the minds of others as well, as it has in my father's. Even that which is untrue, if accepted as true by the world, especially by the elders, becomes the truth. It is publicity—of a fault or virtue—that bears fruit as ill repute or fame. The actual truth may earn its reward in the hereafter, but that is of no use here. Do please make my father give me permission to go and get Vaishampayana back so that I may be able to wipe away the taint on my character. As long as Vaishampayana does not return my father will not be able to get rid of that suspicion from his mind. And, if I do not go Vaishampayana will not come back. If it had been at all possible for them, the thousand princes who serve my father faithfully would have brought him back by now.

'Riding a horse on a route so well known to me I will hardly find the journey irksome. Please rest assured that I will get Vaishampayana back. The pain in my heart over his absence is far more severe than any bodily discomfort that I may have to undergo on the journey. I was so sure that he would quickly follow me with the army that I came away without waiting for him. Have I ever from the time we were born, gone anywhere, stayed anywhere, played or laughed, eaten or drunk slept or remained awake without Vaishampayana at my side? Please save me from the ill fame that would befall me if I did not go for him now. The reason why I did not leave directly from the army encampment after receiving the news was that such an action would have been no different from Vaishampayana's behaviour.'

Shukanasa regarded the flushed face of the troubled prince with great affection and then turned to the king and asked him softly, 'The prince begs permission to go in search of Vaishampayana. What is my lord's command?' King Tarapida thought for a while and said, 'Arya, I was so sure today that very soon I would have the pleasure of seeing Chandrapida married, his bride sparkling like moonlight on a full moon day. But now we have this obstacle, like the rainy season, in the form of the Vaishampayana episode thrown on the path of my wishes by the contrary-minded creator. So let it be as Chandrapida wishes. No one else can bring Vaishampayana back in any case, nor could any one hold this one back here. All the same it is certain that we are going to be plunged into an unfordable sea of anxiety. I know that Devi Vilasavathi too will release him for bringing Vaishampayana home. So let him go. But the boy has to travel far, so fix an auspicious day and hour for departure by consulting the astrologers. Make all preparations for the journey.'

The king then looked at his son with brimming eyes and told him to come closer. He stroked the prince's head and shoulders bent in respect to him and holding the young man's arm with his own hand commanded him: 'My child, go in and tell your mother, who is with Manorama, about your impending departure.'

Chandrapida, joyfully clasping to his heart his father's permission to go, as though it were really the svayamvara garland with which Kadambari would wed him, went into the interior apartments. His eyes however did not reflect the excitement of his heart. He bowed to his mother, sat down near her and sought to console Manorama whose anguish doubled at the sight of Chandrapida. 'Please be consoled. I have been ordered by my father to go and bring Vaishampayana back. I will be back very quickly. I am also eager to see my friend again. Bid me farewell without any qualms.'

Manorama replied: 'Child, is this how you console me, by talking of going away? Is there any difference between you and him as far as I am concerned? That hard-hearted one, he has already disappeared. Now it is only by looking at you that I live. And if you too go away then there would be no reason for me to live any longer. With one of you here both of us, your mother and I are comforted as being blessed with a child.'

Vilasavathi broke in and said firmly: 'My dear friend, you have put into words my very thoughts. But without Vaishampayana whom will this one look up to? Leave things alone. Why do you try to stop him? In any case this one will not be stopped. I feel that is why his father too has granted him permission to go. Let him go. It is far better that for a few days you and I do not see both of them, than having to see this one's long face day after day in the absence of Vaishampayana. Rise now, let us go and prepare for the departure of our son Chandrapida.'

She took Manorama's hands and pulled her up and went back to her palace with Chandrapida following. After discussing his travel plans with her Chandrapida too went home. With mounting excitement in his heart he called over the astrologers secretly and instructed them: 'See to it you find an early date for my departure and inform Arya Shukanasa and my father accordingly.' They replied, 'Deva, according to the configuration of your planets, it is not advisable at present for you to undertake any journey. But if the work is urgent then the time that the king decides upon becomes indeed the right time, for all work. There is really no need to look for an auspicious date now.' Chandrapida replied, 'I spoke to you because my father wished for this. For one involved in the fulfilment of unavoidable and pressing duties that come up every moment how can you fix an auspicious date and hour? So please announce that I can leave as early as tomorrow itself.'

Within a short time the astrologers came back and informed him softly, 'We have carried out Deva's commands thanks to Shukanasa's distracted state of mind, anxious about his son. Let the day be over tomorrow, you can leave at nightfall.' Pleased, Chandrapida thanked them warmly and rewarded them for their labours.

Now both Kadambari and Vaishampayana filled his mind's eye; he saw them as vividly as if they were actually present before him. His mind racing ahead of his body fancied he had already caught up with Patralekha before she reached Kadambari. Realizing he needed fleet-footed horses for the long journey, he selected animals that would match the speed of Indrayudha, made of the essence of the four oceans. He also selected princes who were vigorous men, full of enthusiasm for the journey, and who would not mind the strain of riding such a long distance. Having done that he somehow passed that day and the following night.

Soon it was the evening of the next day. The sun was setting; the russet hues of twilight spread in the western half of the sky like the glow from the funeral pyre of the dead sun. The stars sparkled in the sky like sparks rising from the evening fires. In the enveloping darkness the four heavenly directions seemed to close their eyes, swooning over the disappearance of the day. The noisy birds flying home were heard lamenting the impending separation from the skies. Leaving the light of life the world seemed to retreat into the darkness of the womb. The moon as though returning from a past life climbed the Udayagiri and brightened the face of the maiden of the eastern quarter.

As night fell Chandrapida, ready to leave came to his mother to bid farewell. Vilasavathi was grief-stricken. Her eyes, large as they were, were unable to contain her tears. She tried her best to hold them back, knowing that it was inauspicious to cry at such a moment. Agonized with love for her son she spoke haltingly, chokingly. 'My child, it is but natural that the mother feels deep sorrow when the cherished child leaves her lap for the first time. But this distress of mine, now at this second departure is nothing like what I felt at that first time. My heart seems to split asunder. This distress is piercing my vitals. My body is being consumed by it. My mind is in turmoil. The joints in my body seem to be coming apart. My vital breaths are straining to leave my body. My mind is in total confusion; it sees only emptiness everywhere. I am unable to steady my heart and my tears distress me again and again. I try to prepare for your safe journey but my mind wanders again and again. I have no idea why I am so troubled. What is it that I imagine? Is it that my son who has returned after such a long time is going away again so soon? Or is it that I feel apprehensive of your travelling alone especially in your troubled state of mind? How can my words prevent you from going in search of Vaishampayana? But my heart does not want you to go. You see my agony, son. Do not stay away like last time developing an attachment to some place or the other. I beg of you my child, with folded hands.'

Chandrapida replied kindly. 'Mother, I was then delayed due to the demands of the digvijaya. Now it should take only as much time as is necessary to reach the place where Vaishampayana is and return with him. You should not worry at all about my being delayed.' The mother controlled her tears; but it was only with anguish in her heart that she performed the rites of departure. Her love for her son welled up even as her breasts spouted milk. She held him tightly to her for a long time, kissed his forehead and released him reluctantly as though her own life forces were going away with him.

Chandrapida then went to his father's palace in order to take leave of him. The king who was lying in bed saw his son approach and called out to him to come close. Gazing at his son with love in his eyes the king embraced him. His eyes filled rapidly with tears and his heart with anxiety as he spoke hesitantly. 'My child, you should not take it to heart that your father suspected wrongdoing on your part. From the time you started your studies we have had you constantly under observation. Tested and found fit, you have been entrusted with the responsibility of governing only on the strength of your great qualities, not because of my love for you as my son. To rule is more arduous than to literally carry the earth on your shoulders. The presence of innumerable kings on the earth poses great difficulties; the prevalence of crooked politics renders all movement unsafe. This kingdom that is spread over the entire earth bounded by the four oceans is indeed huge, the establishment of which has been an extremely tough task, that was made possible only by a vast army and great wealth collected with great difficulty. Once established, it is unimaginably difficult to sustain such an empire because of the unrelenting effort, labour coupled with strategy, that is required.

'However, this state has been founded by such an exalted lineage that it is beyond the reach of most; even a thousand enemies cannot capture it and hold it. It is not given to the weak, the unsteady, the unwise, those devoid of vision, the impure, those lacking in valour and enthusiasm, the ill-spoken, the untruthful, the undiscriminating, the ungrateful, the ungenerous who share not the spoils of war with all their subjects, the unrighteous the uncompassionate, those who do not protect the Brahmins, those who stand not by their friends, those incapable of service, to rule over a kingdom of such proportions. It is only in the hands of one, who can, by the excellence of his virtues attract compellingly, the fickle loyalties in the land and bind them all to himself that this kingdom can remain safe.

'It is only in such a one, that the elders of the land, confident that he would not stumble, entrust the responsibility of ruling, after considering all the pros and cons of the step. My son should therefore understand that there is no fault in him. In any case on whom would you shift even a little bit of your responsibility and sit back and nurse your guilt? It is you that ought to strive for the welfare of all in the world. My days are over; I have held things under control for a very long time indeed. My subjects have never been troubled by my greed. I showed no disrespect towards the elders. The saintly were never insulted by my arrogance. No one was harassed by my anger or cruelty. I mocked no one, nor did I destroy my future life with lust. The rule of law and not wilfulness was upheld. I served the elders, not my unruly appetites. I followed the example of the good, and not the dictates of my senses. It was good conduct that I nurtured, not my body. I feared censure, not death. I have experienced all pleasures, even those that may be hard to come by in the divine world; whatever passions rose in me in the first flush of youth were fully satisfied, but never have I indulged in a forbidden act.

'There is only one wish of mine yet to be fulfilled; namely that once you are wed, I would have liked to have handed over completely all my responsibilities to you and gone the way of the *rajarishis* of yore, with a light heart. Vaishampayana's conduct has all of a sudden put paid to the fulfilment of this last desire of mine. I fear it is destined to remain unfulfilled for a long time to come; that is why he has disappeared. How could one have dreamed of such a conduct on his part? And now you have to go away and this desire of mine will lie unrealized in my heart for a long time.' Looking up the king gave tambula to Chandrapida as though he were offering his own heart with it. Then he bade his son farewell.

Feeling immensely elevated by his father's graciousness towards him Chandrapida took his leave with respectful humility and made his way to Shukanasa's residence, where he found them, both the minister and his wife in deep distress. Shukanasa was in a daze as though all his senses had deserted him; Manorama's face was streaked with her incessant tears. Their sorrow-laden blessings adding to the weight of his own grief, Chandrapida quickly turned away from them in order to prevent their following him.

He left their door and saw that an unwilling Indrayudha was being brought forward for mounting. The horse was pulling back; he was making uncharacteristic mournful noises; he did not raise his ears in welcome. It was obvious that his heart was not in the journey and there was no eagerness to be off. He was dispirited and unwilling to go. Chandrapida thought that the horse might refuse to allow him to mount if he delayed any longer. He quickly mounted the steed, and driven by the desire to see Vaishampayana and Kadambari he rode with great speed out of the city.

-59-

Leaving the city, Chandrapida avoided the silk pavilion erected on the banks of the Shipra for performing the farewell rites and rode on, causing great confusion among the attendants and the vassal princes who were waiting there for him. After travelling three kroshas the prince pitched his tents at a place where grass grew plentifully and water was available. However he was too restless to remain inactive for long and resumed the journey even before daybreak.

As he travelled, his imagination grew wings and took flight. 'When I find Vaishampayana' he thought 'I will approach him unannounced; stealing upon him from behind I will put my arms around him and embrace him tightly crying out "Now where will you run away?" Teasing him thus I would remove my friend's embarrassment. After enjoying the reunion with Vaishampayana I would go to meet Mahashveta, that blameless maiden ever accessible and pleasant who would be so thrilled at seeing me so unexpectedly. I would then leave all my army and my princes there at Mahashveta's ashrama and accompanied by her alone proceed to Hemakuta.

'Kadambari's attendants will be taken by such surprise when they recognize me that they will run about in confusion to welcome me. How Kadambari's eyes will widen when she hears of my arrival and how the attendants will grab the *purnapatra* from her. Kadambari will then shoot questions at her friends. "Where is he? Who said he is here? How far is he from here?" and so on. And her love fever will abate immediately; she will at once remove the lotus leaves spread on her chest for coolness and shyly cover her bosom with the utthariya. She will throw away the lotus stalk adornments from her body preferring to show me the natural beauty of her limbs, which far outshines any ornament. She will however first try to remove, by rubbing with her hand, the thick sandalwood paste applied on her so that her limbs would regain their supreme loveliness. She will release the disarranged hair sticking to her cheeks and throw her tresses back on her shoulder, all the while looking at herself in a gem-embedded mirror. She will offer her own tears of joy to quench the fire of Madana; she will abandon her flower-strewn bed and bustle about to welcome me.

'And then my eyes would find their ultimate reward in gazing at Kadambari. I would then salute and hug Madalekha; I would raise Patralekha up affectionately, who by then, would have fallen at my feet. I would then embrace Keyuraka again and again to my heart's content.

'In the meantime Mahashveta would have got things ready for our wedding. Kadambari duly bathed by her attendants and shining like the earth drenched with rain, will be led to me and I will wed her. I will then sit on the bed in the bedchamber of the palace filled with the fragrance of scented powder, flowers, incense and sandalwood that kindled the passions and chat light-heartedly with Madalekha. Madalekha would then go away leaving Kadambari standing with her head lowered in shyness and pretending as if she were unwilling to come to bed. I will take her in my arms and bring her to bed, and from the bed on to my lap and from the lap into my heart. She will then place both her hands on the knot of her garment as though to ward off my hands trying to undo the knot. I will kiss her eyes closed in shyness and my long-cherished dream would then be fulfilled. I will drink the nectar from those lips not available even to the celestials, to my heart's content. I will then embrace her closely and by the melting pleasure of that embrace I will cool her body set on fire by Madana.

'Kadambari was not a free agent yet she followed her own inclination in surrendering to love; while she appeared to be passive she actually wrought for my love; as she seemed to be moving away she kept coming closer to me. She covered her body, but revealed her desire. With such a Kadambari is there any doubt that I would enjoy all the delights of lovemaking, delights that are available to everybody yet experienced only in the privacy of one's own mind? Lovemaking is all about touch alone, yet it captures the heart. It infatuates yet pacifies; it inflames the senses yet relieves the heat of Madana. It tires out the body yet creates great thrills. Enjoyment of it only kindles the desire for more;

even after a thousand times the pleasure does not stale. An intense experience, it remains beyond description, a union that cannot be put into words, an incomparable pleasure of touch, indeed a variation of the supreme bliss nirvana that comes only after a thousand spells of meditation.

'Thus will I enjoy the pleasures of love with Kadambari. Not for a minute will I be away from her. With her by my side I will wander around and delight in all those beautiful spots made more beautiful for us by our youth. After getting really close to her I will beg Kadambari to arrange the marriage of Vaishampayana to Madalekha.'

Chandrapida rode on, lost in such reveries, unaware of hunger or thirst, unmindful of the hot sun with no rest or respite night or day.

—60—

It was a long way to Hemakuta. Although Chandrapida sped along with no breaks in the journey, the rainy season inevitably caught up with him and became an impediment to rapid progress; like a snake lying across one's path; like night obstructing the sun; like Rahu holding the moon in his grip. It was the locked hunters' snare holding captive the deer longing to mate; it was the unbreakable chain, binding the legs of the horses; it was the impenetrable forest desolation confronting the travellers; it was the iron-grilled gaol imprisoning men.

When the rains came, the roaring clouds massed together like the gathering of fierce herds of dark bison; they came like huge swarms of dark bees. Stroking the lightning-strings of the fully pulled bow of Indra, they made the thunder roar, inducing fear, and sent down sharp shower-arrows ceaselessly. Like an enemy of fierce dark mien the rains created a barrier in front, with the blinding showers that fell like a hundred thousand swords.

Troubled by the delay, it was the consciousness-capturing swoon of distress that first darkened the horizons for Chandrapida, the clouds only later. It was his heart that first flew over the slush; the swans only followed suit. His own scented breath blew ahead first, the fragrant wind only later. First his blue-lily-lovely eyes shed their tears only then the clouds their rain. It was his heart that first overflowed with a thousand longings, only later the rivers, with rainwater. As the rivers swelled and became more and more unfordable, his passion too increased. As the rain-lashed field of lotuses drooped, his hopes of union with Kadambari too drowned. As the plantain leaves tore unable to withstand the assault of the showers, his heart too became lacerated. Along with the fluffy *nipa* buds his thrilling body too trembled in the stormy wind. As the malati flowers spread their fragrance, his heart filled with an indescribable anguish. Like the cloud-covered darkness of the skies, the darkness of confusion in him thickened; with lightning that would momentarily lift the darkness, his fever too grew.

Deeply rumbling fresh clouds kept forming in the skies; the unceasing downpour from them seemed to shake the very joints of the earth. Through the excessive showers, the cries of the chataka birds were heard, as were the long shrill calls of the ducks on the ground. The showers falling down with a resounding noise scattered wildly in all directions in the furious monsoon winds. The rain splashed noisily on the stone surface of the peaks high and low, forming into waterfalls. The floodwaters of the swollen rivers broke into fearful roaring waves.

The rain fell everywhere. It spread out evenly on level ground; it gathered itself together in caves. It fell fiercely on the peaks; it fell with a sweet babble on water. It fell sharply on the rocks, softly on grass, charmingly on ponds, darkly on the trees; and it pitter-pattered down on palm groves.

When Chandrapida heard the achingly captivating sounds of rain it only served to intensify his longing for his beloved. There was no relief for him any time, neither at night nor during the day. He found respite nowhere, not in the villages, nor in the forests, not in the gardens, nor on the roads, neither travelling, nor staying still. There was no comfort even in the memories of Vaishampayana or in daydreaming about the union with Kadambari.

The love-fire raged unabated as if seeking to reduce him to ashes. Chandrapida's natural fortitude seemed to wilt, and his very nature seemed to undergo a change. As the rain poured flooding the whole earth he became parched; the lightning that lit up the entire vault of the sky pushed him into the darkness of a swoon. The cool moist winds of the rainy season that delighted the whole world burned him. While the clouds swelled with water he started wasting away. The life-giving rainy season seemed to place his life in grave doubt.

Riding across rivers whose waters were breaking the banks even as his own fortunes seemed to go out of control, sinking into slushy ground as his mind too sank into a stupor, stumbling on tracks submerged in water even as his eyes were blinded with tears, stupefied by the roar of thunder and by the increasing obstacles to travel which it indicated, getting the better of a thousand yearnings with effort even as he managed to cross over a myriad streams, leaving behind the faint hearted among his retinue and the weakening horses, threatened by the streaks of lightning, held back by the ominous clouds, shamed by the thunder that seemed to laugh at him, broken into a thousand pieces by the sword-like showers, impeded in a thousand ways by the inclement rainy season yet his desire to be with Kadambari not weakening, he travelled on. In such conditions when every creature in the land hesitated to move Chandrapida alone pushed on without stopping even for a minute on that road leading to the Acchoda Lake. The only concession he allowed to himself was to eat his meals properly so that he would keep alive until he reached his destination. Although entreated by the princes he cared in no other way for the welfare of his body.

His horses too suffered, their eyes narrowed against the slanting assault of the showers. They shook their heads repeatedly from side to side, or hung them down. The dripping manes clumped together; the hoofs kept sinking into the slush; they often stumbled unable to see the ups and downs on the ground. Often had they to lower their hind parts when crossing the many rivers, one after another. Due to the strain their strength, speed and enthusiasm flagged.

—61—

When a mere third of the total distance was left, Chandrapida encountered Meghanada returning from Acchoda. Chandrapida plied him with impatient questions. 'Let Patralekha's news remain for the time being. I want to know about Vaishampayana. Did you meet him on the shores of the Acchoda? Did you ask him why he has stayed back? Did he say anything at all? Did he at all show any remorse for having thus abandoned us? I hope he still remembers us. Did he ask anything about me? Has he sent any message to his parents? Did you have any conversation with him at all? Did you form any idea as to what might have happened? Have you told him about my coming over soon? I hope he would not go away from that place in order to avoid me. What does he do the whole day? What is it that is keeping him enthralled?'

Meghanada who had left the capital with the returning Keyuraka along with Patralekha before the Vaishampayana story broke did not comprehend any of the questions. He looked confused and said 'Deva, when you sent me to Hemakuta you merely told me that you would soon follow me with the cavalry after meeting Vaishampayana; there was no talk at all of Vaishampayana going back to Acchoda. As your coming was delayed Patralekha and Keyuraka suspected that with the onset of the rains you were perhaps not permitted to undertake this long journey by Deva Tarapida, Devi Vilasavathi and Arya Shukanasa, in spite of having tried hard. They suggested that I return, as it was not wise to stay alone in those regions. They said they too would, in all probability return soon. So here I am on my way back, unwillingly though, without ever reaching the Acchoda Lake.'

Chandrapida realizing his mistake now enquired, 'Do you think Patralekha would have reached her destination by now?'

Meghanada replied, 'If there had been no delays on the road I feel sure she would have reached.'

Imagining Kadambari as having fallen deep into the ocean of passion, swelling like the real one in the rainy season, Chandrapida felt extremely distressed. He now saw the clouds as the messengers of death, the lightning as the flames of the fire of Manmatha and thunder as the drumbeats of Yama. The fragrance of the ketaki turned into a poisonous scent; the cries of the peacocks sounded like the chatter of the messengers of Yama, the formation of the flying cranes appeared like the death god's flag. And the fireflies were like the flying embers of the fire of the final annihilation.

Everything turned upside down in Chandrapida's own personality. His unflinching strength gave place to weakness, his glowing looks to pallor, his clarity of mind to confusion, his optimism to despondency, his laughter to misery, his talkativeness to silence. His senses dulled and a complete indifference to everything came over him. He just sat on his horse like a sculpted figure.

At last Chandrapida was at the familiar lake, but alas, now unfamiliar in its changed appearance. The new grass around the lake had now become submerged in rainwater; it had become slushy around the lake. The wooded shores appeared deserted. The uprooted white lilies were thickly strewn around; decaying lotuses and blue lilies lay scattered. The swans had all flown away. Soggy petals of the lotus and other flowers were bobbing up and down in the water. The restless cranes were calling out piteously. The chakravaka birds crouched in fear among the leaves on the low branches of the trees. The peacocks and the ospreys too were calling out loudly from the trees on the shore. Chandrapida now found it a strange and unfamiliar place. It no longer pleased the eye, nor gladdened the heart; it was not a dear place anymore. In the changed circumstances the very same Acchoda Lake only redoubled his already unbearable agony.

Even while approaching the lake Chandrapida had told his army to stay quiet and spread out around the lake, lest Vaishampayana, seeing the army slip away in embarrassment. Alone, still on horseback he searched everywhere disregarding his tiredness after such a strenuous journey. He looked for him in the dense growth of creepers, under the trees, on the rock surfaces and in the beautiful pavilions. But he could not see anywhere, even signs of anyone living there or ever having lived there earlier. So he thought 'I am sure that this fellow, learning about my coming here from Patralekha, has already gone away somewhere else. But I do not see even indications of his having stayed here. He has gone away somewhere to hide, and that is the reason I have not been able to find him after all this search. What a terrible state of affairs. My feet do not want to take even a single step away from here without meeting Vaishampayana. But how could my vital forces so relentlessly attacked and weakened by Manmatha and holding on only on

the promise of meeting Kadambari brook any delay? I am a
loser in every way. I have failed to trace Vaishampayana and I
have not met Kadambari.' The project had ended in failure, yet
clinging to weakening hope, he wanted to try one last thing. He
thought, 'Perhaps Mahashveta knows something about what
happened to Vaishampayana. I shall see her first and then decide
upon what further to do.'

Having thus made up his mind he stationed his men not too
far away from Mahashveta's ashrama and removed his soldierly
attire and put on garments pure and attractive like moonlight
and fine like snake moult. He then mounted Indrayudha who
still remained saddled and made his way to Mahashveta's ashrama.

— 62 —

At the entrance to the ashrama Chandrapida dismounted
eagerly and went in followed by Indrayudha's attendants.
As soon as he set foot inside he saw her sitting right at the
entrance to the cave on the white stone seat. Her head was
lowered and her whole body was trembling due to some
unbearable emotional turmoil. Her eyes were shedding unceasing
tears. She was like a tender creeper tossed about in a rainstorm.
A tearful Taralika was holding her.

Chandrapida's heart sank when he saw Mahashveta in this
condition. 'I hope nothing dire has befallen Kadambari that has
left Mahashveta in this condition.' His heart nearly breaking at
this possibility, his vital breaths threatening to take flight, with
faltering steps as though about to fall unconscious, he approached
the two women and sat down on one side of the same stone seat.
He then asked Taralika what had happened. Unable to answer
Taralika merely turned and looked at Mahashveta. It was

Mahashveta who replied, still not in control of her distress, in a voice choking with emotion.

Mahashveta Speaks . . .

Distinguished one! What can this wretched woman tell you? With her heart hardened with ill fortune she narrated to you her sad story that first time, even though you did not deserve to listen to such a tale of misery. That same shameless, pitiless woman so attached to life will now tell you yet another tale of sorrow, if you can bear to listen to it.

I learned from Keyuraka that you had gone away. It broke my heart that I had been unable to fulfil the hopes of Chitraratha, or redeem the promises given to Madira. I had not done the right thing by you either, you who had come to me as a guest. I failed to get Kadambari united with her dearly loved one. Dejected by all these failures I cut myself away from the close ties of love binding me to Kadambari in order to begin an even more arduous course of austerities.

It was then I saw a Brahmin youth similar to you in build roaming around looking totally lost; he appeared as if his soul had already fled his body. His face was troubled and his brimming unfocussed eyes wandered vaguely around as though he had lost something. When he saw me he came towards me looking intently at me as though he recognized me. I had never seen him before but he behaved as if he had known me long. I did not welcome him with the rites of hospitality; however, he, despite my coldness seemed to show a great affection for me.

He appeared stunned, yet seemed to remember something. Wordlessly he seemed to beg something of me. I never asked him anything yet he seemed to want to tell me about his situation. It was obvious that he was prey to several conflicting emotions, appearing in turn delighted, depressed, frightened, overpowered, captivated and deprived. He fixed his gaze on me, his long eyes narrowed and wet with unshed tears. He stared at me for a long time with the wild expression of one possessed; he seemed to want to drink me up with his eyes, to pull me to himself, to enter into me. Then he addressed me thus.

'Oh beautiful one! Everyone on the earth leads a life compatible with his or her birth, age and physical qualities and does not incur any censure for doing so. But why are you, like contrary Fate, involved in an effort so unsuitable to you in every respect? This body of yours tender and fresh, is right suited only to wind itself closely round an equally handsome neck, like a soft garland of fresh malati flowers, but you are subjecting it to such severe debilitating austerities. Why do you not look for enjoyment appropriate to your loveliness and youth? Even those born without physical beauty have a right to enjoy first the pleasures this life offers before they take to austerities for the sake of the hereafter. It pains me to see this soft body of yours being subjected to the rigours of penance, like a lotus plant being hit by a shower of hail. If women like you turn away from the pleasures of the world, then the wielder of the floral bow pulls the bowstrings in vain indeed. The moon rises to no purpose; in vain does spring make its appearance and in vain do the lilies and lotuses bloom. Of what purpose is the existence of the gardens, the waterfalls, and the gentle mountain breeze?'

My mind fixed on Pundarika, I never bothered to ask the youth who he was, where he had come from and why he was saying all this to me. I simply went away from his presence and called to Taralika who was collecting flowers for worship and instructed her, 'Taralike, there is a young man who has strayed into our ashrama. He looks like a Brahmin but from his talk I suspect he is not a good fellow. Send him away from here; and do it in such a way that he does not come back here again. I do get the feeling that were he to come here again something terrible might befall him.'

But he did not stop coming after me. It is true Manmatha cannot be warded off so easily; but it could have been the inevitability of the calamity that was to befall him that pulled him back here. A few days later deep in the middle of one night, when Taralika was fast asleep, when the moon's rays were pouring down a flood of moonlight that only served to kindle the fire of Kama, unable to sleep I came out of the cave and threw myself on this very stone seat. A gentle wind blowing in from the lake and bringing with it the soft fragrance of the lotuses soothed me. Looking at the moon painting the skies white with his ray-brush, it occurred to me that Chandrama delighting the entire world with his nectar-showering rays would be drenching my beloved too. My thoughts dwelt on the noble Pundarika; surely it was my wretched misfortune that the words of the divine being that descended from the sky to bear Pundarika's body away had remained unfulfilled so far. What could my lord Pundarika do as he was already dead when taken away. But whatever happened to Kapinjala? He was alive when he left; how could he be so hardhearted as not to send any message all this time? Lost in such thoughts I remained there wide awake.

It was then I saw the same youth again. He had come stepping softly. The hair all over his body stood on edge as if he were carrying the incessantly falling arrows of Kama all on himself. He was pale like the pollen of the ketaki as though Manmatha had already reduced him to ash. He carried in his hands a ring made of lotus stalk; it seemed to symbolize the all powerful death sentence of the one with the floral arrow whose writ ran unchallenged the world over. His extreme emotional state had brought on a flood of tears. His body bathed in sweat, he seemed ready to wed me. His steps were halting as though his strong thighs were pulling him back, admonishing him that it was improper to approach a woman without knowing her mind. Whilst still at a distance from me he spread out his hands expressing eloquently his desperate but futile urge to embrace me. He was trying to cross the unruly ocean of passion filled with a thousand emotional vortices.

His long and deep sighs seemed to be pulling him forward while the flood of moonlight seemed to push him from behind. I could see that he had lost all hold on himself and was totally in the grip of passion. He seemed to have lost all sense of shame, all sense of right and wrong like one possessed by an evil spirit. He was drunk with passion and completely under the spell of Manmatha. I could see him standing there in the moonlight that was as bright as daylight.

I was seized with fear. 'Oh my god! I have a difficult situation here. Should this youth in his frenzy so much as even lay a hand on me I will have to give up this wretched body of mine. All the unbearably painful effort of staying alive in the hope of seeing Pundarika again would be in vain.' The young man in the meantime approached and pleaded, 'Chandramukhi! This moon up there, the friend and collaborator of the one with the flower arrows is determined to finish me off. I have come here seeking refuge in you. I have no other recourse to take, no one to turn to; I suffer terribly and my life is in your hands. Ascetics too are bound by the duty of saving those that approach seeking help. If you do not give yourself to me and rescue me from this predicament, then I am really done for by the two of them, the one with the floral weapon and the other with the cool rays.'

When I heard these words a flaming fury burst out of my head as it were; I was ready to burn him with the fire of my anger.

My body shook and my eyes were filling with tears of rage. I glared at him threateningly and spat out these cruel words without thinking. 'You villain, when you babble on like this why does not lightning strike your head? Why does not your tongue split into a thousand bits? Why does not your voice become enfeebled? Or why do you not forget your words? It is clear that your body is not made of the five elements that bear witness to everything, good and bad. That is why although you prattle on in this fashion agni has not reduced you to ashes; vayu has not blown you away; water has not drowned you, the earth has not swallowed you, nor has akash obliterated you in a moment. In this world of order where have you come from, a specimen of impropriety? Just like the lesser creation of animals and birds, you wander around as you please in complete ignorance. You spout hot passionate words, only thinking of yourself, as though some one taught them to you; you repeat them like a parrot would, unaware of whether they are in or out of context. Why does not that wretched creator push you into the world of parrots where you belong? Then if you keep talking like this it will give rise to laughter and not anger. Your talk has hurt me so much; a proper share of that pain has to go to you too. I shall fix things for you in such a way that you would end up in the kind of life that suits you and in which you would not lust after women like me.' Then I looked at the shining moon and joined my hands in worship and said, 'My god, Parameshvara, the crest jewel of the entire world, the protector of all life. If I have not desired, even in my thoughts, any man other than Lord Pundarika from the minute I saw him, let this crook fall into that level of life that I mentioned earlier.' As soon as I uttered these words, this young man—I do not know if it was due to unbearable love fever, or to some ill deed of his own that was just beginning to give its evil results, or possibly due to my words—fell down on the earth unconscious like an uprooted tree. It was only when I screamed realizing that he was dead that I found out from his attendants that he was your friend.

~

Mahashveta lowered her head in shame; her tears streamed down and flooded the earth; and she fell silent.

~63~

As Chandrapida heard these terrible words spoken by the anguished Mahashveta his long eyes narrowed and filled with tears. He lost the ability to speak clearly. He stammered, 'Madam, you tried your utmost, yet it is not given to this sinner to attain the joy of serving at the feet of Kadambari. Perhaps in my next birth you would be able to make that joy possible for me.' His naturally tender heart, shocked by the realization that Kadambari was forever out of his reach, split into pieces, like a bud just beginning to open being hit by arrows.

Taralika at once dropped Mahashveta and rushed to Chandrapida and held him. She cried out, 'Oh my mistress, this is no time for bashfulness. Deva Chandrapida does not look all right at all. His neck seems broken; it is unable to hold his head. When I shake him he does not know it. The pupils of his eyes have rolled in and his eyes do not see. He does not make an attempt to gather his limp limbs. He is not breathing. Oh my lord Chandrapida! You with the beauty of Chandra! The beloved of Kadambari! What do we do without you?'

While Taralika lamented thus, and Mahashveta stared speechless at the twisted face of Chandrapida, the entourage of the prince raised a heart-rending cry. 'You wicked ascetic woman! What have you done? You have destroyed the noble lineage of

King Tarapida, the king who has spread happiness and prosperity all over the world. The subjects have now been orphaned; all virtuous ways have been destroyed. The door is now closed in the face of those who come seeking succour. Oh lord, whom should the servants serve now? Without you all service has become painful, all appreciation for service has disappeared, and all respect for the serving people has become a mockery. In times of trouble whom would the subjects seek aid from? Who would take care of the virtuous? Generosity has now met with its end. Alas, you have become a mere story now. With you dead who would now relieve King Tarapida of the burden he has been carrying for so long? You were so brave, yet how did your heart break like a weakling's with sorrow?

You are such a compassionate one, yet today you have been so unkind to your servants. Our lord, please take pity on us, command us at least once more, grant the entreaties of the devoted. Please come back to life! Without you no one will survive, neither King Tarapida, nor Devi Vilasavathi, neither Arya Shukanasa nor his wife Manorama, nor any of the subjects. Abandoning all of us where have you gone away all by yourself? Why this sudden aversion towards us?' The grief-stricken attendants fell on the ground. Hearing the wailing of the servants the princes too rushed in with confusion and agitation in their hearts.

Chandrapida's beloved horse Indrayudha moaned piteously and fixed his tear-filled, grief-stricken eyes on his master's face and stamped the ground with his hoofs, one after the other. He pulled at the sharp-edged bit and the golden chain to which it was tied, again and again; it appeared as if he wanted not merely to release himself but to get free of his very horseness.

In the meantime Kadambari had learnt of the arrival of Chandrapida; her heart swelled with joy like the ocean swelling at the rise of the moon. Under the pretext of visiting Mahashveta she hurried down. She had dressed for meeting her lover; her anklets tinkled, her girdle jingled as she tripped along. She carried with her fragrant garlands, sandalwood paste and coloured powders, all for the love-sport. She was accompanied by a few of her attendants. Keyuraka was leading the way. Kadambari held Patralekha's hands and chatted with Madalekha. 'Madalekhe, Patralekha here keeps telling me every day that I did not take in good faith the earlier visit of that exceedingly cruel deceiving prince. Don't you remember how indifferent he was to my condition when I was in the himagriha? That villain spoke so cleverly and deviously as though he was testing my love. And you looked on smilingly and answered him to dispel all his doubts. But it had no effect on him. Even if I had died he would not have believed in my love. Had he only realized that Kadambari was suffering all that agony only on his account he would not have gone away at all. True he has come back now, but it is up to you to talk to him now. I will not utter a word to him. Even if he falls at my feet I shall not be mollified. No, I shall not be cajoled by you either, my friend.' Prattling away in this manner and unmindful of the strain of the journey Kadambari arrived at Mahashveta's ashrama, her heart skipping with joy at the prospect of seeing Chandrapida.

Alas! When she stepped into the ashrama of Mahashveta she saw her beloved lying lifeless on the ground, like the ocean bereft of its nectar, like the night separated from the moon, like a garden with all its flowers plucked away, like a lotus plant all of whose buds have been cut away, like a pearl necklace whose pendant has been taken away. 'Ha!' she cried. 'What has happened?' As she sank to the ground Madalekha screamed and held her at once. Patralekha had dropped Kadambari's hand and had fallen down unconscious.

After what seemed a long time, Kadambari regained consciousness; but she still remained stunned, her eyes dead and expressionless. The weight of her sorrow made her motionless.

She was so still as though she had even forgotten to breathe. Her face was flushed a dark red, like the night of the eclipse of the moon; her eyes were fixed on Chandrapida's face. She was like a creeper on which an axe of deadly sharpness had fallen. Her lips quivered, but she sat there, uncharacteristically quiet for a woman struck with a calamity of such gravity. Seeing her thus stunned, Madalekha cried out. 'Dear friend, please give vent to your sorrow. With unshed tears the weight of your distress would break your heart to pieces. Please think of Devi Madira and Deva Chitraratha. Without you both lineages would be destroyed.'

Kadambari laughed mirthlessly and said, 'You are being silly. Do you really believe this adamantine heart of mine would split now, when it did not break into a thousand bits the moment I saw him lying lifeless? Mother and father, friends and attendants, all these are for those who are going to live. As for me I was going to die anyway; but now I have got my beloved's body. If he came back to life I would enjoy him but as he remains dead I will die with him. Either way it will be the end of my sorrow. It was a great honour that he came here to see me; but by giving up his life for my sake he has now put me on a pedestal. Would I fall from that high position by merely shedding tears over his death? While my lord is going heavenward would I do something so inauspicious as weep? I who want to follow him as the dust on his feet, would I cry when it is an occasion for joy? I have no sorrow now, it is all gone away. I disregarded the honour of my family; I failed to seek my parents' blessings; I crossed the bounds of propriety; I showed no fear for the censure of the people; I abandoned all modesty; I troubled all my friends who had to minister to my love fever. Above all I forgot my promise given to Mahashveta, my dear friend. Now when that very person for whom I did all this has given up his life for me, how can you tell me to keep living? To die now is to live. And to live is really death. Therefore if you have any love for me you should act in such a way that my mother and father would not die grieving for me. Their fond hopes for me will find their fulfilment in you. And to perform my rites a son will be born to you.

It is up to you Madalekhe, to see to it that my friends and my attendants do not miss me. Do not forget to perform the marriage that I have planned, of the madhavi creeper and the little mango sapling grown by me so lovingly. You should never ever pluck the fresh leaves from the branches of the ashoka so often lovingly kicked by me, even to adorn your own ears. The malati flowers may be collected only for worship. And please, tear down the picture of Kama put up at the top of my house. The mango tree grown from the sapling that I had myself created should be looked after well so that it yields plentifully. Release both the poor myna Kalindhi and the parrot Parihasa from the agony of their captivity. The little mongoose that used to sleep in my lap will now sleep in yours. And my little baby, the young deer should be sent away to some hermitage. The chakravaka pair that I used to tend to myself should now be kept on the kridaparvatha so that they do not die. Please take care of that swan that is always at my footsteps. And that poor jungle woman, recently caught and kept in the palace, please arrange to have her released in the forest. And give away my kridaparvatha to some ascetic for his peaceful meditation. All my ornaments and clothes should go to the Brahmins, but my veena, that should now rest on your lap. Do please help yourself to anything else that you may like among my possessions.

As for me, whatever is left of me after the fires of Madana have had their fill these past several day, I shall throw into the pyre with my arms around the neck of my beloved, and then alone shall my love-fevered limbs get their relief.'

Kadambari now pushed Madalekha away, who was still trying to hold her, and went over to Mahashveta, hugged her and said serenely, 'Dear friend, you have been blessed with hope; by the strength of that hope you are putting up with suffering worse than death. You are somehow keeping yourself alive an act that should cause no shame, no dejection, and no mockery or censure. But alas, my hope is all dead. So I take leave of you now, and may we meet in our next birth.'

Kadambari was now in an extreme emotional state. Her body shook, hit by the evil wind of sorrow, like a lily, in the uneven force of a gale. The hair on her throbbing body stood on edge like filaments on the lily. She was being swept away in the flood of her own tears, like a flower being carried away by the waves. Beads of perspiration broke out on her body like drops of honey on a flower. Her lily-eyes narrowed at the death of Chandrapida as the lily would close its petals at the demise of the moon. As she placed her head on Chandrapida's feet, her tresses fell down and showered their flowers on them. With perspiration-drenched hands she took his feet and placed them in her lap.

At the touch of her hands a moonlight-like brightness flowed out of the body and enveloped the whole place in a sort of cool haze. Chandrapida's face too seemed to come alive. Immediately a disembodied voice of ambrosial delectability was heard from the heavens. 'Dear child Mahashvete, it seems I have to console you yet again. Pundarika's body is still in my world doused in my lustre, indestructible, waiting for union with you. This other one, that of Chandrapida, made of my own brilliance is by nature indestructible and now even more so with the touch of Kadambari's hands. It is true that the soul has left it due to a curse but it will be preserved like the bodies of highly evolved ascetics whose souls can go from body to body. It may remain in the care of both of you, so that you might be reassured, until the curse wears out. This body should not be burnt by fire. It should not be thrown away. It has to be looked after carefully until the time for reunion arrives.'

~64~

When they heard the disembodied voice from the heavens everybody, including the entire retinue of Chandrapida, stood transfixed, staring up at the sky in wonder. In the meantime Patralekha had regained her consciousness with the touch of that cool gladdening lustre that arose out of Chandrapida's body. She sprang up as though driven by some force and ran up to Indrayudha. She pulled the horse away from the hand of the groom who held him. 'What becomes of us is not important. But it is not proper for you to stay here any longer as your lord has gone so far away without his transport.' So saying she pulled Indrayudha with her and jumped into the Acchoda Lake.

Then something still stranger happened. As soon as horse and girl disappeared into the water, there arose from it a young ascetic; his hair was plastered down on his head as if weeds from the bottom of the lake had stuck to it. Some strands that had come loose from his topknot fell on his face. It was clear he had not groomed his hair for a long time. The *brahmasutra* stuck to his drenched body like lotus fibre. He was wrapped in an old parijata bark garment that had the dull whiteness of the back of a dried lotus leaf. With one hand he kept pushing away the locks that were falling on his face. The tears streaming out of his slightly reddened eyes made it appear as if he were throwing out all the water that must have collected inside his body. He seemed to be in a state of agitation.

Stepping quickly out of the water he approached Mahashveta whose gaze had been fixed on the young ascetic and who was making a determined effort to stop the flood of tears threatening to rush out of her eyes. The young man's voice shook with emotion as he spoke. 'Gandharva princess, here I am after such a long time, come from another life. Do you recognize me?'

Mahashveta was in the grip of both joy and sorrow. She rose hurriedly and bowed to him and said, 'Venerable Kapinjala, am I such a sinner that I would fail to recognize you? Perhaps you are right in believing such a thing of me as I continue to live, paralysed with indecision, although my lord Pundarika has long since gone to heaven. Please tell me, who took him away? Why has he been taken away? Where is he now? Is he well? What was it with you that for such a long time you never sent any news of yourself or Pundarika to me? And why have you come now alone without my lord?' As Kadambari's attendants and the princes of Chandrapida's entourage looked on in amazement, Kapinjala narrated the incredible story.

Kapinjala Narrates . . .

Gandharva princess, listen carefully to what I have to say. Leaving you to lament alone, impelled by my great love for my friend, I hitched up my garments and shouting, 'Where are you taking my friend?' I sprang up into the sky and chased after that individual. He did not answer me, but went up the heavenly path as riders in other aerial vehicles on the same path looked on in wide-eyed wonder. The apsara women with veiled faces moved out of his way. Others with darting eyes on their way to their assignations bowed to him. He went past the constellations that appeared like clusters of white lilies in the lake that was the vault of the sky, and entered the *chandraloka* drenched in moonlight. There in the famous court called *Mahodaya* he placed Pundarika's body on a great bed of *indukanta* stone. Then he turned to me and said, 'Kapinjala! Let me first introduce myself to you. I am Chandramas. While I went about my own duties showering light on the earth, your friend Pundarika, in the grip of a hopeless passion and about to give up his life to it, cursed me, thus: "You rogue Chandrama, just as I am going to die with my passion roused to an unbearable intensity by your cruel rays, so shall you; you will be born in Bharatavarsha, the land of karma and will undergo extreme mental pain with unfulfilled love and meet your death, in life again and again."

'The fire of that curse seemed to set me ablaze almost immediately; my anger too was roused at once that I had been cursed for no reason at all by this unwise and unreasonable individual who was blaming me who am innocent, for his own failings. In that moment of anger I cursed him in return, that he would find his own sorrow and happiness exactly in the same way and measure as I would.

'By and by, my anger subsided and reason returned, and I found out the connection between this Pundarika and the dear child Mahashveta, daughter of Gauri who belongs to the lineage of apsaras created out of my rays. Mahashveta had chosen this young man as her husband. But with our reciprocal curses Pundarika had now to be born on this earth twice along with me, for otherwise the words "again and again" in the curse would never be fulfilled. Until the complete expiation of his sins this body shed by his soul must be preserved; that is why I picked him up and brought him here. The dear child Mahashveta too was comforted. Let this body remain here basking in my light until the curse passes away. Now you go to Shvetaketu and tell him all that has happened. He has great powers; perhaps he can take some remedial action for mitigating the curse.' Chandrama then dismissed me.

I sped along the aerial pathway, quite oblivious to my surroundings, my mind abstracted with sorrow over my friend's fate. It so happened that as I hurried along I leapt over another such traveller in his aerial carrier, a very short-tempered one, as it turned out. He glared at me, his face distorted with rage and cried, 'You villain, you are swollen with pride over the powers gained by your bogus penance. Rushing about in this very wide aerial path, you jumped over me like a horse. So here is my curse: may you become a horse and go down to the mortal world.'

I joined my hands in supplication and with tears in my eyes I beseeched him: 'My lord, it was my grief over my friend's fate that made me behave with apparent disrespect, and not arrogance. Please do take back your curse.' But he replied, 'The curse is pronounced and cannot be withdrawn. You will spend a while with someone as his vehicle and when he dies you will have a bath and then be freed from the curse.' I requested him further. 'My dear friend Pundarika too has to descend to the mortal world along with Chandramas as a result of a curse. Please discern everything with your divine sight and ordain things in such a way that I too, even as a horse might spend my time on earth close to my friend.' The celestial one was lost in thought for a while and then said, 'I am moved by your devotion to your friend. I have seen everything indeed. In Ujjayini King Tarapida is doing penance for getting a son; Chandramas is to be born as his son. And your friend Pundarika is to be born to the king's minister Shukanasa. You will become the vehicle of that great benefactor, the prince of Ujjaiyini, Chandrapida, the incarnation of Chandramas.'

No sooner had he finished speaking than I fell into the ocean below and as I rose out of the water I had metamorphosed into a horse. But my equestrian exterior did not affect my awareness as Kapinjala. That was why, for the sake of expediting matters, I brought Chandrapida who was chasing the kinnara pair, to this place. Chandrapida's friend Vaishampayana who was really the incarnation of Pundarika fell in love with you due to the force of events in his previous birth. He was, however cursed by you.

~

When she realized that the Brahmin youth whom she had cursed into a parrot was none other than Pundarika himself Mahashveta was demented with grief. 'Oh my lord Pundarika, you never forgot my love even though we were separated by a lifetime. You still looked up to me, you saw me in everything in the world. But what have I done? I am a demon born only to kill you. The wretched Prajapati has created me and endowed me with a long life only to use me to fell you again and again. Since I am the one that destroyed you, on whom shall I cast the blame? Whom shall I curse? Whom shall I turn to? In whom shall I take refuge? Who would have pity on me? Pundarika! I beseech you; please answer me! Are you so disgusted with me that you do not answer me in spite of my lamentations? Oh the agony of still continuing to live!' Mahashveta beat her breasts piteously and threw herself on the ground.

Kapinjala consoled her with compassion. 'Gandharva princess, why do you censure yourself so harshly as though it were entirely your fault when it is not? You are innocent. The time for the fulfilment of your heart's desire is drawing near; this is no time for grief, yet here you are torturing yourself. You have borne a great sorrow with amazing fortitude sustained by the hope of ultimately uniting with your beloved. Your sufferings and Pundarika's are all due to a curse as I have already explained to you. Please stop grieving, it does not benefit you or my friend. Do please continue with whatever penance you have been doing for the welfare of both of you; that would be the proper course of action. Nothing is beyond the power of penance if done with care. Devi Gauri attained half of Hara's body solely by the rigours of her penance. Similarly you too, by the power of your penance, will soon unite with my friend Pundarika.'

As Mahashveta regained her composure Kadambari, looking sad and dejected, asked Kapinjala, 'Venerable one, you jumped into the water of the lake with Patralekha. So what happened to her now?' Kapinjala answered, 'Princess, after I jumped into the lake I was not aware of anything concerning Patralekha. I have no idea either as to where Chandrapida or Vaishampayana has

taken birth. I am now going to Bhagvan Shvetaketu who can see
the past and the future as well as all the three worlds with his
mind's eye to find out what has befallen them.'

Kapinjala then jumped up into the sky and hurried away.

~65~

After Kapinjala had gone Kadambari, who had forgotten
her sad plight when listening to the wondrous events
narrated by Kapinjala, looked at Chandrapida and her eyes filled
once again with tears. She went back to her original place near
the body of her beloved and while her own attendants and the
princely entourage of Chandrapida looked on she said to
Mahashveta, 'My dear friend, the creator wishing to give me a
sorrow equal to yours may have thrust me into this situation
but by no means has he thrown me into any distress. I can now
hold my head high; no longer am I ashamed to look you in the
face and address you as dear friend, for it is only now that I
have truly become your friend. Life or death makes no difference
to me anymore. But I would like to be advised by you, and by
you alone, in this situation. I cannot, on my own, decide what
course is beneficial.'

Mahashveta replied, 'My dear friend, the time for questions
or advice of any kind is past. Only that needs to be done which
is dictated by this insistent desire to unite with the beloved. It is
only now, after all these days, that we have come to know from
Kapinjala what exactly has happened to Pundarika; but at that
time I had to derive all my comfort from the heavenly voice
alone and I was unable to do anything else except hope for the
best. But for you, reassurance lies right there on your lap in the
form of the body of Chandrapida; as long as it lies here
indestructible what else do you want to do except tend to it?

People make images out of mud and stone and wood of the invisible gods in order to pray to them for their personal welfare. But we have here the actual presence of Chandramas in the form of Chandrapida without our ever having propitiated the deity.'

When she heard these words spoken quietly by Mahashveta, Kadambari rose silently, and with the help of Taralika and Madalekha carefully lifted the precious body of Chandrapida and gently placed it on a rock surface, sheltered from extreme heat and cold, wind and rain. Then she removed all the seductive ornaments she had put on when she came down to meet her lover, retaining only a single gem-inlaid bracelet for the sake of auspiciousness. Then she purified herself with a bath and wore clean silken garments. She scrubbed her tender-shoot-soft lips again and again to wash away the redness of the betel leaves from them. It was indeed clear that the creator, that expert mischief maker in typically contrary fashion had set in motion a chain of events in which he had cast Kadambari, a young girl, a mere child in fact, in so unsuitable a role, one that she never thought, never imagined she might ever have to play, and for which she had certainly never been trained.

With all the fragrant flowers, incense and unguents that she had brought with her for love-sport with her beloved, she now performed a rite of worship, fit for a deity, on the body of Chandrapida. A picture of sorrow and distress, her very appearance had undergone a change. Subject to an agony worse than death Kadambari's eyes never left Chandrapida's body. The pain in her heart was intense; yet she controlled her tears. At the end of the worship she sat down as before and placed Chandrapida's feet once again on her lap. The princes who had come with Chandrapida were all still there sparing no thought to their fatigue and hunger after that long journey. They too remained without food or drink keeping vigil along with Kadambari and her attendants.

That night there was a thunderstorm. Dark ominous clouds gathered; the roaring thunder made one's heart tremble. The excited call of the peacocks distracted the mind. The raucous croaking of the frogs was deafening. The blinding streaks of lightning distressed the heavenly directions; innumerable fireflies lit up the trees and lightened somewhat the fearful darkness underneath the canopies. As for Kadambari, she pushed away with determination the fear that women were born with and stayed awake the entire night holding Chandrapida's feet on her lap, unmindful of her own discomfort. In truth she felt that the night was over in minutes.

At dawn, looking at Chandrapida's body as it slowly came into relief as the day brightened, like a painting taking shape, Kadambari gently stroked the body with her hand and said to her dear friend Madalekha who was at her side, 'My dear friend, Madalekhe, look, it may be due to the power of love; on the other hand it may be its innate indestructibility, whatever be the reason for it, his body appears exactly as it has always been, with no signs of deterioration. Look at it attentively and tell me if what I say is true or not.'

Madalekha replied, 'But my dear friend, I was never in doubt. With the vital breath leaving the body he is dead only to the extent his limbs have become still. Otherwise he is just the same as before. Look at his lustrous face, like a fully bloomed lotus; it is not even a little reduced in beauty. And his curly forelocks are still soft and shining. So is his forehead full of brilliance like a piece of the moon. And his long eyes have the lustre of half-opened blue lilies. The corners of his lips seem to be curling up in a smile although he is not smiling. Look at the freshness of his lips like new shoots and his coral-red hands and feet with their shining nails. The natural beauty, softness and health of all his limbs are in no way reduced. Therefore I am sure the pronouncements of the heavenly voice and the account of the

curse narrated by Kapinjala are completely true.' Kadambari
was filled with joy when she heard the words of her friend;
she then pointed out the various parts of Chandrapida's fresh
body to his devoted vassals as well as to Mahashveta in
great delight.

When the princes observed the freshness of Chandrapida's
body their eyes widened in wonder. They placed their heads on
the ground and paid homage to their leader. They remained
kneeling as they said to Kadambari, 'Devi, although our lord
has left us, the unfortunate ones, behind and gone a long way
away, his face here shines with the pure lustre of the moon; his
feet glow with the red brilliance of a fully bloomed lotus. All
this is entirely due to your power. That is why we nurse the
hope that we would be able to enjoy his benevolent presence
once again in our midst. Who else has ever seen, heard or
experienced in this mortal world the wonders that we have had
the fortune to witness?'

Kadambari then set about gathering flowers for worship with
her attendants. She bathed and performed the rites on
Chandrapida's body. She then advised the princes to go ahead
with their daily ablutions. Once they had had their food
Kadambari and her friends partook of the fruits she and
Mahashveta had gathered. After the meal she went back to
Chandrapida and sat down and once again placed his feet on
her lap. That was the second day.

By the third day Kadambari had become fully convinced that
the body of the prince was indeed beyond decay. She then said
to Madalekha, 'My friend, I have realized that we have to attend
to the body of my lord Chandrapida in this manner until the
curse has run its course and so we have to stay here for sometime.
Therefore please go and tell my parents about the wonderful
events that have taken place here. And do so in such a fashion

that they do not misconstrue my action, nor experience any sorrow on my account. But most important, see to it that they do not hurry down here to see me in this bereaved condition. I am not sure that I can control my sorrow if I see my parents now. I did not cry even when I believed Chandrapida to be dead; now that I am no longer in any doubt about his being alive, and that I have taken up a certain discipline why should I cry at all?' Madalakha left immediately on her errand.

Soon she returned and relayed the message from Kadambari's parents. 'Dear friend, your father Chitraratha and your mother Madira want me to tell you that they embrace you very very closely, kiss your forehead and give you this message. 'All these days we did not even entertain the hope that we would see our daughter married. We are indeed delighted that our daughter has chosen her own husband; that our son-in-law is lord Chandramas himself, the protector of the world, is a source of even greater joy. We will therefore wait till after the expiation of the curse to see our joyful daughter along with our son-in-law.' With her mind set at rest Kadambari went back to serving the body of Chandrapida as she would serve a deity.

—66—

The rainy season passed; the world was freed from the restrictions imposed by the heavy clouds. The quarters of the sky once again opened up and appeared expansive in the absence of the lowering clouds. The ripening paddy in the fields around the villages was bent with the weight of the grain; they tinted the boundaries of the villages yellow. In the forests the ground turned white with the kasha flowers. The red lotus bloomed in the little ponds. The nights became cool and carried

the fragrance of the white lilies. The morning breeze wafted in
the scent of the *sephalika* flowers. The evenings became lustrous
and delightful with moonlight. The pollen from the blooming
lotuses scented the days. The waters of the rivers receded
exposing the tide lines on the sand, and it became easy to ford
them. As the slush dried, fresh grass grew without difficulty and
soon covered everything. The wet mud dried and contracted
and new paths appeared on which the princes of the world once
again set off on their marches now that the ground had become
hard enough to bear the stamping hoofs of the horses.

One day Meghanada approached Kadambari, seated as usual
at the feet of Chandrapida and said, 'Devi, worried by the long
absence of Deva Chandrapida, King Tarapida, Devi Vilasavathi
and Arya Shukanasa have sent messengers over to find out what
is holding the prince back. I have told them everything without
actually spelling out the precise nature of the problem in order
to spare Devi Vilasavathi the unbearable details. However, I told
them that at present Deva Chandrapida as well Devi Kadambari
is unable to send any message back through them. I suggested
they return without any delay carrying all the news to King
Tarapida, that great benefactor of the world. But they became
angry and replied. "So that is your story. Leave alone our rank,
our devotion and our long relationship with the prince, the grave
responsibility of carrying out our king's orders alone makes us
anxious to meet the prince. Further, if the information you have
were only what you have heard from others then it would be all
right for us to go back satisfied with it. But you have him with
you, and you see him every day; yet you say that we may not
meet him. We have a right to see him for we too have served
him a long time, and our prince has always been very accessible
to us. What has happened now that we are being dismissed thus
and denied our privilege of meeting our lord? Let the trouble

taken by us travelling all this way bear fruit; allow us to touch the feet of our prince. Besides, if we go back without seeing him what would we say to our king?" It is now up to Devi Kadambari to decide what should be done.'

Kadambari could at once understand the terrible anxiety of her parents-in-law with regard to their son of whom they had had no news at all for such a long while. Her heart melted over their predicament and her eyes rolled up as if she were trying to control the tears welling up from within. She replied, her voice choking with emotion. 'It is only proper that they should be welcomed in here by us. If they go away without seeing their lord what could they tell their king? An incident like this strains the credulity of even those who have actually witnessed it; how much more incredible it would be to people who have not seen it with their own eyes? That apart, when those whose love for him is little more than sham, and those to whom their own lives are much dearer than that of the prince, may be here among those present, is it proper to deny a sight of him to these men with true affection, who serve him with unswerving devotion and who are ready to lay down their lives for him? Please ask them to come in without any more delay. Let them see their lord; let that arduous journey they have undertaken to come here get its reward.'

Led inside by Meghanada, the emissaries from the king entered and fell prostrate at the feet of Chandrapida, with all their limbs touching the ground. The tears flowed from their eyes as their gaze was fixed motionless on the feet of their prince. Kadambari looked at them for a while and then spoke: 'Good sirs, please control your sorrow, which I do realize, is the result of affection born of long association with the prince. There is sorrow that has no end, and there is sorrow that can end only in sorrow; it is these that cause distress to those who fear

death. That sorrow which is expected to end in a happy
denouement does not enter the heart at all, its way being
obstructed by that hope of happiness. In these developments
there is no scope for sorrow at all because of that prospect of
future bliss. Further, this sorrow has become the ground for
very strange and marvellous happenings, the likes of which have
not been witnessed by human beings anywhere. You have now
seen the healthy body of your lord and his face that remains as
fresh as ever; true it is not possible to talk to him now, but that
too will become possible in due course. Therefore good sirs,
all of you now go back to your king who is eagerly waiting for
news of the prince. But please refrain from saying anything either
about the dead body of the prince or the quality of
indestructibility that it possesses. Just say that you have seen
the prince on the shores of the Acchoda Lake. People would
readily believe in the death of anyone, as death is inevitable to
all creatures. But the idea of an indestructible body after life
has fled from it does not carry easy conviction even for those
who have actually seen it. The parents of the prince who are so
far away would be unnecessarily plunged into the dire suspicion
that their son was really dead. Once he gets up from this
"slumber" Chandrapida himself would relate all these
wonderful happenings to his mother and father.'

The king's emissaries replied, 'There are only two ways of
keeping this matter from the elders at Ujjayini, either by not
going back at all, or by not saying anything after getting back.
But both these options are not open to us. King Tarapida, Devi
Vilasavathi and Arya Shukanasa anxious for news about the
prince and Vaishampayana have sent us here, placing great trust
in us to find out what has happened to the young men. In such
a situation the question of our not going back, as long as we are
not dead, does not arise at all. But having gone back, to keep a
straight face in the presence of all of them—so eager for news of

their beloved sons, their faces reflecting the anxiety in their hearts—without revealing anything, that too is equally impossible.'

Kadambari replied, 'Yes, I do understand' and turned to Meghanada and said, 'I do realize that trusted servants will not adopt the course of action I recommended. I suggested it only to prevent the elders undergoing terrible mental agony. Then let someone who has seen everything that took place and whose words will carry conviction and reassurance go with these men to set the elders' minds at rest.'

To which Meghanada replied: 'It would be difficult indeed to find someone who would go back to the capital. For, Devi, it is not just the princes alone, but even the servants of Chandrapida have now taken to eating just roots and fruits and are determined that not one of them would go back without their prince. True servants serve with greater devotion in times of difficulty than in times of happiness. Those who have risen in the service become humble; those who are praised do not become arrogant. Those who are pulled up do not turn away from the master. They work without waiting for explicit orders and having done the work they do not boast about it. They become greedy for service to their master and are always full of praise of their master's qualities. They are so entirely at the disposal of their master that they seem unaware of everything except the needs of their master; they appear to be blind even though they can see, deaf even though they can hear, dumb even though they can speak, lame even though their hands and feet are not impaired. They do not do anything on their own volition but remain like reflections in the mirror of their master's thoughts. Such is now the state of the entire lot of servants of the prince. Only now Devi has taken the place of Deva for them.'

Meghanada then picked out a young man called Tvaritaka to go to Ujjayini along with the returning king's messengers.

— 67 —

Back in Ujjayini, Vilasavathi had gone one day to the temple of Avantimatas, the presiding goddesses of the kingdom of Avanti, in order to pray for the speedy and safe return of her son who had been gone a long time and from whom there had been no news of any kind at all. While she was still at the temple her maids came running to her and cried out, 'Devi, you have indeed been rewarded by the gods. The messengers sent to look for the prince have returned.'

Vilasavathi's long eyes filled with tears of joy and they eagerly scanned the directions like a female deer looking for her young one who had been separated from her. Her searching eyes looked like a dew-drenched garland of blue lily petals. In her excitement and impatience Vilasavathi forgot her dignity as the queen of the land and shouted like a common woman,

'Who has showered this ambrosia on me, in the form of words? Who has taken pity on me? And where are the messengers? Who has seen them? How far away are they as yet? Is my son well?'

As she looked around, the queen saw that the people of Ujjayini too were rushing all over in clusters and heard a confusion of voices questioning, guessing, and answering.

'Has the prince come back?'

'How far behind have you left him?'

'Where did you meet him actually?'

'Was it very tough on him to have spent the entire rainy season on horseback?'

'He must have spent the whole season travelling.'

'Tvaritaka would know all this.'

'But what is the point of all this information? The main question is: Did the prince meet Vaishampayana? And has he brought him back?'

Several in the crowd were also shouting questions at the messengers regarding their own relatives serving in the army.

'Has any message been sent by Devavardhana? Does any one know? He is so immature and impetuous and so likely to meet a violent end that I am afraid even to ask for news of him.

'Will you give me news of my uncle Prithuvarman the best among horsemen?'

'Is Ashvasena the cavalry leader well?'

'Has any one seen my brother Bharatasena who is head of administration in the prince's palace?'

Vilasavathi heard these and many other such questions being hurled at the returning travellers who however, gave no replies. Their sorrowful gaze rested on the tip of their noses. Travel weary they dragged their feet, as though putting one foot in front of the other required a great effort. Their clothes were very dirty; their bodies were unwashed; the hair tied up on top of their heads was stiff with dust. Weariness was writ large on every part of their bodies. They were moving pictures of despondency and a gathering together of sorrows; they were the abodes of wretchedness. Vilasavathi saw them from a distance being led by Tvaritaka. She went back to the temple courtyard and sent word to them to come and meet her where she was.

Soon the messengers were there whose grief had suddenly acquired a fresh sharpness and intensity due to the unexpected meeting with the queen. They looked stunned and lifeless, like figures made of wood; they were moving like corpses. When Vilasavathi saw them tears filled her eyes and blinded her. She stumbled as she approached them because she could not see clearly through the veil of her tears, because she was fearful of the news they had brought her. She cried out even before they saluted her, in a voice that shook with emotion: 'Good sirs, give me quickly just the news of my child. I have a premonition in my heart; I fear something. Have you seen the prince?'

Those good men bowed and placed their heads on the ground, no doubt in salute but also to conceal the tears rushing to their eyes by shedding them on the ground. They then raised their faces with difficulty and said to her, 'Devi, we have seen the prince on the shores of the Acchoda Lake. Tvaritaka here will tell you the rest.'

Vilasavathi looked at their tearful faces and cried out in anguish, 'What else has this poor man got to say that I have not guessed from your demeanour? I have observed you from a distance. You approached reluctantly, cheerlessly and carried no reply from the prince on your head. You were dejected and you were straining to control your tears; you were unable to look me in the eye. All this has told me everything that needs to be told. Alas! My child Chandrapida with the face of Chandra, with the coolness of Chandra, with the lovely qualities of Chandra, the delight of all eyes: what has befallen you that you have not returned? I am speaking with great distress, not out of anger. You promised me that you would not delay even a little; is it fair now to stay away like this? My wretched heart suspected even then, when you left, that it might be difficult for me to see my son's face again. I had no wish to let you go, you tore yourself away. Now what shall I do? But then what is my child's fault in all this? It is my ill luck that is taking this form. There are others in this world dogged by misfortune but none must be so sinful as I, because you, my only son, have been taken away from me. The creator has cheated me.

'My child! You are so far away yet I fall at your feet, come back please, just this once. I long to hear you call me mother. Oh my son, we had you with such difficulty. How should I console myself now? Should I keep remembering your childhood? Or should I think of you as you are now, in the first flush of manhood? Or should I try to imagine, on the basis of your great strength and profundity, what might your future greatness have been? You who are forever enthroned in my heart. Do not for a moment assume, seeing me lament like this, that your mother will live without you. If I continue to live without you how can I face your father? My heart should have split by now, that it has not shows that it refuses to believe any evil could have befallen you. What is the cause of that disbelief? Is it love? Is it some faith in your beautiful face, or is it merely the stupidity that comes over women so easily? I know not. But I do know that I do not want to hear that heartbreaking news brought by Tvaritaka. Isn't it better to die without hearing what would be utterly terrible to hear? Oh my son! What would you say about this shameful weakness of mine so undeserving of my child's love. I have now fallen silent because I know that you disapprove, and I shall say no more, I shall cry no more.' So saying she collapsed on the arms of her attendant and became unconscious.

—68—

In the meantime innumerable attendants of Vilasavathi had rushed to the king with the disquieting news that the prince had not returned nor had sent any letter through the messengers. The king, his mind in turmoil and agitation like the ocean churned by the Mandara Mountain, and seized with bewilderment, mounted an elephant capable of great speed, and accompanied by Shukanasa hurried out of the city of Ujjayini, full of palaces and towers and archways. The swift animal swallowed the miles quickly; on the road there were throngs of people all around also hurrying on, exchanging anxious queries among themselves, creating a murmur that could be heard far and wide.

Reaching the shrine of the Avantimatas, the king found Vilasavathi lying on the ground like a wilted lotus in summer. She was just coming out of her swoon, her stricken twisted face wet with tears. Her maids were ministering to her, sprinkling her with sandalwood water, fanning her with wet plantain leaves and massaging her feet with their soft moistened palms. When the king saw her, his eyes too quickly filled and the teardrops fell on her as though he too were sprinkling her to rouse her from the remnants of her fainting fit. He sat down next to her; gently, soothingly, he stroked her forehead, her eyes, her cheeks, her chest and her hands and spoke gently, 'Devi, if in reality some dire calamity has befallen our son then there is no question of our continuing to live. Since that is the case, why do you faint away like a common woman and draw contempt on yourself? We have performed enough meritorious deeds, and so what more can we do now? We do not seem to deserve any greater happiness. What is not destined to be ours cannot be obtained by any amount of beating of the breast. There is this thing called Fate that does what It pleases; It is not under anyone's control. We have enjoyed the birth of our son, it was a dream come true, a rare blessing. We delighted in his face as he lay in our lap; and when he lay on the ground we lifted and kissed his feet and placed them on our head. When he crawled on his knees and collected dust on his body we gathered him to us and thrilled at the touch. We enjoyed his sweet, heart-warming lisping speech, his first indistinct prattle. As a child we delighted at his mischievous playfulness. Having finished his education he gladdened us by his virtuous conduct. As he grew into young manhood his extraordinary beauty and valour stood revealed. We had the pleasure of anointing him the crown prince of this great realm and kissed his forehead on that occasion. When he returned from the victory march and paid his respects to us we clasped him to our bosom. Among the hundreds of dreams that we had woven around him what did not materialize for us was to enthrone him as the rightful ruler, with his bride by his side and depart in peace to the forest. One needs indeed a huge amount of merit for the fulfilment of all one's dreams.' The king paused and said in a brisk tone, 'Besides, no one has yet stated clearly what exactly has happened to our son. I have heard only the incoherent accounts of the servants. They mentioned a Tvaritaka, a childhood friend of my son's who has arrived with our messengers. You have not asked him anything. Tvaritaka is said to know all the details. So let us now question Tvaritaka. We will listen first to what he has to say and then decide between life and death.'

The pratihari called to a young man standing behind the queen's servants to step forward; as the young man placed his head on the ground in reverence, the pratihari said, 'Here is Tvaritaka.'

The king glanced at the young man who was Chandrapida's childhood friend and placed his hand affectionately on his head and said, 'Come my good fellow, tell me now what has befallen my son that he has not returned even though both of us, the esteemed minister Shukanasa and I wrote letters asking him to come back. Not only has he not returned, he has not sent any letter by way of reply, stating the reasons for having stayed back.'

Thus commanded Tvaritaka started to narrate his story right from the beginning; when he reached the point in the story when Chandrapida's heart broke, the king was overcome with distress. He was completely shaken, and spreading his hands in helpless agony he cried out, 'My dear fellow, please stop now. What you have to say you have said already. And I have heard what I have to hear. My interrogation has attained its result! My ears have achieved their great purpose. My heart ought to be gladdened, and I must be pleased. Oh my dear, dear son when your heart broke how did you bear that agony all alone? How well you have proved your love for Vaishampayana. As for your parents we deserve nothing but sorrow for we are pitiless villains. Our adamantine hearts have not yet shattered to a thousand pieces. Cowards that we are, our vital breaths have not followed you in death.

'So rise my lady! Let us follow our son quickly so that he does not go too far ahead all by himself. Shukanasa! There you stand, still stunned with grief. This is the hour of friendship. Order the servants to start a fire near the temple of Mahakala. Let the woodmen arrange the logs quickly. Why are the kanchukis still here huddled together? Go and get everything ready for us to enter the fire. The time for grieving is now past. Devi! Without delay and demur arrange to give away all the wealth to the Brahmins; do not keep anything back. The time for preserving anything is all over for me, the wretched sinner.

And you princes! Go home now, you have all been discharged. Conduct yourselves in such a manner that my subjects are not troubled. My son's life is now a mere story. On whom shall I shift my burden and go?'

The king lamented uncontrollably; Vilasavathi unmindful of her own grief tried to hold him. Tvaritaka then cried out, 'My lord, although his heart split the prince still has his body intact. Please listen to what I still have to say about the curse on Vaishampayana and where it has now led him.'

As Tvaritaka narrated what he had seen, heard and experienced himself, the king listened; and as he listened he was torn between belief and doubt in the wondrous sequence of events. It caused him unprecedented grief, but along with it his sense of wonder too grew. The story was unbearable to hear; yet it excited his curiosity. When the narration ended he turned his head slightly, his eyes stilled in thought, he let his glance fall on Shukanasa who was in a state no different from his own. That good friend, although in great grief himself controlled his own sorrow and assuming a serenity that he did not feel spoke thus quietly.

'My lord, this phenomenal world is indeed an amazingly strange one, a world in which, dwell the entire creation, divine, human and sub-human in states of happiness or sorrow. Perhaps it is the transformations of *prakriti* consisting of the of the three gunas; or it is the will of Ishvara, the creator, sustainer, and destroyer of everything from the great atom to the cosmic egg; perhaps it is the unfolding of the desirable and the undesirable results of acts of dharma and adharma, in a felicitous or infelicitous denouement; whatever it may be due to, there is no situation in this strange phenomenal world that may be considered impossible of occurrence, among beings that move and that do not, among those that are yet to be born, those that live at present and those that have lived and perished. That being so, why is my lord trying to analyse these events? In a discussion of rationality, events that lack apparent probability of occurrence may gain credence on the basis of the evidence of the scriptures.

By what connection do tantrika mudras and meditation rouse one who has lost his consciousness due to poison? How does a magnet attract iron or make it go round and round? It is known that many a Vedic and non-Vedic chant guarantees success in several undertakings. By combining various substances it is possible to get the power to induce or ward off death and lovesickness, to acquire control over, or to cause enmity between, individuals. The scriptures bear witness to many other such powers.

And there are many instances of curse found in all the scriptures, in the Puranas, and in the Ramayana and the Mahabharata. Nahusha for instance, having attained a status equal to Indra fell into the form of a python due to the curse of Agasthya. Saudasa turned into a cannibal as a result of Vasishtha's sons' curse. Shukracharya cursed Yayati to untimely old age. Trishanku was reduced to an untouchable by the ancestral spirits. Mahamisha, a king dwelling in heaven, had to be born as Shantanu, and his wife Ganga's curse was responsible for the birth of the eight Vasus as humans. There are many other such instances. Ishvara, the One without birth, the Supreme Lord was born as son to Jamadagni; it is said that the Lord then divided Himself fourfold to become the four sons of Dasharatha. And subsequently He was born, as the son of Vasudeva in Mathura.

It is therefore clear that the birth of gods in a human womb is by no means impossible. And you my lord, are in no way inferior to these men of yore in merit and qualities; nor is Chandramas greater than Lord Vishnu, Kamalanabha. Further, do you not remember that when Devi became pregnant with child you saw in your dream, the moon entering her face? I too saw Pundarika in my dream in the form of a white lily. Therefore there is no doubt whatsoever about the divine origin of both the boys.

'That the bodies of the two dead friends remain fresh clearly indicates that they both would regain their lives in some way or the other. One of the important arguments for this is the presence of amrita on the moon whose powers are well known in the world. Therefore you should accept the tale as narrated by Tvaritaka. It is impossible for a son of such splendour and delight as Chandrapida to have been born in this world without any divine connection. Take my word, very soon indeed, after the expiation of the curse, you will, with joyful tears filling your eyes, witness Chandramas, the Lord Protector of the world in the form of Chandrapida, your son, falling at your feet with his wife, the gandharva princess; and then the agony of an entire lifetime would disappear. In fact this curse that has befallen them is a blessing for us. You and Devi should now stop grieving over this matter. On the other hand you should now begin performing auspicious acts; by worshipping your favourite deities and performing acts of charity, enhance further the merits already acquired in a previous birth. Destroy whatever ill luck may still dog you by practising severe austerities and upholding stern spiritual discipline. No effort however strenuous, may be spared; it was only by such unrelenting rigours had the boys' births been brought about.'

The king had listened with attention to the words of Shukanasa. Now he replied sadly, 'Who else can utter such thoughtful words as you have? Who would take the trouble to make us understand things as you do? Whose advice but yours would we strive to follow? Yet, the image of my child's heart breaking at the death of Vaishampayana remains fixed in my mind's eye and hides everything else from sight. I see only that, I hear only that, I imagine only that. Not seeing my son, my heart is stunned and I am unable to act at all. If this is my condition then forget about advising Devi to see things as they are. Therefore there is no other way to keep alive than going there to the shores of Acchoda where lies my son. Arya must understand this.'

─69─

The agony of having endured the long absence of her son gave Vilasavathi courage to speak out. Abandoning her customary reticence born of bashfulness especially in the presence of Arya Shukanasa, she now said to her husband in a loud voice, 'Aryaputra, if that is your decision then why delay any more? We have to leave at once. Please issue your orders for departure. My heart is in intense anguish to see my son. I welcomed death in order to avoid that unbearable sorrow resulting from losing our son. But now that does not appeal to me. If I have survived through this deep anguish of separation and uncertainty all these days it must have been only to see the dear one, at least once more. Even now it is for the sight of him that my heart is holding out, in spite of the terrible grief that is so suddenly upon us. I am now possessed by the desire to see my son who is the only antidote for all our sorrows. In the meantime the travel would divert the heart a little.' At that juncture an elderly man, a respected friend of Arya Shukanasa, a noble Brahmin, a performer of all the six kinds of duties enjoined in the scriptures, approached Vilasavathi and respectfully addressed her thus: 'Devi, disturbed by the vague rumours regarding the messengers who have returned, Manorama has hurried over here, but stands behind the Matrimandir, diffident to appear before the king. She wants Devi to answer these questions for her: What did the messengers say? Is her son Vaishampayana alive and well? Has he joined up with the prince? Would both of them be coming back shortly?'

These words of the Brahmin struck at the king's anguished heart more brutally than the news of his son's death. As for Vilasavathi she trembled all over as her friend's words had now given a fresh edge to her sorrow. The king said to her, 'Devi, your friend is completely in the dark about what has befallen our children. If she hears a garbled version of the story from some outsider she may try to harm herself. Take hold of yourself first and then go and tell her the whole story and help her steady herself. Also, inform her of our decision to go to that place along with Arya Shukanasa.' He helped Vilasavathi up and sent her to Manorama; then he set about getting ready for the journey with the help of the minister.

When the king left for the Acchodasaras the entire population of Ujjayini wanted to leave with him, except those who were caretakers of their homes. Most were, of course, driven by loyalty to the king and affection for the prince. But there were others filled with curiosity to witness the miraculous and still others eager to use this opportunity to go and see their own fathers, brothers or sons who were already there, having accompanied Chandrapida as part of his forces. The king however managed to dissuade most of them on the plea that he had to reach his destination quickly. He took a very light force with him and made haste as if wishing to cover the entire distance in a single day. Every now and then he would ask Tvaritaka how many more miles to go still and how many more days yet to reach the lake. He travelled without a break and arrived at the Acchoda Lake in a very short time indeed, with a hundred misgivings troubling his heart. Stopping at a distance he sent Tvaritaka along with some of his trusted officers to gather information.

The messengers returned in a short while with the princes who had originally accompanied Chandrapida to the lake. Emaciated and unkempt, their woebegone eyes brimming with tears they seemed ready to sink into the bowels of the earth as though to hide their shame at still being alive. Each was trying to hide behind the other in order not to be seen by their king. The more they tried to hurry the more their feet dragged; they appeared defeated yet they were not wounded; with their limbs the enthusiasm too had weakened; they seemed dead as though their lives too had drained away along with their tears. Leading them was Meghanada.

When he saw them the king's agony over his lost son swelled; waves of sorrow seemed to drown him. However, he pulled himself together and at once all his faith in the indestructibility of Chandrapida's body returned. He went to his wife seated in a covered palanquin, and said, 'Devi, our son's body is still preserved. All our son's devoted followers who are still serving at his feet are here to see us.' Vilasavathi drew the curtain aside a little and stared at the gathered princes who looked no different from her own son. She wept and cried out aloud, 'Oh my child, why is it that I do not see you alone in the midst of all these princes who used to play with you in the dust?'

The king consoled her once again and then commanded Meghanada standing a little away with his head lowered, to approach near. Then he asked him, 'Meghanada, now tell me, how is it with our son?' Meghanada replied, 'It is clearly evident that although due to the loss of consciousness there is no movement of the limbs there is daily an increase in the lustre of the body.' With renewed hope the king spoke to his wife again. 'Devi, you heard what Meghanada said. Let us now go and fulfil our long-standing desire of gazing at our son's face.' Goading the elephant to greater speed he proceeded to the hermitage of Mahashveta.

—70—

Mahashveta wept grievously when she heard of the arrival of the parents of Chandrapida, the tears falling like scattering stars. She lamented, 'Ah! Ah! This is the end of me. I have longed for death, but death has eluded me. How much longer and in how many more ways am I going to be persecuted by this cruel Fate, who is such an expert in handing out suffering!' Out of shame she ran and hid herself in her cave. As for Chitraratha's daughter, holding on to her friends who had rushed to her side she fell into a swoon without uttering anything at all.

It was at this juncture that King Tarapida entered the ashrama, his hand resting on the shoulder of Shukanasa; behind him was Vilasavathi held by Manorama. She was asking repeatedly, of no one in particular, where her son was, her eager eyes searching for him everywhere. And there he was still full of that natural lustre with which he had been born, but now lying motionless as though asleep. Before Tarapida could get close to his son, Vilasavathi pushed Manorama away who was trying to hold her back and rushed ahead with outstretched hands. Her streaming eyes drenching the ashrama ground in front of her she cried out. 'Come my precious child. The rare one! I am seeing you after such a long time. Answer me please. Will you not at least look at me once? It is not right my child, for you to remain like this. Please get up now and show me a child's affection by coming to my lap. You have never disregarded my words even as a child. But now here I am lamenting, and you do not seem even to hear me.

'If you are, for any reason, angry with me I seek to dispel that anger by falling at your feet. Please get up, my son

Chandrapida, and salute your poor father who has come such a long way to see you. Ah! What happened to your filial piety and all other good qualities, your affectionate nature, your loyalty to your father, your graciousness to your attendants and your sense of righteousness? Why have you given up everything at one go and remain totally indifferent to everything? All right you remain as you are, I am not going to care what you do.' Vilasavathi fell on her son and embraced him tightly, pressed her face to his head, kissed his cheeks then placed his feet on her head and wept uncontrollably.

The king heard all this quietly; he did not try to embrace the body of his son. He hid his own grief and held his wife in his arms, arms capable of bearing the troubles of all his subjects and said, 'Devi, by some good fortune we, you and I, were blessed with a child and this form here is divine, not human, and therefore there is nothing to grieve about. Now you stop lamenting, for all lamentation belongs strictly to the mortal world. Besides, crying is futile for it is not going to find you a way out of this situation. It will merely split your throat but not your heart. It is not the life forces that come out of the mouth, only meaningless cries. It is the tears that fall to the ground and not one's body. We were distressed because we were unable to see our son for such a very long time; now that we see him, even that cause for distress has disappeared. It is now our duty to support Manorama and Shukanasa whose Vaishampayana is away in another world. That apart, she by whose power the miracle of our son's revival would be celebrated and enjoyed, she, the gandharva princess, your daughter-in-law, overwhelmed with waves of sorrow at our arrival, is still lying unconscious, held by her friends who keep calling out her name. Please get up now, take her in your lap and try to revive her. After that you may cry to your heart's content.'

Thus chided by her husband Vilasavathi got up at once. 'Where is my daughter-in-law, the preserver of my son's life?'

she asked of no one in particular and hurried over to where Kadambari was still lying unconscious; she sat down and placed Kadambari on her lap and gazed at the princess's face; with eyes closed in a swoon, Kadambari's face looked doubly beautiful. Vilasavathi pressed her own cheeks bathed in a ceaseless flow of tears and cool as a piece of the moon to Kadambari's, her forehead to Kadambari's forehead and her eyes to Kadambari's eyes. With her hands rendered cool by the touch of Chandrapida's body she stroked Kadambari's heart and said, 'Hold on, my child. Who else but you can look after my son Chandrapida's body? My daughter, you are indeed a personification of immortality itself and with your help I shall see my son again'.

Kadambari woke up at the mention of her lover's name and the touch of Vilasavathi's body so similar to that of Chandrapida. But her proverbial shyness gripped her and she sat with her head bent, not knowing what to do. Madalekha gently helped her down from Vilasavathi's lap. She then performed mechanically the honours due to the elders under the instruction of Madalekha. They in return wished her long life without widowhood. The king was overjoyed with Kadambari's recovery; he felt as if Chandrapida himself had come back to life. He now embraced his son closely and kissed him and stroked him with his hands for a long time. Then he came to Madalekha and told her, 'We are here merely to derive some joy from the sight of our son and that we have already attained. Whatever regimen our daughter-in-law has been following for the care of the body of our son ought to continue. She should not swerve from it even a little either due to bashfulness or embarrassment resulting from our presence here. We are just useless spectators; what difference would it make whether we stay here or go away? It is by the touch of our daughter-in-law's hands that my son's body has attained this indestructibility; therefore may she remain by his side.'

Then the king left the hermitage. But instead of going to the residence made ready for him he entered a bower of creepers and sat down on a clean rock seat and addressed graciously, the gathering of vassals whose grief was as intense as his own.

'You should not conclude that this step that I am now going to take has been brought on by grief. I had planned for this a long time ago, only I had planned it differently. After seeing Chandrapida happily married I wanted to place my burden on his shoulders and then retire to some hermitage to spend in peace the last days of my life. By the doings of Fate or perhaps by my own actions in the past, those earlier plans have taken this grotesque shape. What has been ordained may not be avoided. It is not given to us to see Chandrapida rise and move about. And the burden of protecting the subjects is already borne by your strong shoulders. Even if I were to act differently the burden will continue to rest on you. That being so, I desire to fulfil now that long cherished wish of mine. Blessed are they, who, their bodies ripened with age, are able to shift their burdens on to the shoulders of their children, and with a feeling of lightness prepare for the future life. The foot of the god of death will stamp down on the throat and cut one down any time he fancies, even if that person were unwilling to die. Having transferred one's responsibilities on to suitable successors, if, with this body, or rather what remains of it after old age has taken its toll making it unfit for worldly pleasures, one can strive to earn the pleasures of the other world, then would it not be a profitable thing? I request you to help me in this matter.'

Having thus relinquished all his regal responsibilities the king also rejected the comforts that were available to him and to which he had been accustomed; in their place he now took on the rigours of a forest life that he was unused to. The shade of a tree took the place of his palace, the forest creepers were now the women of his antapura, and the deer his trusted servants. His taste in food shifted to fruits and roots and his preference in clothes to bark garments. The hands that bore arms now wielded the rosary. His ability for clever conversation turned into a facility for narrating parables. The taste for war changed into a love of serenity, the thirst to conquer was now directed towards a conquest of the other world; the desire for worldly wealth became now a desire for the acquisition of spiritual wealth by penance. Maintaining silence instead of issuing orders as he had been accustomed to do, totally detached, extending the love for his son to the trees of the forest, the king performed all that a hermit was enjoined to do. Accepting only reluctantly the gandharva rites of hospitality performed every day by Kadamabari who had somehow got the better of her shyness, and by Mahashveta as well, his untold agonies ameliorated somewhat with the sight of his son morning and evening, the king stayed on the shores of the Acchoda Lake with his wife, Shukanasa and others of his retinue.

Thus ended the story of the rishi Jabali. A tremulous smile lighting up his aged face, he spoke again to Harita and the other ascetics and to the parrot as well. 'You have seen how captivating such wondrous tales can be. I forgot what I really set out to say and let myself be carried far afield by the emotional content of the story. What I wanted to emphasise was that this person with his mind clouded with passion, lost his position in the heavenly worlds by his own deeds that crossed the bounds of propriety. He was then born in the mortal world as Vaishampayana the son of Shukanasa. And once again by his own deeds he has brought on himself his father's anger and the curse of the chaste Mahashveta, as a result of which he has now fallen into the world of parrots.'

The Parrot Continues

When Jabali finished speaking I felt as though I had been awakened from a long sleep. Although still very young, I now remembered and could command at will all the learning I had acquired in my previous births. I regained my mastery over all the arts and also the ability to speak clearly. I regained knowledge of all the subjects that I had studied earlier. In short, except for the physical body, I regained everything human, everything that had gone into the making of Vaishampayana, his affection for Chandrapida, his tendency to lose himself to passion, his love for Mahashveta and his yearning to win her. Only I lacked my earlier ability to move because I had not as yet grown my wings. With the memories came the yearning for news of my parents, of the venerable Tarapida and Vilasavathi, of my dear friend Chandrapida and my even earlier friend Kapinjala and of course Mahashveta.

Seized with a terrible longing I rested my head on the ground. At the same time I was so overcome with shame for having erred so grievously that I wished I could have hidden myself under the earth. Still I made myself address that great ascetic Jabali, albeit hesitantly. 'Sir, by your infinite grace has enlightenment dawned on me. I now remember all my relatives of my earlier births. When I had no memory of them I had no pain either. But now with this recollection of everything I feel as if my heart would shatter to pieces. The knowledge that Chandrapida's heart broke when he heard of my death is especially unbearable. Please tell me the story of his birth too, so that I may go and live near him; even as a bird, living close to him would alleviate my agony.'

Jabali seemed angry when he looked at me but his reply had tones of pity. 'You villainous wretch, the unsteadiness of mind that has brought you to these straits has still not left you. Your wings have not grown yet. You first grow your wings and get the strength to fly, then you come and ask me about your friend.'

Then Harita sought to satisfy his own curiosity. He asked, 'Father, is it not passing strange that one born of a sage was so powerless against the temptations of the flesh that he could not protect his own life against their onslaught? And how could one who belonged to the divine world have had such a short span of life?'

As Jabali replied a flood of rays issued forth from his teeth and seemed to cleanse the world of all murky sins. 'The reason for that', he said, 'is clear indeed, my son. This one here had been born solely of the weak seed of a woman that carries with it tendencies to lust, blind attachment and delusion. The scriptures tell us that such an individual becomes a prey to all these failings. We know that results partake of the qualities of the causes, as we see even in this world. Ayurveda states that any conception based solely on the female seed without the stabilizing effect of the male sperm is likely either to meet with destruction within the womb itself or to be stillborn. Even if the child lives it is not likely to live long. This one here was such a weakling at birth that he could not resist the desires of the flesh. Unable to bear the heat of Madana he died. Now too his life is short indeed. After the expiation of the curse he would be blessed with long life.'

When I heard this, I laid my head on the ground again and requested the sage. 'Oh my lord, in this wretched body of a bird I am helpless; I am unable to do anything to acquire merit. It is only with your grace that I have got back the power of my speech. If I were to be blessed with a suitable body in my next birth, oh my lord, what should I do to earn a long life for myself?'

Jabali gazed into the distance and replied, 'You will come to know all this by and by. Let the matter rest here for the time being.' Then he turned to his disciples and said, 'The night is almost over; it has passed without our being aware of it as we were in the grip of emotions raised by this strange story. The moon is clinging to the edge of the western sky, and shorn of its lustre it appears like an unpolished silver mirror. As dawn breaks we see the sun rise with the somewhat pallid redness of a fading lotus. The first rays in the east are parting the darkness as if it were a woman's hair. The lingering darkness makes the appearance of the early brilliance of the sun somewhat sudden, into which are entering the clusters of stars and planets looking fainter and fainter. The birds living around the Pampa Lake have woken up as we now hear their delightful calls. The morning breeze has started blowing with the cool touch of the night carrying the fragrance of the flowers swaying in the wind. The time for kindling the fire has arrived.' With these words Jabali got up and dissolved the meeting.

—72—

As Jabali rose to go, the ascetics of the hermitage remained still, caught in the poignancy of the tale they had just heard. They even forgot to pay their respects to their teacher, as it was their wont to do after every meeting. It was true that they had no worldly attachments or longings. Yet this story filled them with an ecstasy of mingled joy and sorrow, their faces expressing their sheer wonderment. They remained there a long time agonizing over the tragic sequence of events before they could tear their minds away from the haunting tale and set about their daily routine.

Harita picked me up and carried me to his hut where he placed me gently on one side of his bed and went off to perform his morning ablutions. Left alone I fell into a reverie; distressing thoughts filled my mind. I pondered sadly over my avian existence which made me unfit for everything. To be born a human being was a rare blessing earned only with meritorious deeds performed in several earlier births. More rare was to take birth in the highest of the *jatis*, as a Brahmin. Still more rare and far more meritorious was to live so close to immortality as an ascetic, and that too in the heavenly world. Having enjoyed that high state, here I was fallen so low due to my own sins. Totally helpless, how could I pull myself out of this bird existence? How was I to enjoy once again the friendships formed in previous existences in this abject condition? If that enjoyment was out of reach, then why preserve this useless existence? Let this body, made only for suffering, perish anywhere, any time; there is anyway no hope for any happiness. I shall get rid of it. Let Fate be satisfied, Fate that is intent only on handing out suffering.

As I lay with my eyes closed and my mind dwelt on such despairing thoughts, Harita entered the hut with his face wreathed in smiles. His words infused new life into me. 'Brother Vaishampayana, there is good news for you. Kapinjala is here looking for you, having been sent by your father Shvetaketu.'

How I then wished I could grow my wings that very instant and fly out to him. But all that I could do at that moment was to raise my head and look all around for Kapinjala. Not seeing him anywhere I asked Harita where my friend was. Harita replied that Kapinjala was with his father. I then pleaded, 'Bhagavan, won't you please take me to him? I cannot wait to see him.' Even while I was uttering these words there he was, standing in front of me.

Kapinjala's hair was disarranged as he had come through the skies; his utthariya too had slipped from its place, as his path must have been windy. His bark cloth was tied tightly round his waist. The half-broken yagnopavita kept his bones company on the emaciated chest. His body was heaving with the effort of flying across the vast expanse of the sky. Although carried along by the wind, he looked tired after his aerial travel. The agony brought on by seeing me in that wretched state expressed itself in the tears that flowed down from his eyes wetting his face.

Dear, dear friend Kapinjala! What a true friend he was. He strove after liberation, yet he allowed himself to be bound by his love for me; he had no desires for himself yet he desired my welfare; he had no attachments yet he loved being with me; he had no ego yet he identified himself with me; he had no worries for himself but he worried about me; he could look upon a clod of earth, a piece of iron and gold with equal indifference but when I suffered he too suffered.

He was all that I was not.

He never forgot a good deed; I was an ungrateful wretch. He was naturally affectionate; I was hard-hearted. He was virtuous; I was a sinner. He was straight; I was devious. He bowed to authority; I transgressed all the time. He was a great soul; I was a villain.

When I saw this good friend Kapinjala my eyes filled with tears. Gasping with the effort of rising I cried out, 'Oh my friend Kapinjala, seeing you thus after two births how I would have run to you, while you were still at a distance with my arms spread widely and pressed you close to myself. How I would have held you by my hand and made you sit on a seat. How I would then have massaged your limbs to remove the fatigue of travelling so far. But look at me now. How helpless I am.'

Kapinjala picked me up while I lamented and placed me on his chest, gaunt with the grief of separation from me. He gazed at me for a long time as though he wished to enter right into my heart by the sheer force of his will and thus enjoy the pleasure of being embraced by me. Soon however, he was overcome with violent grief; he placed me on his head and wept uncontrollably giving in completely to his sorrow like a common individual, forgetting all his tapas and education.

I spoke again for all I could do was speak. 'Dear friend Kapinjala, it is for me to weep in this fashion afflicted as I am with all kinds of ills and sins. But you, even as a child you were never touched by such failings and weaknesses as these which bind one to samsara and act as obstacles in the path of liberation. Why have you now set out on this path frequented only by the deluded? Sit down and tell me the whole story. Is my father well? Does he think of me? Is he saddened by my misfortunes? Is he angry?' Pulling himself together Kapinjala sat down on the leaf seat brought over by a disciple of Harita. He placed me on his lap and then washed his face with water brought over by Harita himself. Then he started his story.

'My friend, your father is well. He had already seen everything that was to happen to us right in the beginning, with his divine sight. And he had immediately started suitable rites as antidote to the calamities.

'As for me, as soon as I was released from the horse body I made haste to his presence. He saw me approaching, dejection writ large on my face, and my eyes brimming with tears; I was also filled with fear. He called to me and quickly sought to remove my dejection and sense of guilt. "My child Kapinjala, please stop blaming yourself. All this is due, in truth, to my foolishness. I knew what might be in store, yet I omitted to perform life-lengthening rites for my son soon after his birth. Anyway, those rites are all now well on their way to completion. One should not dwell on past sufferings. And you Kapinjala, for the time being you stay here with me."

'Reassured I begged him to grant me the favour of allowing me to be with you, wherever you might have taken birth. Father replied, "My child, he is now born among the parrots. Even if you go to him he would not know you, nor would you know him. Wait for a while." This morning he called me and said, "Your friend has now reached the ashrama of the great sage Jabali. He now remembers who he is. You can therefore go to him now. Convey my blessings to him. My child, please tell him that the expiatory rites are now reaching their conclusion. Until they get over he must remain at the hermitage of Jabali under his protection. His mother Shri, equally saddened by his misfortunes, is also working towards his release. Convey her love as well and emphasize that she too wants him to remain for the present at the ashrama of Jabali."' Kapinjala stroked my body, covered with fine hair like the tender shirisha filaments and agonized over my condition in his mind.

Sensing his pain I said to him, 'Friend Kapinjala, why do you distress yourself? You too have suffered a lot thanks to my doings. You had been cursed to exist inside the body of a horse losing all your freedom. Your mouth meant only for the soma drink had suffered lacerations caused by the bit, giving rise to saliva foaming with blood. How your back, used only to the bed of tender leaves, must have hurt, having had to carry the saddle constantly. How could it have borne the pain of the goad? This body of yours used only to the yagnopavita, was made to bear the irritation of the tying rope.' I then spoke of the old times, which enabled me to forget for a little while at least, the agonies of my present existence as a bird.

As the sun rose up to the middle of the sky I was fed in the company of Kapinjala. After the meal was over Kapinjala said, 'I was sent by your father to comfort you and more important, to tell you to remain right here under the protection of Jabali until the expiatory rites reach their conclusion. He does not want you to move from here till then. I am also involved in those rites and so I have to take your leave now.' My face fell when I heard that Kapinjala had to go away. 'My friend,' I said, 'what can I say in this wretched condition? What messages can I send to my father or to my mother? Anyway you know everything.'

Kapinjala then embraced me again and then placed me near Harita. As the wonderstruck young hermits looked on, he rose up in the sky and soon disappeared from sight. Harita consoled me and as he went about his various duties he stationed another young hermit by my side. After completing all his daily duties he himself fed me my evening meal.

─73─

Looked after attentively by Harita I grew wings in a few days. With the ability to fly, the mind became restless. 'I can now fly'. I thought, 'it is true that I do not know where Chandrapida has been born now. But I do know that Mahashveta still lives on Hemakuta. Now that I have got back my memories why should I remain here experiencing the pangs of separation from her? I shall therefore go to Mahashveta and stay with her.' My mind was thus made up to leave the ashrama of Jabali.

Early one morning I left my abode and started flying in a northerly direction. Having acquired the ability to fly only a few days before, I was soon overcome with weariness, after flying a very short distance. I thought my limbs were about to come apart;

my beak had become dry and I was seized with thirst. My neck trembled with my fast breathing. My wings had become weak and powerless. I felt as though I was being carried along by some outside agency and I was sure I was about to fall any moment, perhaps right here this very instant, or perhaps there just a little later. Somehow I managed to carry on and at last threw myself on a tree whose branches were bent with the weight of the dense and dark foliage, one of a forest of trees on the shores of a lake. I sat there for a long time recovering from the fatigue of travel.

Then I came down to the cool shade under the tree where I drank my fill of the cool water fragrant with the pollen of the lotus plants and sharp with the sap of the lotus stalks. The more I drank the more I needed to drink to quench my thirst fully. Then I appeased my hunger with whatever tender lotus seeds that I could find and with the fresh shoots of the bilva tree and its fruits. 'In the afternoon I shall fly some more distance', I decided. I then climbed up another shady branch of the tree close to the ground and remained there; soon sleep stole over my travel-weary body.

After what seemed a long time I woke and found myself bound fast with a rope. There was a man in front of me of terrible mien, the very image of the god of death. His body was dark and hard as though made entirely of the atoms of iron. He appeared the very antithesis of all that was good, a veritable abode of sin. His brows were knitted, and his eyes with mismatched pupils were bloodshot; his face looked angry even though there was no cause for anger. It appeared cruel enough to have instilled fear in Yama himself, whom the whole world held in fear.

His face was clouded and so must his intellect be.
His skin was black and so must his conduct be.
His clothes were soiled and so were his actions.
His body was hard and so were his words.

With a sinking heart losing all hope of ever being free again, I entreated him. 'My good sir, who are you? Why have you tied me up? If it is my flesh that you are after why did you not kill me while I was asleep? Or is it just a cruel impulse? If that is the case you have already satisfied your impulse. So please release me now. I long to see my beloved and I have a long way to go. My heart will not bear any more delay. And you would get the merit of saving a life.'

He replied: 'Great One, it is true I am a man of rough deeds, a *chandala* by caste. But I have not tied you up out of greed for your flesh, or to indulge my sense of cruelty. My master is the headman of the *matanga* settlement not too far from here. His young daughter is now at that stage of life when she is full of eager curiosity. Some evil-minded fellow has gone and told her that a parrot of exceptional qualities resides at the ashrama of the sage Jabali. The matanga girl seized with curiosity has despatched several men like me to catch you and bring you to her. It is my luck that I have accomplished that task today. So I shall now take you to her. It is up to her to release you or keep you bound.'

His words hit me like dry lightning with no rain. My mind fell into turmoil. 'Have things come to such a terrible pass that I, who had been born to Shri at whose lotus feet devas and asuras place their head in worship, I who had been brought up by that great ascetic Shvetaketu revered in all the three worlds, I who had resided at a hermitage in the *devaloka* am about to enter the settlement of the matangas shunned even by the *mlecchas*? I am going to be living with the chandalas. I have to keep my body and soul together by eating food at the hands of old matanga women. I have to be a toy for the amusement of the chandala children. You wretched villain Pundarika, curse upon your birth! It is the result of your own actions that has manifested in this manner. Alas! Why did you not break into a thousand bits as soon as you were conceived. Oh my mother Shri, the refuge of those with no other recourse. Please save me from this horror. Oh my father! You are capable of protecting all the three worlds. Save me, the only living thread of your lineage. You brought me up. Oh my friend Kapinjala! If you do not return and release me from this horrible predicament then you give up the hope of our ever coming together even in future births.' I lamented thus in my heart and tried once again to plead my case with the matanga.

'Oh my good man, I am an ascetic who knows his previous births. If you free me from this calamity you would acquire great merit that would vouch for your pleasures in the hereafter. There is no present danger for you if you release me here without being seen by any one.'

The matanga laughed and said, 'Deluded one, the five guardians of the world who bear witness to all deeds both meritorious and sinful reside within oneself. It is not out of fear of someone else that one refrains from sinful deeds. I am now taking you with me.' He picked me up and started towards the *pakkana*, the matanga settlement.

His words felt like a blow on my head. I wondered silently what particular ill deeds of mine could have led to these dire results. It became clear to me that only death could get me out of this parlous situation. Yet a faint hope lingered in my breast, that perhaps the matanga princess herself might let me go. So I looked straight ahead and soon we arrived at the chandala colony.

When I saw the chandalas I was sure they were possessed by evil spirits. Their clothes and ornaments gave rise to disgust. Mending old nets and snares broken by the animals caught inside, carrying around iron-tipped staffs and bows in their hands and wielding fierce weapons, they went about their business. They were bird catchers skilled at teaching the birds to speak. There were hunters skilled at releasing the hounds for the hunt. Everywhere there were groups of matanga children playing at hunting. The chandala dwellings were hidden in the dense growth of bamboos; only the smoke curling up carrying the smell of flesh indicated their presence. All the paths were full of skulls; the yards of their dwellings were slushy with blood and marrow mixed with pieces of flesh and the rubbish heap consisted mainly of bones.

Hunting was the only livelihood they had, flesh their only food and marrow the only unguent. All their clothes were of silk from the silkworms and all their blankets were of hide and skin. Dogs were their only companions, cows their only vehicles. Women and wine were the only goal of life, blood the only offering to the gods and animal sacrifice the only kind of worship they knew.

A mine of hell fire, a source of all that was unwholesome, a veritable graveyard, an abode of all evil, a temple of agony, the pakkana caused fear in the very imagining of it; just the hearing about it gave rise to agitation. It was sinful merely to look at it for it was home to people soiled both by birth and action. It was a pitiless world where the children, the young and the old carried on with no difference, a world where the men made no discrimination between suitable and unsuitable women in their lascivious enjoyment of them.

Although I was filled with disgust at the sight of the pakkana, a place that could cause fear in the breasts of even the inhabitants of hell, I still nursed the hope that I might be lucky. I hoped that the chandala girl might take pity on me and acting uncharacteristically, release me. 'Would I be as lucky as that?' I wondered. 'If it really happens that way then I shall not tarry here even for a moment,' I told myself fervently. Even as I hoped for some such lucky turn of events, the matanga took me to a girl, ill-favoured and badly dressed and said 'I got him'. The girl looked delighted. 'Well done' she said and took me in her hands and said to me laughingly, 'Ah my child, you are now properly caught. Where will you go now? I shall rid you of all wanderlust.' A chandala boy quickly brought over a cage made with foul smelling ropes made of half-dried hairy skin of cows which contained a wooden vessel for eating and drinking. Opening the door of the cage just a little the girl threw me into it—along with my desire to see Mahashveta—and quickly closed the door and drew the bolt. 'Now you stay there peacefully,' she said.

Imprisoned thus, my mind was in a whirl. 'I have now fallen into very deep trouble indeed. I could tell my story and fall at her feet and beg her to release me but that might be counter-productive for it would only further advertise my ability to talk which has been the chief reason for my capture. Does she suffer any pain by shutting me up like this? None at all.

'For I am not her son or brother, I am not in any way related to her at all. I shall therefore simply remain silent. Very likely, she might, angered by my stubbornness, put me in greater distress. Cruelty is natural to her kind. Never mind if that were to happen, one should not under any circumstance mingle even words with the chandalas. On the other hand, if I persist in my silence she just might out of disappointment, release me. All my tribulations have been the result of my lack of control over my senses. Should I now indulge in speech? No! I shall keep all my sense instruments under control.' Having reasoned thus I remained silent. She tried chatting with me. When she failed to elicit any response from me she threatened me and even tried to beat me and made as if to break my body to pieces; still I never said anything. I merely let out a loud screech. When food and drink were brought to me I left them untouched; I ate nothing the whole day.

The next day after the eating hour was past and my heart was in agony, she brought the food to me herself, various kinds of cooked dishes as well as fresh fruits and fragrant water. She fixed me with a kindly eye and spoke gently. 'Animals and birds with their carefree minds are never known to shun any food brought to them when they are really hungry or thirsty. But you on the other hand seem to know what may be eaten and what may not; it is the knowledge of your previous births that compels you to reject the food offered by us. But having been born among the birds that live under no such restrictions, no food is really ruled out for you. You slipped from the highest order to the level of birds by your own actions; why do you now worry about what may or may not be proper to eat? You failed to conduct yourself with wisdom in the beginning. Now in your avian existence there is no such thing as *dosha,* or fault. Even for those who have to be correct about such things, the rules are relaxed in times of dire difficulties, in order to preserve the life. Besides the food that I have brought for you should not raise the suspicion that it might be of the unacceptable chandala variety. Fruits are always accepted; they say even water once it falls on the ground from the chandala vessels regains its purity. Do stop torturing yourself with hunger and thirst by refusing to partake of forest fruits and seeds, food fit to be consumed by rishis, and pure water.'

I was so wonderstruck by her words of wisdom, so unusual in one of chandala birth that I decided to accept her advice. Rendered powerless by the curse I overcame my disgust and partook of the food she had brought, in the desire to preserve my life. But my silence continued.

~

'The days passed and I entered young manhood. One morning when night was turning into day I opened my eyes and found myself in this golden cage,' said the parrot Vaishampayana. 'And that chandala girl had become transformed into the beautiful woman that your majesty has seen,' continued the parrot. 'The entire chandala settlement had changed into a heavenly city. My distress over having to live in the chandala world disappeared at once. But before I made up my mind to give up my vow of silence and ask her a whole lot of questions about these startling changes, she had brought me to your majesty. Who this woman might be, why she assumed the qualities of a chandala, why I was imprisoned in a cage and why I have now been brought here are questions to which the answers are as unknown to me as they are to your majesty. And I am equally curious to know them.'

~

After narrating his story the bird fell silent.

—74—

King Shudraka and his courtiers had remained oblivious to the world as they listened to this extraordinary tale. Now eager to know all the answers King Shudraka sent his pratihari to fetch the matanga woman. Soon the chandala princess entered the king's apartment, overshadowing the brilliance of the king by her own lustre. She addressed the king with authority while she remained standing. 'You ornament of the world, lord of Rohini, the beloved of the stars, Oo Chandrama, the delight of Kadambari's eyes, you have now listened to the whole story of the previous lives of this wretched one. You have seen how even in this birth, still blinded and deluded by passion, he disobeyed his father's orders and set out to meet his beloved. All this you learned from his own mouth. I am his mother Sri. His father found out by his divine sight that he had flown out of the ashrama of Jabali. He said to me, "Those set on the wrong path will not desist from it unless they are struck with remorse. This son of yours may manage to fall even lower than birds in the scale of creation.

Until the sacrificial rites that I have undertaken reach their conclusion, please keep him on earth under restraint. Arrange things in such a way that he learns to repent his sinful lives." That is why I created the chandala situation, to teach him a lesson in good behaviour. Thankfully the rites are all over now. The time for the lifting of the curse draws close. Once the curse is expiated both of you should experience equal happiness. That is the reason why I brought him here. I created the chandala world also to keep this one secluded so that he might be prevented from getting into more mischief. Now both of you enjoy yourselves in the company of your loved ones having first got rid of these mortal bodies that are subject to the miseries of birth, old age, disease and death.' With these words Sri rose up from the ground, the tinkle of her ornaments creating a commotion in the middle regions, and disappeared into the heavens as the world looked on in wide-eyed wonder.

At that very moment Shudraka remembered his previous births; he exclaimed, 'Oh friend Vaishampayana or Pundarika, how wonderful it is that both of us are being released from our curse at the same time.' Even while the king was uttering these words, there was Kama pulling the bowstring up to his ear with Kadambari as the supreme weapon; at the same time he stepped in like a thief to steal the king's life away closing all avenues of escape. The king's heart, dispossessed of its dwelling as it were, hurried away to the feet of Kadambari. Frightened of being the target of the arrows of Kama, the fiery breaths of Shudraka sought to flee his body. His body trembled as though blown about by the wind raised by the feathers on the speeding arrows. He became languid and the hair all over his body stood on edge. His eyes shed copious tears as though covered with the pollen from Kama's floral arrows. The beauty of his face paled a little. As though his heart was pained by the sound of the bowstring being pulled, Shudraka's eyes narrowed. Could it be the smoke from the fire of passion raging within that made his trembling lips dry? Perspiration poured out of his fevered limbs like sap from wood. As though pinned down by Madana's arrows, he lost control of all his limbs. All the remedial measures to bring down the fever were of no avail.

He stopped all activity. His heart shunned all diversions as painful. He thought of Kadambari all the time and wanted her all the time. In his fevered fancies he was always with her. He would talk to her, he would embrace her, and he would even scold her at times. But soon he would placate her and fall at her feet. He would play with her, make love to her. He was unable to do anything else, his eyes remained closed all through the day, but his nights were sleepless.

He became averse to talking with his friends and failed to respond to those who approached him on business. He stopped paying his respects to his elders, and left all his religious duties unfulfilled. He remained indifferent to pleasure and pain and even to death. In fact he made no attempt even to unite with his beloved Kadambari. He lost consciousness repeatedly as though he were practising how to die. His eyes shed tears constantly yet his face was shrivelling up.

Shudraka's close and trusted attendants did their best to relieve his agony. They smeared his body from head to foot with sandalwood paste. They covered his feet in cool, wet lotus leaves. They placed camphor-powder-covered ice in his hands. On his chest lay a necklace of snow-cool and moist pearls. On his burning cheeks they placed mirrors of crystal, and on his forehead a chandrakanta stone. Cool, wet lotus stalks were draped over his shoulders. He lay on a bed of flowers made with care by his attendants and fanned with plantain leaves and palm leaves which gave rise to a cool moist breeze. The water machines were worked unceasingly to mitigate his agony. The floors were continuously washed and the king's attendants spread on them quantities of lotus flowers with dripping filaments. In such fashion did those who were expert in maintaining the chambers constructed under the ground minister to King Shudraka.

The bowers of creepers near the garden wells were kept well sprinkled. The king was continuously showered with sandalwood water mixed with camphor so that his fever might abate. But despite all these ministrations the king's body dried and the relentless heat of Kama rose and quickly reached the ultimate limits of endurance. Similar was the condition of Vaishampayana-Pundarika pining for Mahashveta.

Epilogue

Epilogue

S pring was setting in with the start of the fragrant month. The southern breeze began to blow, teaching the rhythms of dance to the creepers with lush new leaves. The fresh red shoots of the ashoka tree trembled in the breeze. The young mango trees became laden with the longed-for blossoms, making the branches bend with their weight. The maddening fragrance of the mango flowers filled the air. The *kurabaka*, bakula, tilaka, champaka and nipa trees burst out with buds. The *kinkiratha* flowers painted the atmosphere a pale yellow. The sweet scent of the *atimuktha* pervaded everywhere. The bamboo groves too were in bloom. The kimshuka trees flaunted their flowers like the red flags of Kama. Forests and gardens burgeoned with fresh shoots.

Spring urged the women to break free of restraints; it destroyed all sense of shame and appeased all anger. It swept away bashfulness, drove away modesty and induced violent lovemaking. The world turned golden; love sprang up everywhere. Passion and intoxication were in the air. There was celebration and there was longing. The excited calls of the koels drunk with the nectar in the flowers assaulted the ears of the travellers separated from their beloved women. The constant

shower of honey from the flowers made the entire world mad
with excitement. Spring had indeed arrived, the faithful aide of
Kama, with much fanfare.

Kadambari too found herself troubled by this most potent
weapon of Kamadeva. She had spent the whole day in unease
and in the evening, as it was getting dark, she had a bath and
performed the worship of the god of love. She then bathed
Chandrapida in cool scented water and anointed him all
over with *harichandana* mixed with kasturi. She tied his hair
up with a garland of sweet-scented flowers. On one of his
ears she fixed a bouquet of ashoka flowers and tender
leaves. Finally she adorned him with an ornament made of
karpura blooms.

Then she gazed at him with her eyes full of love. Her heart
was filled with yearning. She sighed again and again. She
trembled and her limbs were washed in perspiration. The hair
on her body stood on edge due to some sort of ecstasy. Her lips
became dry. She cast her eyes all around to make sure
Mahashveta was not looking. She then advanced slowly towards
the recumbent form of Chandrapida, stopping in her tracks every
now and then. It seemed as if she had no control over herself.
Completely under the influence of Madana, the supreme cause
of all love mania in the world, her shyness and timidity vanished.
Suddenly becoming impatient of waiting in that lonely spot
Kadambari went quickly to Chandrapida, and with half-closed
eyes put her arms around his neck and embraced him closely,
tightly, as though he were alive.

That embrace of Kadambari, delightful as nectar, quickened
Chandrapida's apparently lifeless form, and the pulse on his
throat began to throb. Like the wilted blue lily coming to life at
the touch of moonlight his heart too bloomed and began to beat.
His long eyes opened, like lotus buds at the touch of dawn. His
face now sparkled like a lotus flower. Regaining control over his

limbs like one awakening from sleep he put his arms around Kadambari's slender shoulders, rendered frail with all her travails, and held her closely. But now her body shook with fear like wind-blown plantain leaves; her eyes were tightly closed and it appeared as though she wished to enter right into his chest. She was powerless to free herself, or to take herself in hand in any way. Then he spoke, his dear, familiar voice delighting both the ears and heart.

'Timid one! Pray do not be afraid. It is your embrace that has brought me back to life, for you were born of the lineage that sprang from nectar itself. And do you not remember my words uttered at the time of my death, that this lustrous body of mine is by nature indestructible, and now especially so as it would be nourished by the touch of Kadambari's hands? However, all these days, although your hands touched me I could not regain my life because of the weight of the curse. Now, having experienced a second time the unbearable and fevered anguish of separation from you I have been released from the curse. I have given up that human body called Shudraka which experienced such terrible pangs of unfulfilled love. This body called Chandrapida I have preserved and regained only to please you, for you to lavish your love on it. Thus, this world as well as the moon world is now at your feet. And my dear friend, the beloved of your Mahashveta, has also become freed from the curse.'

While these words were being spoken by the lord of the moon in the guise of Chandrapida, there was Pundarika descending from the sky holding Kapinjala's hands, and emanating an intense fragrance about him as a result of contact with the nectar on the moon. He looked no different from what he was when he died of his love for Mahashveta; he had the same single strand of pearls around his neck and he was in the same ruffled condition with pale emaciated cheeks.

When Kadambari saw him she at once released Chandrapida's chest and ran to Mahashveta and embraced her. Even while she was giving Mahashveta the glad news, Pundarika landed and approached that figure of great benevolence, the lord of the moon in the form of Chandrapida. Chandrapida embraced him warmly and said, 'My friend Pundarika, you are already my son-in-law by an earlier birth. But I want you to regard me with the friendship forged in another more recent birth.'

In the meantime Keyuraka had hurried over to Hemakuta to convey the glad tidings to Chitraratha and Hamsa. Madalekha rushed to Tarapida, engrossed in *mrutyunjaya japa,* and Vilasavathi and fell at their feet and exclaimed, 'My lord and lady, I am bringing wonderful news for you! Prince Chandrapida has come back to life and Vaishampayana too.'

The king had been paying scant attention to his physical well-being. His hair, which had turned white, had grown long. His arms too were covered with thick, long, white hair. He caught Madalekha by her shoulders overcome with joy. He embraced his wife with his age-weakened frail arms; he threw his *angavastra* away and began to dance with untrained and ill-timed steps. He asked Madalekha repeatedly, 'Where is he? Where is he?' He hugged his dear friend Shukanasa whose joy was no less than his own. The vassal kings' faces were blooming with joy. When he arrived at the scene of joy he beheld Chandrapida embracing Pundarika. The king cried to Shukanasa, 'Is it not fortunate that I am not the only one to be enjoying the pleasure of a son coming back to life?' Chandrapida turned and saw his father standing there overwhelmed with joy. He immediately released Pundarika, went up to his father and fell at his feet, just as he used to do, with his head touching the ground.

The king lifted him up and said, 'My son, somehow it was given to me to be your father, perhaps due to the curse, perhaps due to some merit earned by me as well. Still, you are the protector of the world, worthy of being worshipped by the world. Whatever authority there was in me as king that commanded your veneration even that I have already passed on to you. Either way therefore it is you who have to be bowed to.' Then the king, along with all the princes, going against all the rules of the world fell at his son's feet.

As for Vilasavathi she was not bothered by her son's divinity. Unable to contain her joy she kissed her son again and again on his head, forehead, and on his cheeks and gathered him close to her and did not release him for a long time. When she finally released him he went to Shukanasa and paid him his respects. Receiving his blessings, Chandrapida introduced Pundarika, holding his head down in shame and shyness, first to his father and then to Shukanasa and Manorama: 'This is your Vaishampayana.'

At once Kapinjala stepped up to Shukanasa and conveyed to him the following message from Bhagwan Shvetaketu. 'This is Pundarika who has merely been raised by me. He is indeed your son. And he too is attached only to you. Know him to be your Vaishampayana and prevent him from further misdemeanours. Please do not ignore him as a stranger. It was because he was your son that I did not get him back to myself even after the expiation of the curse. Having left a part of myself in Pundarika who is blessed with a life as long as the moon exists, the undying spiritual part of me, my atman wishes to ascend to states even higher than this heaven.'

When Shukanasa heard this message he put his arms around Pundarika still standing with his head bent and replied to Kapinjala. 'The great Shvetaketu knows the heart of men well; yet he has sent this message to me. No doubt his own great love for his son makes him worry.'

All is well that ends well. All those gathered there at the ashrama of Mahashveta looked joyfully at each other and exchanged notes about their previous births. In the meantime, the night spent itself out and dawn broke without our characters being quite aware of the passage of time. Soon Chitraratha and Hamsa accompanied by their wives, Madira and Gauri joined them. When they looked at the shy happy faces of their daughters their hearts filled with joy. When they looked at their sons-in-law their faces beamed with happiness. As the parents conversed on matters pertaining to the marriage of their children the intensity of the celebrations increased a thousand fold.

Then Chitraratha said to Tarapida, 'When we have a house of our own why celebrate here in the forest? Although among us gandharvas mutual falling in love by itself constitutes legitimate marriage, one has to abide by the rules of this world. Let us therefore repair to our residence; from there you can go back to your kingdom or to Chandraloka.'

Tarapida replied: 'Oh king of the gandharvas, home is where one finds a wealth of happiness even if it happens to be a jungle. And where else have I found such happiness as this? Besides I have already handed over all my other homes to your son-in-law. So my dear friend, take him and his bride and go back to enjoy the pleasures of your home.' Chitraratha bowed and acquiesced in the wishes of the king.

At Hemakuta, Chitraratha handed over his daughter Kadambari along with his whole kingdom to Chandrapida. Hamsa too was ready to give away his entire kingdom along with his daughter Mahashveta to Pundarika. However, both the young men, considering themselves blessed and fortunate in having gained the women they had set their hearts upon, declined the proffered kingdoms.

Kadambari was supremely happy in the company of her beloved husband and her own people. Yet there was one more thing needed before her cup of joy was completely full. She was sad and tearful as she asked her husband, 'Aryaputra, all our people who were dead have now come back to life and have come together. But that poor girl Patralekha is no longer seen in our midst. It is only of her there is no information.'

Chandrapida, happy that she should have asked, answered, 'My beloved, she is not here any more. She is Rohini who thinks my suffering is her suffering too. When she heard of my curse she was aghast that I would have to live all by myself among the mortals and ignoring all my protests she took birth in the mortal world even before I did in order to be of service to me. When I died and took another birth she too gave up her body and wanted to be born again. But I managed to dissuade her from this and sent her back to my world, where you will see her again.'

Kadambari, wonderstruck and somewhat abashed by Rohini's generosity, affection and nobility, soft-heartedness and loyalty to her husband, remained silent unable to say anything.

The day disappeared quickly as though eager to provide Chandrapida, the Lord of Time, ample scope to experience the joy of union with Kadambari for which he had waited two life spans. Darkness spread everywhere as if to cover the bashfulness of the blushing maiden, the western twilight. When night fell heavily, Chandrapida enjoyed union with Kadambari. Stopping the hand that rushed to hold the loosening knot of the garment, he embraced her and delighed in the bashfulness that came over her after the transports of joy subsided. Enjoying the first thrills of lovemaking with Kadambari, ten nights passed as though they were but one.

Then, taking leave of his overjoyed parents-in-law, he came down to his father. He then suitably rewarded all his princely friends who had suffered equally with him. He entrusted Pundarika with the affairs of state and spent time in the service of his parents who lived a life of renunciation.

Chandrapida the Lord of the Moon divided his time among the many that loved him. Sometimes he was at Ujjayini, his place of birth where the people would gaze at him in wide-eyed admiration; sometimes he was the honoured guest of the gandharva couple enjoying the incomparable beauty of that wonderland Hemakuta. Sometimes he would be on the moon where the cool nectar scented wind blew everywhere, in order to honour Rohini. Out of love for Pundarika he spent some time on the lotus pond where thousand-petal lotuses bloomed and where Lakshmi dwelt. And he was in every other place of beauty according to the wishes of Kadambari, enjoying with her the pleasures for which they had waited for so long, pleasures that never reached satiety.

It was not only Chandramas who enjoyed the pleasures of union with Kadambari; Kadambari enjoyed the pleasure of being with Mahashveta, Mahashveta with Pundarika, and Pundarika too with Chandramas. Thus all of them, with their boundless love for each other, enjoyed their lives together for a long time and reached the ultimate peak of happiness.

Glossary

Adisesha	The great serpent of a thousand hoods on whom Vishnu reclines. He is also supposed to hold the world aloft on his hoods.
Aghamarshana	The most heinous sins are said to be expiated by the recitation of this mantra.
Agni	The god of fire.
aguru	The fragrant aloe wood and tree. *Aquiluria Agallocha*
Aakhandala	Indra
alaktha	The red resin of certain trees, the red lac or sap formerly used by women to dye the soles of their feet.
Ananga	The one without body, Manmatha
anaka	A percussion instrument
Andhaka	Name of a demon killed by Shiva. He is believed to have had 2000 arms, 2000 eyes on 1000 heads and 2000 feet. He was called Andhaka because he walked like a blind man although he could see very well.

angavastra	Upper garment
apsara	Celestial damsels of great beauty often the wives of the Gandharvas
Arundhati	Wife of Vasishta immortalized as a morning star
ashoka tree	It was believed that this tree would burst into red blooms if young women kicked it.
ashvamedha	The horse sacrifice
asuras	Demons or evil spirits, the enemies of the gods
attahasa	The great laughter of Shiva
ayurveda	The Indian system of medicine
bakula	It used to be believed that this tree would burst into blooms if young women spat wine on it.
Bhagiratha	Was a king of the solar dynasty, who with unrelenting efforts and the most arduous penances brought the celestial Ganga down to the earth and thence to the nether regions to purify the ashes of 60,000 of his ancestors. Bhagiratha therefore symbolizes unfailing perseverance.
bhadramusta	Grass: *Cyperus Rotunda*
Bharatavarsha	India
bhasma	sacred ash
Bhargava	A descendant of the sage Bhrigu
bhringaraja	A bird
Bhavanipati	Shiva, the husband of Bhavani, Parvathi
bimba	The fruit of any tree which when ripe turns red and is compared to a woman's lips
bilva	The wood apple tree whose leaves are used in the worship of Shiva
brahmacharya	Celibacy
brahmasutra	The sacred thread
Brhaspati	The preceptor of the gods
Chakradhara	The wielder of the discus, an epithet of Vishnu

chakora	A mythical bird said to feed on moonbeams
chakravaka	The ruddy goose. In literary tradition it is believed that the mating pair is separated from each other at night as they cannot see each other even if they are sitting on the same branch.
chakravartin	Universal monarch, emperor and sovereign of the world
champaka	A tree with yellow fragrant flowers
chamara	Deer tail, also means the fan made out of the tail of a deer.
Chandika	The goddess Kali
Chandra	The lord of the moon
chandala	Lowest and the most despised of the mixed castes, an outcaste.
chandrashala	Room on top of the house.
chandrakanta	Moonstone supposed to ooze in moonlight according to literary tradition.
chaturdashi	The fourteenth day of a lunar fortnight
chataka	A sort of bird that is supposed to live only on raindrops.
chudamani	A crest jewel to be worn on the head.
Daksha Prajapati	One of the ten sons of Brahma born from his right thumb and the chief of the patriarchs of mankind.
darbha	A kind of sacred grass.
durva	Bent grass or panic grass, *Panicum Dactylon*.
Dharma	Righteousness quite often spoken of as a divinity.
dharmashastra	jurisprudence.
Dashratha	A king of the solar dynasty, the father of Rama of the Ramayana.
digvijaya	The victory march of a king.
Dileepa	A king of the solar dynasty and an ancestor of Rama.

dundubhi	A large kettledrum.
gandharvaveda	One of the four subordinate *Vedas* or *Upavedas* that treat of music and ascribed to the divine ascetic Narada.
Garuda	An eagle-like mythical bird with a white face, aquiline beak.
Gauri	Parvathi, wife of Shiva.
Gayatri mantra	A sacred verse that occurs in the Rig Veda that is chanted by the Brahmins morning and evening.
gorochana	A bright yellow pigment prepared from the urine of a cow.
gunja phala	*Gunja* is a small shrub that bears small red-black berries often used as weight.
Hara	Shiva
hara	Necklace
harita	A kind of pigeon.
Hari	Vishnu
himagriha	A cool chamber.
hintala	A variety of palm.
Hrishikesha	Vishnu
hunkara	Growling
Indra	The lord of the gods and also the god of rain.
indukanta	The moonstone
Iravatha	The celestial elephant belonging to Indra
Ishvara	The Supreme Deity
Itihasa	Literally it means 'so it has been', that is history, traditional or legendary.
jaggery	Brown sugar
Jamadagni	The father of Parashurama
jambuphala	The rose-apple tree and fruit of blue-pink lustre
Janardhana	Vishnu
janmas	Births
jata	Matted hair twisted together

jati	Sub-castes
kadamba	*Stephegyne Parviflora Korth*. The tree is said to bloom at the roar of thunderclouds.
kahala	A percussion instrument.
kalakuta	A deadly poison.
Kali Yuga	The last and worst of the four yugas, the current one.
kalpa	A day of Brahma measuring 1000 yugas, 432 million years of the mortals which is supposed to be the duration of the world.
kalpa	Wish-fulfilling tree in Indra's heaven.
kalpalata	A creeper in Indra's paradise.
Kama	Manmatha, the god of love.
Kamalayoni	He whose womb is the lotus, Brahma.
kamandalu	A wooden or mud water pot usually used by the ascetics.
kanchuki	Chamberlain
kankanam	Bracelet
karanja	The flowers of a medicinal tree.
karkandu	The jujube tree and its fruits.
karpasa	Cotton blooms
karpura	Camphor
Kartaviriya	A thousand-handed king who ruled righteously for 85,000 years and was finally killed by Parashurama for having carried away his father Jamadagni's cow.
Kartikeya	Subramania, the son of Shiva and Parvathi.
kasha flowers	The blooms on the grass called *kasha* used for making mats and also for the roofs.
kasturi	Musk
kaustubha	A celebrated mythical gem obtained with thirteen others from the churning of the ocean and worn by Vishnu on his chest.

Kautilya shastra	The *Arthashastra* of Kautilya, a treatise on politics, economics and administration seeking to aggrandize the power of the king.
ketaki	A fragrant succulent.
khandava	A forest sacred to Indra and burnt by Agni with the help of Arjuna and Krishna.
kirata	Mountain tribes who live by hunting.
kimpurusha	Kinnara.
kimshuka	A tree with beautiful blossoms which have no fragrance.
kinnara	Literally 'what sort of a man', a mythical being with the head of a horse on a human body, possibly a kind of monkey.
kridaparvatha	An artificial hill for recreation.
krishnaguru	A kind of sandalwood.
Krita Yuga	The first of the four yugas considered a golden age.
krosha	A distance of a little more than two miles.
Kubera	The god of riches and treasures and regent of the northern quarter.
kundala	Earrings
kungkuma	Saffron or vermilion
kurabaka	A handsome shrub, a species of amaranth with lipped flowers.
kusumbha	Safflower or saffron
kusha	A kind of grass with flowers considered sacred.
Lakshmi	The goddess of wealth and consort of Vishnu.
lavali	A kind of creeper.
lavanga	The clove plant
lavanka	A kind of tree
Madana	Manmatha
madhavi	The spring creeper with fragrant flowers

Madhu and Kaitabha	The demons that Vishnu destroyed.
Madhyadesha	The country lying between the Himalayas and the Vindhyas.
mahadevi	The chief queen
mahisha	The buffalo
Makaradvaja	The flag of Manmatha with the crocodile emblem.
makarika	A particular kind of head dress or a diadem.
malati	A kind of jasmine.
Manasa Lake	A sacred lake on Mount Kailasa, possibly Manasarovar
manashila	Red arsenic
Mandakini	Celestial Ganga whose waters are supposed to be white.
mandala	A charmed circle.
Mandara Mountain	A mythical mountain used as the churning stick by the devas and asuras when they churned the ocean for nectar.
Mandhata	A king of the solar race.
Manmatha	Cupid
matanga	One who belongs to the lowest caste, or a hill tribal or a hunter
mekhala	Girdle
Meru	A fabulous golden mountain of extraordinary height round which the planets and the stars were believed to revolve.
Mimamsa	One of the six systems of Indian philosophy.
mleccha	A foreigner
Mohini	A fascinating female form assumed by Vishnu to cheat the demons of their share of the nectar out of the ocean.

mrtyunjaya japa	The prayer and ritual to conquer death.
muraja	A drum
Nahusha	A wise and powerful king who acted as regent for Indra when the latter had to do penance under the water for having killed the demon Vritra, a Brahmin. Nahusha wanting to win the love of Indrani the wife of Indra rode to her palace in a palanquin carried by hoary sages. When he hurried them on saying 'sarpa, sarpa' sage Agasthya who was one of the carriers cursed him with the words 'sarpo bhava'. Nahusha turned into a snake and fell down into the the mortal world where he was released from the curse after a long time.
Nala	A very virtuous king who went through great suffering losing all his possessions and his wife Damayanti as well, but got everything back finally. Also the name of the monkey that helped Rama build the bridge to Lanka.
Nalakubara	A son of Kubera.
Nandi	The bull of Shiva.
Narada	A sage who is a deified saint and one of the ten mind-born sons of Brahma.
Narasimha	Vishnu as the man-lion avatar.
Narayana	Vishnu
Natyashastra	Treatise on dramaturgy and poetics credited to sage Bharata believed to have lived in the first century BC.
nivara	Wild rice
nipa	A kind of Kadamba said to flower in the rainy season. *Adina Cordifolia Hook.*
nritya	Dance

Nyaya	A system of Hindu philosophy based on logic.
padmasana	Literally the lotus seat. A particular posture in Yoga.
palasha tree	*Butea Frondosa*, also called *shimshuka*.
parijata	One of the five trees of paradise that came out of the ocean when it was churned. It was in Indra's possession until Krishna wrested it from him and planted it in Satyabhama's garden. *Nictanthus Arbor-Tristis*.
Pashupatas	A sect of Shiva worshippers who take special vows.
pataha	A percussion instrument
patala	The nether world
patrabhanga	Designs drawn on the body with pigments, it is also an ornament.
patralata	Another term for the designs drawn on the body.
phanas	Jackfruit
pippala	The holy fig tree
pramathaganas	Goblins devoted to Shiva
pranayama	Breathing exercises in Yoga
priangu	A creeper that is believed to put forth blossoms at the touch of women.
puranam	Name of certain well-known religious works.
purnima	Full moon
purusharthas	the four main objects of human life: *dharma*—righteousness and good works *artha*—attainment of riches *kama*—sensual enjoyment *moksha*—liberation of the soul
putra	Son
raga, ragini	Male and female tonal modes in Indian classical music.
rajahamsa	A species of bird with a red beak and red feet.

Rajyalakshmi	The glory of sovereignty deified as a goddess.
rajarishi	A king of the *kshatriya* caste who by his life of piety and austerity comes to be regarded as a sage.
raktha chandan	Red sandalwood
rallaka	A kind of deer
ranku	Antelope
Rati	Wife of Manmatha. She is represented as grieving because Shiva reduced her husband to ashes when he tried to distract Shiva in his meditation.
rudrakshamala	Rosary made of dried berries of a tree.
sallaki	A kind of tree, *Shorea Robusta*.
sala	A variety of pine
samidh	Fuel for the sacrificial fire, a special collection of twigs.
samsara	The cycle of birth and death.
saptachada	Tree with seven-pronged leaves *Alstonia Scholaris*.
saptarshi	Constellation called Ursa Major, the seven stars of which are believed to be seven hoary sages.
savitr	The sun
sarala	A variety of pine
Sarasvati	The goddess of learning
shabara	A hill tribal
Shaiva	Of Shiva
shalmoli	The silk cotton tree
shami	A tree that is supposed to contain fire within itself.
shakragopa	A kind of red insect.
Sharngapani	Vishnu

Shashanka	The lord of the moon, literally the one with the image of a rabbit marked on him.
shirisha	*Acacia Sirissa*, the tree and its flower which is supposed to be very delicate.
shiva	A kind of thorn apple and the tree.
shramana	An ascetic, a religious mendicant.
shripala	It is either wood apple or coconut.
shruti	An octave
shvetadwipa	White Island, a mythical island, the abode of the blessed.
shyamaka	A kind of edible grain.
Siddhas	Semi divine beings of great purity and holiness.
sinduvara	*Vitex Negundo*
Smriti	The sacred canon
soma	*Sarcostema Viminalis* or *Asclepius Acida*, a climber whose juice was extracted and processed before being offered it to the gods at sacrifices by the priests in ancient time.
suralokha	Heavens
suryakanta	Clear quartz crystal
svayamvara	A noble young woman choosing her husband usually out of a gathering of princes specifically invited for the purpose.
tala	A musical instrument made of bell metal.
tala	The Palmyra tree
tamala	A tree with a dark bark and white blossoms, *Xanthochymus Pictorius*.
tambula	The leaf of the betel with areca nut, catechu and lime chewed after a meal.
tantrika mudra	Certain finger positions assumed in worship in accordance with magical or mystical formulae for attaining supernatural power.

tapas	Penance
tilaka	The mark on the forehead, also the shrub *sesamum indicum* which has beautiful flowers that resemble the mark on the forehead.
torana	Any temporary ornamental arch-like decoration across a doorway.
tripundraka	Mark on the forehead consisting of three lines drawn in the ashes of cow dung.
tripura	Three cities made of gold, silver and iron built for the asuras by their architect Maya that were burnt down by Shiva at the request of the devas.
Trishanku	A king of the solar race who desired to go to heaven in his mortal body. He railed against all his family for refusing to help him realize his wish. Vishvamitra by the power of his own penance raised him to heaven from where he was hurled down head first by Indra and the other gods. But Vishvamitra arrested the king's fall halfway down and there he remains suspended as a constellation in the southern skies.
trishul	Trident
Tumburu	A student of the ancient teacher Kalapin
twice-born	A Brahmin generally but includes all the first three castes.
Udayashaila	The eastern mountain behind which the sun and moon are supposed to rise.
utthariya	The upper cloth
vadava fire	Fire that is believed to be under the waters of the ocean.
vaishvadevas	All the gods
Varuna	A Vedic god, regent of the ocean.
Vasishta	A Rig Vedic sage of great sancity and power and adviser to the solar race of kings.

vastu	Civil engineering
vasuki	The serpent used as the rope to turn the Mandara mountain to churn the ocean.
Vasus	A class of deities usually mentioned in the plural.
Vayu	The god of wind
venu	The bamboo flute
vibhuti	Sacred ash
Vishvamitra	A *kshatriya* by birth became a *brahmarshi* by great penance, and a rival of Vasishtha.
Vishvarupa	Omnipresent, an epithet of Vishnu.
Vrishnis	Name of a tribe or family from which Krishna is descended.
Yagnyopavita	Sacred thread
Yayati	A celebrated king, the son of Nahusha incurred the displeasure of the king of the asuras and was cursed by him to premature old age. One of Yayati's five sons, Puru willingly exchanged his youth for his father's old age. Yayati enjoyed all the pleasures of the world for a thousand years before returning the youth to his son and retiring to the forest.
Yojana	Eight or nine miles equal to four *kroshas*.
yama	1/8th part of a day, three hours.
yama elephant	Elephant that marks the passage of the *yamas* by walking a fixed number of laps.